**Praise for *New York Times* bestselling author
Diana Palmer**

"Palmer [is] the queen of desperado quests for justice
and true love."
—*Publishers Weekly* on *Dangerous*

"Diana Palmer is a mesmerizing storyteller who
captures the essence of what a romance should be."
—*Affaire de Coeur*

"Nobody tops Diana Palmer when it comes to
delivering pure, undiluted romance."
—*New York Times* bestselling author Jayne Ann Krentz

**Praise for *New York Times* bestselling author
Donna Alward**

"Well-defined characters and a powerful conflict drive
the plot, and the story's especially touching because of
Noah's plight and inner strength."
—*RT Book Reviews* on *Her Lone Cowboy*

"Great characters bring life to this beautifully written
story that explores trust, friendship and hope."
—*RT Book Reviews* on *How a Cowboy Stole Her Heart*

## DIANA PALMER

The prolific author of more than one hundred books, Diana Palmer got her start as a newspaper reporter. A multi-*New York Times* and *USA TODAY* bestselling author and voted one of the top ten romance writers in America, she has a gift for telling the most sensual tales with charm and humor. Diana lives with her family in Cornelia, Georgia.

## DONNA ALWARD

A busy wife and mother of three (two daughters and the family dog), Donna Alward believes hers is the best job in the world: a combination of stay-at-home mom and romance novelist. An avid reader since childhood, Donna has always made up her own stories. She completed her arts degree in English literature in 1994, but it wasn't until 2001 that she penned her first full-length novel and found herself hooked on writing romance. In 2006 she sold her first manuscript, and now writes warm, emotional stories for Harlequin.

In her new home office in Nova Scotia, Donna loves being back on the east coast of Canada after nearly twelve years in Alberta, where her career began, writing about cowboys and the West. Donna's debut romance, *Hired by the Cowboy*, was awarded a Booksellers' Best Award in 2008 for Best Traditional Romance.

With the Atlantic Ocean only minutes from her doorstep, Donna has found a fresh take on life and promises even more great romances in the near future!

Donna loves to hear from readers. You can contact her through her website, www.donnaalward.com, or follow @DonnaAlward on Twitter.

New York Times Bestselling Author

# DIANA PALMER

## *The Last Mercenary*

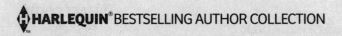HARLEQUIN® BESTSELLING AUTHOR COLLECTION

Recycling programs for this product may not exist in your area.

ISBN-13: 978-0-373-18088-2

THE LAST MERCENARY
Copyright © 2014 by Harlequin Books S.A.

The publisher acknowledges the copyright holders of the individual works as follows:

THE LAST MERCENARY
Copyright © 2001 by Diana Palmer

HER LONE COWBOY
First North American Publication 2010
Copyright © 2010 by Donna Alward

This edition published by arrangement with Harlequin Books S.A.

For questions and comments about the quality of this book, please contact us at CustomerService@Harlequin.com.

® and TM are trademarks of Harlequin Enterprises Limited or its corporate affiliates. Trademarks indicated with ® are registered in the United States Patent and Trademark Office, the Canadian Trade Marks Office and in other countries.

Printed in U.S.A.

www.Harlequin.com

# CONTENTS

Dear Reader,

When I started my second mercenary series for Silhouette Books, I really had no idea exactly which three men I would be writing about. Eb Scott was first. Cy Parks was second. I never planned to have a physician in the company, but the more I thought about it, the more I liked the idea. Micah Steele had turned up in Cy Parks's book, *The Winter Soldier,* and Micah's relationship with his stepsister, Callie, intrigued me. I wanted to explore their antagonism and understand why he hated her so much, when she was obviously crazy about him.

Nothing I planned to do in the book went the way I imagined it. In fact, I found myself on a roller coaster following these two tempestuous people around the world. Characters showed up who weren't even on my radar. Callie's unexpected kidnapping wasn't even in the plot I wrote. Micah's reaction to it was even more amazing.

By the time I got to the end of the book, I felt as if I needed a vacation to recover from the turmoil. And a peculiar, and endearing, twist brought a smile to my face when I took advantage of a stray thought and complicated things even more between Callie and Micah (you'll understand this reference when you get near the end of the book).

I enjoyed Micah Steele more than just about any of the mercenaries I've written about over the years. He's eclipsed only by Cy Parks, and that was more because of a minor character's view of Cy that was endearing to me. Micah, with all his faults, was one of the more capable soldiers when the chips were down. I hope you like him as much as I do.

Love,

Diana Palmer

# THE LAST MERCENARY

# DIANA
# PALMER

In memoriam, Brenda Lou Lilly Rogers.
My friend.

# Chapter 1

It had been a jarring encounter.

Callie Kirby felt chilled, and it wasn't just because it was November in south Texas. She watched the step-brother she worshiped walk away from her as casually as if he'd moved around an obstacle in his path. In many ways, that was what Callie was to Micah Steele. He hated her. Of course, he hated her mother more. The two Kirby women had alienated him from the father he adored. Jack Steele had found his only son wrapped up in the arms of his young wife—Callie's mother—and an ugly scene had followed. Callie's mother, Anna, was sent packing. So was Micah, living mostly at his father's home while he finished his last year of residency.

That had been six years ago, and the breach still hadn't healed. Jack Steele rarely spoke of his son. That suited Callie. The very sound of his name was painful to her. Speaking to him took nerve, too. He'd once called her a gold digger like her mother, among other insults. Words could hurt. His always had. But she was twenty-two now, and she could hold her own with him. That didn't mean that her knees didn't shake and her heartbeat didn't do a tango while she was holding her own.

She stood beside her little second-hand yellow VW and watched Micah bend his formidable height to open the door of the black convertible Porsche he drove. His thick, short blond hair caught the sunlight and gleamed like gold. He had eyes so dark they looked black, and he rarely smiled. She didn't understand why he'd come home to Jacobsville, Texas, in the first place. He lived somewhere in the Bahamas. Jack had said that Micah inherited a trust fund from his late mother, but he'd sounded curious about his son's luxurious lifestyle. The trust, he told Callie privately, wasn't nearly enough to keep Micah in the Armani suits he wore and the exotic sports cars he bought new every year.

Perhaps Micah had finished his residency somewhere else and was in private practice somewhere. He'd gone to medical school, but she remembered that there had been some trouble in his last year of his residency over a lawsuit, stemming from a surgical procedure he refused to do. Neither she nor his father knew the details. Even when he'd been living with his father, Micah was a clam. After he left, the silence about his life was complete.

He glanced back at Callie. Even at a distance he looked worried. Her heart jumped in spite of her best efforts to control it. He'd had that effect on her from the beginning, from the first time she'd ever seen him. She'd only been in his arms once, from too much alcohol. He'd been furious, throwing her away from him before she could drag his beautiful, hard mouth down onto hers. The aftermath of her uncharacteristic boldness had been humiliating and painful. It wasn't a pleasant memory. She wondered why he was so concerned about her. It was probably that he was concerned for his father, and she was his primary caretaker. That had to be it. She turned her attention back to her own car.

With a jerk of his hand, he opened the door of the Porsche, climbed in and shot off like a teenager with his first car. The police would get him for that, she thought, if they saw it. For a few seconds, she smiled at the image of big, tall, sexy Micah being put in a jail cell with a man twice his size who liked blondes. Micah was so immaculate, so sophisticated, that she couldn't imagine him ruffled nor intimidated. For all his size, he didn't seem to be a physical man. But he was highly intelligent. He spoke five languages fluently and was a gourmet cook.

She sighed sadly and got into her own little car and started the engine. She didn't know why Micah was worried that she and his father might be in danger from that drug lord everyone locally was talking about. She knew that Jacobsville mercenaries Cy Parks and Eb Scott had been instrumental in closing down a big drug distribution center, and that the drug lord, Manuel Lopez, had reputedly targeted them for revenge. But that didn't explain Micah's connection. He'd told her that he'd tipped law enforcement officials to a big drug cargo of Lopez's that had subsequently been captured, and Lopez was out for blood. She couldn't picture her so-straitlaced stepbrother doing something so dangerous. Micah wasn't the sort of man who got involved in violence of any sort. Certainly, he was a far cry from the two mercenaries who'd shut down Lopez's operation. Maybe he'd given the information to the feds for Cy and Eb. Yes, that could have happened, somehow. She remembered what he'd said about the danger to his family and she felt chilled all over again. She'd load that shotgun when she and Jack got home, she told herself firmly, and she'd shoot it if she had to. She would protect her stepfather with her last breath.

As she turned down the street and drove out of town, toward the adult day care center where Jack Steele stayed following his stroke, she wondered where Micah was going in such a hurry. He didn't spend a lot of time in the States. He hadn't for years. He must have been visiting Eb Scott or Cy Parks. She knew they were friends. Odd friends for a tame man like Micah, she pondered. Even if they ran cattle now, they'd been professional mercenaries in the past. She wondered what Micah could possibly have in common with such men.

She was so lost in thought that she didn't notice that she was being followed by a dark, late model car. It didn't really occur to her that anyone would think of harming her, despite her brief argument with Micah just now. She was a nonentity. She had short, dark hair and pale blue eyes, and a nice but unremarkable figure. She was simply ordinary. She never attracted attention from men, and Micah had found her totally resistible from the day they met. Why not? He could have any woman he wanted. She'd seen him with really beautiful women when she and her mother had first come to live with Jack Steele. Besides, there was the age thing. Callie was barely twenty-two. Micah was thirty-six. He didn't like adolescents. He'd said that to Callie, just after that disastrous encounter—among other things. Some of the things he'd said still made her blush. He'd compared her to her mother, and he hadn't been kind. Afterward, she'd been convinced that he was having an affair with her mother, who didn't deny it when Callie asked. It had tarnished him in her eyes and made her hostile. She still was. It was something she couldn't help. She'd idolized Micah until she saw him kissing her mother. It had killed something inside her, made her cold. She wondered if he'd been telling the truth when he said he hadn't seen her mother recently. It hurt to think of him with Anna.

She stopped at a crossroads, her eyes darting from one stop sign to another, looking for oncoming traffic. While she was engrossed in that activity, the car following her on the deserted road suddenly shot ahead and cut across in front of her, narrowly missing her front bumper.

She gasped and hit the brake, forgetting to depress the clutch at the same time. The engine died. She reached over frantically to lock the passenger door, and at the same time, three slim, dark, formidable-looking men surrounded her car. The taller of the three jerked open the driver's door and pulled her roughly out of the car.

She fought, but a hand with a handkerchief was clapped over her nose and mouth and she moaned as the chloroform hit her nostrils and knocked her out flat. As she was placed quickly into the back seat of the other car, another man climbed into her little car and moved it onto the side of the road. He joined his colleagues. The dark car turned around and accelerated back the way it had come, with Callie unconscious in the backseat.

Micah Steele roared away from the scene of his latest disagreement with Callie, his chiseled mouth a thin line above his square jaw. His big hands gripped the steering wheel with cold precision as he cursed his own lack of communication skills. He'd put her back up almost at once by being disparaging about the neat beige suit she was wearing with a plain white blouse. She never dressed to be noticed, only to be efficient. She was that, he had to admit. She was so unlike him. He seemed conservative in his dress and manner. It was a deception. He was unconventional to the core, while Callie could have written the book on proper behavior.

She hadn't believed him, about the danger she and her stepfather—his father—could find themselves in. Manuel Lopez wasn't the man to cross, and he wanted blood. He was going to go to the easiest target for that. He grimaced, thinking how vulnerable Callie would be in a desperate situation. She hated snakes, but he'd seen her go out of her way not to injure one. She was like that about everything. She was a sucker for a hard-luck story, an easy mark for a con artist. Her heart was as soft as wool, and she was sensitive; overly sensitive. He didn't like remembering how he'd hurt her in the past.

He did remember that he hadn't eaten anything since breakfast. He stopped to have a sandwich at a local fast-food joint. Then he drove himself back to the motel he was staying at. He'd been helping Eb Scott and Cy Parks get rid of Lopez's fledgling drug distribution center. Just nights ago, they'd shut down the whole operation and sent most of Lopez's people to jail. Lopez's high-tech equipment, all his vehicles, even the expensive tract of land they sat on, had been confiscated under the Rico statutes. And that didn't even include the massive shipment of marijuana that had also been taken away. Micah himself had tipped off the authorities to the largest shipment of cocaine in the history of south Texas, which the

Coast Guard, with DEA support, had appropriated before it even got to the Mexican coast. Lopez wouldn't have to dig too deeply to know that Micah had cost him not only the multimillion-dollar shipment, but the respect of the cartel in Colombia as well. Lopez was in big trouble with his bosses. Micah Steele was the reason for that. Lopez couldn't get to Micah, but he could get to Micah's family because they were vulnerable. The knowledge of that scared him to death.

He took a shower and stretched out on the bed in a towel, his hands under his damp blond hair while he stared at the ceiling and wondered how he could keep an eye on Callie Kirby and Jack Steele without their knowing. A private bodyguard would stick out like a sore thumb in a small Texas community like Jacobsville. On the other hand, Micah couldn't do it himself without drawing Lopez's immediate retaliation. It was a difficult determination. He couldn't make himself go back to the Bahamas while he knew his father and Callie were in danger. On the other hand, he couldn't stay here. Living in a small town would drive him nuts, even if he had done it in the past, before he went off to medical school.

While he was worrying about what to do next, the telephone rang.

"Steele," he said on a yawn. He was tired.

"It's Eb," came the reply. "I just had a phone call from Rodrigo," he added, mentioning a Mexican national who'd gone undercover for them in Lopez's organization. He'd since been discovered and was now hiding out in Aruba.

"What's happened?" Micah asked with a feeling of dread knotting his stomach.

"He had some news from a friend of his cousin, a

woman who knows Lopez. Have you seen Callie Kirby today?" Eb asked hesitantly.

"Yes," Micah said. "About two hours ago, just as she was leaving her office. Why?"

"Rodrigo said Lopez was going to snatch her. He sounded as if they meant to do it pretty soon. You might want to check on her."

"I went to see her. I warned her…!"

"You know Lopez," Eb reminded him somberly. "It won't do her any good even if she's armed. Lopez's men are professionals."

"I'll do some telephoning and get back to you," Micah said quickly, cursing his own lack of haste about safeguarding Callie. He hung up and phoned the adult day care center. Callie would surely be there by now. He could warn her…

But the woman who answered the phone said that Callie hadn't arrived yet. She was two hours late, and her stepfather was becoming anxious. Did Micah know where she was?

He avoided a direct answer and promised to phone her back. Then, with a feeling of utter dread, he climbed into the Porsche and drove past Kemp's law office, taking the route Callie would have taken to the adult day care center.

His heart skipped a beat when he reached the first intersection outside the city. At this time of day, there was very little traffic. But there, on the side of the road, was Callie's yellow VW, parked on the grass with the driver's door wide-open.

He pulled in behind it and got out, cursing as he noted that the keys were still in the ignition, and her purse was lying on the passenger seat. There was no note, no anything.

He stood there, shell-shocked and cold. Lopez had Callie. Lopez had Callie!

After a minute, he phoned Eb on his car phone.

"What do you want me to do?" Eb asked at once, after Micah had finished speaking.

Micah's head was spinning. He couldn't think. He ran a hand through his thick hair. "Nothing. You're newly married, like Cy. I can't put any more women in the firing line. Let me handle this."

"What will you do?" Eb asked.

"My man Bojo's in Atlanta visiting his brother, but I'll have him meet me in Belize tomorrow. If you have a number for Rodrigo, call it, and tell him to meet me in Belize, too, at the Seasurfer's Bar. Meanwhile, I'll call in the rest of my team." He was remembering phone numbers and jotting them down even as he spoke. "They're taking a holiday, but I can round them up. I'll go in after her."

Eb suggested calling the chief of police, Chet Blake, because he had contacts everywhere, including relatives in positions of power—one was even a Texas Ranger. Micah couldn't argue. If Eb wanted to tell the man, let him. He was going to get to Callie while she was still alive.

"Just remember that somebody in law enforcement is feeding information to Lopez, and act accordingly. I've got to make arrangements about Dad before I leave."

"I'm sorry, Micah."

"It's my fault," Micah ground out furiously. "I shouldn't have left her alone for a minute! I warned her, but what good did that do?"

"Stop that," Eb said at once. "You're no good to Callie unless you can think straight. If you need any sort of help, logistical or otherwise, I have contacts of my own in Mexico."

"I'll need ordnance," Micah said at once. "Can you set it up with your man in Belize and arrange to have him meet us at that border café we used to use for a staging ground?"

"I can. Tell me what you want."

Micah outlined the equipment he wanted, including an old DC-3 to get them into the Yucatán, from which his men would drop with parachutes at night.

"You can fly in under the radar in that," Eb cautioned, "but the DEA will assume you're trying to bring in drugs if they spot you. It'll be tricky."

"Damn!" Micah was remembering that someone in federal authority was on Lopez's payroll. "I had a contact near Lopez, but he left the country. Rodrigo's cousin might help, but he'd be risking his life after this latest tip he fed Rodrigo. So, basically, we've got nobody in Lopez's organization. And if I use my regular contacts, I risk alerting the DEA. Who can I trust?"

"I know someone," Eb said after a minute. "I'll take care of that. Phone me when you're on the ground in Cancún and make sure you've got global positioning equipment with you."

"Will do. Thanks, Eb."

"What are friends for? I'll be in touch. Good luck."

"Thanks."

"Want me to call Cy?"

"No. I'll go by his place on my way out of town and catch him up." He hung up.

He didn't want to leave Callie's car with the door

open and her purse in it, but he didn't want to be accused of tampering with evidence later. He compromised by locking it and closing the door. The police would find it eventually, because they patrolled this way. They'd take it from there, but he didn't want anyone in authority to know he was going after Callie. Someone had warned Lopez about the recent devastating DEA raid on his property. That person was still around, and Micah didn't want anyone to guess that he knew about Callie's kidnapping.

It was hard to think clearly, but he had to. He knew that Callie had a cell phone. He didn't know if she had it with her. If Callie had the phone, and Lopez's people didn't know, she might be able to get a call out. He didn't flatter himself that she'd call him. But she might try to call the adult day care center, if she could. It wasn't much, but it gave him hope.

He drove to the center. For one mad instant he thought about speaking to his father in person. But that would only complicate matters and upset the old man; they hadn't spoken in years. He couldn't risk causing his father to have another stroke or a second heart attack by telling him that Callie had been kidnapped.

He went to the office of the nursing director of the center instead and took her into his confidence. She agreed with him that it might be best if they kept the news from his father, and they formulated a cover story that was convincing. It was easy enough for him to arrange for a nurse to go home with his father to Callie's apartment every night and to drive him to the center each day. They decided to tell Jack Steele that one of Callie's elderly aunts had been hurt in a car wreck and she had to go to Houston to see about her. Callie had no elderly aunts, but Jack wouldn't know that. It would placate him and keep him from worrying. Then Micah would have to arrange for someone to protect him from any attempts by Lopez on his life.

He went back to his motel and spent the rest of the night and part of the next day making international phone calls. He knew that Chet Blake, the police chief, would call in the FBI once Callie's disappearance was noted, and that wasn't a bad idea. They would, of course, try to notify Micah, but they wouldn't be able to find him. That meant that Lopez's man in law enforcement would think Micah didn't know that his stepsister had been kidnapped. And that would work to his benefit.

But if Lopez's men carried Callie down to the Yucatán, near Cancún, which was where the drug lord lived these days, it was going to become a nightmare of diplomacy for any U.S. agency that tried to get her out of his clutches, despite international law enforcement co-operation. Micah didn't have that problem. He had Bojo, one of his best mercenaries, with him in the States. It took time to track down the rest of his team, but by dawn he'd managed it and arranged to meet them in Belize that night. He hated waiting that long, and he worried about what Callie was going to endure in the meantime. But any sort of assault took planning, especially on a fortress like Lopez's home. To approach it by sea was impossible. Lopez had several fast boats and guards patrolling the sea wall night and day. It would have to be a land-based attack, which was where the DC-3 came in. The trusty old planes were practically indestructible.

He couldn't get Callie's ordeal out of his mind. He'd kept tabs on her for years without her knowledge. She'd dated one out-of-town auditor and a young deputy sheriff, but nothing came of either relationship. She seemed to balk at close contact with men. That was disturbing to him, because he'd made some nasty allegations about her morals being as loose as her mother's after she'd come on to him under the mistletoe four years ago.

He didn't think words would be damaging, but perhaps they were. Callie had a reputation locally for being as pure as fresh snow. In a small town, where everybody knew everything about their neighbors, you couldn't hide a scandal. That made him feel even more guilty, because Callie had been sweet and uninhibited until he'd gone to work on her. It was a shame that he'd taken out his rage on her, when it was her mother who'd caused all the problems in his family. Callie's innocence was going to cost her dearly, in Lopez's grasp. Micah groaned aloud as he began to imagine what might happen to her now. And it would be his fault.

He packed his suitcase and checked out of the motel. On the way to the airport, he went by Cy Parks's place, to tell him what was going on. Eb was doing enough already; Micah hated the thought of putting more on him. Besides, Cy would have been miffed if he was left out of this. He had his own reasons for wanting Lopez brought down. The vengeful drug lord had endangered the life of Cy's bride, Lisa, and the taciturn rancher wouldn't rest easy until Lopez got what was coming to him. He sympathized with Micah about Callie's kidnapping and Jack Steele's danger. To Micah's relief, he also volunteered to have one of his men, a former law enforcement officer, keep a covert eye on his father, just in case. That relieved Micah's troubled mind. He drove to the airport, left the rented Porsche in the parking lot with the attendant, and boarded the plane to Belize. Then he went to work.

Callie came to in a limousine. She was trussed up like a calf in a bulldogging competition, wrists and ankles bound, and a gag in her mouth. The three men who'd kidnapped her were conversing.

They weren't speaking Spanish. She heard at least one Arabic word that she understood. At once, she knew that they were Manuel Lopez's men, and that Micah had told the truth about the danger she and Jack were in. It was too late now, though. She'd been careless and she'd been snatched.

She lowered her eyelids when one of the men glanced toward her, pretending to still be groggy, hoping for a chance to escape. Bound as she was, that seemed impossible. She shifted a little, noticing with comfort the feel of the tiny cell phone she'd slipped into her slacks' pocket before leaving the office. If they didn't frisk her, she might get a call out. She remembered what she'd heard about Lopez, and her blood ran cold.

She couldn't drag her wrists out of the bonds. They felt like ropes, not handcuffs. Her arm was sore—she wondered if perhaps they'd given her a shot, a sedative of some sort. She must have been out a very long time. It had been late afternoon when she'd been kidnapped. Now it was almost dawn. She wished she had a drink of water....

The big limousine ate up the miles. She had some vague sensation that she'd been on an airplane. Perhaps they'd flown to an airport and the car had picked them up. If only she could see out the window. There were undefined shadows out there. They looked like trees, a lot of trees. Her vision was slightly blurred and she felt as if her limbs were made of iron. It was difficult to concentrate, and more difficult to try to move. What had they given her?

One man spoke urgently to the other and indicated Callie. He smiled and replied with a low, deep chuckle.

Callie noticed then that her blouse had come apart in the struggle. Her bra was visible, and those men were staring at her as if they had every right. She felt sick to her soul. It didn't take knowing the language to figure out what they were saying. She was completely innocent, but before this ordeal was over, she knew she never would be again. She felt a wave of grief wash over her. If only Micah hadn't pushed her away that Christmas. Now it was too late. Her first and last experience of men was going to be a nightmarish one, if she even lived through it. That seemed doubtful. Once the drug lord discovered that Micah had no affection for his stepsister, that he actually hated her and wouldn't soil his hands paying her ransom, she was going to be killed. She knew what happened in kidnappings. Most people knew. It had never occurred to her that she would ever figure in one. How ironic, that she was poor and unattractive, and that hadn't spared her this experience.

She wondered dimly what Micah would say when he knew she was missing. He'd probably feel well rid of her, but he might pay the ransom for her father's sake. Someone had to look after Jack Steele, something his only child couldn't apparently be bothered to do. Callie loved the old man and would have gladly sacrificed her life for him. That made her valuable in at least one way.

The one bright spot in all this was that once word of Callie's kidnapping got out, Micah would hire a bodyguard for Jack whether he wanted one or not. Jack would be safe.

She wished she knew some sort of self-defense, some way of protecting herself, of getting loose from the ropes and the gag that was slowly strangling her. She hadn't had time for lunch the day before and she'd been drugged for the whole night and into the next morning. She was sick and weak from hunger and thirst, and she really had to go to the bathroom. It was a bad day all around.

She closed her eyes and wished she'd locked her car doors and sped out of reach of her assailants. If there was a next time, if she lived to repeat her mistakes, she'd never repeat that one.

She shifted because her legs were cramping and she felt even sicker.

Listening to the men converse in Arabic, she realized her abductors weren't from Mexico. But as she looked out the window now, she could see the long narrow paved ribbon of road running through what looked like rain forest. She'd never been to the Yucatán, but she knew what it looked like from volumes of books she'd collected on Maya relics. Her heart sank. She knew that Manuel Lopez lived near Cancún, and she knew she was in the Yucatán. Her worst fears were realized.

Only minutes later, the car pulled into a long paved driveway through tall steel gates. The gates closed behind them. They sped up to an impressive whitewashed beach house overlooking a rocky bay. It had red ceramic tiles and the grounds were immaculate and full of blooming flowers. Hibiscus in November. She could have laughed hysterically. Back home the trees were bare, and here everything was blooming. She wondered what sort of fertilizer they used to grow those hibiscus flowers so big, and then she remembered Lopez's recent body count. She wondered if she might end up planted in his garden...

The car stopped. The door was opened by a suited dark man holding an automatic rifle of some sort, one of those little snub-nosed machine guns that crooks on television always seemed to carry.

She winced as the men dragged her out of the car and frog-marched her, bonds and all, into the ceramic tile-floored lobby. The tile was black and white, like a chessboard. There was a long, graceful staircase and, overhead, a crystal chandelier that looked like Waterford crystal. It probably cost two or three times the price of her car.

As she searched her surroundings, a small middle-aged man strolled out of the living room with his hands in his pockets. He didn't smile. He walked around Callie as if she were some sort of curiosity, his full lips pursed, his small dark eyes narrow and smugly gleaming. He jerked her gag down.

"Miss Kirby," he murmured in accented English. "Welcome to my home. I am Manuel Lopez. You will be my guest until your interfering stepbrother tries to rescue you," he added, hesitating in front of her. "And when he arrives, I will give him what my men have left of you, before I kill him, too!"

Callie thought that she'd never seen such cruelty in a human being's eyes in her life. The man made her knees shake. He was looking at her with contempt and possession. He reached out a stubby hand and ripped her blouse down in front, baring her small breasts in their cotton bra.

"I had expected a more attractive woman," he said.

"Sadly you have no attractions with which to bargain, have you? Small breasts and a body that would afford little satisfaction. But Kalid likes women," he mused, glancing at the small, dark man who'd been sitting across from Callie. "When I need information, he is the man who obtains it for me. And although I need no information from you, Miss Kirby," he murmured, "it will please Kalid to practice his skills."

A rapid-fire burst of a foreign language met the statement.

"Español!" Lopez snapped. "You know I do not understand Arabic!"

"The woman," one of the other men replied in Spanish. "Before you give her to Kalid, let us have her."

Lopez glanced at the two thin, unshaven men who'd delivered Callie to him and smiled. "Why not? I make you a present of her. It should arouse even more guilt in her stepbrother to find her...used. But not until I tell you," he added coldly. "For now, take her to the empty servant's room upstairs. And put the gag back in place," he added. "I have important guests arriving. I would not want them to be disturbed by any unexpected noise."

"My stepbrother won't come to rescue me," she said hoarsely, shocked. "He isn't a physical sort of man. Aren't you going to ask him to pay ransom?"

Lopez looked at her as if she were nuts. "Why do you think Steele will not come after you?"

"He's a doctor. Or he was studying to be one. He wouldn't know the first thing about rescuing somebody!"

Lopez seemed to find that amusing.

"Besides that," she added harshly, "he hates me. He'll probably laugh his head off when he knows you've got me. He can't stand the sight of me."

That seemed to disturb Lopez, but after a minute he shrugged. *"No importa,"* he said lightly. "If he comes, that will be good. If not, it will make him even more concerned for his father. Who will be," he added with a cold smile, "next to feel my wrath."

Callie had her mouth open to ask another question, but at a signal from Lopez she was half dragged out of the room, her pale blue eyes as wide as saucers as she shivered with fear.

# Chapter 2

Callie had never been in such danger in her life, although she certainly knew what it was to be manhandled. She'd been in and out of foster care since the age of six. On a rare visit home, one of her mother's lovers had broken her arm when she was thirteen, after trying to fondle her. She'd run from him in horror, and he'd caught up with her at the staircase. A rough scuffle with the man had sent her tumbling down the steps to lie sprawled at the foot of the staircase.

Her mother had been furious, but not at her boyfriend, who said that Callie had called him names and threatened to tell her mother lies about him. After her broken arm had been set in a cast, Anna had taken Callie right back to her foster home, making her out to be incorrigible and washing her hands of responsibility for her.

Oddly, it had been Jack Steele's insistence that he

wanted the child that had pushed a reluctant Anna into taking her back, at the age of fifteen. Jack had won her over, a day at a time. When Micah was home for holidays, he'd taunted her, made his disapproval of her so noticeable that her first lesson in the Steele home was learning how to avoid Jack's grown son. She'd had a lot of practice at avoiding men by then, and a lot of emotional scars. Anna had found that amusing. Never much of a mother, she'd ignored Callie to such an extent that the only affection Callie ever got was from Jack.

She closed her eyes. Her own father had ripped her out of his arms when she was six and pushed her away when she begged to stay with him. She was some other man's bastard, he'd raged, and he wanted no part of her. She could get out with her tramp of a mother—whom he'd just caught in bed with a rich friend—and he never wanted to see either of them again. She'd loved her father. She never understood why he couldn't love her back. Well, he thought she wasn't his. She couldn't really blame him for feeling that way.

She was still sitting in a small bedroom that night, having been given nothing to eat or drink. She was weak with hunger and pain, because the bonds that held her wrists and ankles had chafed and all but cut off the circulation. She heard noise downstairs from time to time. Obviously Lopez's visitors had stayed a long time, and been quite entertained, from the sound of things. She could hear the soft whisper of the ocean teasing the shore outside the window. She wondered what they would do with her body, after they killed her. Perhaps they'd throw her out there, to be eaten by sharks.

While she was agonizing over her fate, the sky had darkened. Hours more passed, during which she dozed a little. Then suddenly, she was alone no longer. The door opened and closed. She opened her tired eyes and saw the three men who'd kidnapped her, gathered around her like a pack of dogs with a helpless cat. One of them started stripping her while the others watched. Her cell phone fell out of the pocket of her slacks as they were pulled off her long legs. One of the men tossed it up and laughed, speaking to another man in yet a different foreign language.

Callie closed her eyes, shivering with fear, and prayed for strength to bear what was coming. She wished with all her heart that Micah hadn't pushed her away that last Christmas they'd spent together. Better him than any one of these cold, cruel, mocking strangers.

She heard one of them speaking in rough Spanish, discussing her body, making fun of her small breasts. It was like a playback from one foster home when she was fifteen, where an older son of the family had almost raped her before he was interrupted by the return of his parents. She'd run away afterward, and been sent to another foster home. She'd been saved that time, but she could expect no help now. Micah wouldn't begin to know how to rescue her, even if he was inclined to save her. He probably wouldn't consider ransom, either. She was alone in the world, with no one who would care about her fate. Her mother probably wouldn't even be bothered if she died. Like Micah, she'd blamed Callie for what had happened.

Desperate for some way to endure the ordeal, to block it out, Callie pictured the last time she'd seen her grandmother before she passed away, standing in an arbor of little pink fairy roses, waving. Callie had often stayed with her father's widowed mother when he and Anna were traveling. It was a haven of love. It hadn't lasted. Her grandmother had died suddenly when she was five. Everyone she'd ever loved had left her, in one way or the other. Nobody would even miss her. Maybe Jack would. She spared one last thought for the poor old man who was as alone as she was. But with her out of the way, perhaps Micah would go home again…

There was a loud, harsh shout. She heard the door open, and the men leave. With a shivery sigh, she moved backward until she could ease down into a worn wing chair by the fireplace. It wasn't going to be a long reprieve, she knew. If only she could free herself! But the bonds were cutting into her wrists and ankles. She was left in only a pair of aged white briefs and a tattered white bra, worn for comfort and not for appearance. No one had seen her in her underwear since she was a small child. She felt tears sting her eyes as she sat there, vulnerable and sick and ashamed. Any minute now, those men would be back. They would untie her before they used her. She knew that. She had to try to catch them off guard the instant she was free and run. If she could get into the jungle, she might have a chance. She was a fast sprinter, and she knew woodcraft. It was the last desperate hope she had.

One of the men, the one who'd asked Lopez for her, came back inside for a minute, staring at her. He pulled out a wicked-looking little knife and flicked it at one shoulder strap of her bra, cutting right through it.

She called him a foul name in Spanish, making herself understood despite the gag. Her mind raced along. If she could make him angry enough to free her, which he'd have to do if he had rape in mind… She repeated the foul name, with more fervor.

He cursed. But instead of pulling her up to untie her, he caught her by the shoulder and pressed her hard back into the chair, easing the point of the knife against the soft, delicate upper part of her breast.

She moaned hoarsely as the knife lightly grazed her flesh.

"You will learn manners before we finish with you," he drawled icily, in rough Spanish. "You will do what I tell you!"

He made no move to free her. Instead, he jerked down the side of her bra that had been cut, and stared mockingly at her breast.

The prick from the knife stung. She ground her teeth together. What had she been thinking? He wasn't going to free her. He was going to torture her! She felt sick unto death with fear as she looked up into his eyes and realized that he was enjoying both her shame and her fear.

In fact, he laughed. He went back and locked the door. "We don't need to be disturbed, do we?" he purred as he walked back toward her, brandishing the sharp knife. "I have looked forward to this all the way from Texas..."

Her eyes closed. She said a last, silent prayer. She thought of Micah, and of Jack. Her chin lifted as she waited bravely for the impact of the blade.

There was a commotion downstairs and a commotion outside. She'd hoped it might divert the man standing over her with that knife, but he was too intent on her vulnerable state to care what was going on elsewhere. He put one hand on the back of the chair, beside her head, and placed the point of the knife right against her breast.

"Beg me not to do it," he chuckled. "Come on. Beg me."

Her terrified eyes met his and she knew that he was

going to violate her. It was in his face. He was almost drooling with pleasure. She was cold all over, sick, resigned. She would die, eventually. But in the meantime, she was going to suffer a fate that would make death welcome.

"Beg me!" he demanded, his eyes flashing angrily, and the blade pushed harder.

There was a sudden burst of gunfire from somewhere toward the front of the house. Simultaneously, there was shattering glass behind the man threatening her, and the sudden audible sound of bullets hitting flesh. The man with the knife groaned once and fell into a silent, red-stained heap at her feet.

Wide-eyed, terrified, shaking, Callie cried out as she looked up into a face completely covered with a black mask, except for slits that bared a little of his eyes and mouth. He was dressed all in black with a wicked-looking little machine gun in one hand and a huge knife suddenly in the other. His eyes went to her nicked breast. He made a rough sound and kicked the man on the floor aside as he pulled Callie up out of the chair and cut the bonds at her ankles and wrists.

Her hands and feet were asleep. She almost fell. He didn't even stop to unfasten the gag. Without a word, he bent and lifted her over his shoulder in the classic fireman's carry, and walked straight toward the window. Apparently, he was going out it, with her.

He finished clearing away the broken glass around the window frame and pulled a long black cord toward him. It seemed to be hanging from the roof.

He was huge and very strong. Callie, still in shock from her most recent ordeal, her feet and hands almost numb, didn't try to talk. She didn't even protest. If this was a turf war, and she was being stolen by another drug lord, perhaps he'd just hold her for ransom and not let his men torture her. She had little to say about her own fate. She closed her eyes and noticed that there was a familiar smell about the man who was abducting her. Odd. He must be wearing some cologne that reminded her of Jack, or even Mr. Kemp. At least he'd saved her from the knife.

Her wounded breast hurt, where it was pressed against the ribbed fabric of his long-sleeved shirt, and the small cut was bleeding slightly, but that didn't seem to matter. As long as he got her out of Lopez's clutches, she didn't really care what happened to her anymore. She was exhausted.

With her still over his shoulder, he stepped out onto the ledge, grasped a thick black cord in a gloved hand and, with his rifle leveled and facing forward, he rappelled right out the second-story window and down to the ground with Callie on his shoulder. She gasped as she felt the first seconds of free fall, and her hands clung to his shirt, but he didn't drop her. He seemed quite adept at rappelling.

She'd read about the Australian rappel, where men went down the rope face-front with a weapon in one hand. She'd never seen it done, except on television and in adventure movies. She'd never seen anyone doing it with a hostage over one shoulder. This man was very skillful. She wondered if he really was a rival drug lord, or if perhaps he was one of Eb Scott's mercenaries. Was it possible that Micah would have cared enough to ask Eb to mount her rescue? Her heart leaped at the possibility.

As they reached the ground, she realized that her rescuer wasn't alone. As soon as they were on the ground, he made some sort of signal with one hand, and men dressed in black, barely visible in the security lights dotted along the dark estate, scattered to the winds. Men in suits, still firing after them, began to run toward the jungle.

A four-wheel-drive vehicle was sitting in the driveway with its engine running and the backseat door open, waiting.

Her rescuer threw her inside, climbed in beside her and slammed the door. She pulled the gag off.

"Hit it!" he bit off.

The vehicle spun dirt and gravel as it took off toward the gate. The windows were open. Gunfire hit the side of the door, and was returned by the man sitting beside Callie and the man in the front passenger seat. The other armed man had a slight, neatly trimmed beard and mustache and he looked as formidable as his comrade. The man who was driving handled the vehicle expertly, dodging bullets even as his companions returned fire at the pursuing vehicle. Callie had seen other armed men in black running for the jungle. She revised her opinion that these were rival drug dealers. From the look of these men, they were commandos. She assumed that these three men were part of some sort of covert group sent in to rescue her. Only one person would have the money to mount such an expedition, and she'd have bet money that Eb Scott was behind it somehow. Micah must have paid him to hire these men to come after her.

If he had, she was grateful for his intervention, although she wondered what had prompted it. Perhaps his father had persuaded him. God knew, he'd never have spent that sort of money on her rescue for his own sake.

Her sudden disappearance out of his life would have delighted him.

She was chilled and embarrassed, sitting in her underwear with three strange men, but her clothing had been ripped beyond repair. In fact, her rescuer hadn't even stopped to grab it up on his way out of the room where she was being held. She made herself as inconspicuous as possible, grateful that there was no light inside the vehicle, and closed her eyes while the sound of gunfire ricocheted around her. She didn't say a word. Her companions seemed quite capable of handling this new emergency. She wasn't going to distract them. If she caught a stray bullet, that was all right, too. Anything, even death, would be preferable to what she would endure if Lopez regained custody of her.

Half a mile down the road, there was a deep curve. The big man who'd rescued Callie told the man in front to stop the vehicle. He grabbed a backpack on the floorboard, jumped out, pulled Callie out, and motioned the driver and the man with the beard and mustache to keep going. The big man carried Callie out of sight of the road and dashed her down in the dark jungle undergrowth, his powerful body lying alongside hers in dead leaves and debris while they waited for the Jeep that had been chasing them to appear. Thorns dug into her bare arms and legs, but she was so afraid that she hardly noticed.

Suddenly, the pursuing Jeep came into sight. It braked for the curve, but it barely slowed down as it shot along after the other vehicle. Its taillights vanished around the bend. So far, so good, Callie thought, feeling oddly safe with the warmth and strength of the man lying so close beside her. But she hoped the man who was driving their vehicle and his bearded companion made a clean get-away. She wouldn't want them shot, even to save herself.

"That went well," her companion murmured curtly, rising. He pulled out some sort of electronic gadget and pushed buttons. He turned, sighting along it. "Can you walk?" he asked Callie.

His voice was familiar. Her mind must be playing tricks. She stood up, still in her underwear and barefoot.

"Yes. But I...don't have any shoes," she said hoarsely, still half in shock.

He looked down at her, aiming a tiny flashlight at her body, and a curse escaped his mouth as he saw her mangled bra.

"What the hell did they do to you?" he asked through his teeth.

Amazing, how familiar that deep voice was. "Not as much as they planned to, thanks to you," she said, trying to remain calm. "It's not a bad cut, just a graze. I'll have to have some sort of shoes if we're going to walk. And I...I don't suppose you have an extra shirt?" she added with painful dignity.

He was holding a backpack. He pulled out a big black T-shirt and stuffed her into it. He had a pair of camouflage pants, too. They had to be rolled up, but they fit uncannily well. His face was solemn as he dug into the bag a second time and pulled out a pair of leather loafers and two pairs of socks.

"They'll be too big, but the socks will help them fit. They'll help protect your feet. Hurry. Lopez's men are everywhere and we have a rendezvous to make."

She felt more secure in the T-shirt and camouflage pants. Not wanting to hold him up, she slipped quickly into the two pairs of thick socks and rammed her feet into the shoes. It was dark, but her companion had his small light trained ahead. She noticed that huge knife in his left hand as he started ahead of her. She remembered that Micah was left-handed...

The jungle growth was thick, but passable. Her companion shifted his backpack, so dark that it blended in with his dark gear and the jungle.

"Stay close behind me. Don't speak unless I tell you to. Don't move unless I move."

"Okay," she said in a husky whisper, without argument.

"When we get where we're going, I'll take care of that cut."

She didn't answer him. She was exhausted. She was also dying of thirst and hunger, but she knew there wasn't time for the luxury of food. She concentrated on where she was putting her feet, and prayed that she wouldn't trip over a huge snake. She knew there were snakes and lizards and huge spiders in the jungle. She was afraid, but Lopez was much more terrorizing a threat than a lonesome snake.

She followed her taciturn companion through the jungle growth, her eyes restless, her ears listening for any mechanical sound. The darkness was oddly comforting, because sound traveled so well in it. Once, she heard a quick, sharp rustle of the underbrush and stilled, but her companion quickly trained his light on it. It was only an iguana.

She laughed with delight at the unexpected encounter, bringing a curt jerk of the head from her companion, who seemed to find her amusement odd. He didn't say anything, though. He glanced at his instrument again, stopped to listen and look, and started off again.

Thorns in some of the undergrowth tore at her bare arms and legs, and her face. She didn't complain. Remembering where she'd been just before she was rescued made her grateful for any sort of escape, no matter how physically painful it might be.

She began to make a mental list of things she had to do when they reached safety. First on the list was to phone and see if Jack Steele was all right. He must be worried about her sudden disappearance. She didn't want him to suffer a setback.

Her lack of conversation seemed to puzzle the big man leading her through the jungle. He glanced back at her frequently, presumably to make sure she was behind him, but he didn't speak. He made odd movements, sometimes doubling back on the trail he made, sometimes deliberately snapping twigs and stepping on grass in directions they didn't go. Callie just followed along mindlessly.

At least two hours passed before he stopped, near a small stream. "We should be safe enough here for the time being," he remarked as he put down the backpack and opened it, producing a small bottle of water. He tossed it to Callie. "I imagine you're thirsty."

She opened it with trembling hands and swallowed half of it down at once, tears stinging her eyes at the pleasure of the wetness on her tongue, in her dry mouth.

He set up a small, self-contained light source, revealing his companion. He moved closer, frowning at her enthusiastic swallowing as he drew a first aid kit from his backpack. "When did you last have anything to drink?" he asked softly.

"Day...before yesterday," she choked.

He cursed. In the same instant, he pulled off the mask

he'd been wearing, and Callie dropped the water bottle as her eyes encountered the dark ones of her stepbrother, Micah, in the dim light.

He picked up the water bottle and handed it back to her. "I thought it might come as a shock," he said grimly, noting her expression.

"You came after me yourself?" she asked, aghast. "But, how? Why?"

"Lopez has an agent in one of the federal agencies," he told her flatly. "I don't know who it is. I couldn't risk letting them come down here looking for you and having someone sell you out before I got here. Not that it would have been anytime soon. They're probably still arguing over jurisdictions as we speak." He pulled out a foil-sealed package and tossed it to her. "It's the equivalent of an MRE—a meal ready to eat. Nothing fancy, but if you're hungry, you won't mind the taste."

"Thanks," she said huskily, tearing into it with urgent fingers that trembled with hunger.

He watched her eat ravenously, and he scowled. "No food, either?"

She shook her head. "You don't feed people you're going to kill," she mumbled through bites of chicken and rice that tasted freshly cooked, if cold.

He was very still. "Excuse me?"

She glanced at him while she chewed a cube of chicken. "He gave me to three of his men and told them to kill me." She swallowed and averted her eyes. "He said they could do whatever they liked to me first. So they did. At least, they started to, when you showed up. I was briefly alone with a smaller man, Arabic I think, and I tried to make him mad enough to release me so I had one last chance at escape. It made him mad, all right, but instead of untying me, he…put his knife into me." She chewed another cube of chicken, trying not to break down. "He said it was a…a taste of what to expect if I resisted him again. When you came in through the window, he was just about to violate me."

"I'm going to take care of that cut right now. Infection sets in fast in tropical areas like this." He opened the first-aid box and checked through his supplies. He muttered something under his breath.

He took the half-finished meal away from her and stripped her out of the T-shirt. She grimaced and lowered her eyes as her mutilated bra and her bare breast were revealed, but she didn't protest.

"I know this is going to be hard for you, considering what you've just been through. But try to remember that I'm a doctor," he said curtly. "As near as not, anyway."

She swallowed, her eyes still closed tight. "At least you won't make fun of my body while you're working on it," she said miserably.

He was opening a small bottle. "What's that?"

"Nothing," she said wearily. "Oh God, I'm so tired!"

"I can imagine."

She felt his big, warm hands reach behind her to unfasten the bra and she caught it involuntarily.

He glanced at her face in the small circle of light from the lantern. "If there was another way, I'd take it."

She drew in a slow breath and closed her eyes, letting go of the fabric. She bit her lip and didn't look as he peeled the fabric away from her small, firm breasts.

The sight of the small cut made him furious. She had pretty little breasts, tip-tilted, with dusky nipples. He could feel himself responding to the sight of her, and he had to bite down hard on a wave of desire.

He forced himself to focus on the cut, and nothing else. The bra, he stuffed in his backpack. He didn't dare leave signs behind them. There wasn't much chance that they were closely followed, but he had to be careful.

He had to touch her breast to clean the small cut, and she jerked involuntarily.

"I won't hurt you any more than I have to," he promised quietly, mistaking her reaction for pain. "Grit your teeth."

She did, but it didn't help. She bit almost through her lip as he cleaned the wound. The sight of his big, lean hands on her body was breathtaking, arousing even under the circumstances. The pain was secondary to the hunger she felt for him, a hunger that had lasted for years. He didn't know, and she couldn't let him know. He hated her.

She closed her eyes while he put a soft bandage over the cleaned wound, taping it in place.

"God in heaven, I thought I'd seen every kind of low-life on earth, but the guy who did this to you was in a class all by himself," he growled.

She remembered the man and shuddered. Micah was pulling the shirt down over her bandaged breast. "It probably doesn't seem like it, but I got off lucky," she replied.

He looked into her eyes. "It's just a superficial wound so you won't need stitches. It probably won't even leave a scar there."

"It wouldn't matter," she said quietly.

"It would." He got up, drawing her up with him. "You're still nervous of me, after all this time."

She didn't meet his eyes. "You don't like me."

"Oh, for God's sake," he burst out, letting go of her

shoulders. He turned away to deal with the medical kit. "Haven't you got eyes?"

She wondered what that meant. She was too tired to work it out. She sat down again and picked up her half-eaten meal, finishing it with relish. It was hard to look at him, after he'd seen her like that.

She fingered the rolled-up pair of camouflage pants she was wearing. "These aren't big enough to be yours," she remarked.

"They're Maddie's. She gave me those for you, and the shoes and socks, on the way out of Texas," he commented when he noticed her curious exploration of the pants.

He worked with some sort of electronic device.

"What's that thing?" she asked.

"GPS," he explained. "Global positioning. I can give my men a fix on our position, so they can get a chopper in here to pick us up and pinpoint our exact location. There's a clearing just through there where we'll rendezvous," he added, nodding toward the jungle.

Suddenly she frowned. "Who's Maddie?" she asked.

"Maddie's my scrounger. Anything we need on site that we didn't bring, Maddie can get. She's quite a girl. In fact," he added, "she looks a lot like you. She was mistaken for you at a wedding I went to recently in Washington, D.C."

That was disturbing. It sounded as though he and this Maddie were in partnership or something. She hated the jealousy she felt, when she had no right to be jealous. Old habits died hard.

"Is she here?" she asked, still puzzled by events and Micah's strange skills.

"No. We left her back in the States. She's working

on some information I need, about the mole working for the feds, and getting some of your things together to send on to Miami."

She blinked. "You keep saying 'we,'" she pointed out.

His chin lifted. He studied her, unsmiling. "Exactly what do you think I do for a living, Callie?" In the dim light, his blond hair shone like muted moonlight. His handsome face was all angles and shadows. Her vision was still a little blurred from whatever the kidnapper had given her. So was her mind.

"Your mother left you a trust," she pointed out.

"My mother left me ten thousand dollars," he replied. "That wouldn't pay to replace the engine on the Ferrari I drive in Nassau."

Her hands stilled on the fork and tray. Some odd ideas were popping into her head. "You finished your residency?" she fished.

He shook his head. "Medicine wasn't for me."

"Then, what…?"

"Use your mind, Callie," he said finally, irritated. "How many men do you know who could rappel into a drug lord's lair and spirit out a hostage?"

Her breath caught. "You work for some federal agency?"

"Good God!" He got up, moved to his backpack and started repacking it. "You really don't have a clue, do you?"

"I don't know much about you, Micah," she confided quietly as she finished her meal and handed him the empty tray and fork. "That was the way you always wanted it."

"In some cases, it doesn't pay to advertise," he said carelessly. "I used to work with Eb Scott and Cy Parks, but now I have my own group. We hire out to various world governments for covert ops." He glanced at her stunned face. "I worked for the justice department for a couple of years, but now I'm a mercenary, Callie."

She was struck dumb for several long seconds. She swallowed. It explained a lot. "Does your father know?" she asked.

"He does not," he told her. "And I don't want him to know. If he still gives a damn about me, it would only upset him."

"He loves you very much," she said quietly, avoiding his angry black eyes. "He'd like to mend fences, but he doesn't know how. He feels guilty, for making you leave and blaming you for what…what my mother did."

He pulled out a foil sealed meal for himself and opened it before he spoke. "You blamed me as well."

She wrapped her arms around herself. It was cold in the jungle at night, just like they said in the movies. "Not really. My mother is very beautiful," she said, recalling the older woman's wavy jet-black hair and vivid blue eyes and pale skin. "She was a model just briefly, before she married my…her first husband."

He frowned. "You were going to say, your father."

She shivered. "He said I wasn't his child. He caught her in bed with some rich man when I was six. I didn't understand at the time, but he pushed me away pretty brutally and said not to come near him again. He said he didn't know whose child I was. That was when she put me in foster care."

Micah stared at her, unspeaking, for several long seconds. "Put you in what?"

She swallowed. "She gave me up for adoption on the grounds that she couldn't support me. I went into a juvenile home, and from there to half a dozen foster homes. I only saw her once in all those years, when she took me home for Christmas. It didn't last long." She stared down at the jungle floor. "When she married your father, he wanted me, so she told him I'd been staying with my grandmother. I was in a foster home, but she got me out so she could convince your father that she was a good mother." She laughed hollowly. "I hadn't seen her or heard from her in two years by then. She told me I'd better make a good job of pretending affection, or she'd tell the authorities I'd stolen something valuable—and instead of going back into foster care for two more years, I'd go to jail."

# *Chapter 3*

Micah didn't say a word. He repacked the first-aid kit into his backpack with quick, angry movements. He didn't look at Callie.

"I guess you know how to use that gun," she said quietly. "If we're found, or if it looks like Lopez is going to catch us, I want you to shoot me. I'd rather die than face what you saved me from."

She said it in such a calm, quiet tone that it made all the more impact.

He looked up, scanning her drawn, white face in the soft light from the lantern. "He won't get you. I promise."

She drew a slow breath. "Thanks." She traced a fingernail over the camouflage pants. "And thanks for coming to get me. Lopez said he didn't have any plans to ransom me. He was going to let his men kill me because he thought it would make you suffer."

"What did you tell him?"

"That you were my worst enemy and you wouldn't care if he killed me," she said carelessly. "But he said you did care about your father, and he was the next victim. I hope you've got someone watching Dad," she added fervently. "If anything happens to him…!"

"You really love him, don't you?" he asked in an odd tone.

"He's the only person in my whole life who ever loved me," she said in a strained whisper.

A harsh sound broke from his lips. He got up and started getting things together. He pulled out what looked like a modified cell phone and spoke into it. A minute later, he put it back into the backpack.

"They're on the way in." He stood over her, his face grim as he picked up the small lantern and extinguished the light. "I know you must be cold. I'm sorry. I planned a quick airlift, so I didn't pack for a prolonged trek."

"It's all right," she said at once. "Cold is better than tortured."

He cursed under his breath as he hefted the backpack. "We have to get to that small clearing on the other side of the stream. It isn't deep, but I can carry you…"

"I'll walk," she said with quiet dignity, standing up. It was still painful to move, because she'd been tied up for so long, but she didn't let on. "You've done enough already."

"I've done nothing," he spat. He turned on his heel and led the way to the bank of the small stream, offering a hand.

She didn't take it. She knew he found her repulsive. He'd even told her mother that. She'd enjoyed taunting Callie with it. Callie had never understood why her mother hated her so much. Perhaps it was because she wasn't pretty.

"Walk where I do," he bit off as he dropped his hand. "The rocks will be slippery. Go around them, not over them."

"Okay."

He glanced over his shoulder as they started over the shallow stream. "You're damned calm for someone who's been through what you have in the past two days."

She only smiled. "You have no idea what I've been through in my life."

He averted his eyes. It was as if he couldn't bear to look at her anymore. He picked his way across to the other bank. Callie followed obediently, her feet cold and wet, her body shivering. Only a little longer, she told herself, and she would be home with Jack. She would be completely safe. Except…Lopez was still out there. She shivered again.

"Cold?" he asked when they were across.

"I'll be fine," she assured him.

He led her through one final tangle of brush, which he cut out of the way with the knife. She could see the silver ripple of the long blade in the dim light of the small flashlight he carried. She put one foot in front of the other and tried to blank out what would happen if Lopez's men caught up with them. It was terrifying.

They made it to the clearing just as a dark, noisy silhouette dropped from the sky and a door opened.

"They spotted us on radar!" came a loud voice from the chopper. "They'll be here in two minutes. Run!"

"Run as if your life depended on it!" Micah told Callie, giving her a push.

She did run, her mind so affected by what she'd already endured that she almost kept up with her long-legged stepbrother. He leaped right up into the chopper and gave her a hand up. She landed in a heap on the dirty floor, and laughed with relief.

The door closed and the chopper lifted. Outside, there were sounds like firecrackers in the wake of the noise the propellers made. Gunfire, Callie knew.

"It always sounds like firecrackers in real life," she murmured. "It doesn't sound that way in the movies."

"They augment the sound in movies, mademoiselle." A gentle hand eased her into a seat on the edge of the firing line Micah and two other men made at the door.

She looked up. There was barely any light in the helicopter, but she could make out a beard and a mustache on a long, lean face. "You made it, too!" she exclaimed with visible relief. "Oh, I'm glad. I felt bad that you and the other man had to be decoys, just to get me out."

"It was no trouble, mademoiselle," the man said gently, smiling at her. "Rest now. They won't catch us. This is an Apache helicopter, one of the finest pieces of equipment your country makes. It has some age, but we find it quite reliable in tight situations."

"Is it yours?" she asked.

He laughed. "You might say that we have access to it, and various other aircraft, when we need them."

"Don't bore her to death, Bojo," a younger voice chuckled.

"Listen to him!" Bojo exclaimed. "And do you not drone on eternally about that small computer you carry, Peter, and its divine functions?"

A dark-haired, dark-eyed young man with white teeth came into view, a rifle slung over his shoulder. "Computers are my specialty," he said with a grin. "You're Callie?

I'm Peter Stone. I'm from Brooklyn. That's Bojo, he's from Morocco. I guess you know Micah. And Smith over there—" he indicated a huge dark-eyed man "—runs a seafood restaurant in Charleston, along with our Maddie and a couple of guys we seem to have misplaced…"

"We haven't misplaced them," Micah said curtly. "They've gone ahead to get the DC-3 gassed up."

Bojo grinned. "Lopez will have men waiting at the airport for us."

"While we're taking off where we landed—at Laremos's private airstrip," Micah replied calmly. "And Laremos will have a small army at his airstrip, just in case Lopez does try anything."

"But what about customs?" Callie voiced.

Everybody laughed.

She flushed, realizing now that her captors hadn't gone through customs, and neither had these men. "Okay, I get it, but what about getting back into the States from here? I don't have a passport…"

"You have a birth certificate," Micah reminded her. "It'll be waiting in Miami, along with a small bag containing some of your own clothes and shoes. That's why Maddie didn't come with us," he added smugly.

"Miami?" she exclaimed, recalling belatedly that he'd mentioned that before. "Why not Texas?"

"You're coming back to the Bahamas with me, Callie," Micah replied. "You'll be Lopez's priority now. He'll be out for revenge, and it will take all of us to keep you safe."

She gaped at him. "But, Dad…" she groaned.

"Dad is in good hands. So are you. Now try not to worry. I know what I'm doing."

She bit her lower lip. None of this was making sense,

and she was still scared, every time she thought about Lopez. But all these men surrounding her looked tough and battle-hardened, and she knew they wouldn't let her be recaptured.

"Who's Laremos?" Callie asked curiously, a minute later.

"He's retired now," Micah said, coming away from the door. "But he and 'Dutch' van Meer and J. D. Brettman were the guys who taught us the trade. They were the best. Laremos lives outside Cancún on a plantation with his wife and kids, and he's got the equivalent of a small army around him. Even the drug lords avoid his place. We'll get out all right, even if Lopez has his men tracking us."

She averted her eyes and folded her arms tightly around her body.

"You are shivering," Bojo said gently. "Here." He found a blanket and wrapped it around her.

That one simple act of compassion brought all her repressed fear and anguish to the surface. She bawled. Not a sound touched her lips. But tears poured from her eyes, draping themselves hot and wet across her pale cheeks and down to the corner of her pretty bow mouth.

Micah saw them and his face hardened like rock.

She turned her face toward the other side of the helicopter. She was used to hiding her tears. They mostly angered people, made them more hostile. Or they showed a weakness that was readily exploited. It was always better not to let people know they had the power to hurt you.

She wrapped the blanket closer and didn't speak the rest of the way. She closed her eyes, wiping at them with the blanket. Micah spoke in low tones to the other men, and although she couldn't understand what he was saying, she understood that rough, angry tone. She'd heard it enough at home.

For now, all she wanted to do was get to safety, to a place where Lopez and the animals who worked for him couldn't find her, couldn't hurt her. She was more afraid now than she had been on the way out of Texas, because now she knew what recapture would mean. The darkness was a friend in which she could hide her fear, conceal her terror. The sound of the propellers became suddenly like a mechanical lullaby in her ears, lulling her, like the whispers of the deep voices around her, into a brief, fitful sleep.

She felt an odd lightness in her stomach and opened her eyes to find the helicopter landing at what looked like a small airstrip on private land.

A big airplane, with scars and faded lettering, was waiting with its twin prop engines already running. Half a dozen armed men in camouflage uniforms stood with their guns ready to fire. A tall, imposing man with a mustache came forward. He had a Latin look about him, dark eyes and graceful movement.

He shook hands with Micah and spoke to him quietly, so that his voice didn't carry. Micah listened, and then nodded. They shook hands again. The man glanced at Callie curiously, and smiled in her direction.

She smiled back, her whole young face drawn and fatigued.

Micah motioned to her. "We have to get airborne before Lopez's men get here. Climb aboard. Thanks, Diego!" he called to the man.

*"No es nada,"* came the grinning reply.

"Was that the man you know, with the plantation?"

Callie asked when they were inside and the door was closed.

"That was Laremos," he agreed.

"He and his family won't be hurt on our account, will they?" she persisted.

He glanced down at her. "No," he said slowly. His eyes searched hers until she looked away, made uneasy and shivery by the way he was looking at her.

He turned and made his way down the aisle to the cockpit. Two men poked their heads out of it, grinning, and after he spoke to them, they revved up the engines.

The passengers strapped themselves into their seats. Callie started to sit by herself, but Micah took her arm and guided her into the seat beside his. It surprised her, but she didn't protest. He reached across her to fasten her seat belt, bringing his hard, muscular chest pressing gently against her breasts.

She gasped as the pressure made the cut painful.

"God, I'm sorry! I forgot," he said, his hand going naturally, protectively, to her breast, to cup it gently. "Is it bad?"

She went scarlet. Of course, nobody was near enough to see what was going on, but it embarrassed her to have him touch her with such familiarity. And then she remembered that he'd had her nude from the waist up on one side while he cleaned and bandaged that cut.

Her eyes searched his while she tried to speak. Her tongue felt swollen. Her breath came jerkily into her throat and her lips parted under its force. She felt winded, as if she'd fallen from a height.

His thumb soothed the soft flesh around the cut. "When we get to Miami, I'll take you to a friend of mine who's in private practice. We'll get you checked out before we fly out to the Bahamas."

His other arm, muscular and warm, was under her head. She could feel his breath, mint-scented and warm, on her lips as he searched her eyes.

His free hand left her breast and gently cupped her softly rounded chin. "Soft skin," he whispered deeply. "Soft heart. Sweet, soft mouth…"

His lips pressed the words against her mouth, probing tenderly. He caught her upper lip in both of his and tasted it with his tongue. Then he lifted away to look down into her shocked, curious eyes.

"You should hate me," he whispered. "I hurt you, and you did nothing, nothing at all to deserve it."

She winced, remembering how it had been when he'd lived with his father. "I understood. You resented me. My mother and I were interlopers."

"Your mother, maybe. Never you." He looked formidable, angry and bitter. But his black eyes were unreadable. "I've hesitated to ask. Maybe I don't really want to know. When Lopez had you," he began with uncharacteristic hesitation, "were you raped?"

"No," she said quietly. "But I was about to be. I remember thinking that if it hadn't all gone wrong that Christmas…" Her voice stopped. She was horrified at what she was about to say.

"I know," he interrupted, and he didn't smile. "I thought about it, too. What Lopez's damned henchmen did to you at least wouldn't have been your first experience of intimacy, if I hadn't acted like a prize heel with you!"

He seemed maddened by the knowledge. His hand on her face was hard and the pressure stung.

"Please," she whispered, tugging at his fingers.

He relaxed them at once. "I'm sorry," he bit off. "I'm still on edge. This whole thing has been a nightmare."

"Yes." She searched his black eyes, wishing she knew what he was thinking.

His thumb brushed softly over her swollen mouth. "Lopez will never get the chance to hurt you again," he said quietly. "I give you my word."

She bit her lower lip when his hand lifted away, shy of him. "Do you really think he'll come after me again?"

"I think he'll try," he said honestly.

She shivered, averting her eyes to the aisle beside them. "I hate remembering how helpless I was."

"I've been in similar situations," he said surprisingly. "Once I was captured on a mission and held for execution. I was tied up and tortured. I know how it feels."

She gaped at him, horrified. "How did you escape?"

"Bojo and the others came in after me," he said simply. "Under impossible odds, too." He smiled, and it was the first genuine smile he'd ever given her. "I guess they missed being yelled at."

She smiled back, hesitantly. It was new to relax with Micah, not to be on her guard against antagonistic and sarcastic comments.

He touched her face with a curious intensity in his eyes. "You must have been terrified when you were kidnapped. You've never known violence."

She didn't tell him, but she had, even if not as traumatically as she had at Lopez's. She lowered her gaze to his hard, disciplined mouth. "I never expected to be rescued at all, least of all by you. I wasn't even sure you'd agree to pay a ransom if they'd asked for one."

He scowled. "Why not?"

"You don't like me," she returned simply. "You never did."

He seemed disturbed. "It's a little more complicated than that, Callie."

"All the same, thank you for saving me," she continued. "You risked your own life to get me out."

"I've been risking it for years," he said absently while he studied her upturned face. She was too pale, and the fatigue she felt was visible. "Why don't you try to sleep? It's going to be a long flight."

Obviously he didn't want to talk. But she didn't mind. She was worn-out. "Okay," she agreed with a smile.

He moved back and she leaned her head back, closed her eyes, and the tension of the past two days caught up with her all at once. She fell asleep almost at once and didn't wake up until they were landing.

She opened her eyes to find a hard, warm pillow under her head. To her amazement, she was lying across Micah's lap, with her cheek on his chest.

"Wakey, wakey," he teased gently. "We're on the ground."

"Where?" she asked, rubbing her eyes like a sleepy child.

"Miami."

"Oh. At the airport."

He chuckled. "*An* airport," he corrected. "But this one isn't on any map."

He lifted her gently back into her own seat and got to his feet, stretching hugely. He grinned down at her. "Come on, pilgrim. We've got a lot to do, and not much time."

She let him lead her off the plane. The other men had

all preceded them, leaving behind automatic weapons, pistols and other paraphernalia.

"Aren't you forgetting your equipment?" she asked Micah.

He smiled and put a long finger against her mouth. His eyes were full of mischief. He'd never joked with her, not in all the years they'd known each other.

"It isn't ours," he said in a stage whisper. "And see that building, and those guys coming out of it?"

"Yes."

"No," he corrected. "There's no building, and those guys don't exist. All of this is a figment of your imagination, especially the airplane."

"My gosh!" she exclaimed with wide eyes. "We're working for the CIA?"

He burst out laughing. "Don't even ask me who they are. I swore I'd never tell. And I never will. Now let's go, before they get here."

He and the others moved rapidly toward a big sport utility vehicle sitting just off the apron where they'd left the plane.

"Are you sure you cleared this with, uh—" Peter gave a quick glance at Callie "—the man who runs this place?"

"Eb did," Micah told him. "But just in case, let's get the hell out of Dodge, boys!"

He ran for the SUV, pushing Callie along. The others broke into a run as well, laughing as they went.

There was a shout behind them, but it was still hanging on the air when the driver, one of the guys in the cockpit, burned rubber taking off.

"He'll see the license plate!" Callie squeaked as she saw a suited man with a notepad looking after them.

"That's the idea," the young man named Peter told her with a grin. "It's a really neat plate, too. So is this vehicle. It belongs to the local director of the—" he hesitated "—of an agency we know. We, uh, had a friend borrow it from his house last night."

"We'll go to prison for years!" Callie exclaimed, horrified.

"Not really," the driver said, pulling quickly into a parking spot at a local supermarket. "Everybody out."

Callie's head was spinning. They got out of the SUV and into a beige sedan sitting next to it, with keys in the ignition. She was crowded into the back with Micah and young Peter, while the two pilots, one a Hispanic and the other almost as blond as Micah, crowded Bojo on either side in the front. The driver took off at a sedate pace and pulled out into Miami traffic.

That was when she noticed that all the men were wearing gloves. She wasn't. "Oh, that's lovely," she muttered. "That's just lovely! Everybody's wearing gloves but me. My fingerprints will be the only ones they find, and *I'll* go to prison for years. I guess you'll all come and visit me Sundays, right?" she added accusingly.

Micah chuckled with pure delight. "The guy who owns the SUV is a friend of Eb's, and even though he doesn't show it, he has a sense of humor. He'll double up laughing when he runs your prints and realizes who had his four-wheel drive. I'll explain it to you later. Take us straight to Dr. Candler's office, Don," he told the blond guy at the wheel. "You know where it is."

"You bet, boss," came the reply.

"I'm not going to prison?" Callie asked again, just to be sure.

Micah pursed his lips. "Well, that depends on whether

or not the guy at customs recognizes us. I was kidding!" he added immediately when she looked ready to cry.

She moved her shoulder and grimaced. "I'll laugh enthusiastically when I get checked out," she promised.

"He'll take good care of you," Micah assured her. "He and I were at medical school together."

"Is he, I mean, does he do what you do?"

"Not Jerry," he told her. "He specializes in trauma medicine. He's chief of staff at a small hospital here."

"I see," she said, nodding. "He's a normal person."

Micah gave her a speaking glance while the others chuckled.

The hospital where Micah's friend worked was only a few minutes from the airport. Micah took Callie inside while the others waited in the car. Micah had a private word with the receptionist, who nodded and left her desk for a minute. She came back with a tall, darkheaded man about Micah's age. He motioned to Micah.

Callie was led back into an examination room. Micah sank into a chair by the desk.

"Are you going to sit there the whole time?" Callie asked Micah, aghast, when the doctor asked her to remove the shirt she was wearing so he could examine her.

"You haven't got anything that I haven't seen, and I need to explain to Jerry what I did to treat your wound." He proceeded to do that while Callie, uncomfortable and shy, turned her shoulder to him and removed the shirt.

After checking her vital signs, Dr. Candler took the bandage off and examined the small red cut with a scowling face. "How did this happen?" he asked curtly.

"One of Lopez's goons had a knife and liked to play games with helpless women," Micah said coldly.

"I hope he won't be doing it again," the physician murmured as he cleaned and redressed the superficial wound.

"That's classified," Micah said simply.

Callie glanced at him, surprised. His black eyes met hers, but he didn't say anything else.

"I'm going to give you a tetanus shot as a precaution," Dr. Candler said with a professional smile. "But I can almost guarantee that the cut won't leave a scar when it heals. I imagine it stings."

"A little," Callie agreed.

"I need to give her a full examination," Dr. Candler told him after giving Callie the shot. "Why don't you go outside and smoke one of those contraband Cuban cigars I'm not supposed to know you have?"

"They aren't contraband," Micah told him. "It isn't illegal if you're given one that someone has purchased in Cuba. Cobb was down there last month and he brought me back several."

"Leave it to you to find a legal way to do something illegal," Candler chuckled.

"Speaking of which, I'd better give a mutual acquaintance a quick call and thank him for the loan of his equipment." He glanced at Callie and smiled softly. "Then maybe Callie can relax while you finish here."

She didn't reply. He went out and closed the door behind him. She let out an audible sigh of relief.

"Now," Dr. Candler said as he continued to examine her. "Tell me what happened."

She did, still shaken and frightened by what she'd experienced in the last two days. He listened while he worked, his face giving nothing away.

"What happened to the man who did it?" he persisted.

She gave him an innocent smile. "I really don't know," she lied.

He sighed. "You and Micah." He shook his head. "Have you known him long?"

"Since I was fifteen," she told him. "His father and my mother were briefly married."

"You're Callie!" the doctor said at once.

# Chapter 4

The look on Callie's face was priceless. "How did you know?" she asked.

He smiled. "Micah talks about you a lot."

That was a shocker. "I didn't think he wanted anybody to know I even existed," she pointed out.

He pursed his lips. "Well, let's just say that he has ambiguous feelings about you."

Ambiguous. Right. Plainly stated, he couldn't stand her. But if that was true, why had he come himself to rescue her, instead of just sending his men?

She drew in a breath as he tended to her. "Am I going to be okay?"

"You're going to be good as new in a few days." He smiled at her. "Trust me."

"Micah seems to."

"He should. I taught him everything he knows about

surgery," he chuckled. "I was a year ahead of him when we were in graduate school, and I took classes for one of the professors occasionally."

She smiled. "You're very good."

"So was he," he replied grimly.

She hesitated, but curiosity prodded her on. "If it wouldn't be breaking any solemn oath, could you tell me why he didn't finish his residency?"

He did, without going into details. "He realized medicine wasn't his true calling."

She nodded in understanding.

"But you didn't hear that from me," he added firmly.

"Oh, I never tell people things I know," she replied easily, smiling. "I work for a lawyer."

He chuckled. "Do tell?"

"He's something of a fire-eater, but he's nice to me. He practices criminal law back in Jacobsville, Texas."

He put the medical equipment to one side and told her she could get dressed.

"I'm going to put you on some antibiotics to fight off infection." He studied her with narrowed eyes. "What you've been through is traumatic," he added as he handed her the prescription bottle. "I'd advise counseling."

"Right now," she said on a long breath, "I'm occupied with just trying to stay alive. The drug dealer is still after me, you see."

His jaw tautened. "Micah will take care of you."

"I know that." She stood up and smiled, extending her hand. "Thanks."

He shook her hand and shrugged. "Think nothing of it. We brilliant medical types feel obliged to minister to the masses..."

"Oh, for God's sake!" Micah groaned as he entered the room, overhearing his friend.

Dr. Candler gave him a look full of frowning mock-hauteur. "And aren't you lucky that I don't have to examine *you* today?" he drawled.

"We're leaving. Right now." He took Callie by the hand and gave the other man a grin. "Thanks."

"Anytime. You take care."

"You do the same."

Callie was herded out the door.

"But, the bill," she protested as he put her out a side door and drew her into the vehicle that was waiting for them with the engine running.

"Already taken care of. Let's get to the airport."

Callie settled into the seat, still worrying. "I don't have anything with me," she said miserably. "No papers, no clothes, no shoes…"

"I told you, Maddie got all that together. It will be waiting for us at the airport, along with tickets and boarding passes."

"What if Lopez has people there waiting for us?" she worried aloud.

"We also have people waiting there for us," Bojo said from the front seat. "Miami is our safest domestic port."

"Okay," she said, and smiled at him.

He smiled back.

Micah and Bojo exchanged a complicated glance. Bojo turned his attention back to the road and didn't say another word all the way to the airport. Callie understood. Micah didn't want her getting too friendly with his people. She didn't take offense. She was used to rejection, after so many years in foster care. She only shrugged and looked out the window, watching palm trees and colorful buildings slide past as they wove through side streets and back onto the expressway.

The airport was crowded. Micah caught her by the arm and guided her past the ticket counter on the way to the concourses.

"But…" she protested.

"Don't argue. Just walk through the metal detector."

He followed close behind her. Neither of them was carrying anything metallic, but Micah was stopped when a security woman passed a wand over the two of them and her detector picked up the residual gunpowder on his hands and clothing. The woman looked at her instrument and then at him, with a wary, suspicious stare.

He smiled lazily at the uniformed woman holding the wand. "I'm on my way to a regional skeet shooting tournament," he lied glibly. "I sent my guns on ahead by express, unassembled. Can't be too careful these days, where firearms are concerned," he added, catching Callie's hand in his. "Right, honey?" he murmured softly, drawing her close.

To Callie's credit, she didn't faint at the unexpected feel of Micah's arm around her, but she tingled from head to toe and her heart went wild.

The airport security woman seemed to relax, and she smiled back. She assumed, as Micah had intended, that he and Callie were involved. "Indeed you can't. Have a good trip."

Micah kept that long, muscular arm around Callie as they walked slowly down the concourse. He looked down, noting the erratic rhythm of her heartbeat at her neck, and he smiled to himself.

"You have lightning-quick reflexes," he remarked

after a minute. "I noticed that in Cancún. You didn't argue, you didn't question anything I told you to do, and you moved almost as fast as I did. You're good company in tight corners."

She shrugged. "When you came in through the window, I didn't know who you were, because of that face mask. Actually," she confessed with a sheepish smile, "at first, I figured you were a rival drug dealer, but I had high hopes that you might be kind enough to just kill me and not torture me first if I didn't resist."

He drew in a sharp breath and the arm holding her contracted with a jerk. "Strange attitude, Callie," he remarked.

"Not at the time. Not to me, anyway." She shivered at the memory and felt his arm tighten almost protectively. They were well out of earshot and sight of the security guard. "Micah, what was that wand she was checking us with?"

"It detects nitrates," he replied. "With it, they can tell if a passenger has had any recent contact with weapons or explosives."

She was keenly aware of his arm still holding her close against his warm, powerful body. "You can, uh, let go now. She's out of sight."

He didn't relent. "Don't look, but there's a security guard with a two-way radio about fifteen feet to your right." He smiled down at her. "And I'll give you three guesses who's on the other end of it."

She smiled back, but it didn't reach her eyes. "The lady with the nitrate wand? We're psyching them out, right?"

He searched her eyes and for a few seconds he stopped

walking. "Psyching them out," he murmured. His gaze fell to her soft, full mouth. "Exactly."

She couldn't quite get her breath. His expression was unreadable, but his black eyes were glittering. He watched her blouse shake with the frantic rate of her heartbeats. He was remembering mistletoe and harsh words, and that same look in Callie's soft eyes, that aching need to be kissed that made her look so very vulnerable.

"What the hell," he murmured roughly as his head bent to hers. "It's an airport. People are saying hello and goodbye everywhere…"

His warm, hard mouth covered hers very gently while the sounds of people in transit all around them faded to a dull roar. His heavy brows drew together in something close to anguish as he began to kiss her. Fascinated by his expression, by the warm, ardent pressure of his mouth on hers, she closed her eyes tight, and fantasized that he meant it, that he wasn't pretending for the benefit of security guards, that he was enjoying the soft, tremulous response of her lips to the teasing, expert pressure of his own.

"Boss?"

They didn't hear the gruff whisper.

It was followed by the loud clearing of a throat and a cough.

They didn't hear that, either. Callie was on tiptoe now, her short nails digging into the hard muscles of his upper arms, hanging on Micah's slow, tender kiss with little more than willpower, so afraid that he was going to pull away…!

"Micah!" the voice said shortly.

Micah's head jerked up, and for a few seconds he

seemed as disoriented as Callie. He stared blankly at the dark-headed man in front of him.

The man was extending a small case toward him. "Her papers and clothes and shoes and stuff," the man said, nodding toward Callie and clearing his throat again. "Maddie had me fly them over here."

"Thanks, Pogo."

The big, dark man nodded. He stared with open curiosity at Callie, and then he smiled gently. "It was my pleasure," he said, glancing again at Micah and making an odd little gesture with his head in Callie's direction.

"This is Callie Kirby," Micah said shortly, adding, "my...stepsister."

The big man's eyebrows levered up. "Oh! I mean, I was hoping she wasn't a real sister. I mean, the way you were kissing her and all." He flushed, and laughed self-consciously when Micah glared at him. Callie was scarlet, looking everywhere except at the newcomer.

"You'll miss your flight out of here," Micah said pointedly.

"What? Oh. Yeah." He grinned at Callie. "I'm Pogo. I'm from Saint Augustine. I used to wrestle alligators until Micah here gave me a job. I'm sort of a bodyguard, you know..."

"You're going to be an unemployed bodyguard in twenty seconds if you don't merge with the crowd," Micah said curtly.

"Oh. Well...sure. Bye, now," he told Callie with an ear-to-ear smile.

She smiled back. He was like a big teddy bear. She was sorry they wouldn't get to know each other.

Pogo almost fell over his own feet as he turned, jerking both busy eyebrows at his boss, before he melted into the crowd and vanished.

"Stop doing that," Micah said coldly.

She looked up at him blankly. "Doing what?"

"Smiling at my men like that. These men aren't used to it. Don't encourage them."

Her lips parted on a shaken breath. She looked at him as if she feared for his sanity. "Them?" she echoed, dazed.

"Bojo and Peter and Pogo," he said, moving restlessly. He was jealous, God knew why. It irritated him. "Come on."

He moved away from her, catching her hand tightly and pulling her along with him.

"And don't read anything into what just happened," he added coldly, without looking at her.

"Why would I?" she asked honestly. "You said it was just for appearances. I haven't forgotten how you feel about me, Micah."

He stopped and stared intently down into her eyes. His own were narrow, angry, impatient. She wore her heart where anyone could see it. Her vulnerability made him protective. Odd, that, when she was tough enough to survive captivity by Lopez and still keep her nerve during a bloody breakout.

"You don't have a clue how I feel about you," he said involuntarily. His fingers locked closer into hers. "I'm thirty-six. You're barely twenty-two. The sort of woman I prefer is sophisticated and street-smart and has no qualms about sex. You're still at the kissing-in-parked-cars stage."

She flushed and searched his eyes. "I don't kiss people in parked cars because I don't date anybody," she told him with blunt honesty. "I can't leave Dad alone in the evenings. Besides, too many men around Jacobsville remember my mother, and think I'm like her." Her face stiffened and she looked away. "Including you."

He didn't speak. There was little softness left in him after all the violent years, but she was able to touch some last, sensitive place with her sweet voice. Waves of guilt ran over him. Yes, he'd compared her to her mother that Christmas. He'd said harsh, cruel things. He regretted them, but there was no going back. His feelings about Callie unnerved him. She was the only weak spot in his armor that he'd ever known. And what a good thing that she didn't know that, he told himself.

"You don't know what was really going on that night, Callie," he said after a minute.

She looked up at him. "Don't you think it's time I did?" she asked softly.

He toyed with her fingers, causing ripples of pleasure to run along her spine. "Why not? You're old enough to hear it now." He glanced around them cautiously before he looked at her again. "You were wearing an emerald velvet dress that night, the same one you'd worn to your eighteenth birthday party. They were watching a movie while you finished decorating the Christmas tree," he continued absently. "You'd just bent over to pick up an ornament when I came into the room. The dress had a deep neckline. You weren't wearing a bra under it, and your breasts were visible in that position, right to the nipples. You looked up at me and your nipples were suddenly hard."

She gaped at him. The comment about her nipples was disturbing, but she had no idea what he meant by emphasizing them. "I had no idea I was showing like that!"

"I didn't realize that. Not at first." He held her fingers tighter. "You saw me and came right up against me, drowning me in that floral perfume you wore. You stood on tiptoe, like you did a minute ago, trying to tempt me into kissing you."

She averted her embarrassed eyes. "You said terrible things…"

"The sight of you like that had aroused me passionately," he said frankly, nodding when her shocked eyes jumped to his face. "That's right. And I couldn't let you know it. I had to make you keep your distance, not an easy accomplishment after the alcohol you'd had. For which," he added coldly, "your mother should have been shot! It was illegal for her to let you drink, even at home. Anyway, I read you the riot act, pushed you away and walked down the hall, right into your mother. She recognized immediately what you hadn't even noticed about my body, and she thought it was the sight of her in that slinky silver dress that had caused it. So she buried herself against me and started kissing me." He let out an angry breath. "Father saw us like that before I could push her away. And I couldn't tell him the truth, because you were just barely eighteen. I was already thirty-two."

The bitterness in his deep voice was blatant. She didn't feel herself breathing. She'd only been eighteen, but he'd wanted her. She'd never realized it. Everything that didn't make sense was suddenly crystal clear—except that comment about his body. She wondered what her mother had seen and recognized about him that she hadn't.

"You never told me."

"You were a child, Callie," he said tautly. "In some ways, you still are. I was never low enough to take advantage of your innocence."

She was almost vibrating with the turmoil of her emotions. She didn't know what to do or say.

He drew in a long, slow breath as he studied her. "Come on," he said, tugging her along. "We have to move or we'll miss our flight." He handed her the case and indicated the ladies' room. "Get changed. I'll wait right here."

She nodded. Her mind was in such turmoil that she changed into jeans and a long-sleeved knit shirt, socks and sneakers, without paying much attention to what was in the small travel case. She didn't take time to look in any of the compartments, because he'd said to hurry. She glanced at herself in the mirror and was glad she had short hair that could do without a brush. Despite all she'd been through, it didn't look too bad. She'd have to buy a brush when they got where they were going, along with makeup and other toiletries. But that could wait.

Micah was propping up the wall when she came out. He nodded, approving what Maddie had packed for her, and took the case. "Here," he said, passing her a small plastic bag.

Inside were makeup, a brush, a toothbrush, toothpaste and deodorant. She almost cried at the thoughtful gift.

"Thanks," she said huskily.

Micah pulled the tickets and boarding passes out of his shirt pocket. "Get out your driver's license and birth certificate," he said. "We have to have a photo ID to board."

She felt momentary panic. "My birth certificate is in

my file at home, and my driver's license is still in my purse, in my car…!"

He laid a lean forefinger across her pretty mouth, slightly swollen from the hard contact with his. "Your car is at your house, and your purse is inside it, and it's locked up tight. I told Maddie to put your birth certificate and your driver's license in the case. Have you looked for them?"

"No. I didn't think…"

She paused, putting the case down on the carpeted concourse floor to open it. Sure enough, her driver's license was in the zipped compartment that she hadn't looked in when she was in the bathroom. Besides that, the unknown Maddie had actually put her makeup and toiletries inside as well, in a plastic bag. She could have wept at the woman's thoughtfulness, but she wasn't going to tell Micah and make him feel uncomfortable that he'd already bought her those items. She closed it quickly and stuck her license in her jeans pocket.

"Does Maddie really look like me?" she asked on the way to the ticket counter, trying not to sound as if she minded. He'd said they resembled one another earlier.

"At a distance," he affirmed. "Her hair is shorter than yours, and she's more muscular. She was a karate instructor when she signed on with me. She's twenty-six."

"Karate."

"Black belt," he added.

"She seems to be very efficient," she murmured a little stiffly.

He gave her a knowing glance that she didn't see and chuckled softly. "She's in love with Colby Lane, a guy I used to work with at the justice department," he told her. "She signed on with us because she thought he was going to."

"He didn't?"

He shook his head. "He's working for Pierce Hutton's outfit, as a security chief, along with Tate Winthrop, an acquaintance of mine."

"Oh."

They were at the ticket counter now. He held out his hand for her driver's license and birth certificate, and presented them along with his driver's license and passport and the tickets to the agent on duty.

She put the tickets in a neat folder with the boarding passes in a slot on the outside, checked the ID, and handed them back.

"Have a nice trip," she told them. "We'll be boarding in just a minute."

Callie hadn't looked at her boarding pass. She was too busy trying to spot Bojo and Peter and the others.

"They're already en route," Micah told her nonchalantly, having guessed why she was looking around her.

"They aren't going with us?"

He gave her a wry glance. "Somebody had to bring my boat back. I left it here in the marina when I flew out to Jacobsville to help Eb Scott and Cy Parks shut down Lopez's drug operation. It's still there."

"Why couldn't we have gone on the boat, too?"

"You get seasick," he said before he thought.

Her lips fell open. She'd only been on a boat once, with him and her mother and stepfather, when she was sixteen. They'd gone to San Antonio and sailed down the river on a tour boat. She'd gotten very sick and thrown up. It had been Micah who'd looked after her, to his father's amusement.

She hadn't even remembered the episode until he'd said that. She didn't get seasick now, but she kept quiet.

"Besides," he added, avoiding her persistent stare, "if Lopez does try anything, it won't be on an international flight out of the U.S. He's in enough trouble with the higher-ups in his organization without making an assault on a commercial plane just to get even for losing a prisoner."

She relaxed a little, because that had been on her mind.

He took her arm and drew her toward a small door, where a uniformed man was holding a microphone. He announced that they were boarding first-class passengers first, and Micah ushered her right down the ramp and into the plane.

"First class," she said, dazed, as he eased her into a wide, comfortable seat with plenty of leg room. Even for a man of his height, there was enough of it.

"Always," he murmured, amused at her fascination. "I don't like cramped places."

She fastened her seat belt with a wry smile. "Considering the size of you, I can understand that. Micah, what about Dad?" she added, ashamed that she was still belaboring the point.

"Maddie's got him under surveillance. When Pogo goes back, he'll work a split shift with her at your apartment to safeguard him. Eb and Cy are keeping their eyes out, as well. I promise you, Dad's going to be safe." He hesitated, searching her wide, pale blue eyes. "But you're the one in danger."

"Because I got away," she agreed, nodding.

He seemed worried. His dark eyes narrowed on her face. "Lopez doesn't lose prisoners, ever. You're the first.

Someone is going to pay for that. He'll make an example of the people who didn't watch you closely enough. Then he'll make an example of you and me, if he can, to make sure his reputation doesn't suffer."

She shivered involuntarily. It was a nightmare that would haunt her forever. She remembered what she'd suffered already and her eyes closed on a helpless wave of real terror.

"You're going to be safe, Callie. Listen," he said, reading her expression, "I live on a small island in the Bahamas chain, not too far from New Providence. I have state-of-the-art surveillance equipment and a small force of mercenaries that even Lopez would hesitate to confront. Lopez isn't the only one who has a reputation in terrorist circles. Before I put together my team and hired out as a professional soldier, I worked for the CIA."

Her eyes widened. She hadn't known that. She hadn't known anything about him.

"They approached me while I was in college, before I changed my course of study to medicine. I was already fluent in French and Dutch, and I picked up German in my sophomore year. I couldn't blend in very well in an Arabic country, but I could pass for German or Dutch, and I did. During holidays and vacations, I did a lot of traveling for the company." He smiled, reminiscing. "It was dangerous work, and exciting. By the time I was in my last year of residency, I knew for a fact that I wouldn't be able to settle down into a medical practice. I couldn't live without the danger. That's when I left school for good."

She was hanging on every word. It was amazing to have him speak to her as an equal, as an adult. They'd never really talked before.

"I wondered," she said, "why you gave it up."

He stretched his long legs out in front of him and crossed his arms over his broad chest. "I had the skills, but as I grew older, the less I wanted roots or anything that hinted at permanence. I don't want marriage or children, so a steady, secure profession seemed superfluous. On the other hand, being a mercenary is right up my alley. I live for those surges of adrenaline."

"None of us ever knew about that," she said absently, trying not to let him see how much it hurt to know that he couldn't see a future as a husband and father. Now that she knew what he really did for a living, she could understand why. He was never going to be a family man. "We thought it was the trust your mother left you that kept you in Armani suits," she added in a subdued tone.

"No, it wasn't. I like my lifestyle," he added with a pointed glance in her direction. He stretched lazily, pulling the silk shirt he was wearing taut across the muscles of his chest. A flight attendant actually hesitated as she started down the aisle, helplessly drinking in the sight of him. He was a dish, all right. Callie didn't blame the other woman for staring, but the flight attendant had blond hair and blue eyes and she was lovely. Her beauty was like a knife in the ribs to Callie, pointing out all the physical attributes she herself lacked. If only she'd been pretty, she told herself miserably, maybe Micah would have wanted more than an occasional kiss from her.

"Would you care for anything to drink, sir?" the flight attendant asked, smiling joyfully as she paused by Micah's side.

"Scotch and soda," he told her. He smiled ruefully. "It's been a long day."

"Coming right up," the woman said, and went at once to get the order.

Callie noticed that she hadn't been asked if she wanted anything. She wondered what Micah would say if she asked for a neat whiskey. Probably nothing, she told herself miserably. He might have kissed her in the airport, but he only seemed irritated by her now.

The flight attendant was back with his drink. She glanced belatedly at Callie and grimaced. "Sorry," she told the other woman. "I didn't think to ask if you'd like something, too?"

Callie shook her head and smiled. "No, I don't want anything, thanks."

"Are you stopping in Nassau or just passing through?" the woman asked Micah boldly.

He gave her a lingering appraisal, from her long, elegant legs to her full breasts and lovely face. He smiled. "I live there."

"Really!" Her eyes lit as if they'd concealed fires. "So do I!"

"Then you must know Lisette Dubonnet," he said.

"Dubonnet," the uniformed woman repeated, frowning. "Isn't her father Jacques Dubonnet, the French ambassador?"

"Yes," he said. "Lisette and I have known each other for several years. We're…very good friends."

The flight attendant looked suddenly uncomfortable, and a little flushed. Micah was telling her, in a nice way, that she'd overstepped her introduction. He smiled to soften the rejection, but it was a rejection, just the same.

"Miss Dubonnet is very lovely," the flight attendant said with a pleasant, if more formal, smile. "If you need anything else, just ring."

"I will."

She went on down the aisle. Beside him, Callie was
staring out the window at the ocean below without any
real enthusiasm. She hated her own reaction to the news
that Micah was involved with some beautiful woman in
Nassau. And not only a beautiful woman, but a poised
sophisticate as well.

"You'll like Lisse," he said carelessly. "I'll ask her to
go shopping with you. You'll have to have a few clothes.
She has excellent taste."

Implying that Callie had none at all. Her heart felt
like iron in her chest, heavy and cold. "That would be
nice," she said, lying through her teeth. "I won't need
much, though," she added, thinking about her small sav-
ings account.

"You may be there longer than a day or two," he said
in a carefully neutral voice. "You can't wear the same
clothes day in and day out. Besides," he added curtly,
"it's about time you learned how to dress like a young
woman instead of an elderly recluse!"

# Chapter 5

Callie felt the anger boil out of her in waves. "Oh, that's nice, coming from you," she said icily. "When you're the one who started me wearing that sort of thing in the first place!"

"Me?" he replied, his eyebrows arching.

"You said I dressed like a tramp," she began, and her eyes were anguished as she remembered the harsh, hateful words. "Like my mother," she added huskily. "You said that I flaunted my body..." She stopped suddenly and wrapped her arms around herself. She stared out the porthole while she recovered her self-control. "Sorry," she said stiffly. "I've been through a lot. It's catching up with me. I didn't mean to say that."

He felt as if he'd been slapped. Maybe he deserved it, too. Callie had been beautiful in that green velvet dress. The sight of her in it had made him ache. She had the grace and poise of a model, even if she lacked the necessary height. But he'd never realized that his own anger had made her ashamed of her body, and at such an impressionable age. Good God, no wonder she dressed like a dowager! Then he remembered what she'd hinted in the jungle about the foster homes she'd stayed in, and he wondered with real anguish what she'd endured before she came to live in his father's house. There had to be more to her repression than just a few regretted words from him.

"Callie," he said huskily, catching her soft chin and turning her flushed face toward him. "Something happened to you at one of those foster homes, didn't it?"

She bit her lower lip and for a few seconds, there was torment in her eyes.

He drew in a sharp breath.

She turned her face away again, embarrassed.

"Can you talk about it?" he asked.

She shook her head jerkily.

His dark eyes narrowed. And her mother—her own mother—had deserted her, had placed her in danger with pure indifference. "Damn your mother," he said in a gruff whisper.

She didn't look at him again. At least, she thought mistakenly, he was remembering the breakup of his father's marriage, and not her childhood anymore. She didn't like remembering the past.

He leaned back in his seat and stretched, folding his arms over his broad chest. One day, he promised himself, there was going to be a reckoning for Callie's mother. He hoped the woman got just a fraction of what she deserved, for all the grief and pain she'd caused. Although, he had to admit, she had changed in the past year or so.

He wondered if her mother's first husband, Kane Kirby, had contacted Callie recently. Poor kid, he thought. She really had gone through a lot, even before Lopez had her kidnapped. He thought about what she'd suffered at Lopez's hands, and he ached to avenge her. The drug lord was almost certain to make a grab for her again. But this time, he promised himself, Lopez was going to pay up his account in full. He owed Callie that much for the damage he'd done.

It was dark when the plane landed in Nassau at the international airport, and Micah let Callie go ahead of him down the ramp to the pavement. The moist heat was almost smothering, after the air-conditioned plane. Micah took her arm and escorted her to passport control. He glanced with amusement at the passengers waiting around baggage claim for their bags to be unloaded. Even when he traveled routinely, he never took more than a duffel bag that he could carry into the airplane with him. It saved time waiting for luggage to be offloaded.

After they checked through, he moved her outside again and hailed a cab to take them to the marina, where the boat was waiting.

Another small round of formalities and they boarded the sleek, powerful boat that already contained Micah's men. Callie went below and sat quietly on a comfortable built-in sofa, watching out the porthole as the boat flew out of Prince George Wharf and around the bay. From there, it went out to sea.

"Comfortable?" Micah asked, joining her below.

She nodded. "It's so beautiful out there. I love the way the ships light up at night. I knew cruise ships did, but

I didn't realize that smaller ones did, too." She glanced at him in the subdued light of the cabin. "You don't light yours, do you?"

He chuckled. "In my line of work, it wouldn't be too smart, would it?"

"Sorry," she said with a sheepish smile. "I wasn't thinking."

He poured himself a scotch and water and added ice cubes. "Want something to drink? If you don't want anything alcoholic, I've got soft drinks or fruit juice."

She shook her head. "I'm fine." She laughed. Her eyes caught and held on a vessel near the lighted dock. "Look! There's a white ship with black sails flying a skull and crossbones Jolly Roger flag!"

He chuckled. "That would be Fred Spence. He's something of a local eccentric. Nice boat, though."

She glanced at him. "This one is nice, too."

"It's comfortable on long hauls," he said noncommittally. He dropped down onto the sofa beside her and crossed his long legs. "We need to talk."

"About what?"

"Lopez. I'm putting you under twenty-four-hour surveillance," he said somberly. "If I'm not within yelling distance, one of my men will be. Even when you go shopping with Lisse, Bojo or Peter will go along. You aren't to walk on the beach alone, ever."

"But surely that would be safe…?"

He sat forward abruptly, and his black eyes glittered. "Callie, he has weapons that could pinpoint your body heat and send a missile after it from a distance of half a mile," he said curtly.

She actually gasped. That brought to mind another

worry. She frowned. "I'm putting you in jeopardy by being with you," she said suddenly.

"You've got that backward, honey," he said, the endearment coming so naturally that he wasn't even aware he'd used it until he watched Callie's soft complexion flush. "You were in jeopardy in the first place because of me. Why does it make you blush when I call you honey?" he added immediately, the question quick enough to rattle her.

"I'm not used to it."

"From me," he drawled softly. "Or from any man?"

She shifted. "From Dad, maybe."

"Dad doesn't count. I mean single, datable bachelors."

She shook her head. "I don't date."

He'd never connected her solitary existence with himself. Now, he was forced to. He drew his breath in sharply, and got up from the sofa. He took a long sip from his drink, walking slowly over to stare out the porthole at the distant lights of the marina as they left it behind. "I honestly didn't realize how much damage I did to your ego, Callie. I'm really sorry about it."

"I was just as much at fault as you were," she replied evenly. "I shouldn't have thrown myself at you like some drunk prostitute..."

"Callie!" he exclaimed, horrified at her wording.

She averted her eyes and her hands clenched in her lap. "Well, I did."

He put his drink on the bar and knelt just in front of her. He was so tall that his black eyes were even with soft blue ones in the position. His lean hands went to her waist and he shook her very gently.

"I pushed you away because I wanted you, not because I thought you were throwing yourself at me," he said bluntly. "I was afraid that I wouldn't be able to re-sist you if I didn't do something very fast. I would have explained it to you eventually, if your mother hadn't stepped in and split the family apart, damn her cold heart!"

Her hands rested hesitantly on his broad shoulders, lifted and then rested again while she waited to see if she was allowed to touch him.

He seemed to realize that, because he smiled very slowly and his thumbs edged out against her flat belly in a sensuous stroking motion. "I like being touched," he murmured. "It's all right."

She smiled nervously. "I'm not used to doing it."

"I noticed." He stood up and drew her up with him. The top of her head only came to his nose. He framed her face in his warm, strong hands and lifted it gently. "Want to kiss me?" he asked in a husky whisper, and his eyes fell to her own soft mouth.

She wasn't sure about that. Her hands were on his chest now, touching lightly over the silky fabric. Under it, she could feel thick hair. She was hopelessly curious about what he looked like bare-chested. She'd never seen Micah without a shirt in all the time she'd lived in his house with his father.

"No pressure," he promised, bending. "And I won't make fun of you."

"Make fun of me?" she asked curiously.

"Never mind." He bent and his lips closed tenderly on her upper lip while he tasted the moist inside of it with his tongue. His lips moved to her lower lip and repeated the arousing little caress. His hands were at her waist, but they began to move up and down with a lazy, sen-sual pressure that made her body go rigid in his arms.

He lifted his mouth from her face and looked down at her with affectionate amusement. "Relax! Why are you afraid of me?" he asked gently. "I wouldn't hurt you, Callie. Not for any reason."

"I know. It's just that…"

"What?" he asked.

Her eyes met his plaintively. "Don't…tease me," she asked with dignity. "I'm not experienced enough to play that sort of game."

The amusement left his face. "Is that what it seems like to you?" he asked. He searched her worried eyes. "Even if I were into game-playing, you'd never be a target. I do have some idea now of what you've been through, in the past and just recently."

She let out the breath she'd been holding. "This Lisette you mentioned. Is she…important to you?"

"We're good friends," he said, and there was a new remoteness in his expression. "You'll like her. She's outgoing and she loves people. She'll help you get outfitted."

Now she was really worried. "I have my credit card, but I can't afford expensive shops," she emphasized. "Could you tell her that, so I won't have to?"

"I can tell her." He smiled quizzically. "But why won't you let me buy you some clothes?"

"I'm not your responsibility, even if you have been landed with me, Micah," she replied. "I pay my own way."

He wondered if she had any idea how few of his female acquaintances would ever have made such a statement to him? It occurred to him that he'd never had a woman refuse a wardrobe.

He scowled. "You could pay me back, if you have to."

She smiled. "Thanks. But I'll buy my own clothes."

His black eyes narrowed on her face. "You were always independent," he recalled.

"I've had to be. I've been basically on my own for a long time," she said matter-of-factly. "Since I was a kid, really, and my father—I mean, Mother's first husband—threw us out. Mother didn't want the responsibility for me by herself and Kane Kirby didn't want me at all."

"If your father didn't think you were his, why didn't he have a DNA profile run?" he asked with a watchful look.

She drew away from him. "There was no such thing fifteen years ago in Jacobsville."

"You could insist that he have it done now, couldn't you?" He gave her an odd look. "Have you spoken to him?"

"He phoned me recently. But I didn't call him back," she said unwillingly. She'd seen her mother's first husband once or twice, during his rare visits to his Jacobsville home. He'd actually phoned her apartment a few weeks ago and left a strange, tentative message asking her to call him back. She never had. His rejection of her still hurt. She didn't see him often. He lived mostly in Miami these days.

"Why not talk to him and suggest the DNA test?" he persisted.

She looked up at him with tired, sad eyes. "Because it would probably prove what my mother said, that I'm not related to him at all." She smiled faintly. "I don't know whose child I am. And it really doesn't matter anymore. Please, just…leave it alone."

He sighed with irritation, as if he knew more than he was telling her. She wondered why he was so interested in her relationship with the man who was supposed to be her own father.

He saw that curiosity in her eyes, and he closed up. He could see years of torment in that sad little face. It infuriated him. "Your mother should be horsewhipped for what she did to you," he said flatly.

She folded her arms across her chest, remembering the loneliness of her young life reluctantly. New homes, new faces, new terrors. She turned back to the porthole. "I used to wish I had someplace to belong," she confessed. "I was always the outsider, in any home where I lived. Until my mother married your father," she added, smiling. "I thought he'd be like all the others, that he'd either ignore me or be too familiar, but he just sort of belonged to me, from the very beginning. He really cared about me. He hugged me, coming and going." She drew in a soft breath. "You can't imagine what it feels like, to have someone hug you, when you've hardly been touched in your whole life except in bad ways. He was forever teasing me, bringing me presents. He became my family. He even made up for my mother. I couldn't help loving him." She turned, surprised to see an odd look of self-contempt on Micah's strong face. "I guess you resented us…"

"I resented your mother, Callie," he interrupted, feeling icy-cold inside. "What I felt for you was a lot more complicated than that."

She gave him a surprised little smile. "But, I'm still my mother's daughter, right? Don't they say, look at the mother and you'll see the daughter in twenty years or so?"

His face hardened. "You'll never be like her. Not in your worst nightmares."

She sighed. "I wish I could be sure of that."

He felt like hitting something. "Do you know where she is?"

"Somewhere in Europe with her new husband, I suppose," she said indifferently. "Dad's lawyer heard from her year before last. She wanted a copy of the final divorce decree, because she was getting married again, to some British nobleman, the lawyer said."

He remembered his own mother, a gentle little brown-eyed woman with a ready smile and open arms. She'd died when he was ten, and from that day on, he and his father had been best friends. Until Anna showed up, with her introverted, nervous teenage daughter. The difference between Anna and his own mother was incredible. Anna was selfish, vain, greedy…he could have laid all seven deadly sins at her feet with ease. But Callie was nothing like her, except, perhaps, her exact opposite.

"You're the sort of woman who would love a big family," he murmured thoughtfully.

She laughed. "What do I know about families?" she responded. "I'd be terrified of bringing an innocent child into this sort of world, knowing what I know about the uncertainties of life."

He shoved his hands into his pockets. Children. He'd never thought about them. But he could picture Callie with a baby in her arms, and it seemed perfectly natural. She'd had some bad breaks, but she'd love her own child. It was sad that she didn't want kids.

"Anyway, marriage is dead last on my list of things to do," she added, uncomfortable because he wasn't saying anything.

"That makes two of us," he murmured. It was the sort

of thing he always said, but it didn't feel as comfortable suddenly as it used to. He wondered why.

She turned away from the porthole. "How long will it take us to get to your place?" she asked.

He shrugged. "About twenty more minutes, at this speed," he said, smiling. "I think you'll like it. It's old, and rambling, and it has a history. According to the legend, a local pirate owned it back in the eighteenth century. He kidnapped a highborn Spanish lady and married her out of hand. They had six children together and lived a long and happy life, or so the legend goes." He studied her curiously. "Isn't there Spanish in your ancestry somewhere?"

Her face closed up. "Don't ask me. My mother always said she descended from what they call 'black Irish,' from when the Spanish armada was shipwrecked off the coast of Ireland. I know her hair was jet-black when she was younger, and she has an olive complexion. But I don't really know her well enough to say whether or not it was the truth."

He bit off a comment on her mother's penchant for lying. "Your complexion isn't olive," he remarked quietly. "It's creamy. Soft."

He embarrassed her. She averted her eyes. "I'm just ordinary."

He shook his head. His eyes narrowed on her pretty bow of a mouth. "You always were unique, Callie." He hesitated. "Callie. What's it short for?" he asked, suddenly curious.

She drew in a slow breath. "Colleen," she replied reluctantly. "But nobody ever calls me that. It's been Callie since I was old enough to talk."

"Colleen what?"

"Colleen Mary," she replied.

He smiled. "Yes. That suits you."

He was acting very strangely. In fact, he had been ever since he rescued her. She wondered if he was still trying to take her mind off Lopez. If he was, it wasn't working. The nightmarish memories were too fresh to forget.

She looked at him worriedly. "Lopez will be looking for me," she said suddenly.

He tautened. "Let him look," he said shortly. "If he comes close enough to make a target, I'll solve all his problems. He isn't getting his hands on you again, Callie."

She relaxed a little. He sounded very confident. It made her feel better. She moved back into the center of the room, wrapping her arms around herself. "How can people like that exist in a civilized world?" she wanted to know.

"Because governments still can't fight that kind of wealth," he said bluntly. "Money and power make criminals too formidable. But we've got the Rico statutes which help us take away some of that illegal money," he added, "and we've got dedicated people enforcing the law. We win more than we lose these days."

"You sound like a government agent," she teased.

He chuckled. "I do, don't I? I spent several years being one. It sticks." He moved forward, taking his hands out of his pockets to wrap them gently around her upper arms. "I give you my word that I won't let Lopez get you. In case you were worrying about that."

She grimaced. "Does it show?"

"I don't know. Maybe I can read your mind these days," he added, trying to make light of it.

"You're sure? About Dad being safe, I mean?"

"I'm sure about Dad," he returned at once. "Gator may look dumb, but he's got a mind like a steel trap, and he's quick on the draw. Nobody's going to get past him—certainly nobody's going to get past him and Maddie at the same time."

"You like her a lot, I guess?"

He chuckled. "Yes, I do. She's hell on two legs, and one of the best scroungers I've ever had."

"What does Bojo do?"

He gave her a wary appraisal, and it seemed as if he didn't like the question. "Bojo is a small arms expert," he replied. "He also has relatives in most of the Muslim nations, so he's a great source of information as well. Peter, you met him on the plane, is new with the group. He's a linguist and he's able to pass for an Arab or an Israeli. He's usually undercover in any foreign operation we're hired to undertake. You haven't met Rodrigo yet— he was the pilot of the DC-3 we flew back to Miami. He does undercover work as well. Don, the blond copilot, is a small arms expert. We have another operative, Cord Romero, who does demolition work for us, but he had an accident and he's out of commission for a while."

"What you and your men do—it's dangerous work."

"Living is dangerous work," he said flatly. "I like the job. I don't have any plans to give it up."

Her eyebrows arched and her pale blue eyes twinkled. "My goodness, did I propose marriage just now and get instant amnesia afterward? Excuse *me!*"

He gaped at her. "Propose marriage...?"

She held up both hands. "Now, don't get ruffled. I understand how men feel about these things. I haven't asked you out, or sent you flowers, or even bought you a nice pair of earrings. Naturally you're miffed because I put the cart before the horse and asked you to give up an exciting job you love for marriage to a boring paralegal."

He blinked. "Callie?" he murmured, obviously fearing for her sanity.

"We'll just forget the proposal," she offered generously.

"You didn't propose!" he gritted.

"See? You've already forgotten. Isn't that just like a man?" she muttered, as she went back to the sofa and sat down. "Now you'll pout for an hour because I rejected you."

He burst out laughing when he realized what she was doing. It took the tension away from their earlier discussion and brought them back to normal. He dropped down into an armchair across from her and folded his arms over his chest.

"Just when I think I've got you figured out, you throw me another curve," he said appreciatively.

"Believe me, if I didn't have a sense of humor, I'd already have smeared Mr. Kemp with honey and locked him in a closet with a grizzly bear."

"Ouch!"

"I thought you lived in Nassau?" She changed the subject.

He shrugged. "I did. This place came on the market three years ago and I bought it. I like the idea of having a defendable property. You'll see what I mean when we get there. It's like a walled city."

"I'll bet there are lots of flowers," she murmured hopefully.

"Millions," he confirmed. "Hibiscus and orchids and

bougainvillea. You'll love it." He smiled gently. "You were always planting things when I lived at home."

"I didn't think you noticed anything I did," she replied before she thought.

He watched her quietly. "Your mother spent most of that time ordering you around," he recalled. "If she wanted a soft drink, or a scarf, or a sandwich, she always sent you after it. I don't recall that she ever touched a vacuum cleaner or a frying pan the whole time she was around."

"I learned to cook in the last foster home I stayed in," she said with a smile. "It was the best of the lot. Mrs. Toms liked me. She had five little kids and she had arthritis real bad. She was so sweet that it was a joy to help her. She was always surprised that anyone would want to do things for her."

"Most giving people are," he replied. "Ironically they're usually the last ones people give to."

"That's true."

"What else did she teach you?" he asked.

"How to crochet," she recalled. She sighed. "I can't make sweaters and stuff, but I taught myself how to make hats. I give them to children and old people in our neighborhood. I work on them when I'm waiting for appointments with Dad. I get through a lot."

It was another reminder that she was taking care of his father, something he should have been doing himself—something he would be doing, if Callie's mother hadn't made it impossible for him to be near his parent.

"You're still bitter about Dad," she said, surprising him. "I can tell. You get this terrible haunted look in your eyes when I talk about him."

It surprised him that at her age she could read him

so well, when his own men couldn't. He wasn't sure he liked it.

"I miss him," he confessed gruffly. "I'm sorry he won't let me make peace."

She gaped at him. "Whoever told you that?"

He hesitated. "I haven't tried to talk to him in years. So I phoned him a few days ago, before you were kidnapped. He listened for a minute and hung up without saying a word."

"What day was it?"

"It was Saturday. What difference does that make?"

"What time was it?" she repeated.

"Noon."

She smiled gently. "I go to get groceries at noon on Saturdays, because Mrs. Ruiz, who lives next door, comes home for lunch and makes it for herself and Dad and stays with him while I'm away."

"So?"

"So, Mrs. Ruiz doesn't speak English yet, she's still learning. The telephone intimidates her. She'll answer it, but if it's not me, she'll put it right down again." She smiled. "That's why I asked when you called."

"Then, Dad might talk to me, if I tried again," he said after a minute.

"Micah, he loves you," she said softly. "You're the only child he has. Of course he'll talk to you. He doesn't know what really happened with my mother, no more than I did, until you told me the truth. But he realizes now that if it hadn't been you, it would have been some other younger man. He said that, after the divorce was final, she even told him so."

"He didn't try to get in touch with me."

"He was upset for a long time after it happened. So

was I. We blamed you both. But that's in the past. He'd love to hear from you now," she assured him. "He didn't think you'd want to talk to him, after so much time had passed and after what he'd said to you. He feels bad about that."

He leaned forward. "If that's so, when he had the heart attack, why wasn't I told?"

"I called the only number I had for you," she said. "I never got an answer. The hospital said they'd try to track you down, but I guess they didn't."

Could it really be that simple? he wondered. "That was at the old house, in Nassau. It was disconnected three years ago. The number I have now is unlisted."

"Oh."

"Why didn't you ask Eb Scott or Cy Parks?"

"I don't know them," she said hesitantly. "And until very recently, when this Lopez thing made the headlines, I didn't know they were mercenaries." She averted her eyes. "I knew you were acquainted with them, but I certainly didn't know that you were one of them."

He took a slow breath. No, he remembered, she didn't know. He'd never shared that bit of information with either her or Jack Steele.

"I wrote to you, too, about the heart attack, at the last address you left us."

"That would have been forwarded. I never got it."

"I sent it," she said.

"I'm not doubting that you did. I'm telling you that it never got to me."

"I'm really sorry," she told him. "I did try, even if it doesn't look like it. I always hoped that you'd eventually phone someone and I'd be able to contact you. When you didn't, well, I guess Dad and I both figured that you weren't interested in what happened back here. And he did say that he'd been very cruel in what he said to you when you left."

"He was. But I understood," he added.

She smiled sadly. "He loves you. When this is over, you should make peace with him. I think you'll find that he'll more than meet you halfway. He's missed you terribly."

"I've missed him, too." He could have added that he'd missed her as well, but she wasn't likely to believe him.

He started to speak, but he felt the boat slowing. He smiled. "We must be coming up to the pier. Come on. It will be nice to have a comfortable bed to sleep in tonight."

She nodded, and followed him up to the deck.

Her eyes caught sight of the house, on a small rise in the distance, long and low and lighted. She could see arches and flowers, even in the darkness, because of the solar-powered lights that lined the walkway from the pier up to the walled estate. She caught her breath. It was like a house she'd once seen in a magazine and daydreamed about as a child. She had the oddest feeling that she was coming home...

## Chapter 6

"What do you think?" Micah asked as he helped her onto the ramp that led down to the pier.

"It's beautiful," she said honestly. "I expect it's even more impressive in the daylight."

"It is." He hesitated, turning back toward the men who were still on the boat. "Bojo! Make sure we've got at least two guards on the boat before you come up to the house," he called to his associate, who grinned and replied that he would. "Peter can help you," he added involuntarily.

Callie didn't seem to notice that he'd jettisoned both men who'd been friendly with her. Micah did. He didn't like the idea of his men getting close to her. It wasn't jealousy. Of course it wasn't. He was…protecting her from complications.

She looked around as they went up the wide graveled

path to the house, frowning as she became aware of odd noises. "What's that sound?" she asked Micah.

He smiled lazily. "My early warning radar."

"Huh?"

He chuckled. "I keep a flock of geese," he explained, nodding toward a fenced area where a group of big white birds walked around and swam in a huge pool of water. "Believe it or not, they're better than guard dogs."

"Wouldn't a guard dog or two be a better idea?"

"Nope. I've got a Mac inside."

Before she could ask any more questions, the solid wood front door opened and a tall, imposing man in khakis with gray-sprinkled black wavy hair stood in their path. He was holding an automatic weapon in one big hand.

"Welcome home, boss," he said in deep, crisply accented British. He grinned briefly and raised two bushy eyebrows at the sight of Callie. "Got her, did you?"

"Got her, and with no casualties," Micah replied, returning the grin. "How's it going, Mac?"

"No worries. But it'll rain soon." He shifted his weight, grimacing a little.

"At least you're wearing the prosthesis, now," Micah muttered as he herded Callie into the house.

Mac rubbed his hip after he closed the door and followed them. "Damned thing feels funny," he said. "And I can't run." He glowered at Micah as if the whole thing was his fault.

"Hey," Micah told him, "didn't I say 'duck'? In fact, didn't I say it twice?"

"You said it, but I had my earphones in!"

"Excuses, excuses. We even took up a collection for

your funeral, then you had to go mess everything up by living!" Micah grumbled.

"Oh, sure, after you lot had divided up all my possessions! Bojo's still got my favorite shirt and he won't give it back! And he doesn't even wear shirts!"

"He's using it to polish his gun," Micah explained. "Says it's the best shine he's ever put on it."

Callie was openly gaping at them.

Micah's black eyes twinkled. "We're joking," he told her gently. "It's the way we let off steam, so that we don't get bogged down in worry. What we do is hard work, and dangerous. We have to have safety valves."

"I'll blow Bojo's safety valve for him if he doesn't give back my shirt!" Mac assured his boss. "And you haven't even introduced us."

Callie smiled and held out her hand. "Hi! I'm Callie Kirby."

"I'm MacPherson," he replied, shaking it. "I took a mortar hit on our last mission, so I've got KP until I get used to this damned prosthesis," he added, lifting his right leg and grimacing.

"You'd better get used to it pretty soon, or you're going to be permanent in that kitchen," Micah assured him. "Now I'd like to get Callie settled. She's been through a lot."

The other man became somber all at once. "She's not what I expected," Mac said reluctantly as he studied her.

"I can imagine," she said with a sad little smile. "You were expecting a woman who was blond and as good-looking as Micah. I know I don't look like him…"

Before she could add that they weren't related, the older man interrupted her. "That isn't what I meant," Mac replied at once.

She shrugged and smiled carelessly. "Of course not. I really am tired," she added.

"Come on," Micah said. "Have you got something for sandwiches?" Micah asked Mac. "We didn't stop for food."

"Sure," Mac replied, visibly uncomfortable. "I'll get right to it."

Micah led Callie down the long hall and turned her into a large, airy room with a picture window overlooking the ocean. Except for the iron bars, it looked very touristy.

"Mac does most of the cooking. We used to take turns, but after he was wounded, and we found out that his father once owned a French restaurant, we gave him permanent KP." He glanced at her with a wry smile. "We thought it might encourage him to put on the prosthesis and try to be rehabilitated. Apparently it's working."

"He's very nice."

He closed the door and turned to her, his face somber. "He meant that the sort of woman I usually bring here is blond and long-legged and buxom, and that they usually ignore the hired help."

She flushed. "You didn't have to explain."

"Didn't I?" His eyes narrowed on her face as a potential complication presented itself when he thought about having Lisette take Callie on that shopping trip. The woman was extremely jealous, and Callie had been through enough turmoil already. "I haven't told Mac or Lisette that we aren't related. It might be as well to let them continue thinking we are, for the time being."

She wondered why, but she wasn't going to lower her pride by asking. "Sure," she said with careful indifference. "No problem." Presumably this Lisette would be jealous of a stepsister, but not of a real one. Micah obviously didn't want to cause waves. She smiled drowsily. "I think I could sleep the clock around."

"If Maddie's her usual efficient self, she should have packed a nightgown for you."

"I don't have a gown," she murmured absently, glancing at the case he'd put down beside the bed.

"Pajamas, then."

"Uh, I don't wear those, either."

He stood up and looked at her pointedly. "What *do* you sleep in?"

She cleared her throat. "Never mind."

His eyebrows arched. "Well, well. No wonder you locked your bedroom door when you lived with us."

"That wasn't the only reason," she said before she thought.

His black eyes narrowed. "You've had a hell of a life, haven't you? And now this, on top of the past."

She bit her lower lip. "This door does have a lock?" she persisted. "I'm sorry. I've spent my life behind locked doors. It's a hard habit to break, and not because of the way I sleep."

"The door has a lock, and you can use it. But I hope you know that you're safe with me," he replied quietly. "Seducing innocents isn't a habit with me, and my men are trustworthy."

"It's not that."

"If you're nervous about being the only woman here, I could get Lisette to come over and spend the night in this room with you," he added.

"No," she said, reluctant to meet his paramour. "I'll be fine."

"You haven't been alone since it happened," he reminded her. "It may be more traumatic than you think, especially in the dark."

"I'll be all right, Micah," she said firmly.

He drew in an irritated breath. "All right. But if you're frightened, I'm next door, through the bathroom."

She gave him a curious look.

"I'll wear pajama bottoms while you're in residence," he said dryly, reading her mind accurately.

She cleared her throat. "Thanks."

"Don't you want to eat something before you go to bed?"

She shook her head. "I'm too tired. Micah, thanks for saving me. I didn't expect it, but I'm very grateful."

He shrugged. "You're family," he said flatly, and she grimaced when he wasn't looking. He turned and went out, hesitating before he closed the door. "Someone will be within shouting distance, night or day."

Her heart ached. He still didn't see her as a woman. Probably, he never would. "Okay," she replied. "Thanks."

He closed the door.

She was so tired that she was sure she'd be asleep almost as soon as her head connected with the pillow. But that wasn't the case. Dressed only in her cotton briefs, she lay awake for a long time, staring at the ceiling, absorbing the shock of the past two days. It seemed unreal now, here where she was safe. As her strung muscles began to relax, she tugged the cool, expensive designer sheet in a yellow rose pattern over her and felt her mind begin to drift slowly into peaceful oblivion.

"Callie? Callie!"

The deep forceful voice combined with steely fingers on her upper arms to shake her out of the nightmare she'd been having. She was hoarse from the scream that had dragged Micah from sleep and sent him running to the connecting door with a skeleton key.

She was sitting up, both her wrists in one of his lean, warm hands, her eyes wide with terror. She was shaking all over, and not from the air-conditioning.

He leaned over and turned on the bedside lamp. His eyes went helplessly to the full, high thrust of her tip-tilted little breasts, their nipples relaxed from sleep. She was so shaken that she didn't even feel embarrassment. Her pale blue eyes were wild with horror.

"You're safe, baby," he said gently. "It's all right."

"Micah!" came a shout from outside the bedroom door. It was Bojo, alert as usual to any odd noise.

"Callie just had a nightmare, Bojo. It's okay. Go back to bed!"

"Sure thing, boss."

Footsteps faded down the corridor.

"I was back in the chair, at Lopez's house. That man had the knife again, and he was cutting me," she choked. Her wild, frightened eyes met Micah's. "You'll shoot me, if they try to take me and you can't stop them, right?" she asked in a hoarse whisper.

"Nobody is going to take you away from here by force," he said gently. "I promise. I can protect you on this island. It's why I brought you here in the first place."

She sighed and relaxed a little. "I'm being silly. It was the dream. It was so real, and I was scared to death, Micah! It all came back the minute I fell asleep!" She shivered. "Can't you hold me?" she asked huskily, her eyes on his muscular, hair-roughened chest. Looking at it made her whole body tingle. "Just for a minute?"

"Are you out of your mind?" he ground out.

She searched his eyes. He looked odd. "Why not?"

"Because…" His gaze fell to her breasts. They were hard-tipped now, visibly taut with desire. His jaw clenched. His hands on her wrists tightened roughly.

"Oh, for heaven's sake. I forgot! Sorry." She tried to cover herself, but his hands were relentless. She cleared her throat and grimaced. "That hurts," she complained on a nervous laugh, tugging at his hands. They loosened, but only a fraction.

"Did you take those pills I gave you to make you sleep?" he asked suddenly.

"Yes. But they didn't keep me asleep." She blinked. She smiled drowsily. She felt very uninhibited. He was looking at her breasts and she liked it. Her head fell back, because he hadn't turned her loose. His hands weren't bruising anymore, but they were holding her wrists firmly. She arched her back sensuously and watched the way his eyes narrowed and glittered on her breasts. She saw his body tense, and she gave a husky, wicked little laugh.

"You like looking at me there, don't you?" she asked, vaguely aware that she was being reckless.

He made a rough sound and met her eyes again. "Yes," he said flatly. "I like it."

"I wanted to take my clothes off for you when I was just sixteen," she confided absently as her tongue ran away with her. "I wanted you to see me. I ached all over when you looked at me that last Christmas. I wanted you to kiss me so hard that it would bruise my mouth. I wanted to unbutton your shirt and pull my dress down and let you hold me like that." She shivered helplessly at the images that rushed into her reeling mind. "You're so sexy, Micah," she whispered huskily. "So handsome.

And I was just plain and my breasts were small, nothing like those beautiful, buxom women you always dated. I knew you'd never want me the way I wanted you."

He shook her gently. "Callie, for God's sake, hush!" he grated, his whole body tensing with desire at the imagery she was creating.

She was too relaxed from the sleeping pills to listen to warnings. She smiled lazily. "I never wanted anybody to touch me until then," she said softly. "Men always seemed repulsive to me. Did I ever tell you that my mother's last lover tried to seduce me? I ran from him and he knocked me down the stairs. I broke my arm. My mother said it was my fault. She took me back to the foster home. She said I was a troublemaker, and told lies about what happened."

"Dear God!" he exclaimed.

"So after that, I wore floppy old clothes and no makeup and pulled my hair back so I looked like the plainest old maid on earth, and I acted real tough. They left me alone. Then my mother married your dad," she added. "And I didn't have to be afraid anymore. Except it was worse," she murmured drowsily, "because I wanted you to touch me. But you didn't like me that way. You said I was a tramp, like my mother…"

"I didn't mean it," he ground out. "I was only trying to spare you more heartache. You were just a baby, and I was old enough to know better. It was the only way I knew to keep you at arm's length."

"You wanted my mother," she accused miserably.

"Never!" he said, and sounded utterly disgusted. "She was hard as nails, and her idea of femininity was complete control. She was the most mercenary human being I ever met."

Her pale blue eyes blinked as she searched his black ones curiously. "You said I was, too."

"You're not mercenary, honey," he replied quietly. "You never were."

She sighed, and her breasts rose and fell, drawing his attention again. "I feel so funny, Micah," she murmured.

"Funny, how?" he asked without thinking.

She laughed softly. "I don't know how to describe it. I feel…like I'm throbbing. I feel swollen."

She was describing sexual arousal, and he was fighting it like mad. He drew in a long, slow breath and forced himself to let go of her wrists. Her arms fell to her sides and he stared helplessly at the thrust of her small, firm breasts.

"It's so sad," she sighed. "The only time you've ever looked at me or touched me was because I was hurt and needed medical attention." She laughed involuntarily.

"You have to stop this. Right now," he said firmly.

"Stop what?" she asked with genuine curiosity.

He lifted the sheet and placed it over her breasts, pulling one of her hands up to hold it there.

She glowered at him as he got to his feet. "That's great," she muttered. "That's just great. Are you the guy at a striptease who yells 'put it back on'?"

He chuckled helplessly. "Not usually, no. I'll leave the door between our rooms and the bathroom open. You can sing out if you get scared again."

"Gosh, you're brave," she said. "Aren't you afraid to leave your door unlocked? I might sneak in and ravish you in your sleep."

"I wear a chastity belt," he said with a perfectly straight face.

Her eyes widened and suddenly she burst out laughing.

He grinned. "That's more like it. Now lie back down and stop trying to seduce me. When you wake up and remember the things you've said and done tonight, you'll blush every time you look at me."

She shrugged. "I guess I will." She frowned. "What was in those pills?"

"A sedative. Obviously it has an unpredictable reaction on you," he commented with a long, amused look. "Either that or I've discovered a brand-new aphrodisiac. It makes retiring virgins wanton, apparently."

She glared up at him. "I am not wanton, and it wasn't my fault, anyway. I was very scared and you came running in here to flaunt your bare chest at me," she pointed out.

"You were the one doing the flaunting," he countered. "I'm going to have Lisette buy you some gowns, and while you're here, you'll wear them. I don't keep condoms handy anymore," he added bluntly.

She flushed and gasped audibly. "Micah Steele!" she burst out, horrified at the crude remark.

"Don't pretend you don't know what one is. You're not that naive. But that's the only way I'd ever have sex with you, even if I lost my head long enough to stifle my conscience," he added bluntly. "Because I don't want kids, or a wife, ever."

"I've already told you that I'm not proposing marriage!"

"You tried to seduce me," he accused.

"You tempted me! In fact, you drugged me!"

He was trying valiantly not to laugh. "I never!" he

defended himself. "I gave you a mild sedative. A very mild sedative!"

"It was probably Spanish Fly," she taunted. "I've read about what it's supposed to do to women. You gave it to me deliberately so that I'd flash my breasts at you and make suggestive remarks, no doubt!"

He pursed his lips and lifted his chin, muffling laughter. "For the record, you've got gorgeous breasts," he told her. "But I've never seen myself as a tutor for a sensuous virgin. In case you were thinking along those lines."

She felt that compliment down to her toes and tried not to disgrace herself by showing it. Apparently he didn't think her breasts were too small at all. Imagine that! "There are lots of men who'd just love to have sex with me," she told him haughtily.

"What a shame that I'm the only one you'd submit to."

She glared at him. "Weren't you going back to bed?" she asked pointedly.

He sighed. "I might as well, if you're through undressing for me."

"I didn't undress for you! I sleep like this."

"I'll bet you didn't before you moved in with my father and me," he drawled softly.

Her flush was a dead giveaway.

"*And* you never locked your bedroom door at home," he added.

"For all the good it did me," she said grimly.

"I never got my kicks as a voyeur, especially with precocious teenagers," he told her. "You're much more desirable now, with a little age on you. Not," he added, holding up one lean hand, "that I have any plans to succumb. You're a picket-fence sort of woman."

"And you like yours in combat gear, with muscles," she retorted.

His eyes sketched her body under the sheet. "If I ever had the urge to marry," he said slowly, "you'd be at the top of my list of prospects, Callie. You're kindhearted and honest and brave. I was proud of you in the jungle."

She smiled. "Were you, really? I was terribly scared."

"All of us are, when we're being hunted. The trick is to keep going anyway." He pushed her down gently with the sheet up to her neck and her head on the pillow, and he tucked her in very gently. "Go back to sleep," he said, tracing a path down her cheek with a lean forefinger. He smiled. "You can dream about having wild sex with me."

"I don't have a clue about how to have wild sex," she pointed out. She lifted both eyebrows and her eyes twinkled as she gave him a wicked smile. "I'll bet you're great in bed."

"I am," he said without false modesty. "But," he added somberly, "you're a virgin. First times are painful and embarrassing, nothing like the torrid scenes in those romance novels you like to read."

She drew in a drowsy breath. "I figured that."

He had to get out of here. He was aroused already. It wouldn't take much to tempt him, and she'd been through enough already. He tapped her on the tip of her nose. "Sleep well."

"Micah, can I ask you something?" she murmured, blinking as she tried to stay awake.

"Go ahead."

"What did my mother see that made her think she'd enticed you that night we had the blowup?"

"Are you sure you want to know?" he asked. "Because if you do, I'll show you."

Her breath caught in her throat and her heart pounded. She looked at him with uninhibited curiosity and hunger. "I'm sure."

"Okay. Your choice." He unsnapped his pajama bottoms, and let them fall. "She saw this," he said quietly.

Her eyes went to that part of him that the pajamas had hidden. She wasn't so naive that she hadn't seen statues, and photographs in magazines, of naked men. But he sure didn't look like any of the pictures. There were no white lines on him anywhere. He was solid muscle, tanned and exquisitely male. Her eyes went helplessly to that part of him that was most male, and she almost gasped. He was impressive, even to an innocent.

"Do you understand what you're seeing, Callie?" he asked quietly.

"Yes," she managed in a husky whisper. "You're... you're aroused, aren't you?"

He nodded. "When I got away from you that Christmas night, I was like this, just from being close to you," he explained quietly, his voice strained. "The slacks I was wearing were tailored to fit properly, so it was noticeable. Your mother was experienced, and when she saw it, she thought it was because of her. She was wearing a strappy little silver dress, and she had an inflated view of her own charms. I found her repulsive."

"I didn't know men looked like that." Her lips parted as she continued to stare at him. "Are you...I mean, is that...normal?"

"I do occasionally inspire envy in other men," he murmured with a helpless laugh. He pulled his pajama trousers back up and snapped them in place, almost shivering with the hunger to throw himself down on top of her and ravish her. She had no idea of the effect that wide-eyed curiosity had on him. "Now I'm getting out of here before it gets any worse!" he said in a tight voice. "Good night."

She stretched, feeling oddly swollen and achy. She stretched, feeling unfamiliar little waves of pleasure washing over her at the intimacy they'd just shared. She noticed that his face went even tauter as he watched her stretch. It felt good. But she was really sleepy and her eyelids felt heavy. Her eyes began to close. "Gosh, I'm tired. I think I can sleep…now." Her voice trailed off as she sighed heavily and her whole body relaxed in the first stages of sleep.

He looked at her with pure temptation. She'd been sedated, of course, or she'd never have been so uninhibited with him. He knew that, but it didn't stop the frustrated desire he felt from racking his powerful body.

"I'm so glad that one of us can sleep," he murmured with icy sarcasm, but she was already asleep. He gave her one last, wistful stare, and went out of the room quickly.

The next morning, Callie awoke after a long and relaxing sleep feeling refreshed. Then she remembered what had happened in the middle of the night and she was horrified.

She searched through the bag Micah's friend had packed for her, looking for something concealing and unnoticeable, but there wasn't a change of clothing. She only had the jeans and shirt she'd been wearing the day before. Grimacing, she put them back on and ran a brush through her short dark hair. She didn't bother with makeup at all.

When she went into the kitchen, expecting to find

it empty, Micah was going over several sheets of paper with a cup of black coffee in one big hand. He gave her a quick glance and watched the blush cover her high cheekbones. His lean, handsome face broke into a wicked grin.

"Good morning," he drawled. "All rested, are we? Ready for another round of show and tell?"

She ground her teeth together and avoided looking directly at him as she poured herself a cup of coffee from the coffeemaker on the counter and added creamer to it.

"I was drugged!" she said defensively, sitting down at the table. She couldn't make herself look him in the eye.

"Really?"

"You should know," she returned curtly. "You drugged me!"

"I gave you a mild sedative," he reminded her. He gave her a mischievous glance. "But I'll be sure to remember the effects."

She cleared her throat and sipped her coffee. "Can you find me something to do around here?" she asked. "I'm not used to sitting around doing nothing."

"I phoned Lisse about thirty minutes ago," he said. "She'll be over at ten to take you shopping."

"So soon?" she asked curiously.

"You don't have a change of clothes, do you?" he asked.

She shook her head. "No."

"Maddie travels light and expects everyone else to, as well," he explained. "Especially in tight corners. I'll give you my credit card…"

"I have my own," she said at once, embarrassed. "Thanks, but I pay my own way."

"So you said." He eyed her over his coffee cup. "I

won't expect anything in return," he added. "In case that thought crossed your mind."

"I know that. But I don't want to be obligated to you any more than I already am."

"You sound like me, at your age," he mused. "I never liked to accept help, either. But we all come to it, Callie, sooner or later."

She let out a slow breath and sipped more coffee. "I couldn't repay you in a hundred years for what you did for me," she said gently. "You risked your life to get me out of there."

"All in a day's work, honey," he said, and smiled. "Besides," he added, "I had a score to settle with Lopez." His face hardened. "I've got an even bigger one to settle, now. I have to put him out of action, before he organizes his men and goes after Dad!"

# *Chapter 7*

Callie felt her heart go cold at the words. She'd been through so much herself that she'd forgotten briefly that Jack Steele was in danger, too. Micah had said that Pogo and Maddie would watch over him, but obviously he still had fears.

"You don't think he'll be safe with your people?" she asked worriedly.

"Not if Lopez gets his act together," he said coolly. "Which is why I've had Bojo send him a message in the clear, rubbing it in that I took you away from him."

She felt uneasy. "Isn't that dangerous, with a man like Lopez?"

"Very," he agreed. "But if he's concentrating on me, he's less likely to expend his energy on Dad. Right?"

"Right," she agreed. "What do you want me to do?"

He lowered his eyes to his coffee cup and lifted it to

his chiseled mouth. "You do whatever you like. You're here as my guest."

She frowned. "I don't need a holiday, Micah."

"You're getting one, regardless. Today you can go shopping with Lisse. Tomorrow, I'll take you sightseeing, if you like."

"Is it safe?"

He chuckled. "We won't be alone," he pointed out. "I intend to take Bojo and Peter and Rodrigo along with us."

"Oh."

"Disappointed?" he asked with faint arrogance. "Would you rather be alone with me, on a deserted beach?"

She glared at him. "You stop that."

"Spoilsport. You do rise to the bait so beautifully." He leaned back in his chair and the humor left his eyes. "Bojo's going with you to Nassau. Buy what you like, but make sure you don't bring home low-cut blouses and short-shorts or short skirts. There aren't any other women on this island, except a couple of married middle-aged island women who live with their husbands and families. I don't want anything to divert the men's attention with Lopez on the loose."

"I don't wear suggestive clothing," she pointed out.

"You do around me," he said flatly. "Considering last night's showing, I thought the warning might be appropriate."

"I was drugged!" she repeated, flushing.

"I don't mind if you show your body to me," he continued, as if she hadn't spoken. "I enjoy looking at it. But I'm not sharing the sight. Besides, for the next week or two, you're my sister. I don't want anyone speculating about our exact relationship."

"Why? Because of your friend Lisette?" she asked bitterly.

"Exactly," he said with a poker face. "Lisette and I are lovers," he added bluntly. "The last thing I need is a jealous tug-of-war in a crisis."

She caught her breath audibly. It was cruel of him to say such a thing. Or maybe he was being cruel to be kind, making sure that she didn't get her hopes up.

She lifted her head with postured arrogance. "That's wishful thinking," she said firmly. "I know you're terribly disappointed that I haven't proposed, but you'd better just deal with it."

For an instant he looked shocked, then he laughed. It occurred to him that he'd never laughed as much in his life as he had with her, especially the past couple of days. Considering the life or death situation they'd been in, it was even more incredible. Callie was a real mate under fire. He'd heard stories about wives of retired mercs walking right into fire with their husbands. He'd taken them with a grain of salt until he'd seen Callie in a more desperate situation than any of those wives had ever been in.

"You made me proud, in Cancún," he said after a minute. "Really proud. If we had campfires, you're the sort of woman we'd build into legend around them."

She flushed. "Like Maddie?"

"Maddie's never been in the situation you were in," he said somberly. "I don't even know another woman who has. Despite the nightmares, you held up as well as any man I've ever served with."

She smiled slowly. "A real compliment, wow," she

murmured. "If you'll write all that down, I'll have it notarized and hang it behind my desk. Mr. Kemp will be very impressed."

He glowered at her. "Kemp's more likely to hang you on the wall beside it. You're wasted in a law office."

"I love what I do," she protested. "I dig out little details that save lives and careers. Law isn't dry and boring, it's alive. It's history."

"It's a job in a little hick Texas town while you'll eventually dry up and blow away like a sun-scorched creosote bush."

She searched his dark eyes. "That's how it felt to you, I know. You never liked living in Jacobsville. But I'm not like you," she added softly. "I want a neat little house with a flower garden and neighbors to talk to over the fence, and a couple of children." Her face softened as she thought about it. "Not right away, of course. But someday."

"Just the thought of marriage gives me chest pain," he said with veiled contempt. "More often than not, a woman marries for money and a man marries for sex. What difference does a sheet of paper with signatures make?"

"If you have to ask, you wouldn't understand the answer," she said simply. "I guess you don't want kids."

He frowned. He'd never thought about having kids. It was one of those "someday" things he didn't give much time to. He studied Callie and pictured her again with a baby in her arms. It was surprisingly nice.

"It would be hard to carry a baby through jungle undergrowth with a rifle under one arm," she answered her own question. "And in your line of work, I don't suppose leaving a legacy to children is much of a priority."

He averted his head. "I expect to spend what I make while I'm still alive," he said.

She looked out over the bay, her eyes narrowing in the glare of the sunlight. The casuarinas lining the beach were towering and their feathery fronds waved gracefully in the breeze that always blew near the water. Flowers bloomed everywhere. The sand was like sugar, white and picturesque.

"It's like a living travel poster," she remarked absently. "I've never seen water that color except in postcards, and I thought it was just a bad color job."

"There are places in the Pacific and the Caribbean like it," he told her. He glanced toward the pier as he heard the sound of a motor. "There's Lisse," he said. "Come and be introduced."

She got up and followed along behind him, feeling like a puppy that couldn't be left alone. As she watched, a gorgeous blonde in a skimpy yellow sundress with long legs and long hair let Micah help her onto the pier. Unexpectedly he jerked her against him and kissed her so passionately that Callie flushed and looked away in embarrassment. He was obviously terrified that she might read something into last night, so he was making his relationship with Lisse very plain.

A few minutes later, Micah put something into Lisse's hand and spoke softly to her. Lisse laughed breathily and said something that Callie couldn't hear. Micah took the blonde by the hand and led her down the pier to where Callie was waiting at a respectful distance.

Up close, the blonde had a blemishless complexion and perfect teeth. She displayed them in a smile that would do credit to a supermodel, which was what the woman really looked like.

"I'm Lisette Dubonnet, but everyone calls me Lisse," she introduced herself and held out a hand to firmly shake Callie's.

"I'm Callie…" she began.

"My sister," Micah interrupted, obviously not trusting her to play along. "She's taking a holiday from her job in Texas. I want you to help her buy some leisure wear. Her suitcase didn't arrive with her."

"Oh," Lisse said, and laughed. "I've had that happen. I know *just* how you feel. Well, shall we go? Micah, are you coming with us?"

Micah shook his head. "I've got things to do here, but Bojo wants to come along, if you don't mind. He has to check on a package his brother is sending over from Georgia."

"He's perfectly welcome," Lisse said carelessly. "Come along, Callie. Callie…what a pretty name. A little rare, I should say."

"It's short for Colleen," Callie told her, having to almost run to keep up with the woman's long strides.

"We'll go downtown in Nassau. There are lots of chic little boutiques there. I'm sure we can find something that will do for you."

"You're very kind…"

Lisse held up an imperative hand as they reached the boat she'd just disembarked from. "It's no bother. Micah never speaks of you. Did he have you hidden in a closet or something?"

"We don't get along very well," Callie formulated. It was the truth, too, mostly.

"And that's very odd. Micah gets along wonderfully with most women."

"But then you're not related to him," Callie pointed

out, just managing to clamber aboard the boat before the line was untied by Bojo, who was already there and waiting to leave.

"No, thank God I'm not." Lisse laughed. Even her laugh was charming. "I'd kill myself. Hurry up, Bojo, Dad and I have to go to an embassy ball tonight, so I'm pressed for time!"

"I am coming, mademoiselle!" he said with a grin and leaped down into the boat.

"Let's go, Marchand!" she called to the captain, who replied respectfully and turned the expensive speedboat back into the bay and headed it toward Nassau.

"We could postpone this trip, if you don't have time," Callie offered.

"Not necessary," Lisse said. "I'll have less time later on. I try to do anything Micah asks me to. He's always *so* grateful," she added in a purring tone.

And I can just imagine what form that takes, Callie thought, but she didn't say it. Even so, Bojo heard their conversation, caught Callie's eye, and grinned so wickedly that she cleared her throat and asked Lisse about the history of Nassau to divert her.

Nassau was bustling with tourists. The colorful straw market at the docks was doing a booming business, and fishing boats rocked gently on the waves made by passing boats. Seagulls made passes at the water and flew gracefully past the huge glass windows of the restaurant that sat right on the bay. It was beautiful. Just beautiful. Callie, who'd never been anywhere—well, except for the road trip to Cancún with the drug lord's minions while she was unconscious—thought it was pure delight.

"Don't gawk like a tourist, darling," Lisse scoffed as

they made their way past the fishing boats and into an arcade framed in an antique stone arch covered in bougainvillea. "It's only Nassau."

But Callie couldn't help it. She loved the musical accents she caught snatches of as they strolled past shops featuring jewelry with shell motifs and handcrafts from all over Europe, not to mention dress shops and T-shirt shops galore. She loved the stone pathways and the flowers that bloomed everywhere. They went past a food stand and her nose wrinkled.

"I thought I smelled liquor," she said under her breath.

"You did," Lisse said nonchalantly, waving her painted fingernails in the general direction of the counter. "You can buy any sort of alcoholic drink you want at any of these food stands."

"It's legal?"

"Of course it's legal. Haven't you been anywhere?"

Callie smiled sheepishly. "Not really. Now this is the sort of shop I need," she said suddenly, stopping at a store window displaying sundresses, jeans and T-shirts and sneakers. It also displayed the cards it accepted, and Callie had one of them. "I'll only be a minute…"

"Darling, not there!" Lisse lamented. "It's one of those cheap touristy shops! Micah wants you to use his charge card. I've got it in my pocket. He wants you to wear things that won't embarrass him." She put her fingers over her mouth. "Oh, dear, I forgot, I wasn't to tell you that he said that." She grimaced. "Well, anyway…"

"Well, anyway," Callie interrupted, following Lisse's lead, "this is where I'm shopping, with *my* card. You can wait or come in. Suit yourself."

She turned and left Lisse standing there with her

mouth gaping, and she didn't care. The woman was horrible!

After she'd tried on two pairs of jeans, two sundresses, a pair of sandals, one of sneakers and four T-shirts, she felt guilty for the way she'd talked to Micah's woman. But Lisse was hard-going, especially after that kiss she'd witnessed. It had hurt right to the bone, and Lisse's condescending, snappy attitude didn't endear her to Callie, either.

She came back out of the shop with two bags. "Thank you very much. I'd like to go back to the house, now," she told Lisse, and she didn't smile.

Lisse made a moue with her perfect mouth. "I've hurt your feelings. I'm sorry. But Micah told me what to do. He'll be furious with me now."

What a pity. She didn't say it. "He can be furious with me," Callie said, walking ahead of Lisse back the way they'd come. "I buy my own clothes and pay my own way. I'm not a helpless parasite. I don't need a man to buy things for me."

There was a stony silence from behind her. She stopped and turned and said, "Oh, my, did I hurt your feelings? I'm sorry." And with a wicked gleam in her eyes at the other woman's furious flush, she walked back toward the boat.

Bojo knew something was going on, but he was too polite to question Lisse's utter silence all the way back to the pier. He got out first to tie up the boat and reached down to help Callie out, relieving her of her packages on the way. Micah had heard the boat and was strolling down the pier to meet them. There was a scramble as Lisse climbed out of the boat, cursing her captain for not being quick enough to spare her a stumble. She sounded like she was absolutely seething!

"We'd better run for it," Callie confided to Bojo.

"What did you do?" he asked under his breath.

"I called her a parasite. I think she's upset."

He muffled a laugh, nodded respectfully at his boss and herded Callie down the pier at very nearly a run while Micah stood staring after them with a scowl. Seconds later Lisse reached him and her voice carried like a bullhorn.

"She's got the breeding of a howler monkey, and the dress sense of an octopus!" she raged. "I wouldn't take her to the nearest tar pit without a bribe!"

Callie couldn't help it. She broke down and ran even faster, with Bojo right beside her.

Later, of course, she had to face the music. She'd changed into a strappy little blue-and-white-striped sundress. It was ankle-length with a square bodice and wide shoulder straps. Modest even enough for her surroundings. She was barefoot, having disliked the fit of the sandals she'd bought that rubbed against her big toe. Micah came striding toward her where she was lounging under a sea grape tree watching the fishing boats come into the harbor.

Micah was in cutoff denims that left his long, powerful legs bare, and he was wearing an open shirt. His chest was broad and hair-roughened and now Callie couldn't look at it without feeling it under her hands.

"Can't you get along with anyone?" he demanded, his fists on his narrow hips as he glared down at her.

"My boss Mr. Kemp thinks I'm wonderful," she countered.

His eyes narrowed. "You gave Lisse fits, and she only came over to do you a favor, when she was already pressed for time."

Her eyebrows arched over shimmering blue eyes. "You don't think I'm capable of walking into a shop and buying clothes all by myself? Whatever sort of women are you used to?"

"And you called her a parasite," he added angrily.

"Does she work?"

He hesitated. "She's her father's hostess."

"I didn't ask you about her social life, I asked if she worked for her living. She doesn't. And she said that when she did you favors, you repaid her handsomely." She cocked her head up at him. "I suppose, in a pinch, you could call that working for her living. But it isn't a profession I'd want to confess to in public."

He just stood there, scowling.

"I make my own living," she continued, "and pay my own way. I don't rely on men to support me, buy me clothes, or chauffeur me around."

"Lisse is used to a luxurious lifestyle," he began slowly, but without much conviction.

"I'm sure that I've misjudged her," she said placatingly. "Why, if you lost everything tomorrow, I know she'd be the first person to rush to your side and offer to help you make it all back with hard work."

He pursed his lips and thought about that.

"That's what I thought," she said sweetly.

He was glaring again. "I told you to put everything on my card, and get nice things."

"You told Lisse to take me to expensive dress shops so that I wouldn't buy cheap stuff and embarrass you," she countered, getting to her feet. She brushed off her skirt, oblivious to the shocked look on his face, before she lifted her eyes back to his. "I don't care if I embarrass you," she pointed out bluntly. "You can always hide me in a closet when you have guests if you're ashamed of me."

He made a rough sound. "You'd walk right into the living room and tell them why you were hidden."

She shrugged. "Blame it on a rough childhood. I don't like people pushing me around. Especially model-type parasites."

"Lisse is not—" he started.

"I don't care what she is or isn't," she cut him off, "she's not bossing me around and insulting me!"

"What did you tell her about our relationship?" he demanded, and he was angry.

"I told her nothing," she countered hotly. "It's none of her business. But, for the record, if you really were my brother, I'd have you stuffed and mounted and I'd use you for an ashtray!"

She walked right past him and back into the house. She heard muffled curses, but she didn't slow down. Let him fume. She didn't care.

She didn't come out for supper. She sat in a peacock chair out on the patio overlooking the bay and enjoyed the delicious floral smell of the musty night air in the delicious breeze, while sipping a piña colada. She'd never had one and she was curious about the taste, so she'd had Mac fix her one, along with a sandwich. She wasn't really afraid of Micah, but she was hoping to avoid him until they both cooled down.

He came into her room without knocking and walked right out onto the patio. He was wearing a tuxedo with a fine white cotton shirt, and he looked so handsome that her heart stopped and fluttered at just the sight of him.

"Are you going to a funeral, or did you get a job as a waiter?" she asked politely.

He managed not to laugh. It wasn't funny. She wasn't funny. She'd insulted Lisse and the woman was going to give him fits all night. "I'm taking Lisse to an embassy ball," he said stiffly. "I would have invited you, but you don't have anything to wear," he added with a vicious smile.

"Just as well," she murmured, lifting her glass to him in a mock toast. "It would have blood all over it by the end of the night, if I'm any judge of miffed women."

"Lisse is a lady," he said shortly. "Something you have no concept of, with your ignorance of proper manners."

That hurt, but she smiled. "Blame it on a succession of foster homes," she told him sweetly. "Manners aren't a priority."

He hated being reminded of the life she'd led. It made him feel guilty, and he didn't like it. "Pity," he said scathingly. "You might consider taking lessons."

"I always think that if you're going to fight, you should get down in the mud and roll around, not use words."

"Just what I'd expect from a little savage like you," he said sarcastically.

The word triggered horrible memories. She reacted to it out of all proportion, driven by her past. She leaped to her feet, eyes blazing, the glass trembling in her hand. "One more word, and you'll need a shower and a dry cleaner to get out the door!"

"Don't you like being called a savage?" He lifted his chin as her hand drew back. "You wouldn't daaa....re!"

He got it right in the face. It didn't stay there. It dribbled down onto his spotless white shirt and made little white trickles down over his immaculate black tuxedo.

She frowned. "Damn. I forgot the toast." She lifted the empty glass at him. *"Salud y pesetas!"* she said in Spanish, with a big furious smile. Health and wealth.

His fists clenched at his sides. He didn't say a word. He didn't move a muscle. He just looked at her with those black eyes glittering like a coiling cobra.

She wiggled her eyebrows. "It will be an adventure. Lisse can lick it off! Think of the new experiences you can share…now, Micah," she shifted gears and started backing up.

He was moving. He was moving very slowly, very deliberately, with the steps of a man who didn't care if he had to go to jail for homicide. She noticed that at once.

She backed away from him. He really did look homicidal. Perhaps she'd gone a little too far. Her mouth tended to run away from her on good days, even when she wasn't insulted and hadn't had half a glass of potent piña colada to boot. She wasn't used to alcohol at all.

"Let's be reasonable," she tried. She was still backing up. "I do realize that I might have overreacted. I'll apologize."

He kept coming.

"I'm really sorry," she tried again, holding up both hands, palms toward him, as if to ward him off.

He still kept coming.

"And I promise, faithfully, that I will never do it… *aaaaahh!*"

There was a horrific splash and she swallowed half the swimming pool. She came up soaked, sputtering, freezing, because the water was cold. She clamored over the softly lit water to the concrete edge and grabbed hold of the ladder to pull herself up. It was really hard, because her full skirt was soaked and heavy.

"Like hell you do," he said fiercely, and started to push her back in.

She was only trying to save herself. But she grabbed his arms and overbalanced him, and he went right into the pool with her, headfirst.

This time when she got to the surface, he was right beside her. His black eyes were raging now.

She pushed her hair out of her eyes and mouth. "I'm *really* sorry," she panted.

He was breathing deliberately. "Would you like to explain why you went ballistic for no reason?" he demanded.

She grimaced, treading water and trying not to sink. She couldn't swim *very well.* She was ashamed of her behavior, but the alcohol had loosened all her inhibitions. She supposed she owed him the truth. She glanced at him and quickly away again. "When that man hit on me and made me break my arm, he told my mother I was a lying little savage and that I needed to be put away. That's when my mother took me back to my foster family and disowned me," she bit off the words, averting her eyes.

There was a long silence. He swam to the ladder, waiting for her to join him. But she was tired and cold and emotionally drained. And when she tried to dog-paddle, her arms were just too tired. She sank.

Powerful arms caught her, easing her to the surface effortlessly so that she could breathe. He sat her on the edge and climbed out, reaching down to lift her out beside him. He took her arm and led her back up the cob-blestoned walkway to the patio.

"I can pack and go home tomorrow," she offered tautly.

"You can't leave," he said flatly. "Lopez knows where you are."

She lifted her weary eyes to his hard, cold face. "Poor you," she said. "Stuck with me."

His eyes narrowed. "You haven't dealt with any of it, have you?" he asked quietly. "You're still carrying your childhood around on your back."

"We all do, to some extent," she said with a long sigh. "I'm sorry I ruined your suit. I'm sorry I was rude to Lisse. I'll apologize, if you like," she added humbly.

"You don't like her."

She shrugged. "I don't know her. I just don't have a high opinion of women who think money is what life is all about."

He scowled. "What *is* it all about?" he challenged.

She searched his eyes slowly. "Pain," she said in a husky tone, and she winced involuntarily before she could stop herself. "I'm going to bed. Good night."

She was halfway in the door when he called her back. She didn't turn. "Yes?"

He hesitated. He wanted to apologize, he really did. But he didn't know how. He couldn't remember many regrets.

She laughed softly to herself. "I know. You wish you'd never been landed with me. You might not believe it, but so do I."

"If you'll give me the name of the shop where you

bought that stuff, I'll have them transfer it to my account."

"Fat chance, Steele," she retorted as she walked away.

## Chapter 8

After a restless night, but thankfully with no night-mares, Callie put on a colorful sundress and went out onto the beach barefoot to pick up shells. She met Bojo on the way. He was wearing the long oyster silk hooded djellaba she'd never seen him out of.

He gave her a rueful glance. "The boss had to send to town for a new tuxedo last night," he said with twinkling dark eyes. "I understand you took him swimming."

She couldn't help chuckling. "I didn't mean to. We had a name-calling contest and he lost."

He chuckled, too. "You know, his women rarely accost him. They fawn over him, play up to him, stroke his ego and live for expensive presents."

"I'm his sister," she said neutrally.

"You are not," he replied gently. He smiled at her surprised glance. "He does occasionally share things with me," he added. "I believe the fiction is to protect you from Lisse. She is obsessively jealous of him and not a woman to make an enemy of. She has powerful connections and little conscience."

"Oh, I got to her before I got to him, if you recall," Callie said with a wry glance. She scuffed her toes in the sand, unearthing part of a perfect shell. She bent to pick it up. "I guess I'll be fish food if she has mob connections."

He chuckled. "I wouldn't rule that out, but you are safe enough here," he admitted. "What are you doing?"

"Collecting shells to take back home," she said, her eyes still on the beach. "I've lived inland all my life. I don't think I've ever even seen the ocean. Galveston is on the bay, and it isn't too far from Jacobsville, but I've never been there, either. It just fascinates me!" She glanced at him. "Micah said you were from Morocco. That's where the Sahara Desert is, isn't it?"

"Yes, but I am from Tangier. It is far north of the desert."

"But it's desert, too, isn't it?" she wondered.

He laughed pleasantly. "Tangier is a seaport, mademoiselle. In fact, it looks a lot like Nassau. That's why I don't mind working here with Micah."

"Really?" She just stared at him. "Isn't it funny, how we get mental pictures of faraway places, and they're nothing like what you see when you get there? I've seen postcards of the Bahamas, but I thought that water was painted, because it didn't even look real. But it is. It's the most astonishing group of colors..."

"Bojo!"

He turned to see his boss coming toward them, taciturn and threatening. It was enough for Callie to hear the tone of his voice to know that he was angry. She didn't turn around, assuming he had chores for Bojo.

"See you," she said with a smile.

He lifted both eyebrows. "I wonder," he replied enigmatically, and went down the beach to speak to Micah.

Minutes later, Micah strolled down the beach where Callie was kneeling and sorting shells damp with seawater and coated with sand. He was wearing sand-colored slacks with casual shoes and an expensive silk shirt under a sports coat. He looked elegant and so handsome that Callie couldn't continue looking at him without letting her admiration show.

"Are you here for an apology?" she asked, concentrating on the shells instead of him. Her heart was pounding like mad, but at least her voice sounded calm.

There was a pause. "I'm here to take you sightseeing."

Her heart jumped. She'd thought that would be the last thing on his mind after their argument the night before. She glanced at his knees and away again. "Thanks for the offer, but I'd rather hunt shells, if it's all the same to you."

He stuck his hands into his pockets and glared at her dark, bent head, his mouth making a thin line in a hard face. He felt guilty about the things he'd said to her the night before, and she'd made him question his whole lifestyle with that remark about Lisse. When he looked back, he had to admit that most of the women in his life had been out for material rewards. Far from looking for love, they'd been looking for expensive jewelry, nights out in the fanciest nightclubs and restaurants, sailing trips on his yacht. Callie wouldn't even let him buy her a decent dress.

He glared at the dress she was wearing with bridled fury. Lisse had spent the evening condemning Callie for everything from her Texas accent to her lack of style. It had been one of the most unpleasant dates of his life, and when he'd refused her offer to stay the night at her apartment, she'd made furious comments about his "unnatural" attraction to his sister. Rather than be accused of perversion, he'd been forced to tell the truth. That had only made matters worse. Lisse had stormed into her apartment house without a word and he knew that she was vindictive. He'd have to watch Callie even more carefully now.

"I guess she gave you hell all night, huh?" Callie asked his shoes. "I'm really sorry."

He let out a harsh breath. His dark eyes went to the waves caressing the white sand near the shore. Bits of seaweed washed up over the occasional shell, along with bits of palm leaves.

"Why don't you want to see Nassau?"

She stood up and lifted one of her bare feet. There was a noticeable blister between her big toe and the next one, on both feet. "Because I'd have to go barefoot. I got the wrong sort of sandals. They've got a thong that goes between your toes, and I'm not used to them. Sneakers don't really go with this dress."

"Not much would," he said with a scathing scrutiny of it. "Half the women on New Providence are probably wearing one just like it."

She glared at him. "Assembly line dresses are part of my lifestyle. I have to live within my means," she said with outraged pride. "I'm sorry if I don't dress up to your exacting standards, but I can't afford haute couture on take-home pay of a little over a hundred and fifty dollars a week!" Her chin tilted with even more hostility. "So spare your blushes and leave me to my shells. I'd hate to embarrass you by wearing my 'rags' out in public."

"Oh, hell!" he burst out, eyes flashing.

He was outraged, but she knew she'd hit the nail on the head. He didn't even try to pretend that he wasn't ashamed to take her out in public. "Isn't it better if I stay here, anyway? Surely I'm safer in a camp of armed men that I would be running around Nassau."

"You seem to be surgically attached to Bojo lately," he said angrily.

She lifted both eyebrows. "I like Bojo," she said. "He doesn't look down on the way I dress, or make fun of my accent, or ignore me when I'm around."

He was almost vibrating with anger. He couldn't remember any woman in his life making him as explosively angry as Callie could.

"Why don't you take Lisse sight-seeing?" she suggested, moving away from him. "You could start with the most expensive jeweler in Nassau and work your way to the most expensive boutique…Micah!"

He had her up in his arms and he was heading for the ocean.

She pushed at his broad chest. "Don't you dare, don't…you…dare, Micah!"

It didn't work. He swung her around and suddenly was about to toss her out right into the waves when the explosion came. There was a ricochet that was unmistakable to Micah, and bark flew off a palm tree nearby. "Bojo!" Micah yelled.

The other man, who was still within shouting distance, came running with a small weapon in his hands. Out beyond the breakers, there was a ship, a yacht, moving slowly. A glint of sunlight reflecting off metal was visible on the deck and the ricocheting sound came again.

"What the…!" she exclaimed, as Micah ran down the beach with her in his arms.

"This way!" Bojo yelled to him, and a sharp, metallic ripple of gunfire sounded somewhere nearby.

The firing brought other men to the beach, one of whom had a funny-looking long tube. It was Peter. Bojo called something to him. He protested, but Bojo insisted. He knelt, resting the tube on his shoulder, sighted and pulled the trigger. A shell flew out of it with a muffled roar. Seconds later, there was a huge splash in the water just off the yacht's bow.

"That'll buy us about a minute. Let's go!" Micah grabbed Callie up in his arms and rushed up the beach to the house at a dead run. His men stopped firing and followed. Micah called something to Bojo in a language Callie had never heard before.

"What was that?" she asked, shocked when he put her down inside the house. "What happened?"

"Lopez happened, unless I miss my guess. I was careless. It won't happen twice," Micah said flatly. He walked away while she was still trying to form questions.

Moments later, Micah went to find Bojo.

"The yacht is gone now, of course," Bojo said angrily. "Peter is upset that I refused to let him blow her up."

"Some things require more authority than I have, even here," Micah said flatly. "But don't think I wasn't tempted to do just that. Lopez knows I have Callie, and he knows where she is now. He'll make a try for her."

He looked at Bojo. "She can't be out of our sight again, not for a second."

"I am aware of that," the other man replied. His dark eyes narrowed. "Micah, does she have any idea at all that you're using her as bait?"

"If you so much as mention that to her…!" Micah threatened softly.

"I would not," he assured the older man. "But you must admit, it hardly seems the action of someone who cares for her."

Micah stared him down. "She's part of my family and I'll take care of her. But she's only part of my family because my father married her tramp of a mother. She's managed to endear herself to my father and it would kill him if anything happened to her," he said in a cold tone. "I can't let Lopez get to my father. Using Callie to bait him here, where I can deal with him safely, is the only way I have to get him at all, and I'm not backing down now!"

"As you wish," Bojo said heavily. "At least she has no idea of this."

Micah agreed. Neither of them saw the shadow at the door behind them retreat to a distance.

Callie went back to her room and closed the door very quietly before she let the tears roll down her white face. She'd have given two years of her life not to have heard those cold words from Micah's lips. She knew he was angry with her, but she didn't realize the contempt with which he was willing to risk her life, just to get Lopez. All he'd said about protecting her, keeping her safe, not letting Lopez get to her—it was all lies. He wanted her for bait. That was all she meant to him. He was doing it to save his father from Lopez, not to save her. Apparently she was expendable. Nothing in her life had ever hurt quite so much.

She seemed to go numb from the pain. She didn't feel anything, except emptiness. She sat down in the chair beside the window and looked out over the ocean. The ship that had been there was gone now, but Lopez knew where the house was, and how well it was guarded. Considering his record, she didn't imagine that he'd give up his quest just because Micah had armed men. Lopez had armed men, too, and all sorts of connections. He also had a reputation for never getting bested by anyone. He would do everything in his power to get Callie back, thinking Micah really cared for her. After all, he'd rescued her hadn't he?

She wrapped her arms around herself, remembering how it had been at Lopez's house, how that henchman had tortured her. She felt sick all over. This was even worse than being in the foster care system. She was all alone. There was no one to offer her protection, to comfort her, to value her. Her whole life had been like that. For just a little while, she'd had some wild idea that she mattered to Micah. What a joke.

At least she knew the truth now, even if she'd had to eavesdrop to learn it. She could only depend on herself. She was going to ask Bojo for a gun and get him to teach her to shoot it. If she had to fend for herself, and apparently she did, she wanted a chance for survival. Micah would probably turn her over to Lopez if he got a guarantee that Lopez would leave his father alone, she reasoned irrationally. The terror she felt was so consuming that she felt her whole body shaking with it.

When Micah opened the door to her room, she had to fight not to rage at him. It wasn't his fault that he didn't care for her, she told herself firmly. And she loved his father as much as he did. She managed to look at him without flinching, but the light in her eyes had gone out. They were quiet, haunted eyes with no life in them at all.

Micah saw that and frowned. She was different. "What's wrong? You're safe," he assured her. "Lopez was only letting us know he's nearby. Believe me, if he'd wanted you dead, you'd be dead."

She swallowed. "I figured that out," she said in a subdued tone. "What now?"

The frown deepened. "We wait, of course. He'll make another move. We'll draw back and let him think we didn't take the threat seriously. That will pull him in."

She lifted her eyes to his face. "Why don't you let me go sight-seeing alone?" she offered. "That would probably do the trick."

"And risk letting him take you again?" he asked solemnly.

She laughed without humor and turned her eyes back to the ocean. "Isn't that what you have in mind already?"

The silence behind her was arctic. "Would you like to explain that question?"

"In ancient times, when they wanted to catch a lion, they tethered a live kid goat to a post and baited him with it. If the goat lived, they turned him loose, but if the lion got him, it didn't really matter. I mean, what's a goat more or less?"

Micah had never felt so many conflicting emotions at the same time. Foremost of them was shame. "You heard me talking to Bojo?"

She nodded.

His indrawn breath was the only sound in the room.

"Callie," he began, without knowing what he could say to repair the damage.

"It's okay," she said to the picture window. "I never had any illusions about where I fit in your family. I still don't."

His teeth ground together. Why should it be so painful to hear her say that? She was the interloper. She and her horrible mother had destroyed his relationship with his own father. He was alone because of her, so why should he feel guilty? But he did. He felt guilty and ashamed. He hadn't really meant everything he'd said to Bojo. Somewhere there was a vague jealousy of the easy friendship she had with his right-hand man, with the tenderness she gave Bojo, when she fought Micah tooth and nail.

"I'll do whatever you want me to," she said after a minute. "But I want a gun, and I want to learn how to use it." She stood up and turned to face him, defiant in the shark-themed white T-shirt and blue jeans she'd changed into. "Because if Lopez gets me this time, he's getting a dead woman. I'll never go through that again."

Micah actually winced. "He's not getting you," he said curtly.

"Better me than Dad," she said with a cold smile. "Right?"

He slammed the door and walked toward her. She didn't even try to back up. She glared at him from a face that was tight with grief and misery, the tracks of tears still visible down her cheeks.

"Do you actually think I'd let him take you, even to save Dad?" he demanded furiously. "What sort of man do you think I am?"

"I have no idea," she said honestly. "You're a stranger. You always have been."

He searched her blue eyes with irritation and impatience. "You're a prime example of the reason I prefer mercenary women," he said without thinking. "You're nothing but a pain in the neck."

"Thank you. I love compliments."

"You probably thrive on insults," he bit off. Then he remembered how she'd had to live all those years, and could have slapped himself for taunting her.

"If they're all you ever hear, you get used to them," she agreed without rancor. "I'm tough. I've had to be. So do your worst, Micah," she added. "Tie me to a palm tree and wait in ambush for Lopez to shoot at me, I don't care."

But she did care. There was real pain in those blue eyes, which she was trying so valiantly to disguise with sarcasm. It hurt her that Micah would use her to draw Lopez in. That led him to the question of why it hurt her. And when he saw that answer in her eyes, he could have gone through the floor with shame.

She...loved him. He felt his heart stop and then start again as the thought went through him like electricity. She almost certainly loved him, and she was doing everything in her power to keep him from seeing it. He remembered her arms around him, her mouth surrendering to his, her body fluid and soft under his hands as she yielded instantly to his ardor. A woman with her past would have a hard time with lovemaking, yet she'd been willing to let him do anything he liked to her. Why hadn't he questioned that soft yielding? Why hadn't he known? And she'd heard what he said to Bojo, feeling that way...

"I swear to you, I won't let Lopez get you," he said in a firm, sincere tone.

"You mean, you'll try," she replied dully. "I want a gun, Micah."

"Over my dead body," he said harshly. "You're not committing suicide."

Her lower lip trembled. She felt trapped. She looked trapped.

That expression ignited him like fireworks. He jerked her into his tall, powerful body, and bent to her mouth before she realized his intent. His warm, hard mouth bit into her lips with ardent insistence as his arms enveloped her completely against him. He felt his body swell instantly, as it always did when he touched her. He groaned against her mouth and deepened the kiss, lost in the wonder of being loved…

Dizzily he registered that she was making a half-hearted effort to push him away. He felt her cold, nervous hands on his chest. He lifted his head and looked at her wary, uncertain little face.

"I won't hurt you," he said softly.

"You're angry," she choked. "It's a punishment…"

"I'm not and it isn't." He bent again, and kissed her eyelids. His hands worked their way up into the thickness of her hair and then down her back, slowly pressing her to him.

She shivered at the feel of him against her hips.

He chuckled at that telltale sign. "Most men would kill to have such an immediate response to a woman. But I don't suppose you know that."

"You shouldn't…"

He lifted his head again and gave her a look full of

amused worldly wisdom. "You think I can will it not to happen, I guess?"

She flushed.

"Sorry, honey, but it doesn't work that way." He moved away just enough to spare her blushes, but his hands slid to her waist and held her in front of him. "I want you to stay in the house," he said, as if he hadn't done anything outrageous at all. "Stay away from windows and porches, too."

She searched his eyes. "If Lopez doesn't see me," she began.

"He knows you're here," he said with faint distaste. "I don't want him to know exactly where you are. I'll have men on every corner of the property and the house for the duration. I won't let you be captured."

She leaned her forehead against him, shivering. "You can't imagine...how it was," she said huskily.

His arms tightened, holding her close. He cursed himself for ever having thought of putting her deliberately in the line of fire. He couldn't imagine he'd been that callous, even briefly. It had been the logical thing to do, and he'd never let emotion get in the way of work. But Callie wasn't like him. She had feelings that were easily bruised, and he'd done a lot of damage already. Those nightmares she had should have convinced him how traumatic her captivity had been, but he hadn't even taken that into consideration when he was setting up Lopez by bringing Callie here.

"I'm sorry," he bit off the words. He wondered if she knew how hard it was to say that.

She blinked away sudden tears. "It's not your fault, you're just trying to save Dad. I love Dad, too, Micah," she said at his chest. "I don't blame you for doing everything you can to keep him safe."

His eyes closed and he groaned silently. "I'm going to do everything I can to keep you safe, too," he told her.

She shrugged. "I know." She pulled away from him with a faint smile to soften the rejection. "Thanks."

He studied her face and realized that he'd never really looked at her so closely before. She had a tiny line of freckles just over her straight little nose. Her light blue eyes had flecks of dark blue in them and she had the faintest little dimple in her cheek when she smiled. He touched her pretty mouth with his fingertips. It was slightly swollen from the hungry, insistent pressure of his lips. She looked rumpled from his ardor, and he liked that, too.

"Take a picture," she said uncomfortably.

"You're pretty," he murmured with an odd smile.

"I'm not, and stop trying to flatter me," she replied, shifting away from him.

"It isn't flattery." He bent and brushed his mouth lightly over her parted lips. She gasped and hung there, her eyes wide and vulnerable on his face when he drew back. Her reaction made him feel taller. He smiled softly. "You don't give an inch, do you? I suppose it's hard for you to trust anyone, after the life you've led."

"I trust Dad," she snapped.

"Yes, but you don't trust me, do you?"

"Not an inch," she agreed, pulling away. "And you don't have to kiss me to make me feel better, either."

"It was to make me feel better," he pointed out, smiling at her surprise. "It did, too."

She shifted her posture a little, confused.

His dark eyes slid over her body, noting the little

points that punctuated her breasts and the unsteady breathing she couldn't control. Yes, she wanted him.

She folded her arms over her breasts, curious about why he was staring at them. They felt uncomfortable, but she didn't know why.

"I didn't tell Lisse that you were an embarrassment to me," he said suddenly, and watched her face color.

"It's okay," she replied tersely. "I know I don't have good dress sense. I don't care about clothes most of the time."

"I'm used to women who do, and who enjoy letting men pay for them. The more expensive they are, the better." He sounded jaded and bitter.

She studied his hard face, recognizing disillusionment and reticence. She moved a step closer involuntarily. "You sound...I don't know...cheated, maybe."

"I feel cheated," he said shortly. His eyes were full of harsh memories. "No man likes to think that he's paying for sex."

"Then why do you choose women who want expensive gifts from you?" she asked him bluntly.

His teeth met. "I don't know."

"Don't you, really?" she asked, her eyes soft and curious. "You've always said you don't want to get married, so you pick women who don't want to, either. But that sort of woman only lasts as long as the money does. Or am I wrong?"

He looked down at her from his great height with narrowed eyes and wounded pride. "I suppose you're one of those women who would rush right over to a penniless man and offer to get a second job to help him out of debt!"

She smiled sheepishly, ignoring the sarcasm. "I guess

I am." She shrugged. "I scare men off. They don't want me because I'm not interested in what sort of car they drive or the expensive places they can afford to take me to. I like to go walking in the country and pick wildflowers." She peered up at him with a mischievous smile. "The last man I said that to left town two days before he was supposed to. He was doing some accounts for Mr. Kemp and he left skid marks. Mr. Kemp thought it was hilarious. He was a notorious ladies' man, it seems, and he'd actually seduced Mr. Kemp's last assistant."

Micah didn't smile, as she'd expected him to. He looked angry.

She held up a hand. "I don't have designs on you, honest. I know you don't like wildflowers and Lisse is your sort of woman. I'm not interested in you that way, anyhow."

"Considering the way you just kissed me, you might have trouble proving that," he commented dryly.

She cleared her throat. "You kiss very nicely, and I have to get experience where I can."

"Is that it?" he asked dubiously.

She nodded enthusiastically. She swallowed again as the terror of the last hour came back and the eyes she lifted to his were suddenly haunted. "Micah, he's never going to stop, is he?"

"Probably not, unless he has help." He lifted an eyebrow. "I have every intention of helping him, once I've spoken with the authorities."

"What authorities?"

"Never mind. You know nothing. Got it?"

She saluted him. "Yes, sir."

He made a face. "Come on out. We'll have Mac make

some sandwiches and coffee. I don't know about you, but I'm hungry."

"I could eat something."

He hesitated before he opened her door. "I really meant what I told you," he said. "Lopez won't get within fifty yards of you as long as there's a breath in my body."

"Thanks," she said unsteadily.

He felt cold inside. He couldn't imagine what had made him tell such lies to Bojo, where she might overhear him. He hadn't meant it, that was honest, but he knew she thought he had. She didn't trust him anymore.

He opened the door to let her go through first. A whiff of the soft rose fragrance she wore drifted up into his nostrils and made his heart jump. She always smelled sweet, and she had a loving nature that was miraculous considering her past. She gave with both hands. He thought of her with Bojo and something snapped inside him.

"Bojo's off limits," he said as she slid past him. "So don't get too attached to him!"

She looked up at him. "What a bunch of sour grapes," she accused, "just because I withdrew my proposal of marriage to you!" She stalked off down the hall.

He opened his mouth to speak, and just laughed instead.

# Chapter 9

They ate lunch, but conversation among the mercenaries was subdued and Callie got curious glances from all of them. One man, the Mexican called Rodrigo, gave her more scrutiny than the rest. He was a handsome man, tall, slender, dark-haired and dark-eyed, with a grace of movement that reminded her of Micah. But he had a brooding look about him, and he seemed to be always watching her. Once, he smiled, but Micah's appearance sent him away before he could speak to her.

After lunch, Callie asked Bojo about him.

"Rodrigo lost his sister to Lopez's vicious temper," he told her. "She was a nightclub singer who Lopez took a fancy to. He forced himself on her after she rejected Lopez's advances and... She died trying to get away from him. Rodrigo knows what was done to you, and he's angry. You remind him of his sister. She, too, had blue eyes."

"But he's Latin," she began.

"His father was from Denmark," he said with a grin. "And blond."

"Imagine that!"

He gave her a wry glance. "He likes you," he said. "But he isn't willing to risk Micah's temper to approach you."

"You do," she said without thinking.

"Ah, but I am indispensable," he told her. "Rodrigo is not. He has enemies in many countries overseas and also, Lopez has a contract out on him. This is the only place he has left to go where he has any hope of survival. He wouldn't dare risk alienating Micah."

She frowned. "I can't think why approaching me would do that. Micah tolerates me, but he still doesn't really like me," she pointed out. "I overheard what he said to you, about using me as bait."

He smiled. "Yes. Curious, is it not, that when one of the other men suggested the same thing, he paid a trip to the dentist?"

"Why?"

"Micah knocked out one of his teeth," he confided. "The men agreed that no one would make the suggestion twice."

She caught her breath. "But I heard him tell you that very thing…!"

"You heard what he wanted me to think," he continued. "Micah is jealous of me," he added outrageously, and grinned. "You and I are friendly and we have no hostility between us. You don't want anything from me, you see, or from him. He has no idea how to deal with such a woman. He has become used to buying expensive things at a woman's whim, yet you refuse even the gift of a few items of necessary clothing." He shrugged. "It is new for him that neither his good looks nor his wealth make an impression on you. I think he finds that a challenge and it irritates him. He is also very private about his affairs. He doesn't want the men to see how vulnerable he is where you are concerned," he mused. "He had to assign me, along with Peter and Rodrigo, to keep a constant eye on you. He didn't like that. Peter and Rodrigo are no threat, of course, but he is afraid that you are attracted to me." He grinned at her surprise. "I can understand why he thinks this. I hardly need elaborate on my attributes. I am urbane, handsome, sophisticated, generous…" He paused to glance at her wide-eyed, bemused face. "Shall I continue? I should hate to miss acquainting you with any of my virtues."

She realized he was teasing then, and she chuckled. "Okay, go ahead, but I'm not making you any marriage proposals."

His eyebrows arched. "Why not?"

"Micah's put me off men," she said, tongue-in-cheek. "He's already upset because I won't propose to him." She gave him a wicked grin. "Gosh, first Micah, then you! Having this much sex appeal is a curse. Even Lopez is mad to have me!"

He grinned back. She was a unique woman, he thought, and bristling with courage and character. He wondered why Micah didn't see her as he did. The other man was alternately scathing about and protective of Callie, as if his feelings were too ambiguous to unravel. He didn't like Bojo spending time with her, but he kept her carefully at arm's length, even dragging Lisse over for the shopping trip and using her as camouflage. Callie didn't know, but Lisse had been a footnote in Micah's life even in the days when he was attracted to her. She hadn't been around much for almost a year now.

"After we deal with Lopez, you must play down your attractions," he teased. "Providing twenty-four-hour protection is wearing on the nerves."

"You're not kidding," she agreed, wandering farther down the beach. "I'm getting paranoid about dark corners. I always expect someone to be lurking in them." She glanced up at him. "Not rejected suitors," she added wryly.

He clasped his hands behind him and followed along with her, his keen eyes on the horizon, down the beach, up the beach—everywhere. Bojo was certain, as Micah was, that Lopez wasn't likely to give them time to attack him. He was going to storm the island, and soon. They had to be constantly vigilant, if they wanted to live.

"Do you know any self-defense?" Bojo asked her curiously.

"I know a little," she replied. "I took a course in it, but I was overpowered too fast."

"Show me what you know," he said abruptly. "And I will teach you a little more. It never hurts to be prepared.

She did, and he did. She learned enough to protect herself if she had time to use it. She didn't tell him, but she was really scared that Lopez might snatch her out of sight and sound of the mercs. She prayed that she'd have a fighting chance if she was in danger again.

Callie had convinced herself that an attack would come like a wave, with a lot of men and guns. The last thing she expected was that, when she was lying in her own bed, a man would suddenly appear by the bed and slap a chloroformed handkerchief over her mouth and nose. That was what happened. Outside her patio a wait-ing small boat on the beach was visible only where she was situated. The dark shadow against the wall man-aged to bypass every single safeguard of Micah's se-curity system. He slipped into Callie's bedroom with a cloth and a bottle of chloroform and approached the bed where she was asleep.

The first Callie knew of the attack was when she felt a man's hand holding her head steady while a foul-smelling cloth was shoved up under her nose. She came awake at once, but she kept her head, even when she felt herself being carried roughly out of her bedroom onto the stone patio. She knew what to expect this time if she were taken, and she remembered vividly what Bojo had taught her that afternoon. She twisted her head abruptly so that the chloroform missed her face and landed in her hair. Then she got her hands up and slammed them against her captor's ears with all her might.

He cried out in pain and dropped her. She hit the stone-floored patio so hard that she groaned as her hip and leg crashed down onto the flagstones, but she dragged herself to her feet and grabbed at a shovel that the yardman had left leaning against a stone bench close beside her. As her assailant ignored the pain in his fury to pay her back, she swung the shovel and hit him right in the head with it. He made a strange sound and crum-pled to the patio. Callie stared out toward the boat, where a dark figure was waiting.

Infuriated by the close call, and feeling very proud of the fact that she'd saved herself this time, she raised the shovel over her head. "Better luck next time, you son of a bitch!" she yelled harshly. "If I had a gun, I'd shoot you!"

Her voice brought Micah and two other men running out onto the patio. They were all armed. The two mercs ran toward the beach, firing as they made a beeline toward the little boat, which had powered up and was sprinting away with incredible speed and very little noise.

Micah stood in front of Callie wearing nothing but a pair of black silk boxer shorts. He had an automatic pistol in one hand. His hair was tousled, as if he'd been asleep. But he was wide-awake now. His face was hard, his dark eyes frightening.

He moved close to her, aware of her body in the thin nylon gown that left her breasts on open display in the light from inside the house. She didn't seem to notice, but he did. He looked at them hungrily before he dragged his gaze back up to her face, fighting a burst of desire as he tried to come to grips with the terror he'd felt when he heard Callie yelling. Thank God she'd had the presence of mind to grab that shovel and knock the man out.

"Are you okay?" he asked curtly.

"I'm better off than he is," she said huskily, swallowing hard. Reaction was beginning to set in now, and her courage was leaking away as the terror of what had almost happened began to tear at her nerves. "He had chloroform. I…I fought free, but…oh, Micah, I was scared to…death!"

She threw herself against him, shuddering in the aftermath of terror. Now that the danger was past, reaction set in with a vengeance. Her arms went under his and around him. Her soft, firm breasts were flattened against his bare stomach because she was so much shorter than he was. Her hands ran over the long, hard muscles of his back, feeling scars there as she pressed closer. He felt the corner of her mouth in the thick hair that covered

the hard muscles of his chest. His body reacted predict-
ably to the feel of a near-naked woman and he gasped
audibly and stiffened.

Her hips weren't in contact with his, but she felt a
tremor run through his powerful body and she pulled
back a little, curious, to look up at his strained face.
"What's wrong?"

He drew in a steadying breath and moved back.
"Nothing! We'll get this guy inside and question him.
You don't need to see it," he added firmly. "You should
go back into your room…"

"And do what?" she asked, wide-eyed and hurt by his
sudden withdrawal. "You think I can go to sleep now?"

"Stupid assumption," he murmured, moving restively
as his body tormented him. "I can call Lisse and let her
stay with you."

"No!" She lifted her chin with as much pride as she
had left. "I'll get dressed. Bojo will sit up with me if I
ask him…"

"The hell he will!" he exploded, his eyes glittering.

She took a step backward. He was frightening when
he looked like that. He seemed more like the stranger
he'd once been than the man who'd been so kind to her
in past days.

"I'll get dressed and you can stay with me tonight,"
he snapped. "Obviously it's asking too much to expect
you to stay by yourself!" That was unfair, he realized
at once, and he ground his teeth. He couldn't help it. He
was afraid to be in the same room with her in the dark,
but not for the reason she thought.

She took another step backward, pride reasserting itself. Her chin came up. "No, thanks!" she said. "If you'll

just get me a gun and load it and show me how to shoot it, I won't have any problem with being alone."

She sounded subdued, edgy, still frightened despite that haughty look she was giving him. He was overreacting. It infuriated him that she'd had to rescue herself. It infuriated him that he wanted her. He was jealous of his men, angry that she was vulnerable, and fighting with all his might to keep from giving in to his desire for her. She was a marrying woman. She was a virgin. It was hopeless.

Worst of all, she'd almost been kidnapped again and on his watch. He'd fallen asleep, worn-out by days of wear and tear and frustrated desire. Lopez had almost had her tonight. He blamed himself for not taking more precautions, for putting her in harm's way. He should have protected her. He should have realized that Lopez was desperate enough to try anything, including an assault on the house itself. So much for his security net. Upgrades were very definitely needed. But right now, she needed comfort, and he wasn't giving it to her.

He glanced toward the beach. Out beyond it, the little boat had stilled in the water and seemed to be sinking. A dark figure struck out toward the shore.

"Peter, get him!" Micah yelled.

The young man gave him a thumbs-up signal. The tall young man tossed down his weapon, jerked off his boots and overclothes and dived into the water. The assailant tried to get away, but Peter got him. There was a struggle and seconds later, Peter dragged the man out of the water and stood over him where he lay prone on the beach.

Rodrigo came running back up from the beach just

about the time the man who'd tried to carry Callie off woke up and rubbed his aching head.

"I told Peter to take the other man around the side of the house to the boat shed."

"Good work," Micah said.

"Oh, look, he's all right," Callie murmured, her eyes narrowed on the downed man who was beginning to move and groan. "What a shame!"

Micah glanced at her. "Bloodthirsty girl," he chided, and grinned despite his churning emotions.

"Well, he tried to kidnap me," she bit off, finally getting her nerve and her temper back. She remembered the chloroform and her eyes blazed. "All I had to hand was a lousy shovel, that's why he's all right."

He turned to the other man. "Rodrigo, get this guy around to the boat shed to keep Peter's captive company. Strip them both, tie them up and gag them. I've got to make a few preparations and I'll be along to question them. Do *not* tell Bojo anything, except that the police have been notified. You can phone them to pick up Lopez's henchmen an hour from now, no sooner."

"I know what you're thinking. It won't work," Rodrigo said, trying to reason with him. "Lopez will be expecting his men back, if he hasn't already seen what happened."

"Have you got the infrareds on you?"

Rodrigo nodded and pulled out what looked like a fancy pair of binoculars.

"Check the area off the beach for Lopez's yacht."

"It's clear for miles right now. No heat signatures."

"Heat signatures?" Callie murmured.

"We have heat-seeking technology," Micah explained.

"We can look right into a house or a room in the dark and see everything alive in it, right through the walls."

"You're kidding!" she exclaimed.

"He's not," Rodrigo said, his dark eyes narrowing as he noted the gown and the pretty form underneath.

Micah knew what the other man was seeing, and it angered him. He stepped in front of Callie, and the action was blatant enough to get Rodrigo moving.

"Where do you think Lopez's yacht is?" Callie asked.

"It'll be somewhere close around. Let's just hope the man Peter caught was too rattled to call Lopez while he was being shot at. I'm sure he had a cell phone. Get out my diving gear and some C-4. And don't say a word to Bojo. Got that? It will work."

"What will work?" Callie asked.

"Never mind," Micah said. "Thanks, Rodrigo. I'm going to get Callie back inside."

"I'll deal with our guest," Rodrigo said, and turned at once to his chore.

Micah drew Callie along with him, from the patio to the sliding glass doors her assailant had forced, and down the hall to her bedroom. On the way, he noticed that two other doors had been opened, as if her captor had looked in them in search of her. His bedroom was closer to the front of the house.

He drew her inside her room and closed the door behind them, pausing to lay the automatic on a table nearby. "Did he hurt you?" he asked at once.

"He dropped me on the patio. I bruised my hip... Micah, no!" she exclaimed, pushing at the big, lean hand that was pulling up her nylon gown.

"I've seen more of you than this," he reminded her.

"But..."

He swept her up in his arms and carried her to the bed, easing her down gently onto the sheet where the covers had been thrown back by her captor. He sat down beside her and pulled up the gown, smiling gently at the pale pink cotton briefs she was wearing.

"Just what I'd expect," he murmured. "Functional, not sexy."

"Nobody sees my underthings except me," she bit off. "Will you stop?"

He pushed the gown up to her waist, ignoring her protests, and winced when he saw her upper thigh and hip. "You're going to have a whopper of a bruise on your leg," he murmured, drawing down the elastic of the briefs. "Your hip didn't fare much better."

His thumb was against the soft, warm skin of her lower stomach and the other one was poised beside her head on the pillow while he looked at her bruises. She didn't think he was doing it on purpose, but that thumb seemed to be moving back and forth in a very arousing way. Her body liked it. She moved restlessly on the sheet, shivering a little with unexpected pleasure.

"A few bruises are…are better than being kidnapped," she whispered shakily. Her wide eyes met his. "I was so scared, Micah!"

His hand spread on her hip. His narrow black eyes met hers. "So was I, when I heard you shouting," he said huskily. "He almost had you!"

"Almost," she agreed, her breath jerking out. "I'm still shaking."

His fingers contracted. "I'm going to give you a sedative," he said, rising abruptly. "You need to sleep. You never will, in this condition."

He left her there and went to get his medical kit. He

was back almost at once. He opened the bag and drew out a small vial of liquid and a prepackaged hypodermic syringe. This would alleviate her fear of being alone tonight and give him time to get his rampaging hormones under control.

She watched him fill the syringe effortlessly. It was a reminder that he'd studied medicine.

"Have you ever thought of going back to finish your residency?" she asked him.

He shook his head. "Too tame." He smiled in her general direction as he finished filling the syringe. "I don't think I could live without adrenaline rushes."

"Doctors have those, too," she pointed out, watching him extend her arm and tap a vein in the curve of her elbow. "You're going to put it in there?" she asked worriedly.

"It's quicker. You won't get addicted to this," he added, because she looked apprehensive. "Close your eyes. I'll try not to hurt you."

She did close her eyes, but she felt the tiny prick of the needle and winced. But it was over quickly and he was dabbing her arm with alcohol on a cotton ball.

"It won't knock you out completely," he said when he'd replaced everything in the kit. "But it will relax you."

She blinked. She felt *very* relaxed. She peered up at him with wide, soft eyes. "I wish you liked me," she said.

His eyebrows levered up. "I do."

"Not really. You don't want me around. I'm not pretty like her."

"Her?"

"Lisse." She sighed and stretched lazily, one leg rising so that the gown fell away from her pretty leg, leaving it bare. "She's really beautiful, and she has nice, big breasts. Mine are just tiny, and I'm so ordinary. Gosh, I'd love to have long blond hair and big breasts."

He glanced at the bag and back at her. "This stuff works on you like truth serum, doesn't it?" he murmured huskily.

She sat up with a misty smile and shrugged the gown off, so that it fell to her waist. Her breasts had hard little tips that aroused him the instant he saw them. "See?" she asked. "They look like acorns. Hers look like cantaloupes."

He couldn't help himself. He stared at her breasts helplessly, while his body began to swell with an urgency that made him shiver. He was vulnerable tonight.

"Yours are beautiful," he said softly, his eyes helplessly tracing them.

"No, they're not. You don't even like feeling them against you. You went all stiff and pushed me away, out on the patio. It's been like that since...Micah, what are you...doing?" she gasped as his hungry mouth abruptly settled right on top of a hard nipple and began to suckle it. "Oh...glory!" she cried out, arching toward him with a lack of restraint that was even more arousing. Her nails bit into his scalp through his thick hair, coaxing him even closer. "I like that. I...really like that!" she whispered frantically. "I like it, I like it, I...!"

"I should be shot for this," he uttered as he suckled her. "But I want you. Oh God, I want you so!" His teeth opened and nipped her helplessly.

She drew back suddenly, apprehensively as she felt his teeth, her eyes questioning.

He could barely breathe, and he knew there was no way on earth he was going to be able to stop. It was already too late. Danger was an aphrodisiac. "You don't like my teeth on you," he whispered. "All right. It's all right. We'll try this."

His fingers traced around her pert breast gently and he bent to take her mouth tenderly under his lips. She had no willpower. She opened her lips for him and clung as he eased her down onto the cool sheets.

"Don't let me do this, Callie," he ground out in a last grab at sanity, even as he shed his boxer shorts. "Tell me to stop!"

"I couldn't, not if it meant my life," she murmured, her body on fire for him. Her mind wasn't even working. She held on for dear life and pulled his mouth down harder on hers. She was shivering with pleasure. "I want you to do it," she whispered brazenly. "I want to feel you naked in my arms. I want to make love…!"

"Callie. Sweet baby!" he whispered hoarsely as he felt her hands searching down his flat belly to the source of his anguish. She touched him and he was lost, totally lost. He pressed her hard into the mattress while his mouth devoured hers. It was too late to pull back, too late to reason with her. She was drugged and uninhibited, and her hands were touching him in a way that pushed him right over the edge.

Callie lifted against him, aware of his nudity and the delight of touching him where she'd never have dreamed of touching him if she hadn't been drugged. But she'd always wanted to touch him like that, and it felt wonderful. Her body moved restlessly with little darts of pleasure as he began to discover her, too.

She enjoyed the feel of his body, the touch of his hands. Her skin felt very hot, and when she realized that the gown and her underwear were gone, it didn't matter, because she felt much more comfortable. Then he started touching her in a way she'd never been touched. She gasped. Her body tensed, but she moved toward his hand, burying her face in his neck as the delicious sensations made her pulse with delight. His skin was damp and very hot. She could hear the rasp of his breathing, she could feel it in her hair as he began to caress her very intimately.

Of course, it was wrong to let him do something so outrageous, but it felt too good to stop. She kept coaxing him with sharp little movements of her hips until he was touching her where her body wanted him to. Now the pleasure was stark and urgent. She opened her legs. Her nails bit into his nape and she clung fiercely.

"It's all right," he whispered huskily. "I won't stop. I'll be good to you."

She clung closer. Her body shivered. She was suddenly open to his insistent exploration and with embarrassment she felt herself becoming very damp where his fingers were. She stiffened.

"It's natural," he breathed into her ear. "Your body is supposed to do this."

"It is?" She couldn't look at him. "It isn't repulsive to you?"

"It's the most exciting thing I've ever felt," he whispered. His powerful body shifted so that he was lying directly over her, his hair-roughened legs lazily brushing against hers while he teased her mouth with his lips and her body with his fingers.

Her arms were curled around his neck and the sensations were so sweet that she began to gasp rhythmically. Her hips were lifting and falling with that same rhythm as she fed on the delicious little jabs of pleasure that accompanied every sensual movement.

He began to shudder, too. It was almost as if he weren't in control of himself. But that was ridiculous. Micah was always in control.

His teeth tugged at her upper lip and then at her lower one, his tongue sliding sinuously inside her mouth in slow, teasing thrusts. She felt her breasts going very tight. He was lying against her in an unexpectedly intimate way. She felt body hair against her breasts and her belly. Then she felt him there, *there,* in a contact that she'd never dreamed of sharing with him.

Despite her languor, her eyes opened and looked straight into his. She could actually see the desire that was riding him, there in his taut face and glittering eyes and flattened lips. He was shivering. She liked seeing him that way. She smiled lazily and deliberately brushed her body up against him. He groaned.

Slowly he lifted himself just a little. "Look down," he whispered huskily. "Look at me. I want you to see how aroused I am for you."

Her eyes traced the path of thick, curling blond-tipped hair from the wedge on his muscular chest, down his flat belly, and to another wedge...heavens! He had nothing on. And more than that, he was...he was...

Her misty gaze shot back up to meet his. She should be protesting. He was so aroused that a maiden lady with silver hair couldn't have mistaken it. She felt suddenly very small and vulnerable, almost fragile. But he wanted her, and she wanted him so badly that she couldn't find a single word of protest. Even if he never touched her again, she'd have this one time to live on for the rest of her miserable, lonely life. She'd be his lover, if only this once. Nothing else mattered. Nothing!

Her body lifted to brush helplessly against his while she looked at him. She was afraid. She was excited. She was on fire. She was wanton…

His hand went between their hips and began to invade her body, where it was most sensitive. Despite the pleasure that ensued, she felt a tiny stab of discomfort.

"I can feel it," he whispered, his eyes darkening as his body went taut. "It's wispy, like a spiderweb." He shifted sensuously. His body began to invade hers in a slow, teasing motion, and he watched her the whole time. "Are you going to let me break it, Callie?" he whispered softly.

"Break…it?"

"Your maidenhead. I want it." He moved his hips down and his whole face clenched as he felt the veil of her innocence begin to separate. His hands clenched beside her head on the pillow and the eyes that looked down into hers were tortured. His whole body shuddered with each slow movement of his hips. "I want…you! Callie!" he groaned hoarsely, his eyes closing. "Callie … baby…let me have you," he whispered jerkily. "Let me have…all of you! Let me teach you pleasure…"

He seemed to be in pain. She couldn't bear that. She slid her calves slowly over his and gasped when she felt his body tenderly penetrating hers with the action, bringing a tiny wave of pleasure. She gasped again.

He arched above her, groaning. His eyes held hers as he moved slowly, carefully. She watched her wince and he hesitated. He moved again, and she bit her lip. He moved one more time, and she tensed and then suddenly relaxed, so unexpectedly that his possession of her was complete in one involuntary movement.

It was incredible, he thought, his body as taut as steel as he looked down into her wide, curious eyes with awe as he became her lover. He could feel her, like a warm silk glove. She was a virgin. He was having her. She was giving herself. He moved experimentally, and her lips parted on a helpless breath.

His lean hands slid under her dark hair and cradled her head while he began to move on her. One of his thighs pushed at hers, nudging it further away from the throbbing center of her body. The motion lifted her against him in a blind grasp at pleasure.

"I never thought...it would be you," she whispered feverishly.

"I never thought it would be anyone else," he replied, his eyes hot and narrow and unblinking. "I watched you when I went completely into you," he whispered and smiled when she gasped. "Now, you can watch me," he murmured roughly. "Watch me. I'll let you see...everything I feel!"

She shivered as his hips began to move sinuously, more insistently, increasing the pleasure.

He caught one of her hands and drew it between them, coaxing it back to his body. He groaned at the contact and guided her fingers to the heart of him.

She let him teach her. It was so sweet, to lie naked in his arms, and watch him make love to her. He was incredibly tender. He gave her all the time in the world before he became insistent, before his kisses devoured, before his hand pinned her hips and his whole body became an instrument of the most delicious torture. He looked down at her with blazing dark eyes, his face clenched in passion, his body shivering with urgency as he poised over her.

"Don't close your eyes," he groaned when stars were exploding in his head. "I want to see them…the very second…that you go over the edge under me!"

The words were as arousing as the sharp, violent motion of his hips as he began to drive into her. She thought he became even more potent as the tempo and the urgency increased. He held her eyes until she became blind with the first stirrings of ecstasy and her sharp, helpless cry of surprised pleasure was covered relentlessly by his mouth.

She writhed under him, sobbing with the sensation of fulfillment, her body riveted to his as convulsions made her ripple like a stormy wave. She clutched his upper arms, her nails biting in, as the ripples became almost painful in their delight. Seconds later, she felt him climax above her. His harsh, shuddering groan was as alien a sound as her own had been seconds before. She wrapped her arms around him and held on for dear life, cuddling him, cradling him, as he endured the mindless riptide and finally, finally, went limp and heavy in her arms with a whispery sigh.

"You looked at me…when it happened," she whispered with wonder. "And I saw you, I watched you." She shivered, holding him tight. Her body rippled with the tiny movement, and she laughed secretly and moaned as she felt the pleasure shoot through her. "Do it again," she pleaded. "Make me scream this time…!"

He was still shivering. "Oh, God…no!" he bit off. "Be still!" He held her down, hard, drawing in a sharp breath as he fought the temptation to do what she asked.

He closed his eyes and his teeth clenched as he jerked back from her abruptly.

She gasped as his weight receded. There was a slight discomfort, and then he was on his feet beside the bed, grabbing up his boxer shorts with a furious hand.

She stared at him with diminishing awareness. She was deliciously relaxed. She felt great. Why was he cursing like that. She blinked vacantly. "You're very angry. What's wrong?"

"What's wrong!" He turned to look down at her. She was sprawled nude in glorious abandon, looking so erotic that he almost went to his knees with the arousal that returned with a vengeance.

She smiled lazily and yawned. "Gosh, that was good. So good!" Her eyelids felt very heavy. She sprawled even more comfortably. "Even better than the last time."

"What last time?" he demanded, outraged.

She yawned again. "That other dream," she mumbled, rolling onto her side. "So many dreams. So embarrassing. So erotic! But this was the best dream, though. The very…best…"

Her voice trailed away and he realized all at once that she'd fallen asleep. She didn't understand what had happened. She'd been full of sedative and she'd let him seduce her, thinking she was just dreaming. She thought the whole thing was nothing more than another dream. No wonder she hadn't protested!

"God in heaven, what have I done!" he asked her oblivious form. There was a smear of blood on the white sheet.

Micah ground his teeth together and damned his lack of control. He hadn't had a woman in a very long time, and he'd wanted Callie since the day he'd met her. But that was no excuse for taking advantage of her while she was under the influence of a sedative. Even if she had come on to him with the most incredibly erotic suggestions. He'd seduced her and that was that.

He went to the bathroom, wet a washcloth and bathed her body as gently as he could. She was sleeping so soundly that she never noticed a thing. He put her briefs and gown back on her and put her under the sheet. He'd have to hope she didn't notice the stain, or, if she did, assumed it was an old one.

He dressed, hating himself, and went out of the room after checking the security net. He still had to go after Lopez, and now his mind was going to be full of Callie sobbing with pleasure under the crush of his body. And what if there were consequences?

## Chapter 10

With a face as grim as death, Micah pulled on his black wet suit and fins and checked the air in his tanks and the mouthpiece and face mask. He sheathed the big knife he always carried on covert missions. To the belt around his waist, he attached a waterproof carry pack. He'd interrogated one of the men, who'd been far too intimidated not to tell him what he wanted to know about Lopez's setup on the yacht, the number and placement of his men and his firepower.

"I should go with you," Rodrigo told him firmly.

"You can't dive," Micah said. "Besides, this is a one-man job. If I don't make it, it will be up to you and Bojo to finish it. But whatever happens," he added curtly, and with a threatening stare, "don't let them get Callie."

"I won't. I swear it," Rodrigo said heavily.

"Tell Bojo where I've gone after I've gone, but only

after I'm gone," he added. "Don't let him follow me." He picked up a small device packed with plastique and shoved it into the waterproof bag on his belt and sealed it.

"Once you set the trigger, you'll only have a few minutes to get free of the ship. If the engines fire up while you're placing the bomb, you'll be chum," Rodrigo said worriedly. "You already look exhausted. Even if everything goes right, how will you make that swim and turn around and come back in time?"

"If I can't get free in that amount of time, I'm in the wrong business," he told Rodrigo. "I'd disgrace my expensive government training. How many men on the yacht right now?"

Rodrigo nodded toward the yacht, which had just come into view in the past ten minutes. It was out very far, almost undetectable without exotic surveillance devices. But they had a device that used a heat sensor with a telescopic lens, and they could see inside the ship. "The crew, Lopez, and six henchmen. It's suicide to do this alone."

"I'm not letting him try again," he said shortly, and his eyes were blazing. "I've put Callie's life at risk already, because I was arrogant enough to think she was safe here. She could have been killed tonight while I was asleep in my bed. I won't get over that in a hurry. I'm not going to give her to Lopez, no matter what it costs me." He put a hand on Rodrigo's shoulder. "Listen to me. If anything goes wrong, you tell Bojo that I want him to take care of her from now on. There's enough money in my Swiss account to support her and my father for life, in any style they like. You tell Bojo I said to see that she gets it, less the sum we agreed on for all of you. Promise me!"

"Of course I promise." Rodrigo's eyes narrowed. "You look...different."

*I've just seduced a virgin who thinks she was having an erotic dream,* he thought with black humor. *No wonder I look different.* "It's been a long night," he said. "Call the police an hour from now." He looked at his expensive commando watch, the one with a tiny sharp knife blade that could be released from the edge of the face with a light touch. "Coming up on fourteen hundred and ten hours...almost...almost...hack!"

Rodrigo had set his watch to the same time. He gave Micah a long, worried look as the taller man put on his face mask and adjusted the mouthpiece.

*"Dios te protégé,"* Rodrigo said gently. God protect you.

Micah smiled and put the mouthpiece in. Seconds later, he was in the water, under the water, headed out toward the yacht. It was a distance of almost half a mile, and Rodrigo was uneasy. But Micah had been a champion swimmer in his school days, and he held some sort of record for being able to hold his breath underwater. He looked very tired, though, and that was going to go against him. Odd, Rodrigo thought, that a man who'd just gotten out of bed should look exhausted. And after the culprits had been dealt with so quickly and effectively, which couldn't have tired him. He hoped Micah would succeed. He checked his watch, glanced at the bound and gagged captives in their underwear, and shrugged.

"How sad for you, *compadres,* that your futures will

be seen through vertical bars. But, then, your choice of employer leaves so much to be desired!"

He turned away, recalling that Micah had told him to phone the police an hour after he'd gone. But he hesitated to do that, orders or not. Timing was going to be everything here. If there was a holdup planting the charge, and if Lopez had someone on the payroll in Nassau, the show was over. Lopez would get word of the failed kidnapping attempt in time to blow Micah out of the water. Micah couldn't have been thinking straight. Rodrigo would do that for him. He would watch Micah's back. Now he prayed that his boss could complete this mission without discovery. If ever a man deserved his fate, it was Manuel Lopez. He gave Mexicans a bad name, and for that alone Rodrigo was anxious to see him go down.

It took Micah a long time to reach the boat. He was exhausted from the mindless pleasure Callie had given him. Making love with her just before the most dangerous mission of recent years had to be evidence of insanity. But it had been so beautiful, so tender. He could still hear her soft, surprised cries of pleasure. The memory was the sort a man wouldn't mind going down into the darkness for. Of course, it wasn't helping him focus on the task at hand. He forcibly put the interlude to the back of his mind and swam on.

He paused as he reached the huge yacht, carefully working his way toward the huge propellers at the stern, which were off right now but would start again eventually. If they started while he was near them, he'd be caught in their turbulent wake and dragged right into those cruel blades to be dismembered before he set the charge. *Not* the end he hoped for.

He kept himself in place with slow movements of his fins while he shone an underwater light hooked to his belt on the bomb package enclosed in the waterproof bag. He drew it out, very carefully, and secured it to a metallic connection behind the propellers. It stuck like glue. He positioned the light so that he could work with his hands while he wired the charge into the propeller system. It was meticulous work, and he was really tired. But he finally secured the connection and double-checked the explosive package. Yes. The minute the turbine engines fired, the ship would blow up.

The problem was, he was almost too tired to swim back. He was going to have to give himself thirty minutes to get back to the shore, and pray that Lopez didn't have his men fire up those propellers until he was out of harm's way.

He gave the ship's hull a gentle pat, with a momentary twinge of regret at having to destroy such a beautiful yacht. Then he turned and moved slowly, cautiously, around toward the bow of the ship. There was a ladder hanging down from the side. He passed it with idle curiosity and held onto it while he floated, letting his body relax and rest. He just happened to look up while he was hanging from it.

Just above the surface, a man was aiming an automatic weapon down at him through the water.

He couldn't get away. He was too tired. Besides, the man wasn't likely to miss at this range. Salute the flag and move on, he mused philosophically. Nobody lived forever, and his death would serve a noble cause. All he had to do was make them think he'd come aboard to use the knife on Lopez, so they wouldn't start looking for bombs. They had enough time to find and disarm it if he didn't divert them. The waterproof bag on his hip was going to be hard to explain. So was his flashlight. Fortunately the light fit into the bag and weighed it down. He unhooked the bag and closed it out of sight while the man above motioned angrily for him to come up the ladder. He let the bag drop and it sank even as he started the climb to his own death. He might get a chance at Lopez before they killed him, because Lopez would want to gloat.

He padded onto the deck in his breathing equipment and fins, which the man ordered him in Spanish to take off.

Micah tossed his gear aside, carefully, because the man with the gun was nervous. If he had any chance at all to escape, he could make the distance without his equipment if he swam—assuming he wasn't shot to death in the process. He had to hope for a break, but it wasn't likely. This was the situation that every working mercenary had to consider when he chose the lifestyle. Death could come at any moment, unexpectedly.

He stood glaring down at the smaller man. Even with his automatic weapon, the drug lord's man didn't seem too confident. He backed up two more steps. Micah noted the hasty retreat and tensed to make his move. But only seconds later, Lopez and two more men—armed men—came up on deck.

Lopez stared at Micah for a minute and then recognition flashed in his dark eyes. "Micah Steele, I presume," he drawled in accented English. He put his hands behind him and walked around Micah like an emperor inspecting a new slave. "You lack proficiency, don't you? Were you planning to use this on me while I slept?" he added, jerking the big bowie knife out of its sheath. "A nasty weapon. Very nasty." He put the point against Micah's wet suit just below the nipple. "A hard thrust, and you cease to exist. You were careless. Now you will pay the price for it." His face hardened. "Where are my two men that I sent to reclaim your stepsister?"

Micah smiled calmly. "The police have them by now. I expect they'll spill their guts trying to save themselves."

"They would not dare," Lopez said easily. "They fear me."

"They won't fear you if you're in prison," he replied easily. "Or dead."

Lopez laughed. It amused him that this mercenary wasn't begging for his life. He was used to men who did.

"Your attempt at diversion serves no purpose. We both know that my men are on the way back with their captive even now. In fact," he added with a deliberate smile, "I had a phone call just before you were discovered, telling me that she was safely bound and gagged. Your men are too numerous for them to fight, so they are hiding her some distance from your house until the coast is clear and they can get here with the boat." He chuckled maliciously.

Micah surmised that a cell phone had been discovered on one of the men, and Rodrigo had used it to reassure Lopez. A stroke of genius, and it might have worked, if Micah hadn't been careless and let himself get captured like a raw recruit.

"I am fond of knives," Lopez murmured, and ran his fingers over the carved bone handle almost like a caress. He looked at Micah as he traced the pattern in it. "This time, I will not give your stepsister to my men. I will use the knife on her myself." His eyes were cold, hard, unfeeling. "I will skin her alive," he said softly. "And with every strip that comes off, I will remind her that you were careless enough to let her be apprehended a second time." His eyes blazed. "You invaded my home to take her from me. No one humiliates me in such a manner and lives to gloat about it. You will die and your sister will die, and in such a way that it will frighten anyone who sees it."

Micah studied the little man with contempt, seeing the years of death and torture that had benefited Lopez. The drug lord could buy people, yachts, countries. He had enormous power. But it was power built on a foundation of greed, floored with blood and tears. If ever a man deserved to go down, it was Lopez.

"You are very quiet, Micah Steele," Lopez said suddenly, and his eyes narrowed suspiciously.

"I was thinking that I've never encountered anyone as evil as you, Lopez," he said quietly. "You have no conscience at all."

Lopez shrugged. "I am what I am," he said simply. "In order to accumulate great wealth, one has to be willing to take great risks. I have been poor. I never want to be poor again."

"Plenty of people prefer it to murder."

Lopez only laughed. "You are, how is it said, stalling for time," he said abruptly. "Are you hoping to be rescued? Or are you hoping that perhaps one of your men has checked on your stepsister and found her missing from her room? That is not likely. My men are quite expert. Playing for time will avail you nothing."

Micah could have told him that he was using the time to rest from his exhaustive swim, marshaling his strength for an all-out assault. If they took him down, he vowed, he was at least going to take Lopez with him, even if he died with the drug lord's neck in his hands.

"Or you might think it possible to overpower all of us and escape." He laughed again. "I think that I will wait to begin your interrogation until your stepsister is on board with us. Carlos!" he called to a henchman. "Tell the captain to start the engines and move us a little closer to the island."

Micah's heart stopped dead, but not a trace of fear or apprehension showed on his face. Lopez was watching him very closely, as if he suspected something. Micah simply smiled, considering that it was the fortunes of war that sometimes you didn't win. At least Callie was safe. He hadn't lost completely as long as she survived. He took a relaxing breath and waited for the explosion.

Lopez's henchman was almost up the steps to the pilothouse when Lopez wheeled suddenly.

"Wait!" Lopez called his man back suddenly and Micah fought to keep from showing his relief. "I do not trust you, Steele," Lopez added. "I think perhaps you want me to go closer to your island, to give your men a shot at us, here on the deck. If so, you are going to be disappointed." He turned to the man, Carlos. "Take him below and tie him up. Then I want you and Juan to take one of the boats and follow in the steps of Ramon and Jorge. They must be somewhere near the house waiting for the mercenaries to give up the search or locate it elsewhere. You can help them bring the girl back."

*"Si, señor,"* Carlos said at once, and stuck the automatic weapon in Micah's back. "You will go ahead of me, *señor*," he told Micah. "And remember, there will be an armed man at the foot of the steps. Escape is not possible. *¡Vaya!*"

Micah gave Lopez one last contemptuous look before he went down the steps into the bowels of the ship. So far, so good. They were convinced that their men on shore were safe and had Callie. They weren't going to start the ship just yet, thank God. He had one last chance to absolve himself. He was going to take it, regardless of the price.

The henchman tied him up in a chair with nylon cord at his wrists and ankles. The cord was tight enough to cut off the circulation. Micah felt his hands and feet going numb, but he wasn't going to protest.

"What a nice fish we caught," Lopez's man chuckled. "And soon, big fish, we will fillet you and your stepsister together." His eyes narrowed and he smiled coldly. "You have embarrassed my boss. No one is allowed to do that. You must be made an example of. I would not wish to be in your shoes." He looked pointedly at Micah's bare feet. "Hypothetically speaking," he added. "Enjoy your last minutes of life, *señor*."

The small man left Micah in the stateroom, which was obviously some sort of guest room. There was a bed and a dresser and this chair in it, and it was very small. One of the officers of the ship might sleep here, he reasoned.

Now that he was alone—and he wouldn't be for long—he might have just enough time to free himself. Micah touched the button on his watch that extended the small but very sharp little knife blade concealed in the watch face. He cut himself free with very little effort. But the most dangerous part was yet to come. There were men everywhere, all armed. The one thing he had going for him was that it was dark and Lopez had very few lights on deck at the moment, hoping not to be noticed by Micah's men.

He eased out into the corridor and listened. He heard a man's voice humming a Mexican drinking song off-key nearby. Watching up and down the hall with every step, he eased into the galley. A man just a little smaller than he was stirring something in a very big stainless-steel pot. He was wearing black slacks and a black sweater with an apron over them. Micah smiled.

He caught the man from behind and stunned him. Carefully he eased the cook back behind the stove and began to strip him. He pulled off his scuba gear and donned the cook's outerwear, taking time to dress the cook in his own diving suit. The cook had dark hair, but it wouldn't matter. All he had to do was look like Micah at a distance.

He got the cook over his shoulder and made his way carefully to the ladder that led up onto the deck. Lopez was talking to two other men, and not looking in Micah's direction. What supreme self-confidence, Micah thought. Pity to spoil it.

He slapped the cook and brought him around. In the next instant, he threw the man overboard on the side that faced away from Micah's island.

*"¡Steele ha escapado!"* Micah yelled in Spanish. *"¡Se fue alla, a la izquierda, en el Mar!"* Steele has escaped, he went there, to the left, in the sea!

There was a cry of fury from Lopez, followed by harsh orders, and the sound of running feet. Micah followed the other men, managing to blend in, veering suddenly to the other side of the ship.

Just as he got there, he was faced with a henchman who hadn't followed the others. The man had an automatic weapon in his hands and he was hesitating, his eyes trying to see Micah, who was half in shadow so that his blond hair didn't give the game away. If the man pulled that trigger…

*"Es que usted esta esperando una cerveza?"* he shot at the man angrily. *"¡Vaya! ¡Steele esta alla!"* What are you waiting for, a beer? Get going, Steele's over there!

He hesitated with his heart in his throat, waiting, waiting…

All at once, there was a shout from the other side of the ship. The man who was holding Micah at bay still hesitated, but the noise got louder.

*"¡Vaya!"* he repeated. He waved the man on urgently with a mumbled Spanish imprecation about Steele and his useless escape attempt. In that space of seconds before they discovered the man in the water was not Micah, their escaping captive got over the rail and into the ocean and struck out back toward the shore. He kept his strokes even and quick, and he zigzagged. Even if Lopez's men spotted him, they were going to have to work at hitting him from that distance. Every few yards, he submerged and swam underwater. Any minute now, he told himself, and thanked God he'd had just enough rest to allow him a chance of making it to shore before he was discovered and killed.

He heard loud voices and a searchlight began sweeping the water. Micah dived under again and held his breath. With a little bit of luck, they might pass right over him, in his black clothing. He blended in very well with the ocean.

There was gunfire. He ground his teeth together and prayed they'd miss him. Probably they were shooting blind, hoping to hit him with a lucky shot.

Odd, though, the gunfire sounded closer than that…

He came up for air, to snatch a breath, and almost collided with his own swift motorboat, with Bojo driving it and firing an automatic rifle toward Lopez and his men at the same time.

"Climb in, boss!" Bojo called, and kept shooting.

"Remind me to give you a raise," Micah panted as he dragged himself over the side and into the rocking boat. "Good work. Good work! Now get the hell out of here before they blow us out of the water!"

Bojo swung the boat around masterfully and imitated the same zigzag pattern that Micah had used when he swam.

"Lopez is mad now," Micah said with a glittery smile. "If there's any justice left in the world, he'll try to move in closer to get a better shot at us."

"We hope," Bojo said solemnly, still dodging bullets.

Micah looked back toward the ship, now clearly visible against the horizon. He thought of all Lopez's helpless victims, of whole families in tiny little Mexican towns who had been mowed down with automatic weapons for daring to help the authorities catch the local pushers. He thought of the hard fight to shut down Lopez's distribution network slated for operation in Jacobsville, Texas. He thought of Callie in that murderous assassin's hands, of the knife cut on her pretty little breast where the point had gone in. He thought of Callie dead, tortured, an anguished expression locked forever into those gentle features. He thought of his father, who would have been Lopez's next target. He thought of Lisa Monroe Parks's young husband in the DEA who'd been killed on Lopez's orders. He thought of all the law enforcement people who'd risked their lives and the lives of their families to stop Lopez.

"It's retribution time, Lopez," Micah said absently, watching the big ship with somber eyes. "Life calls in the bets for us all, sooner or later. But you're overdue, you drug-dealing son of a…!"

Before the last word left his lips, there was a huge fireburst where the ship had been sitting in the water. Flames rolled up and up and up, billowing black smoke into the atmosphere. The sound rocked the boat, and pieces of the yacht began falling from the sky in a wide circumference. Micah and Bojo ducked down in the boat and covered their heads as Bojo increased their speed and changed direction, hoping to miss the heavier metal parts that were raining down with wood and fabric.

They made it to the boat dock and jumped out as the last pieces of what had been Lopez's yacht fell into the water.

Mercenaries came rushing down from the house, all armed, to see what had happened.

"Say goodbye to Lopez," Micah told them, eyes narrowed with cold scrutiny.

They all watched the hull of the ship, still partially intact, start to sink. To their credit, none of them cheered or laughed or made a joke. Human lives had been lost. It was no cause for celebration, not even when the ringleader was as bad as Lopez. It had been necessary to eliminate him. He was crazed with vengeance and dangerous to the world at large.

Rodrigo came up beside them. "Glad to see you still alive, boss," he said.

Micah nodded. "It was close. I was too tired to swim back. He caught me at the ladder like a raw recruit."

There was a faint sound from Peter, the newest of the group. "I thought slips were my signature," he told Micah.

"Even veterans can step the wrong way and die for it," Micah told him gently. "That's why you always do it by the book and make sure you've got backup. I broke all the rules, but I didn't want to put anyone else at risk. I got lucky. Sometimes you don't." He watched the last of Lopez's yacht sink. "What about our two guests?"

"They're still in the shed."

"Load them up and take them in to Nassau and say we'll file charges for trespassing," Micah told Rodrigo.

"I'm on my way."

"We'll have federal agents combing the island by dawn, I guess," one of the other mercenaries groaned.

Micah shook his head. "I was sanctioned. And that's all I intend to say about this, ever," he added when the man seemed set to protest. "Let's see if we can get a little more sleep before dawn."

Mumbled agreement met the suggestion. He walked back into the house and down the hall to his bedroom. Callie's door was still closed. He felt a horrible pang of guilt when he remembered what had happened before he went after Lopez. He was never going to get over what he'd done.

He took a shower and changed into a pair of white shorts and a white-and-red patterned silk shirt. He padded down the hall to the kitchen and started to get a beer out of the refrigerator. But it hadn't been a beer sort of night. He turned on his heel and went to the liquor cabinet in his study. He poured himself two fingers of Kentucky bourbon with a little ice and took it back down the hall with him.

At the door of Callie's room, he paused. He opened
the door gently and moved in to stand by the bed and
look down at her. She was sound asleep, her cheek pil-
lowed on a pretty hand devoid of jewelry. She'd kicked
off the sheet and bedspread and her long legs were visible where the gown had fallen away from them. She
looked innocent, untouched. He remembered the feel
of that soft mouth under his lips, the exquisite loving
that had driven every sane thought out of his mind. His
body went rigid just from the memory.

She stirred, as if she sensed his presence, but she
didn't wake up. The sedative had really kicked in now.
She wouldn't wake until dawn, if then.

He reached down a gentle hand and brushed the hair
away from the corner of her mouth and her cheek. She
wasn't conventionally pretty, but she had an inner beauty
that made him feel as if he'd just found spring after a
hard winter. He liked to hear her laugh. He liked the way
she dressed, so casually and indifferently. She didn't
take hours to put on makeup, hours to dress. She didn't
complain about the heat or the cold or the food. She was
as honest as any woman he'd ever known. She had wonderful qualities. But he was afraid of her.

He'd been a loner most of his life. His mother's
death when he was ten had hit him hard. He'd adored
his mother. After that, it had been Jack and himself,
and they'd grown very close. But when Callie and her
mother moved in, everything had changed. Suddenly he
was an outsider in his own family. He despised Callie's
mother and made no secret of his resentment for both
women. That had caused a huge rift between his father
and himself, one that had inevitably grown wide enough
to divide them altogether.

He'd blamed Callie for the final blow, because he'd convinced himself that she'd found Jack and sent him to the hall to find Micah and Anna kissing. Callie had always denied it, and finally he believed her. It hadn't been pique because he'd rejected her.

He took a sip of the whiskey and stared down at her broodingly. She was part of his life, part of him. He hated knowing that. He hated the memory of her body moving sensuously under his while he seduced her.

And she thought she'd been dreaming. What if she woke up still believing that? They'd not only had sex, but thanks to him they'd had unprotected sex. His dark eyes slid down her body to her flat belly. Life might already be growing in her womb.

His breath caught. Callie might have his baby. His lips parted as he thought about a baby. He'd never wanted one before. He could see Callie with an infant in her arms, in her heart, in her life. Callie would want his baby.

He felt an alien passion gripping him for the first time. And just as quickly, he considered the difficulty it would engender. Callie might be pregnant. She wouldn't remember how she got that way, either.

He pursed his lips, feeling oddly whimsical for a man who was facing the loss of freedom and perhaps even the loss of his lifestyle and his job. Wouldn't it be something if Callie was pregnant and he was the only one who knew?

# *Chapter 11*

Callie felt the sun on her face. She'd been dreaming. She'd been in Micah's warm, powerful arms, held tight against every inch of him, and he'd been making ardent love to her. He'd looked down into her wide eyes at the very instant he'd possessed her. He'd watched her become a woman. It seemed so real…

Her eyes opened. Sure it was real. And any minute now, the tooth fairy was going to fly in through the open patio windows and leave her a shiny quarter!

She sat up. Odd, that uncomfortable feeling low in her belly. She shifted and she felt sore. Talk about dreams that seemed real!

She swung her legs off the bed and stood up, stilling for a moment so that the sudden dizziness passed. She turned to make up the bed and frowned. There was a stain on the bottom sheet. It looked like dried blood.

Well, so much for the certainty that her period wasn't due for another two weeks, she thought. Probably all the excitement had brought it on sooner. She went into the bathroom, wondering what she was going to do for the necessary equipment in a house full of men.

But she wasn't having her period. That would mean some spotting had occurred and that frightened her because it wasn't natural. She'd always been regular. She'd have to see a doctor when she got home, she supposed.

She bathed and frowned when she was standing in front of the mirror. There were some very bad bruises on her hip and thigh, and that was when she remembered the terror of the night before. Half asleep, she hadn't really been thinking until she saw the bruises and it began to come back. A man, Lopez's man, had tried to kidnap her. She'd actually knocked him out with a shovel. She smiled as she remembered it. Sadly she'd been less brave when Micah came running out to see about her. He'd carried her in here and given her a sedative. She hoped she hadn't said anything revealing to him. Sedatives made her very uninhibited. But she had no memory past the shot. That might, she concluded, be a good thing.

Dressed in a pink Bermuda shorts set that she'd bought on her shopping trip in Nassau, she put her feet into a new pair of sneakers. Unlike the sandals she couldn't wear, the sneakers were a perfect fit.

She walked back into the bedroom worriedly, wondering what Micah had done with Lopez's men. It seemed very quiet this morning. She was certain Micah had all sorts of surveillance systems set up to make sure Lopez couldn't sneak anybody else in here to make another attempt at kidnapping her. But she felt uneasy, just the same. Lopez would never stop. She knew that she was still in the same danger she'd been in when she first arrived here with Micah.

She felt as if she had a hangover, probably because of that sedative Micah gave her. That explained the erotic dream as well. She blushed, remembering what an erotic dream it was, too. She brushed her hair, not bothering with makeup, and went down the hall to the kitchen to see if coffee was available.

Bojo was helping himself to a cup. He grinned as she came into the room. "You slept very late."

"I was very tired. Besides, Micah drugged me. That's the second time he's given me a sedative since I've been here. I'm not used to them." She laughed as she took the fresh cup of coffee Bojo handed her. "It's a good thing I fell asleep right away, too, because sedatives generally have a very odd effect on me. I get totally swept away. Where is everybody?" she added, noting that Bojo was the only person in the house.

"Micah has gone to Nassau on business," he told her with a grin. "Lopez seems to have vanished in the night. Not only Lopez, but his very expensive yacht and several of his men. The authorities are justifiably curious."

"Lopez has gone?" she asked, excited. "You mean, he's gone away?"

"Very far away," he said with a grin.

"But he'll just come back." He gave her a wry look and she frowned. "Don't you still have his two henchmen? Micah was going to give those two men to the police," she reminded him. "Maybe they know where he is."

"They were handed over to the police," he agreed. "But they don't know where Lopez is, either."

"You look smug," she accused.

He smiled. "I am. I do know where Lopez is. And I can promise you that he won't be making any more raids on this island."

"Great!" she exclaimed, relieved. "Can you hand him over to the police, too?"

"Lopez can't be handed over." He paused to think. "Well, not in one piece, at least," he added.

"You're sounding very strange," she pointed out.

He poured his own cup of coffee and sat back down at the table. "Lopez's yacht went up in flames last night," he said matter-of-factly. "I am amazed that you didn't hear the explosion. It must have been a fault in the engine, or a gas leak," he added, without meeting her eyes. He shook his head. "A very nasty explosion. What was left of the yacht sank within sight of here."

"His boat sank? He was on it? You're sure? Did you see it go down?" she asked, relieved and horrified at the same time.

"Yes, yes, and yes." He studied her. "Lopez will never threaten you or Micah's father again. You will be able to return home now, to your job and your stepfather. I shall miss you."

"I'll miss you, too, Bojo," she said, but her mind was racing ahead. Lopez was dead. She was out of danger. She could go home. She had to go home, she amended. She would never see Micah again…

Bojo was watching the expressions chase themselves across her face. She was vulnerable, and besides that, she was in love with Micah. It didn't take much guesswork to figure that out, or to make sense of Micah's strange attitude about her. Obviously the boss knew she was in love with him, and he was trying to be kind while making his position to her clear.

He grimaced. The musical tones of his cell phone interrupted his gloomy thoughts. He answered it quickly.

"Yes," he said, glancing warily at Callie. "She's here, having coffee. I'll ask her." He lifted both eyebrows. "Micah is having lunch with Lisse on the bay in Nassau. If you want to join them, I can take you over in the small boat."

Lisse. Why should she think anything had changed? she wondered. Lisse was beautiful and Micah had told her at the beginning that he and Lisse were lovers. They'd been together for a long time, and she was important in the Bahamas as well as being beautiful. A few teasing kisses for Callie meant nothing to him. She'd been a complete fool. Micah had been kind to her to get her to stay and bait Lopez. That was all it had been. It was an effort to smile, but she did.

"Tell him thanks, but I've got to start packing. If Lopez is really out of the way, I have to go home. Mr. Kemp won't keep my job open forever."

Bojo looked really worried. "Boss, she says she'd rather not." He hesitated, nodded, glanced again at Callie. "Okay. I'll make sure he knows. We'll expect you soon. Yes. Goodbye."

"You look like a bad party," she commented.

"He's bringing Lisse here for lunch," he said reluctantly.

Her heart jumped but she only smiled. "Why not? It's obvious to anybody that he's crazy about her. She's a dish," she added, and then wondered why she should suddenly think about Lisse's bust size when compared to her own.

"She's a cat," Bojo replied tersely. "Don't let her walk on you."

"I never have," she commented. "If we're having lunch, I guess I need to get started fixing it, huh?"

"We have a cook…"

"I'm good," she told him without conceit. "I cook for Dad and me every night. I'm not *cordon-bleu,* but I get compliments."

"Very well." Bojo gave in, hoping the boss wasn't going to fire him for letting her into the kitchen. "Mac went to Nassau with the boss and the other guys, so it would have been cold cuts anyway."

"I make homemade rolls," she told him with a grin. "And I can bake a pound cake."

She got up, looked through the cupboards and refrigerator, found an apron and got busy. It would give her something to do while her heart was breaking.

Two hours later, Micah and Lisse came into the living room together, laughing. Callie peered out from the kitchen. "Food's on the table if you want to sit down," she called gaily.

Micah gaped at her. He'd told Bojo to get Mac to fix lunch. What was Callie doing in the kitchen?

Bojo came out of it, and Micah's face hardened. "I thought I told you to monitor communications for traffic about Lopez," he said coldly.

Bojo knew what was eating him, so he only smiled. "I am. I was just asking Callie for another pot of coffee. We drank the other, between us," he added deliberately.

Micah's eyes flashed like black lightning, but he didn't say another word as Bojo nodded politely at Lisse and walked back toward the communications room.

"Sit down, Lisse," Micah said quietly, pulling out a chair for her at the dining-room table, already laid with silverware and plates and fresh flowers. "I'll be back in a minute."

"I do hope it's going to be something light," Lisse said airily. "I can't bear a heavy meal in the middle of the day."

Micah didn't answer her. He'd run into Lisse in town and she'd finagled him into lunch. He'd compromised by bringing her here, so that he could see how Callie was feeling after the night before. He was hoping against hope that she remembered what had happened. But the instant she looked at him, he knew she hadn't.

"Hi," she said brightly and with a forced smile. "I slept like two logs. I hope you've got an appetite. I made homemade bread and cake, and steak and salad."

"Lisse will probably only want the salad," he murmured. "But I love cake."

"I remember. Go sit down. I'll bring it."

"You only set two places," he said quietly.

She shrugged. "I'm just cooking it. I wouldn't want to get in the way…Micah!"

While she was talking, he picked her up and carried her out of the kitchen the back way and into the first sprawling bathroom he came to, closing the door behind them.

"You're not the hired help here," he said flatly, staring into her eyes without putting her down. "You don't wait at table. You don't cook. I have a man for that."

"I'm a good cook," she pointed out. "And it's going to get cold if you don't put me down and let me finish."

His eyes dropped to her mouth and lingered there hungrily. "I don't want food." He brought her close and his mouth suddenly went down against hers and twisted ardently, until he forced her lips apart and made her respond to him. He groaned under his breath as her arms reached up to hold him. She made a husky little sound and gave in all at once. It felt so familiar to be held like this, kissed like this. She opened her mouth and felt his tongue go into it. Her body was on fire. She'd never felt such desire. Odd, that her body seemed to have a whole different knowledge of him than her mind did.

He couldn't get enough of her mouth. He devoured it. His powerful arms had a faint tremor when he was finally able to draw back. He looked straight into her eyes, remembering her headlong response the night before, feeling her body yield to him on crisp, white sheets in the darkness. He'd thought of nothing else all day. It was anguish to know that she was totally oblivious to what they'd done together, when the memories were torturing him.

"How long have you been talking to Bojo?" he demanded gruffly.

"Just…just a little while." Her mouth was swollen, but her body was shivering with secret needs. She looked at the tight line of his lips and impulsively reached up to kiss him. Amazingly he kissed her back with ardent insistence.

"Micah!" Lisse's strident voice came floating down the hall, followed by the staccato sound of high heels on wood.

Micah heard her and lifted his head. His mouth, like Callie's, was swollen. He searched her misty eyes intently.

"It's Lisse," she whispered dazedly.

"Yes." He bent and brushed his lips lazily over her own, smiling as she followed them involuntarily.

"She wants her lunch," she persisted.

"I want you," he murmured against her mouth.

The words shocked. Her fingers, linked behind his nape, loosened and she looked worried. "I can't!" she whispered huskily.

"Why can't you?"

"Because I've never…" she began.

*Until last night.* He almost said it. He thought it. His face hardened as he forced his tongue to be silent. He couldn't tell her. He wanted to. But it was too soon. He had to show her that it wasn't a one-night thing with him. Even more important, he had to convince himself that he could change enough, settle down enough, to give her some security and stability. He knew that he could have made her pregnant. Oddly it didn't worry him. The thought of a child was magical, somehow. He didn't know much about children, except that he was certain he'd love his own. Callie would make a wonderful mother.

He smiled as he bent and kissed her eyelids shut. "Wouldn't you?" he whispered. "If I insisted?"

"I'd hate you," she bit off, knowing that she wouldn't. She loved him endlessly.

"Yes, you might," he said after a minute. "And that's the last thing I want."

"Micah!" Lisse's voice came again, from even farther down the hall.

"Sit. Stay," Callie whispered impishly.

He bit her lower lip and growled deep in his throat. "She insisted on lunch. I compromised. Kiss me again." His mouth drifted lazily over hers.

She did kiss him, because she had no willpower when it came to this. She loved being in his arms, being held by him. She loved him!

After a minute he lifted his head and put her down, with obvious reluctance. "We'd better go before she starts opening doors," he said in a husky tone.

"Would she?" she asked, curious.

"She has before," he confessed with a wry grin. He brushed back her hair with exquisite tenderness. His eyes held an expression she'd never seen in them. "You look like I've been making love to you," he whispered with a faint smile. "Better fix your face before you come out."

She reached up and touched his swollen mouth with wonder. She was still trying to make herself believe that he'd dragged her in here and kissed her so hungrily. There was something in the back of her mind, something disturbing. She couldn't grasp it. But the most amazing thing was the tenderness he was showing her. It made her breathless.

His lean hand spread against her cheek. His thumb parted her lips as he bent again, as if he couldn't help himself. He kissed her softly, savoring the trembling response of her lips.

*"Micah!"* Lisse was outside, almost screeching now.

He lifted his head again with a long sigh. "I need to take you out in the boat and drop anchor five miles out," he said heavily. He tapped her nose. "Okay, let's go see if everything's cold before Lisse loses her voice."

He opened the door, checking to see if the coast was clear. "Fix your face," he whispered with a wicked grin and closed the door behind him.

She heard his footsteps moving toward the dining room. Two minutes later, staccato heels made an angry sound passing the bathroom door.

"Micah…!"

"I'm in the dining room, Lisse! Where were you? I've been looking everywhere!"

He was good at improvising, Callie thought as she repaired the damage to her face. She combed her hair with a comb from a tray on the vanity table and wondered at the change in her relationship with Micah. He was very different. He acted as if she'd become suddenly important to him, and not in a conventional way. She couldn't help smiling. It was as if her whole life had changed.

She went back into the kitchen and put everything on the table, after checking that the steak had kept warm on the back of the stove. It had.

Micah got up and set a third place at the table, giving Callie a deliberate look. "You eat in here with us," he said firmly, ignoring Lisse's glare.

"Okay." She put out the last of the food, and butter for the rolls, and sat down. "Micah, will you say grace?" she added.

*"Grace?"* Lisse's beautiful face widened into shock.

Micah flashed her a disapproving glance and said a brief prayer. He was digging into the food while Lisse, in her gold-trimmed white pantsuit, was still gaping.

"We're very conventional at home," Callie pointed out.

"And traditional," Micah added. "Tradition is important for families."

"But you don't have a family, really, darling," Lisse protested. She helped herself to a couple of forkfuls of salad and a hint of dressing. "Rolls? Thousands of calories, darling, especially with butter!" she told Micah.

"Callie made them for me, from scratch," he said imperturbably. He bit into one and smiled. "These are good," he said.

Callie shrugged. "It's the only thing I do really well. My mother couldn't boil water." That had slipped out and she looked horrified as she met Micah's eyes.

"I think Micah could do very well without hearing about your tramp of a mother, dear," Lisse said haughtily. "He's suffered enough at her hands already. Who was it she threw you over for, darling, that British earl?"

"She didn't throw me over," Micah said through his teeth.

"But she was staying here with you last year…?"

Callie's eyes exploded. She got up, throwing down her napkin. "Is that true?" she demanded.

"It is, but not the way you're assuming it is," he said flatly. "Callie, there's something you need to know."

She turned and walked out of the room.

"What the hell was that in aid of?" Micah demanded of Lisse, with real anger.

"You keep secrets, don't you?" she asked with cold delight. "It's dangerous. You've even slept with her, haven't you, darling?" she added venomously.

Micah threw down his own napkin and got to his feet. *"Bojo!"* he yelled.

The tall Berber came rushing into the room. His boss never raised his voice!

Micah was almost vibrating with rage. "See Lisse back to Nassau. She won't be coming here again," he added with ice dropping from every syllable.

Lisse put down her fork and wiped her mouth before she got leisurely to her feet. She gave him a cool look. "You use people," she accused quietly. "It's always what *you* want, what *you* need. You manipulate, you control, you…use. I loved you," she added in a husky undertone. "But you didn't care. I was handy and good in bed, and that was what mattered to you. When you didn't want me so much anymore, you threw me out. I was only invited over here this time so that you could show your houseguest that she wasn't the only egg in your basket." She gave him a cold smile. "So how does it feel to be on the receiving end for once, Micah? It's your turn. I wish, I really wish, I could stick around to see the result. She doesn't look like the forgiving sort to me. And I'd know, wouldn't I?"

She turned, leaving Bojo to follow her after a complicated glance in Micah's direction. The boss didn't say a word. Not a single word.

Callie was packing with shaking hands. Micah came to the doorway and leaned against it with his hands in his pockets, watching her glumly.

"Nothing to say?" she asked curtly.

"Nothing you'd listen to," he replied. He shrugged. "Lisse just put me in my place. I didn't realize it, but she's right. I do use people. Only I never meant to use you, in any way."

"You said you weren't having an affair with my mother," she accused as she folded a pair of slacks and put them in her case.

"I'm not. I never have." His chest rose and fell heavily. "But you're not in any mood to listen, are you, baby?"

Baby. She frowned. Baby. Why did that word make her uneasy? She looked at him with honest curiosity.

"I called you that," he said quietly. "You don't remember when, do you?"

She sighed, shaking her head.

"It may be just as well," he said, almost to himself. "For now, it's safe for you to go home. Lopez is dead.

His top lieutenants died with him. There's no longer any threat to you or to Dad."

"Yes. What a lucky explosion it was," she added, busy with her case.

"It wasn't luck, Callie," he said shortly. "I swam out to the yacht and planted a block of C-4 next to his propeller shaft."

She turned, gasping. Her hands shook as she fumbled the case closed and sat down heavily on the bed. So that was what they'd been talking about the night before, when Micah had said that "it might work." He could have been killed!

"It was a close call," he added, watching her. "I let myself get caught like a rank beginner. I was too tired to make it back in a loop, so I stopped to rest. One of Lopez's men caught me. Lopez made a lot of threats about what he planned to do to you and Dad, and then he got stupid and had me tied up down below." He extended his arm, showed her his watch, pressed a button, and watched her expression as a knife blade popped out. "Pity his men weren't astute enough to check the watch. They knew what I do for a living, too."

Her eyes were full of horror. Micah had gone after Lopez alone. He'd been captured. If it hadn't been for that watch, he'd be dead. She stared at him as if she couldn't get enough of just looking at him. What difference did it make if he'd had a full-blown affair with her mother? He could be out there with Lopez, in pieces...

She put her face in her hands to hide the tears that overflowed.

He went to the bed and knelt beside her, pulling her wet face into his throat. He smoothed her hair while she clung to him and let the tears fall. It had been such a traumatic week for her. It seemed that her whole life had been uprooted and stranded. Micah could have been dead. Or, last night, she could have been dead. Pride seemed such a petty thing all of a sudden.

"You could have died," she whispered brokenly.

"So could you." He moved, lifting her into his arms. He dropped into a wide cushioned rattan chair and held her close while the anguish of the night before lanced through her slender body like a tangible thing. She clung to him, shivering.

"I wish I'd known what you were planning," she said. "I'd have stopped you, somehow! Even if it was only to save you so you could go to my…my mother."

He wrapped her up even closer and laid his cheek against her hair with a long sigh. "You still don't trust me, do you, honey?" he murmured absently. "I suppose it was asking too much, considering the way I've treated you over the years." He kissed her dark hair. "You go back home and settle into your old routine. Soon enough, this will all seem like just a bad dream."

She rubbed her eyes with her fists, like a small child. Curled against him, she felt safe, cherished, treasured. Odd, to feel like that with a man who was a known playboy, a man who'd already told her that freedom was like a religion to him.

"You'll be glad to have your house to yourself again," she said huskily. "I guess it really cramped your style having me here. With Lisse, I mean."

He chuckled. "I lied."

"Wh…what?"

"I lied about Lisse being my lover now. What was between us was over years ago." He shrugged. "I brought her over here when you arrived as a buffer."

She sat up, staring at him like a curious cat. "A buffer?"

He smiled lazily. His fingers brushed away the tears that were wetting her cheeks. "Bachelors are terrified of virgins," he commented.

"You don't even like me," she protested.

His dark eyes slid down to her mouth, and even farther, over her breasts, down to her long legs. "You have a heart like marshmallow," he said quietly. "You never avoid trouble or turn down people in need. You take in all sorts of strays. Children love you." He smiled. "You scared me to death."

"Past tense?" she asked softly.

"I'm getting used to you." He didn't smile. His dark eyes narrowed. "It hurt me that Lopez got two men onto my property while I was lying in bed asleep. You could have been kidnapped or killed, no thanks to me."

"You were tired," she replied. "You aren't superhuman, Micah."

He drew in a slow breath and toyed with the armhole of her tank top. His fingers brushed against soft, warm flesh and she had to fight not to lean toward them. "I didn't feel comfortable resting while we were in so much danger. It all caught up with me last night."

She was remembering something he'd said. "You were almost too tired to swim back from Lopez's yacht, you said," she recalled slowly. She frowned. "But you'd just been asleep," she added. "How could you have been tired?"

"Oh, that's not a question you should ask yet," he said heavily. "You're not going to like the answer."

"I'm not?"

He searched her eyes for a long moment. All at once,

he stood up, taking her with him. "You'd better finish getting your stuff together. I'll put you on a commercial flight home."

She didn't want to go, but she didn't have an excuse to stay. She looked at him as if she were lost and alone, and his face clenched.

"Don't do that," he said huskily. "The idea is to get you out of here as smoothly as possible. Don't invite trouble."

She didn't understand that taut command. But then, she didn't understand him, either. She was avoiding the one question she should be asking. She gave in and asked it. "Why was my mother here?"

"Her husband has cancer," he said simply. "She phoned here and begged for help. It seems the earl is penniless and she does actually seem to love him. I arranged for him to have an unorthodox course of treatment from a native doctor here. They both stayed with me until he got through it." He put his hands in his slacks pockets. "As much as I hate to admit it, she's not the woman she was, Callie," he added. "And she did one other thing that I admired. She phoned your father and told him the truth about you."

Her heart skipped. "What father? What truth?" she asked huskily.

"Your father was going to phone you and ask you to meet him. Did he?"

She moved restlessly back to her packing. "He phoned and left a message. I didn't have anything to say to him, so I didn't call him back."

"He knows that you're his child," he told her. "Your mother sent him your birth certificate. That's why he's trying to contact you. I imagine he wants to apologize.

Your mother does, too, to you and Dad, but she told me she wasn't that brave."

Her eyes met his, haunted. "I went through hell because of her and my father," she said in a tight tone. "You don't know...you can't imagine...what it was like!"

"Yes, I can," he said, and he sounded angry. "He's apparently counting his regrets. He never remarried. He doesn't have any children, except you."

"Then he still doesn't have a child," she said through her teeth.

He didn't reply for several long seconds. "I can understand why you feel that way, about him and your mother. I don't blame you. I just thought I'd tell you what I know. It's up to you, what you do or don't do about it."

She folded one last shirt and put it into the case. "Thanks for telling me." She glanced at him. "Lisse wanted to make trouble."

"Yes, she did, and she was entitled. She's right. I did use her, in a way. Your mother left me very embittered about women," he confessed. "I loved my own mother, but I lost her when I was still in grammar school. In later years, your mother was the very worst example of what a wife should be. She made a very bad impression on me."

"On me, too." She closed the case and turned back to him, her eyes trying to memorize his lean face. "I wish you'd liked me, when I lived in your house," she said abruptly. "It would have meant more than you know."

His eyes narrowed. "I couldn't afford to like you, Callie," he said quietly. "Every time I looked at you, I burned like fire inside. You were just a teenager, a virgin. I couldn't take advantage of you that way."

"We could have been friends," she persisted.

He shook his head. "You know we couldn't. You know why."

She grimaced, averting her face. "It's always sex with you, isn't it?"

"Not anymore." His voice was quiet, solemn. "Those days are past. I'm looking ahead now. I have a future to build."

A bigger army of mercenaries, she decided, and more money. She smiled to herself. Once a mercenary, always a mercenary. He'd be the last mercenary who would ever be able to give up the lifestyle.

"I wish you well," she said. She picked up her case and looked around to make sure she hadn't left anything. "Thanks for saving my life. Twice," she added with a forced grin.

"You're welcome." He moved forward to take the case from her. He studied her face for a long time with narrowed eyes. It was as if he was seeing her for the first time. "It's amazing," he murmured involuntarily, "that it took me so long."

"What took you so long?"

"Never mind," he murmured, and he smiled. "You'll find out soon enough. Come on. I'll drive you into Nassau to the airport."

"Bojo could…"

He put his fingers against her soft mouth, and he didn't smile. "I'll drive you."

She swallowed. The tip of his finger was tracing her upper lip, and it was making her knees weak. "Okay," she said.

He took her hand and led her out to the car.

## Chapter 12

Two weeks later, Callie was back at work and it was as if she'd never been kidnapped by Lopez's men or gone to Nassau with Micah. Despite the excitement and adventure, she hadn't told anyone except Mr. Kemp the truth about what had happened. And she let him think that Lopez had died in a freak accident, to protect Micah.

Micah had walked her to the concourse and kissed her goodbye in such a strange, breathlessly tender way that it had kept her from sleeping much since she'd been back. The look in his eyes had been fascinating, but she was still trying to decide what she'd seen there. He'd said he'd see her soon. She had no idea what he meant. It was like leaving part of herself behind when she got on the plane. She cried all the way to Miami, where she got on a plane to San Antonio and then a charter flight to Jacobsville from there.

Micah's father was much better, and so glad to see her that he cried, too. She dismissed the nurse who'd been staying with him with gratitude and a check, but the nurse refused the check. She'd already been paid her fee, in advance, she told a mystified Callie. She left, and Callie and Jack Steele settled back into their comfortable routine.

"I feel better than I have in years," Jack Steele told her with a grin at supper one evening. "It makes me proud that my son wanted to protect me as well as you."

"Micah loves you terribly," she assured him. "He just has a hard time showing it, that's all."

"You really think so?"

"I do. I'm sure he'll come and see you, if you'll let him."

He gave her a peculiar look and pursed his lips. "I'll let Micah come here if you'll do something for me."

"What?"

He leaned back in his chair, and his features reminded her of Micah in a stubborn mood. "If you'll make peace with your father," he said.

She let out a surprised gasp.

"I knew you'd take it like that," he said. "But he's phoned here every single day since you left. He told me some cock-and-bull story about a drug dealer named Lopez. He said he'd heard from a friend in law enforcement that Lopez had kidnapped you and taken you to Mexico. I thought he was full of bull and I told him so. But he kept phoning. I guess it was a good excuse to mend fences. A man that persistent should at least have a hearing."

She gaped at him. "You...didn't believe him, about Lopez?"

Her tone surprised him. "No, of course not." Her expression was very disturbing. He scowled. "Callie…it wasn't true? You really did go to take care of that aunt Micah told me about?"

"Jack, I don't have an aunt," she said heavily. "Lopez did kidnap me. Micah came and got me out himself. He went right into Lopez's house and rescued me."

"My son, storming drug dealers' lairs?" he exclaimed. "Are you kidding?"

"Oh, I didn't want you to have to find out like this," she groaned. "I should have bitten my tongue through!"

He was shocked. "Micah got you out," he repeated.

She leaned across the table and took his arthritic hands in hers and held them tight. "There's no easy way to say this, but you'll have to know. I'm not sure Micah wants you to know, but I don't have a choice anymore. Dad, Micah is a professional mercenary," she told him evenly. "And he's very good at it. He rappelled from Lopez's roof right into a bedroom and rescued me from a man who was going to kill me. We're both fine. He got me away and out of the country, and took me home with him to Nassau. He lured Lopez in, and…Lopez's boat was blown up in a freak accident."

Jack let out the breath he'd been holding. "The things you learn about people you thought you knew. My own son, and he never told me."

She grimaced. "I'm not sure he ever would. He's very brave, Jack. He isn't really money-hungry, although it sounds as if he is. I'd never have survived without him. His men are just the same, dedicated professionals who really care about what they do. They're not a gang of thugs."

Jack sat back in his chair again, scowling. "You know,

it does make some sort of sense. He came home bandaged, you remember that time? And he said he'd had a bad fall. But I saw him accidentally without the bandage and it looked like a bullet wound to me."

"It probably was," she said. "He has scars on his back, too."

She frowned, trying to understand how she knew that. She'd seen Micah with his shirt unbuttoned in Nassau, but never with it off completely. How would she know he had scars down his back?

She put that thought out of her mind. "There's something else I found out," she added. "My mother was there last year, staying with him."

Jack's face hardened at once.

"No, it's not what you're thinking," she said quickly. "That was my thought, too, but she asked Micah for help. She's married to a British earl who has cancer. There was a clinic near Micah and he let them stay with him while the earl was treated. He's impoverished, and I suspect that Micah paid for the treatments, too, although he didn't admit it." She smiled. "He says Mother is really in love this time. She wanted to make peace with both of us as well, but she didn't think it would be possible."

"Not for me," Jack said quietly. "She cost me a lot."

"She cost me more," she agreed. "But you can't hate people forever. It only hurts you in the end. You have to forgive unless you want to live in torment forever."

"How did you get so wise, at your age?" he asked, smiling as he tried to lighten the mood.

"I had a lot of hard knocks. I learned early how terrible a thing hatred is." She touched his hand gently. "Micah loves you so much. You can't imagine how it hurt him when we thought he'd betrayed you with Mother. He's been bitter, too."

"I wouldn't let him talk about it," he said. "I should have listened. He's never lied to me, except maybe by omission." He sighed with a wry smile. "I never would have guessed he'd have been in such a profession."

She laughed. "Neither would I." She sighed. "He can't give it up, of course. He told me he had no ambition whatsoever to settle down and have a family. I never really saw him as a family man."

He studied her curiously. "But you wish he was," he said perceptibly.

Her gaze fell to the table. "I love him," she said heavily. "I always have. But he's got all the women in his life that he needs already. Beautiful women. One of them took me shopping when we first got to Nassau."

"You have ties with him that no other woman will ever have. If he didn't care about you, he certainly wouldn't have risked his own life to rescue you," he remarked.

"He did it for you, because he knows you love me," she said. "That's why."

He pursed his lips and his eyes narrowed as he studied her. "Think so? I wonder."

She got up. "I'll fix dinner. Then I guess I'll try to phone my father."

"Remember what you said, about forgiving people, Callie," he reminded her. "Your mother told him a lot of lies. He believed her, but maybe it was easier to believe her, when he knew she was taking you away. He was going to lose you anyway."

"She didn't take me away," she said coldly. "He threw me out, and she put me in foster care immediately."

He grimaced. "Yes, I know. Your father told me. He'd only just found out."

"Found out, how?" she exclaimed.

"Apparently he hired a private detective," he said gently. "He was appalled at how you'd been treated, Callie. He blames himself."

She moved restlessly, her eyes glancing at him. "You're the only father I've ever known."

He grinned. "You'll always have me. But give the man a chance. He's not as bad as you remember him being." The smile faded. "Maybe, like your mother, he's found time to face himself and his mistakes."

She turned away. "Okay. I guess it wouldn't hurt to talk to him."

She phoned, but her father was out of the country. She left a message for him on his answering machine, a stumbling sort of greeting and her phone number. If he hadn't given up on her, he might try again.

The next week dragged. She missed Micah. She felt tired. She wondered if all the excitement of the past few weeks wasn't catching up with her. She also seemed to have stopped having a period. She'd always been regular and never skipped, and then she remembered that odd spotting in Nassau. She grimaced. It must be some sort of female problem. She'd have to make an appointment to see Dr. Lou Coltrain.

She made the appointment from work, just after she got back from lunch. When she hung up, her boss, Blake Kemp, was speaking to someone in his office, the door just having opened so that he could show his client out.

"...yes, he phoned me a couple of days ago," the client

was saying. "He used to hate Jacobsville, which makes it even stranger. We were all shocked."

"Yes," Kemp replied. "He had a whole island, didn't he? He's already sold up there, and he's got big plans for the Colbert Ranch property. He owns several thoroughbreds, which he's having shipped here from New Providence. He plans to have one of the best racing stables in Texas, from what he says."

"He says he's giving up the business as well and coming back here to live."

"That's another odd thing, he mentioned going back to medical school and finishing his residency," Kemp chuckled.

"He's good at what he used to do. He's patched me up enough over the years." The tall man with the green eyes, favoring a burned forearm and hand glanced at Callie and noted her shocked face. "Yes, Callie, I'm talking about your stepbrother. I don't guess you and Jack Steele knew a thing about this, did you?"

She shook her head, too stunned to speak.

"That's like Micah." The client chuckled. "He always was secretive. Well, Callie, you look none the worse for wear after your ordeal."

She finally realized who the client was. That was Cy Parks! She knew that he and Micah were friends, but until recently she hadn't known that they shared the same profession.

"Micah's moving here?" she asked involuntarily.

"He is," Cy told her. "But don't tell him you heard me say so," he added with a twinkle in his green eyes. "I don't need to lose any more teeth."

"Sure thing, Mr. Parks," she said with a smile.

"He couldn't stop talking about how brave you were,

you know," he added unexpectedly. "He was so proud of you."

She flushed. "He never said so."

"He doesn't, usually." He smiled. "Your father will enjoy having him home, too."

She nodded. "He's proud of Micah. I had to tell him the truth. He'll be over the moon to think that Micah's coming home. He's missed him."

"That cuts both ways. I'm glad to see him making an attempt to settle down," he added with a chuckle. "I can recommend it highly. I never expected so much happiness in my own life. Lisa's pregnant, you know," he added. "It's going to be a boy. We're both over the moon."

"Babies are nice," Callie said wistfully. "Thanks for telling me about Micah, Mr. Parks."

"Make it Cy," he told her. "I expect we'll be seeing each other again. Kemp, walk me out, I want to ask you something."

"Sure thing."

The men walked out onto the sidewalk and Callie stared at her computer screen with trembling fingers on the keyboard. Micah had sold his island. He was coming to live in Jacobsville. Was Lisse coming with him? Had they made up in spite of what he'd said about her? Was he going to marry the beautiful blonde and set up housekeeping here? If he was, she couldn't bear to stay in Jacobsville!

She felt like bawling. Her emotions had been all over the place lately. Along with the sudden bouts of fatigue and an odd nausea at night, and a missing period, she was likely to cry at the drop of a hat. She remembered a girlfriend having all those same symptoms, but of course, the girlfriend had been pregnant. That wasn't possible in her case. An erotic dream did not produce conception, after all. She was going to see the doctor the next day, anyway. She'd know what was wrong then, if anything was. She hoped it was nothing too terrible.

When she got home that evening, the doctor, the office, everything went right out of her head. There was a black Porsche convertible sitting in the driveway. With her heart pounding like mad, she got out and rushed up the front steps and into the apartment house.

She opened her own door, which was unlocked, and there was Micah, sitting at the dining-room table with Jack Steele while they shared a pot of coffee.

"Micah!" she exclaimed, everything she felt showing helplessly on her face.

He got to his feet, his face somber and oddly watchful. "Hello, Callie," he said quietly.

"I thought…I mean, I didn't think…" The room was swirling around her. She felt an odd numbness in her face and everything went white.

Micah rushed forward and caught her up in his arms before she hit the floor.

"Her bedroom's through there," Jack told him. "She's been acting very odd, lately. Tired and goes to bed early. I'll make another pot of coffee."

"Thanks, Dad."

Micah carried her to her room and laid her down gently on the white coverlet of her bed. Her fingers were like ice. He brushed back her disheveled hair and his heart clenched at just the sight of her. He'd missed her until it was anguish not to hear her voice, see her face.

She moaned and her eyes opened slowly, looking up

into his. She was faintly nauseous and her throat felt tight.

"I feel awful, Micah," she whispered. "But I'm so happy to see you!"

"I'm happy to see you, too," he replied, but he didn't look it. He looked worried. His big hand flattened on her belly, resting there very gently. He leaned close and his lips touched her eyelids, closing them. They moved down her face, over her cheeks, to her soft lips and he kissed her with breathless tenderness. "Callie," he whispered, and his lips became hard and insistent, as if he couldn't help himself.

She opened her mouth to him unconsciously, and her arms went around his neck, pulling him down. She forgot about Lisse, about everything. She kissed him back hungrily. All the weeks apart might never have been. She loved him so!

After a long minute, he forced himself to lift his head. He drew in a long, hard breath. He looked down where his hand was resting on her belly. It wasn't swollen yet, but he was certain, somehow, that she was carrying his child.

"Why…are you doing that?" she asked, watching his hand smooth over her stomach.

"I don't know how to tell you," he replied gently. "Callie…do you remember the night Lopez's men tried to kidnap you again? Do you remember that I gave you a sedative?"

"Yes," she said, smiling nervously.

"And you had an…erotic dream," he continued.

"Yes." She shifted on the cover. "I'd rather not talk about it."

"But we have to. Callie, I…"

"How about some coffee?" Jack Steele asked, poking his head through the doorway. "I just made a fresh pot."

"I'd like some," Callie said with a forced smile. "I'd like something to eat, too. I'm so empty!"

"That's what you think," Micah said under his breath. He stared down at her with twinkling eyes and a smile unlike any smile she'd ever seen on his lips before.

"You look very strange," she commented.

He shrugged. "Don't I always?"

She laughed gently. "Cy Parks was in Mr. Kemp's office today," she said as he helped her to her feet. "He said you were moving here…oops! I promised not to say anything, too. Please don't get mad at him, Micah."

"It's no big secret," he said gently. "In small towns, everybody knows what's going on. It's all right."

"You really are coming back here?"

Her wide eyes and fascinated expression made him tingle all over. "I am. I'm going to breed thoroughbreds. It's something I've always had an interest in. I might finish my residency as well. Jacobsville can always use another doctor."

"I guess so. I have to go see Dr. Lou Coltrain tomorrow. I think I may have a female problem," she said absently as they started out of the bedroom.

"Tomorrow?"

"After lunch," she said. "Don't tell Dad," she said, holding him back by the sleeve before they left the room. "I don't want him to worry. It probably scared him when I fainted. It scared me, too," she confessed.

He touched her hair gently. He wanted to tell her, but he didn't know how. He needed to talk to Lou Coltrain first. This had to be done very carefully, so that Callie didn't feel he was being forced into a decision he didn't want to make.

She searched his eyes. "You look so tired, Micah," she said softly.

"I don't sleep well since you left the island," he replied. "I've worried about you."

"I'm doing okay," she said at once, wanting to reassure him. "I don't even have nightmares." She looked down at her hand on his sleeve. "Micah, is Lisse…I mean, will she come, too?"

"Lisse is history. I told you that when you left. I meant it."

"She's so beautiful," she said huskily.

He frowned, tipping her face up to his with a hand under her chin. "You're beautiful yourself. Didn't you know?" he asked tenderly. "You have this big, open heart that always thinks of other people first. You have a generosity of spirit that makes me feel selfish by comparison. You glow, Callie." He smiled softly. "That's real beauty, the kind you don't buy in the cosmetic section of the department store. Lisse can't hold a candle to you." The smile faded. "No woman on earth could, right now. You're pure magic to me, Callie. You're the whole world."

That sounded serious. She just stared at him, transfixed, while she tried to decipher what he was saying.

"Coffee?" Jack Steele repeated, a little more loudly.

They both jumped when they saw him there. Then they laughed and moved out of the bedroom. Jack poured coffee into mugs and Micah carried Callie hers.

"Feeling better?" Jack asked.

"Oh, yes," she said, the excitement she was feeling so plain on her face that Micah grinned. "Much better!"

\* \* \*

Micah stayed near Callie for the rest of the evening, until he had to go. She'd fixed them a meal and had barely been able to eat a bite of it. She had little appetite, but mostly she was too excited. Micah was watching her as if everything she did fascinated him. All her dreams of love seemed to be coming true. She couldn't believe the way he was looking at her. It made her tingle.

She walked out with him after he'd said his goodnights to his father. "You could stay," she said.

"I can't sleep on that dinky little sofa, and Dad's in a twin bed. So unless you're offering to share your nice big double bed…?" he teased as they paused by the driver's side of his car.

She flushed. "Stop that."

He touched her cheek with his fingertips. "There's something I wanted to ask you. I can't seem to find a way to do it."

"What? You can ask me anything," she said softly.

He bent and brushed his mouth over hers. "Not yet. Come here and kiss me."

"We have neighbors…" she protested weakly.

But he'd already lifted her clear of the ground and he was kissing her as if there was no tomorrow. She held on and kissed him back with all her might. Two young boys on skateboards went whizzing by with long, insinuating wolf whistles.

Micah lifted his head and gave them a hard glare. "Everyone's a critic," he murmured.

"I'm not complaining," she whispered. "Come back here…"

He kissed her again and then, reluctantly, put her back on her feet. "Unless you want to make love on the hood of the car, we'd better put on the brakes." He looked around. More people had appeared. Incredible that there would be hordes of passersby at this hour in a small Texas town. He glared at two couples saunter-ing by. They grinned.

"That's Mr. and Mrs. Harris, and behind them is Mr. Harris's son and Jill Williams's daughter. They're going steady," she explained. "They know me, but I'm not in the habit of being kissed by handsome men in Porsches. They're curious."

He nodded over her shoulder. "And her?"

She followed where he was looking. "That's old Mrs. Smith. She grows roses."

"Yes. She seems to be pruning them." He checked his watch. "Ten o'clock at night is an odd hour to do that, isn't it?"

"Oh, she just doesn't want to look as if she's staring," she explained. "She thinks it would embarrass us." She added in a whisper, "I expect she thinks we're courting."

He twirled a strand of dark hair around his fingers. "Aren't we?" he asked with a gentle smile.

"Courting?" She sounded breathless. She couldn't help it.

He nodded. "You're very old-fashioned, Callie. In some ways, so am I. But you'd better know up-front that I'm not playing."

"You already said you didn't want to settle down," she said, nodding agreement.

"That isn't what I mean."

"Then what do you mean?"

"Hello, Callie!" came an exuberant call from the win-dow upstairs. It was Maria Ruiz, who was visiting her aunt who lived upstairs. She was sixteen and vivacious. "Isn't it a lovely night?"

"Lovely."

"Who's the dish?" the younger woman asked with an outrageous grin. "He's a real hunk. Does he belong to you, or is he up for grabs?"

"Sorry, I'm taken," Micah told her.

"Just my luck," she sighed. "Well, good night!"

She closed the window and the curtain and went back inside.

Callie laughed softly. "She's such a doll. She looks in on Dad when her aunt's working. I told you about her aunt, she doesn't speak any English."

He bent again and kissed her lazily. "You taste like roses," he whispered against her mouth. He enfolded her against him, shivering a little as his body responded instantly to the feel of hers against it and began to swell. He groaned softly as he kissed her again.

"Micah, you're…" She felt the hard crush of his mouth and she moaned, too. It was as if she'd felt him like this before, but in much greater intimacy. It was as if they'd been lovers. She held on tight and kissed him until she was shivering, too.

His mouth slid across her cheek to her ear, and he was breathing as roughly as she was. "I want you," he bit off, holding her bruisingly close. "I want you so much, Callie!"

"I'm sorry," she choked. "I can't…!"

He took deep breaths, trying to keep himself in check. He had to stop this. It was too soon. It was much too soon.

"It may not seem like it, but I'm not asking you to,"

he said. "It's just that there are things you don't know, Callie, and I don't know how to tell them to you."

"Bad things?"

He let out a slow breath. "Magical things," he whispered, cradling her in his arms as he thought about the baby he was certain she was carrying. His eyes closed as he held her. "The most magical sort of things. I've never felt like this in my life."

She wanted, so much, to ask him what he was feeling. But she was too shy. Perhaps if she didn't push him, he might like her. He sounded as if he did. She smiled, snuggling close to him, completely unintimidated with the hard desire of his body. She loved making him feel this way.

He smoothed over her hair with a hand that wasn't quite steady. His body ached, and even that was sweet. The weeks without her had been pure hell.

"Soon," he said enigmatically. "Very soon."

"What?"

He kissed her hair. "Nothing. I'd better go. Mrs. Smith is cutting the tops off the roses. Any minute now, there won't even be a bud left."

She glanced past his shoulder. She giggled helplessly. The romantic old woman was so busy watching them that she was massacring her prize roses!

"She wins ribbons for them, you know," she murmured.

"She won't have any left."

"She's having the time of her life," she whispered. "Her boyfriend married her sister. They haven't spoken in thirty years and she's never even looked at another man. She reads romance novels and watches movies and dreams. This is as close as she's likely to get to a hot romance. Even if it isn't."

"It certainly is," he whispered wickedly. "And if I don't get out of here *very* soon, she's going to see more than she bargained for. And so are you."

"Really?" she teased.

His hand slid to the base of her spine and pushed her close to him. His eyes held a very worldly amusement at her gasp. "Really," he whispered. He bent and kissed her one last time. "Go inside."

She forced herself to step back from him. "What about Bojo and Peter and Rodrigo and Pogo and Maddie?" she asked suddenly.

"Bojo was being groomed to take over the group. He's good at giving orders, and he knows how we operate. I'll be a consultant."

"But why?" she asked, entranced. "And why come back to Jacobsville to raise horses?"

"When you're ready for those answers I'll give them to you," he said with a gentle smile. "But not tonight. I'll be in touch. Good night."

He was in the car and gone before she could get another word out. Several doors down, Mrs. Smith was muttering as she looked at the rosebuds lying heaped around her feet. The skateboarders went past again with another round of wolf whistles. The couples walking gave her long, wicked grins. Callie went back inside, wondering if she should give them all a bow before she went inside.

## Chapter 13

Micah was ushered back into Dr. Lou Coltrain's office through the back door, before she started seeing her patients. He shook hands with her and took the seat she indicated in her office. She sat down behind her desk, blond and attractive and amused.

"Thanks for taking time to see me this morning," he said. He noted her wry look and chuckled. "Is my head on backward?" he asked.

"You may wish it was," she replied with twinkling dark eyes. "I think I know why you're here. At least two people have hinted to me that Callie Kirby's having what sounds like morning sickness."

He sighed and smiled. "Yes."

"And you're the culprit, unless I miss my guess. Are you here to discuss alternatives?" she asked, suddenly serious.

"I am not!" he said at once. "I want a baby as much as Callie will, when she knows about it."

"When she knows? She doesn't suspect?" she asked, wide-eyed.

He grimaced. "Well, it's like this. Lopez and his thugs—you know about them?" When she nodded, he sighed. "I was careless and they almost got her a second time in Nassau. She knocked her assailant out with a shovel, but she was really shaken up afterward. I gave her a sedative." His high cheekbones colored and he averted his eyes. "She got amorous and I was already upset and on the edge, and I'd abstained for so damned long. And…well…"

"Then what?" she asked, reading between the lines with avid curiosity.

He shifted in the chair, still avoiding eye contact. "She doesn't remember anything. She thinks it was an erotic dream."

Her intake of breath was audible. "In all my years of medicine…" she began.

"I haven't had that many, but it's news to me, too. The thing is, I'm sure she's pregnant, but she'll have a heart attack if you tell her she is. I have to break it to her. But first I have to find a way to convince her to marry me," he added. "So that she won't spend the rest of our lives together believing that the baby forced me into marriage. It's not like that," he said. He rubbed at a spot on his slacks so that he wouldn't have to meet Lou's intent stare. "She's everything. Everything in the world."

Lou smiled. He wasn't saying the words, but she was hearing them. He loved Callie. So it was like that. The mercenary was caught in his own trap. And, amazingly, he didn't want to get out of it. He wanted the baby!

"What do you want me to do?" she asked.

"I want you to do a blood test and see if she really is pregnant. But if she is, I want you to make some excuse about the results being inconclusive, and you can give her a prescription for some vitamins and ask her to come back in two weeks."

"She'll worry that it's something fatal," Lou advised. "People do."

"Tell her you think it's stress, from her recent ordeal," he persisted. "Please," he added, finding the word hard to say even now. "I just need a little time."

"Just call me Dr. Cupid Coltrain," she murmured. "I guess I'll get drummed out of the AMA, but how can I say no?"

"You're in the business of saving lives," he reminded her. "This will save three of them."

"I hear you're moving back here," she said.

"I am. I'm going to raise thoroughbreds," he added, smiling. "And act as a consultant for Eb Scott when he needs some expertise. That way, I'll not only settle down, I'll have enough of a taste of the old life to satisfy me if things get dull. I might even finish my residency and hit you and Coltrain up for a job."

"Anytime," she said, grinning. "I haven't had a day off in two years. I'd like to take my son to the zoo and not have to leave in the middle of the lions on an emergency call."

He chuckled. "Okay. That's a dare."

She stood up when he did and shook hands again. "You're not what I expected, Mr. Steele," she said after a minute. "I had some half-baked idea that you'd never give up your line of work, that you'd want Callie to do something about the baby."

"I do. I want her to have it," he said with a smile. "And a few more besides, if we're lucky. Callie and I were only children. I'd like several, assorted."

"So would we, but one's all we can handle at the moment. Of course, if you finish your residency and stand for your medical license, that could change," she added, tongue-in-cheek.

He grinned. "I guess it's contagious."

She nodded. "Very. Now get out of here. I won't tell Callie I've ever seen you in my life."

"Thanks. I really mean it."

"Anything for a future colleague," she returned with a grin of her own.

Callie worried all morning about the doctor's appointment, but she relaxed when she was in Lou's office and they'd drawn blood and Lou had checked her over.

"It sounds to me like the aftereffects of a very traumatic experience," Lou said with a straight face. "I'm prescribing a multiple vitamin and I want you to come back and see me in two weeks."

"Will the tests take that long?" Callie asked.

"They might." Lou sighed. "You're mostly tired, Callie. You should go to bed early and eat healthy. Get some sun, too. And try not to worry. It's nothing serious, I'm positive of that."

Callie smiled her relief. "Thanks, Dr. Coltrain!" she said. "Thanks, so much!"

"I hear your stepbrother's moving back to town,' Lou said as she walked Callie to the door of the cubicle. "I guess you'll be seeing a lot of him now."

Callie flushed. "It looks that way." Her eyes lit up.

"He's so different. I never could have imagined Micah settling for small-town life."

"Men are surprising people," Lou said. "You never know what they're capable of."

"I suppose so. Well, I'll see you in two weeks."

"Count on it," Lou said, patting her on the shoulder. "Lots of rest. And take those vitamins," she added, handing over the prescription.

Callie felt as if she were walking on air. No health problems, just the aftereffects of the kidnapping. That was good news indeed. And when Micah phoned and asked her to come out to the ranch with him and see the house, she was over the moon.

He picked her up after work at her apartment house. "I took Dad out there this morning," he told her with a grin. "He's going to move in with me at the weekend."

Callie's heart jumped. "This weekend?"

He nodded, glancing at her. "You could move in, too."

Her heart jumped, but she knew he didn't mean that the way it sounded. "I like living in town," she lied.

He smiled to himself. He knew what she was refusing. She wasn't about to live in sin with him in Jacobsville, Texas.

He reached for her hand and linked her fingers with his. "Did you go see the doctor?"

"Yes. She said it was stress. I guess it could be. At least, it's nothing extreme."

"Thank God," he said.

"Yes."

He turned down onto a long winding graveled road. Minutes later, they pulled up in front of a big white Victorian house with a turret room and a new tin roof. "It's really old-fashioned and some of the furniture will have to be replaced," he said, helping her out of the car. "But it's got potential. There's a nice rose garden that only needs a little work, and a great place out to the side for a playground. You know, a swing set and all those nice plastic toys kids love so much."

She stared at him. "You have kids?" she asked with an impish smile.

"Well, not yet," he agreed. "But they're definitely in the picture. Don't you like kids?" he asked with apparent carelessness.

"I love them," she said, watching him warily. "I didn't think you did."

He smiled. "I'll love my own, Callie," he said, his fingers contracting in hers. "Just as you'll love them."

"I'll love your kids?" she blurted out.

He couldn't quite meet her eyes. He stared down toward the big barn a few hundred yards behind the house and he linked his fingers tighter with hers. "Have you ever thought," he said huskily, "about making a baby with me?"

Her heart went right up into her throat. She flushed scarlet. But it wasn't embarrassment. It was pure, wild, joy.

He looked down at her then. Everything she thought, felt, was laid out there for him to see. He caught his breath at the depth of those emotions she didn't know he could see. It was more than he'd ever dared hope for.

"I want a baby, Callie," he whispered huskily. He framed her red face in his hands and bent to kiss her eyelids closed. His fingers were unsteady as he held her where he wanted her, while his mouth pressed tender, breathless little kisses all over her soft skin. "I want one so much. You'd make…the most wonderful little mother," he bit off, choked with emotion. "I could get up with you in the night, when the baby cried, and take turns walking the floor. We could join the PTA later. We could make memories that would last us forever, Callie—you and me and a little boy or a little girl."

She slid her arms tight under his and around him and held on for dear life, shaking with delighted surprise. He wasn't joking. He really meant it. Her eyes closed. She felt tears pouring down her cheeks.

He felt them against his thin silk shirt and he smiled as he reached in his pocket for a handkerchief. He drew her away from him and dabbed at the tears, bending to kiss away the traces. "We can build a big playground here," he continued, as if he hadn't said anything earth-shaking. "Both of us were only kids. I think two or three would be nice. And Dad would love being a grandfather. He can stay with us and the kids will make him young again."

"I'd love that. I never dreamed you'd want to have a family or settle down. You said…"

He kissed the words back against her lips. "Freedom is only a word," he told her solemnly. "It stopped meaning anything to me when I knew that Lopez had you." The memory of that horror was suddenly on his face, undisguised. "I couldn't rest until I knew where you were. I planned an assault in a day that should have taken a week of preparation. And then I went in after you myself, because I couldn't trust anyone to do it but me." His hands clenched on her shoulders. "When I saw you like that, saw what that animal had done to you…" He stopped and swallowed hard. "My God, if he'd killed you, I'd have cut him to pieces! And then," he whispered, folding her close, shivering with the depth of his feelings, "I'd have picked you up in my arms and I'd have jumped off the balcony into the rocks with you. Because I wouldn't want to live in a world…that didn't hold us both. I couldn't live without you. Not anymore."

There was a faint mist in his black eyes. She could barely see it for the mist in her own. She choked on a sob as she looked up at him. "I love you," she whispered brokenly. "You're my whole life. I never dared to hope that you might care for me, too!"

He folded her against him and held her close, rocking her, his cheek on her dark hair as he counted his blessings. They overwhelmed him. She loved him. His eyes closed. It seemed that love could forgive anything, even his years of unkindness. "I wish I could take back every single hurtful thing I've ever done or said to you."

She smiled tearfully against his broad chest. "It's all right, Micah. Honest it is. Do you really want babies?" she asked dreamily, barely aware of anything he'd said.

"More than anything in the world!"

"I won't sleep with you unless you marry me," she said firmly.

He chuckled. "I'll marry you as soon as we can get a license. But," he added on a long sigh, drawing back, "I'm afraid it's too late for the sleeping together part."

Her thin eyebrows arched up. "What?"

He traced around her soft lips. "Callie, that erotic dream you had…" He actually flushed. "Well, it wasn't a dream," he added with a sheepish grin.

Her eyes widened endlessly. All those explicit things he'd done and said, that she'd done and said, that had seemed like something out of a fantasy. The fatigue, the spotting, the lack of a period, the…

"Oh my God, I'm pregnant!" she exclaimed in a high-pitched tone.

"Oh my God, yes, you are, you incredible woman!" he said with breathless delight. "I'm sorry, but I went to Lou Coltrain behind your back and begged her not to tell you until we came to an understanding. I was scared to death that you'd be off like a shot if you knew it too soon." He shook his head at her surprise. "I've never wanted anything as much as I want this child—except you," he added huskily. "I can't make it without you, Callie. I don't want to try." He glanced around them at the house and the stable. "This is where we start. You and me, a new business, a new life—in more ways than one," he added with a tender hand on her soft abdomen. "I know I'm something of a risk. But I'd never have made the offer to come here unless I'd been sure, very sure, that I could make it work. I want you more than I want the adventure and the freedom. I love you with all my heart. Is that enough?"

She smiled with her heart in her eyes. "It's enough," she said huskily.

He seemed to relax then, as if he'd been holding his breath the whole while. His eyes closed and he shivered. "Thank God," he said reverently.

"You didn't think I was going to say no?" she asked, shocked. "Good Lord, the sexiest man in town offers me a wedding ring and you think I'm going to say no?"

He pursed his lips. "Sexy, huh?"

"You seduced me," she pointed out. "Only a very sexy man could have managed that." She frowned. "Of course, you did drug me first," she added gleefully.

"You were hysterical," he began.

"I was in love," she countered, smiling. "And I wasn't

all that sedated." She blushed. "But I did think it was a dream. You see, I'd had sort of the same dream since I was…well, since I was about sixteen."

His lips parted on a shocked breath. "That long?"

She nodded. "I couldn't even get interested in anybody else. But you didn't want me…"

"I did want you," he countered. "That's why I was horrible to you. But never again," he promised huskily. "Never again. I'm going to work very hard at being a good husband and father. You won't regret it, Callie. I swear you won't."

"I know that. You won't regret it, either," she promised. She placed her hand over his big one, that still lay gently against her stomach. "And I never guessed," she whispered, smiling secretly. Her eyes brimmed over with excitement. "I'm so happy," she told him brokenly. "And so scared. Babies don't come with instruction manuals."

"We have Lou Coltrain, who's much better than an instruction manual," he pointed out with a grin. "And speaking of Lou, did you get those vitamins she prescribed?"

"Well, not yet," she began.

"They're prenatal vitamins," he added, chuckling. "You're going to be amazed at how good you feel. Not to mention how lucky you are," he added blithely, "to have a husband who knows exactly what to expect all through your pregnancy." He kissed her softly. "After the baby comes, I might finish my residency and go into practice with the Coltrains," he added.

That meant real commitment, she realized. He was giving up every vestige of the old life for her. Well, almost. She knew he'd keep his hand in with Eb Scott's operation. But the last of Jacobsville's mercenaries was ready to leave the past behind and start again.

So many beautiful memories are about to be created here, she thought as she looked around her from the shelter of Micah's hard arms. She pressed close with a sigh. "After the pain, the pleasure," she whispered.

"What was that?"

"Nothing. Just something I heard when I was younger." She didn't add that it was something her father had said. That was the one bridge she hadn't yet crossed. It would have to be faced. But, she thought, clinging to Micah in the warmth of the sun, not right now...

Micah drove her by the pharmacy on the way back to her apartment. He stood with her while Nancy, the dark-haired, dark-eyed pharmacist filled the prescription, trying not to grin too widely at the picture they made together.

"I suppose you know what these are for?" Nancy asked Callie.

Callie smiled and looked up at Micah, who smiled back with the same tenderness. "Oh, yes," she said softly.

He pulled her close for an instant, before he offered his credit card to pay for them. "We're getting married Sunday at the Methodist church," Micah told her and the others at the counter. "You're all invited... 2:00 p.m. sharp."

Nancy's eyes twinkled. "We, uh, heard that from the minister already," she said, clearing her throat as Callie gaped at her.

Micah chuckled at Callie's expression. "You live in a small town, and you didn't think everybody would know already?"

"But you hadn't told me yet!" she accused.

He shrugged. "It didn't seem too smart to announce that I'd arranged a wedding that you hadn't even agreed to yet."

"And they say women keep secrets!" she said on a rough breath.

"Not half as good as men do, sweetheart," Micah told her gently. He glanced around at a sudden commotion behind them. Two of the Hart brothers, Rey and Leo, were almost trampling people in their rush to get to the prescription counter.

"Have to have this as soon as possible, sorry!" Rey exclaimed, pressing a prescription into Nancy's hands with what looked like desperation.

"It's an emergency!" Leo seconded.

Nancy's eyes widened. She looked at the brothers with astonishment. "An emergency? This is a prescription for anti-inflammatories…"

"For our cook," Leo said. "Her hands hurt, she said. She can't make biscuits. We rushed her right over to Lou Coltrain and she said it was arthritis." He grimaced. "*Pleaaase* hurry? We didn't get any breakfast at all!"

Callie had her hand over her mouth trying not to have hysterics. Micah just looked puzzled. Apparently he didn't know about the famous biscuit mania.

Leo sounded as if he was starving. Amazing, a big, tall man with a frame like that attempting to look emaciated. Rey was tall and thin, and he did look as if he needed a feeding. Nancy went to fill the prescriptions.

"Sorry," Rey muttered as he glanced behind him and Leo at the people they'd rushed past to get their prescription filled. He tried to smile. He wasn't really good at it. He cleared his throat self-consciously. "Chocolates," he reminded Leo.

"Right over there," Leo agreed somberly. "We'd better get two boxes. And some of that cream stuff for arthritis, and there's some sort of joint formula…"

"And the We're Sorry card," Rey added, mumbling something about shortsightedness and loose tongues as they stomped off down the aisle with two pairs of spurs jingling musically from the heels of their boots.

Nancy handed Micah the credit card receipt, which he signed and gave Callie a pert grin as she went back to work.

Callie followed Micah out the door, letting loose a barrage of laughter when they reached the Porsche. By the time they got to her apartment, he was laughing, too, at the town's most notorious biscuit eaters.

Jack Steele was overjoyed at the news they had for him. For the next week he perked up as never before, taking a new interest in life and looking forward to having a daughter-in-law and a grandchild. The news that he was going to live with them disturbed him, he thought they needed privacy, but they insisted. He gave in. There was no mistaking their genuine love for him, or their delight in his company. He felt like the richest man on earth.

Callie, meanwhile, had an unexpected phone call from her father, who was back in town and anxious to see her. She met him in Barbara's café on her lunch hour from the law office, curious and nervous after so many years away from him.

Her father had black hair with silver at his temples and dark blue eyes. He was somber, quiet, unassuming and guilt was written all over him.

After they'd both ordered salads and drinks, her father gave her a long, hesitant scrutiny.

"You look so much like my mother," he said unexpectedly. "She had the same shaped eyes you do, and the same color."

Callie looked down at her salad. "Do I?"

He laid down his fork and leaned forward on his elbows. "I've been an idiot. How do I apologize for years of neglect, for letting you be put through hell in foster homes?" he asked quietly. "When I knew what had happened to you, I was too ashamed even to phone. Your mother had only just told me the truth and after the private detective I hired gave me the file on you, I couldn't take it. I went to Europe and stayed for a month. I don't even remember what I did there." He grimaced at Callie's expression. "I'm so ashamed. Even if you hadn't been my biological child, you'd lived in my house, I'd loved you, protected you." He lowered his shamed eyes to his plate. "Pride. It was nothing but pride. I couldn't bear thinking that you were another man's child. You paid for my cruelty, all those years." He drew in a long breath and looked up at her sadly. "You're my daughter. But I don't deserve you." He made an awkward motion. "So if you don't want to have anything to do with me, that's all right. I'll understand. I've been a dead bust as a father."

She could see the torment in his eyes. Her mother had done something unspeakably cruel to both of them with her lies. The bond they'd formed had been broken, tragically. She remembered the loneliness of her childhood, the misery of belonging nowhere. But now she had Micah and a child on the way, and Jack Steele as well. She'd landed on her feet, grown strong, learned to cope with life. She'd even fought off drug dealing thugs, all by herself, that night in Nassau when her child had been conceived. She felt so mature now, so capable. She smiled slowly. She'd lectured Micah about forgiveness. Here was her best chance to prove that she believed her own words.

"You're going to be a grandfather," she said simply. "Micah and I are getting married Sunday afternoon at two o'clock in the Methodist church. You and Jack Steele could both give me away if you like." She grinned. "It will raise eyebrows everywhere!"

He seemed shocked. His blue eyes misted and he bit his lip. "A grandfather." He laughed self-consciously and looked away long enough to brush away something that looked suspiciously wet. "I like that." He glanced back at her. "Yes. I'd like to give you away. I'd like to get you back even more, Callie. I'm…sorry."

When he choked up like that, she was beyond touched. She got up from her seat and went around to hug him to her. The café was crowded and she didn't care. She held him close and laid her cheek on his hair, feeling his shoulders shake. It was, in so many ways, one of the most poignant experiences of her young life.

"It's okay, Papa," she whispered, having called him that when she was barely school age. "It's okay now."

He held her tighter and he didn't give a damn that he was crying and half of Jacobsville could see him. He had his daughter back, against all the odds.

Callie felt like that, too. She met Barbara's eyes over the counter and smiled through her tears. Barbara nodded, and smiled, and reached for a napkin. It was so much like a new start. Everything was fresh and sweet and life was blessed. She was never again going to take anything for granted as long as she lived!

The wedding was an event. Callie had an imported gown from Paris, despite the rush to get it in time. Micah wore a morning coat. All the local mercenaries and the gang from the island, including Bojo, Peter, Rodrigo and Mac were there, along with Pogo and Maddie. And, really, Callie thought, Maddie did resemble her, but the older woman was much more athletic and oddly pretty. She smiled broadly at Callie as she stood beside a man Callie didn't recognize, with jet-black hair and eyes and what was obviously a prosthetic arm. There were a lot of men she didn't know. Probably Micah had contacts everywhere, and when word of the marriage had gotten out, they all came running to see if the rumors were true. Some of them looked astonished, but most were grinning widely.

The ceremony was brief, but beautiful. Micah pulled up the veil Callie wore, and kissed her for the first time as his wife.

"When we're finished, you have to read the inscription in your wedding band," he whispered against her soft mouth.

"Don't make me wait," she teased. "What does it say?"

He clasped her hand to his chest, ignoring the glowing faces of the audience. "It says 'forever,' Callie. And it means forever. I'll love you until I close my eyes for the last time. And even afterward, I'll love you."

She cried as he kissed her. It was the most beautiful thing he'd ever said to her. She whispered the words back to him, under her breath, while a soft sound rippled through the church. The couple at the rose-decked altar were so much in love that they fairly glowed with it.

They walked out under a cloud of rose petals and rice and Callie stopped and threw her bouquet as they reached the limousine that would take them to the airport. They were flying to Scotland for their honeymoon, to a little thatched cottage that belonged to Mac and had been loaned to them for the occasion. A romantic gesture from a practical and very unromantic man, that had touched Callie greatly.

Jack Steele, who was staying at the ranch with Micah's new foreman and his wife, waved them off with tears in his eyes, standing next to Kane Kirby, who was doing the same. The two men had become friends already, both avid poker players and old war movie fanatics.

"The last mercenary," she whispered. "And you didn't get away, after all."

"Not the last," he murmured, glancing toward his old comrades and Peter, their newest member, all of whom were silently easing away toward the parking lot. He smiled down at her. "But the happiest," he added, bending to kiss her. "Wave bye at both our papas and let's go. I can't wait to get you alone, Mrs. Steele!"

She chuckled and blushed prettily. "That makes two of us!"

She waved and climbed into the car with her acres of silk and lace and waited for Micah to pile in beside her. The door closed. The car drove away to the excited cries of good luck that followed it. Inside, two newlyweds were wrapped up close in each others' arms, oblivious to everything else. Micah cradled Callie in his arms and thanked God for second chances. He recalled Callie's soft words: After the pain, the pleasure. He closed his eyes and sighed. The pleasure had just begun.

\* \* \* \* \*

Dear Reader,

Every once in a while, a character stands out for an author and becomes unforgettable. Noah Laramie was one of those characters, and he remains one of my favorites. You see, Noah is a little bit different. He's an amputee.

But you know, Noah is so much more than his disability. He's a brother and a soldier, a cowboy and a friend and, despite the fact that he is missing an arm, I think he's drop-dead sexy. Lily Germaine thinks so, too. As I was writing, I found his handicap fading into the background as I got caught up in telling their love story. Which is just as it should be—looking beyond the physical imperfections to the heart within.

You can find out more about my Larch Valley stories and all my series—including the Cadence Creek Cowboys series and my new books in the Harlequin American Romance line—by visiting my website at www.donnaalward.com. Just head on over to the Bookshelf page for more information and links.

Happy reading,

Donna

# HER LONE COWBOY

**Donna Alward**

In memory of Justice and Juliana.
Always loved.

# *Chapter 1*

The blade nicked the skin, turning the shaving cream around it pink. Noah swore, rinsed the razor in the sink of hot water, angled his head and tried again.

He felt like a baby, learning everything again for the first time. Letting out a breath, he jutted his chin and swiped the blade over his jaw once more, this time the path even and smooth. It was a good thing. He had three other nicks to attest to the poor job he was doing.

He made faces, attempting to make the skin taut where he needed it to be. In the hospital, a pretty young nurse had always come around to shave him. She'd even cut his hair when he'd asked. All he'd had to do was hold the mirror. At the time he'd enjoyed the attention. But it had worn thin. He was a man used to doing things himself. The fact that a simple morning shave caused him to break out in a sweat made him angry. At himself. At the world in general.

He held the razor in midair as there was a knock on the door.

It had to be Andrew, he reasoned. No one else really knew he was back, and that was just the way he wanted it. He scraped more cream off his face, cleaning the blade in the water. Andrew, with the familiarity of being a younger brother, would let himself in. And Andrew wouldn't care about the mess around the place.

But then the knock came again and his stomach did a slow twist. What if it wasn't Andrew? He wrinkled his brow. It could be Andrew's fiancée, Jen. Jen had been with Andrew the day they'd picked him up at the airport. Noah was only *slightly* self-conscious around Jen.

A third time it sounded, and with a growl he put down the razor and grabbed a hand towel, stomping out of the bathroom. If people with two good arms couldn't open a door…or take a hint for that matter…

Holding the towel in his fingers, he reached out and turned the knob. "Keep your pants on," he commanded, and then froze.

Not Andrew. Not even Jen. Instead, the most beautiful woman he'd seen in forever stood on his doorstep. For a moment his gaze caught on her long, dark hair, clear skin, and finally a pair of brilliant blue eyes. Her eyebrows raised, making him feel like a child caught in a tantrum. And with a huffy sound, she brushed by him carrying a cardboard box.

Noah stared at the figure which was now heading toward his very small kitchen. What the hell? Wordlessly she put the box down and started unpacking it. In his kitchen. On his countertop.

He went to slam the door and realized he would have to forgo the satisfaction. At least he'd remembered to pin up his shirtsleeve this morning. He looked back at the kitchen. The woman had stopped her unpacking and was watching him now with undisguised interest. He felt color and heat infuse his cheeks. The last thing he wanted was morbid curiosity about his condition, or worse…pity.

He affected his best scowl. "Did you come to get a good look at the cripple?"

Lily saw Noah Laramie blush, saw him struggle and then heard the harsh words. Noah was a bad-tempered bear with a chip on his shoulder the size of a brick. So far he'd yelled at her at the door and then accused her of coming here to gawk. It was just too bad for him she was used to dealing with teenagers all day, and the way Noah was looking at her right now said *belligerence covering insecurity.* Not that she could blame him. She was a complete stranger. A smile quivered at the corner of her lips. "Are you trying to scare me away?"

His mouth dropped open for the smallest second, then he put his guard back up again and scowled. "Is it working?"

"No. You need to work on your big bad wolf impression."

"Where I come from people wait to be invited in."

Lily fired straight back, "Where I come from, people don't get yelled at, at the door."

She left the supplies on the counter and went out into the living room. She gave the pinned-up sleeve where his arm used to be no more than a glance, determined not to stare. Curiosity about how it had happened burned within her, but it would be the height of impoliteness to ask. Neither Jen nor Andrew had mentioned anything about it beyond that it had happened.

She caught her breath as they seemed to square off. His build was imposing despite the obvious. Taller than his brother, Andrew, she guessed him to be at least six-two, and even though there had to have been a distinct lack of physical activity since his injury, he was still lean and muscled. His short, dark hair was a rumpled mess, and his chin was still covered in shaving cream.

Her smile blossomed completely at the sight. "It's hard to be afraid of a man whose face resembles Santa Claus."

"Dammit," he mumbled, taking the towel and hastily wiping off the remnants of white foam. "Who *are* you?"

"I'm Lily Germaine." Without thinking, she held out her hand. Only to realize that Noah did not have a right hand to shake hers with. This time it was her cheeks that flushed and she dropped the hand back to her side.

"It's all right. I forget sometimes, too."

The quietly spoken response did more to elicit her sympathy than the sight of him had.

"I'm a friend of Jen and Andrew's. They asked me to stop by."

"Why?"

She took another step forward and looked up into his face. There were patches where he'd missed with the razor, the dark stubble shadowing a strong jaw. "Jen wanted me to deliver some groceries." She hesitated for a second. "She said you found shopping difficult and could use…"

Again she faltered. Ordinary sayings now suddenly

took on new meaning. The last thing she wanted to do was insult him.

"Use a hand?"

His lips were a hard line, and the dark look in his eyes nearly sent her scuttling back to her car. But he couldn't ignore the obvious. He couldn't drive himself to the grocery store, and carting bags inside would be a definite chore. She lifted her chin. "In a manner of speaking."

He dropped the towel on the top of an armchair, putting his left hand in his jeans pocket. "Let's just get it out of the way. I'm Noah Laramie, and I've lost an arm. It is what it is. No need to dance around it. Or worry about what's going to come out of your mouth."

"It's not the appendage coming *out* of my mouth that's the problem at the moment. It's the one I keep putting *in* it." She tried a hopeful smile, relieved when the hard lines of his face relaxed. Goodness, he *was* handsome when he wasn't being so sharp and abrasive.

"Jen's a mother hen," he stated. "I'm fine. So no need to bring in whatever it is you've brought in."

Lily's smile faded. Jen hadn't said anything about the resistance Lily was suddenly facing. Oh, no. Jen had said what a teasing, easygoing guy Noah had been when they had all been growing up together—a time well before Lily had come to Larch Valley. Despite his earlier frankness in speaking, she got the feeling that trying to convince him of anything was about as effective as talking to a turnip and expecting a response. Once Noah Laramie made up his mind, she doubted anyone could budge it.

"I'm also supposed to give you a ride to Lazy L today."

"Andrew will come and get me."

"Andrew had to go to Pincher Creek."

"Then Jen."

"Jen has a bakery to open, and she asked if I'd drop these things over and give you a lift. You might as well get used to it, Laramie. I'm your chauffeur, like it or not."

After one hard, brittle glare, he stalked back down the hall toward the bathroom. "Fine. For *today*."

She heard him shutting doors—loudly—while she put away the groceries Jen had asked her to deliver. Oh, he was a tough one. She shook her head as she opened the fridge. Inside was half a brick of cheese, a bottle of ketchup, a jar of mustard and perhaps three tablespoons of milk left in a plastic jug. She sighed, then stocked the shelves with milk, fruit, fresh vegetables and several small packages of meat. What on earth was the man eating? Clearly he'd managed, because the sink was full of dirty dishes. The furniture needed a dusting, and she wondered if he'd managed to do any laundry.

There'd been no thought of turning down Jen's request, though. Jen was her best friend and she'd do anything for her.

Even if this was the first real day of summer vacation. She could have been sleeping in, drinking coffee on her patio, sunbathing in her backyard.

She sighed. It all seemed frivolous beside Noah's problems. Losing an arm in combat and then coming home after so many years away… She couldn't blame him if housework really wasn't on the top of his list of things to do. Right now his job was to get better. Maybe he could use some help keeping the house shipshape.

When he came back out, she'd managed to finish putting groceries away and tidied the living room. She was fluffing a cushion when his deep voice sounded behind her.

"Don't do that."

She straightened and turned. He'd finished shaving, his freshly bladed face clean and smooth, with only a few telltale blemishes where he'd nicked himself. His eyes were a deep blue, dark enough that the color was nearly indiscernible. As he stood at the gap between the hall and living room, she realized once more how imposing a figure he really was. He was a big man, a man who'd been a soldier since he'd turned nineteen. His raw masculinity did queer things to her insides, and she unconsciously took a step backward. Where had that flare of attraction come from? It certainly didn't make sense. And it was very unwelcome. She definitely couldn't be *interested*.

Besides, she didn't take well to the way he seemed to demand things. As if he were giving an order. She leveled her gaze. "Why not?"

"Because I can do it myself."

She made a wrinkle above her nose. "And you haven't been because?"

That seemed to make him pause. He stared at her and she was determined not to look away. She wasn't used to giving in to intimidation. She never would have lasted through three years of sixteen-year-olds otherwise! She hadn't really considered that teaching high school would be good preparation for dealing with garrulous ex-soldiers. Go figure.

"Because I haven't bothered."

She smiled frostily. "So now you needn't bother. I'm perfectly capable."

He came farther into the room. "Don't you have a job?"

She straightened a throw blanket along the back of the sofa, trying to slow the beating of her heart. Something had happened in the moment when he'd taken a step toward her. Something had passed between his eyes and hers and had set her pulse stammering.

"I'm a home economics teacher at the high school."

He snorted. "You're barely older than they are."

She smoothed a hand over the blanket and tilted her nose into the air. "I'm twenty-seven, thank you. I've been teaching there for three years."

"So this is how you spend your summer vacation. Charity?" He said it as if it was a dirty word.

"It's hardly charity, Noah." His name sounded foreign on her tongue, as though she shouldn't be using it. What was the other option? Mr. Laramie? Captain? That had been his rank. Neither name seemed to fit the enigmatic stranger before her.

"How much did Andrew pay you to come here today?" His gaze was sharp, pinning her and making a lie impossible.

"Nothing. I did Jen a favor, delivering some groceries and giving you a ride. Although from the looks of this place, it could stand some cleaning up. I could do that, too," she offered.

"What would you charge?"

Charge? Lily stared at him, trying to puzzle him out. The carefree, fun boy Jen had described was nothing like the Noah she was meeting. She wondered if combat had changed him. Or if it was just leaving a piece of himself on the battlefield that had done it. Either way, taking money for a few hours' worth of tidying just felt wrong.

"I wouldn't dream of charging you a penny."

He turned away. "That's charity. I won't have it." He paused, considering, and faced her again. His eyes flickered over the tidy living room and the chaotic kitchen beyond, assessing the mess. "If you were to stay, just for today, I'll write you a check. I am able."

Goodness, Lily knew that. Everyone in Larch Valley knew that Andrew had bought out Noah's half of the ranch. Plus, Noah had been a single officer without a family to support at home. But that was hardly the point.

"Friends help friends," she replied simply.

"Yes, but you are not my friend. You are Jen's friend, and that is different."

She absorbed the snub. It wasn't different, not really. Did he have no concept of doing a favor for a friend? By helping him she was also putting Jen's and Andrew's minds at ease.

And yet, she somehow knew that to say either of those things would cause him to protest further. His pride would demand it.

"If that's the way it must be, then fine." She simply wouldn't cash any check that he wrote. Besides, it was only this one time. It wasn't as though this would be an ongoing issue.

"Agreed." He gave a sharp nod. "Now, if you'll run me out to Lazy L, seeing as I have no other way of getting there today, that will be the end of it."

She watched with barely concealed curiosity as he went to the door and got his boots, then sat on a nearby stool to put them on. It took him a little longer than it normally would have, but he gripped the pullstrap with his left hand and shoved his foot inside. He did the same with the other foot, and then spent several moments trying to fit his pant leg over top.

She almost offered to help, but if he didn't want her to tidy a cushion, he certainly would take offense to her offer to straighten the hem of his jeans.

"If you're ready," she said quietly.

He stomped out the door without a backward glance. Lily shut the door behind her with a sigh.

She had made a promise to a friend. And she wouldn't go back on it, no matter how stubborn Noah might be.

After she'd dropped him off at Lazy L, Lily went back to the house. He hadn't bothered to lock the door—many people didn't in the small town—and so she went back inside to continue what she'd started while he'd been getting ready.

She ran the sink full of hot, soapy water and began washing the pile of dishes. Jen had called her last night, sounding utterly exhausted, needing to get up at 4:00 a.m. to be at Snickerdoodles for the day. Lily hadn't thought twice about saying yes to what sounded like a simple request.

Jen had befriended Lily when she'd first come to town, had introduced her around and made her feel that she'd finally found a home. The kind of home she'd never had growing up in Toronto. Home, hah. Home had consisted of a series of apartments, never settling in one place for long. It had meant a new school more years than not, new classmates, new routines. Lily had read *Anne of Green Gables* as a child and had keenly felt Anne's longing for a "bosom friend." But Lily had always been hesitant, knowing that she would end up leaving friends behind when they moved again.

But then she'd come to Larch Valley for her job, and had fallen in love with the town and its people. Jen was the closest thing Lily had ever had to a sister, when it came right down to it. And now Lily was an adult and could make her own choices. And if now and then her town house felt a bit lonely, that was okay. Having a place to belong was enough. And she had a good life. She enjoyed her job. She had friends. She filled her spare time with fun projects.

Not that dealing with Noah Laramie this morning could be classified as fun.

As she wiped a plate and placed it in the cupboard, she decided that the best thing to do was ignore the fact that this person happened to be a very tall, very handsome ex-soldier who'd been a hero on the battlefield. He was the brother of a friend. A cranky, proud brother at that.

Lily worked clear through the afternoon, cleaning the small house until it sparkled, feeling a sense of satisfaction at the shining floors and gleaming appliances. She put some of the chicken breasts she'd brought in to marinate. From the look of it, Noah had been eating simple meal-in-a-box type food. A decent dinner would do him good. She was putting together a salad when Andrew's truck drove in the yard, and Noah got out—along with Andrew and Jen. She thought of the chicken on the grill out back. She'd made four breasts so he would have leftovers. Oh, well. At least there was enough if they all stayed for dinner.

Noah stomped inside, using his toes to push off his boots. "You're still here?"

She wiped her hands on a dish towel and opened her mouth to retort when Jen stepped in.

"Noah! What a greeting!"

His gaze skittered away from Lily's as he colored. "Sorry," he murmured. Andrew paid no attention, and Jen blew by through to the kitchen, a parcel in her hands. Lily waited for Noah to look back at her.

When he did, she saw he was embarrassed at the harsh tone he'd used. He shifted his weight on his heels. "I spoke sharply. I just…I figured you'd be finished by now."

"I made you dinner," she said. And yet she was compelled to say more. He had to know this wasn't about the money. "I also made a promise," she said softly, so the others couldn't hear. "And I don't go back on my promises. Not ever." She swallowed, knowing exactly how true that was. Her mind flitted back to the day everything in her life had changed. She had been the one who'd stayed. Who'd waited, hoping. Who had kept her promise. Curtis was the one who had left without a word, breaking her heart in the process.

"Your promise wasn't to me." Noah interrupted her thoughts.

"A promise is a promise just the same."

The words hung for a few moments, until Noah seemed to accept that she meant them. "I didn't know they were both coming," he said gruffly.

"It's your house. You don't need to apologize to me. I was going to leave leftovers for you to have another time, but there's enough food for the three of you. Which reminds me, I need to check on the barbecue."

She disappeared outside, going to flip the chicken and taking a breath, happy to get away from the tense atmosphere that had seemed to envelop her both times she'd been with Noah. For a man in such a predicament, he certainly was independent. He was prepared to fight her every step of the way, it seemed. That was fine. She even admired his tenacity—it spoke of a strength of character. As she turned the chicken over with tongs, she thought of the long days of her summer vacation and wondered how he was going to manage here. There was nothing that said she couldn't help him out while he was away at Lazy L. Cleaning, cooking, sewing…the domestic arena was her specialty. It would give her something to keep busy with until school went back in September.

She got the feeling that convincing him would be quite another matter.

When she went back inside, Jen had set the table for four. "Oh," Lily said, surprised. "I'm not staying. You three enjoy."

"But of course you're staying." Jen butted in again, sticking her head in the refrigerator for the salad dressing Lily had brought in with the groceries. She turned around with the bottle in her hand. "We both came because we want to talk to you and Noah about something."

Lily got a strange, dark feeling in the middle of her chest, and she didn't need to look to feel Noah's eyes on her. What on earth could they want to speak to both of them about? Lily swallowed. Today had shown that she and Noah had next to nothing in common.

She got out a plate for the chicken and a bowl for the pilaf that was finishing up on the stove. "And I need to stay for dinner for this?"

Andrew broke in. "Yep, 'fraid so, Lil. You got a corkscrew around here?"

Lily looked at Noah and raised an eyebrow, questioning. Whatever it was, Andrew and Jen were in on it together. Noah seemed to sense it, too, and for a second she felt a brief sense of solidarity with him. Considering their inauspicious beginning today, Lily did not have a good feeling.

"Try the second drawer," Noah suggested, his face unreadable. "If not, I have a multi-tool with one on it somewhere."

She couldn't tell if he wanted her to stay or not. Surely not, after the rude reception she'd received both times he'd found her here. Her earlier thought about helping him more seemed foolish now. She opened the second drawer he'd nodded at and scrounged around, finally finding a corkscrew. She handed it to Andrew, who uncorked a bottle of white wine while Jen took out glasses.

"I recognize these," Noah said suddenly, as Jen handed out the wine.

"They were Mom and Dad's," Andrew answered. He shared a look with Jen and smiled. "When you asked me to find you a place to rent, Jen thought bringing some things over from the house might make you feel at home."

Noah stared at the wineglass, his lips a thin, inscrutable line.

Jen stepped forward. "We're in the process of combining the two houses anyway, with the wedding coming up."

Again Jen and Andrew shared a look, and Lily got that unsettled feeling in her chest again. It was plain as day Jen and Andrew were ecstatic about their upcoming nuptials, but the mere mention of the word *wedding* made Lily uncomfortable. It brought back so many memories, and none of them good. "Jen, can you put the pilaf in a bowl? I'm going to get the chicken off the grill."

Lily escaped to the backyard, only to realize she'd forgotten the plate for the meat. When she turned around, Noah was behind her, holding it out, a dry, amused smile barely quivering at the edges of his mouth.

"Thank you."

She took the plate and went back to the barbecue. Noah stepped up behind her, and she tried to ignore his presence even though she could feel him there. The air was different somehow.

"They're up to something."

His deep voice came from behind her, and she stifled a shiver that slid deliciously along her spine. "I agree."

"Any idea what that might be?"

Her cheeks flamed, and it had nothing to do with the heat from the barbecue and a lot more to do with the intimate tone of his voice. "No idea," she replied, sounding slightly strangled.

She put the breasts one by one on the plate.

"Hmm," came his voice again, not as harsh but definitely speculative. "Lily Germaine, who seemed completely unflappable to me today, is suddenly put off her stride with wedding talk. Interesting."

She focused on placing the meat on the plate. "Don't be silly." *And don't psychoanalyze me,* she thought.

"I'm many things, Miss Germaine, but silly is one I've yet to be called. I know what a tactical retreat looks like."

She put the cover down on the barbecue and faced him. Granted, wedding talk did tend to put her off the mark. Some disappointments left scars that would never be completely healed. But she'd never say a word to Jen about it. It was her past, her problem, not Jen's. She was happy for her and for Andrew.

"I am thrilled for both of them. They love each other very much."

She went to go by him, but he stopped her with his hand on her arm. "I wasn't talking about them. I was talking about you. I saw the look on your face just now."

Lily looked up, found his eyes serious. As if she were going to tell him anything. If she hadn't breathed a word to her best friend, she certainly wasn't going to spill her guts to some grumpy stranger she'd met less than twelve hours earlier.

"You know as much about me as you need to," she replied carefully, moving away from the warm feel of his hand on her bicep.

"I doubt that," he replied, following her to the back steps.

"And I know next to nothing about you," she said, desperately trying to change the subject. "Besides the fact that you are very grumpy in the morning. Actually, not just the morning, it seems."

They paused, she on the first step and he on the soft grass beneath her, so that their eyes were nearly level. Her heart thumped against her ribs.

"I *am* sorry about today," he said quietly, and Lily knew he was sincere.

"Apology accepted," she breathed. His gaze bored into her and she nibbled on her lower lip.

"The thing is, Lily, I never used to be this moody." Once he admitted it he stepped back, surprise blanking his face. "I don't know why I just said that."

Lily's teeth released her lip and she tried a tentative smile. "Maybe you're trying to make a good impression?"

"I think that ship already sailed."

Then they were smiling at each other. When Lily realized it, and also that they'd been standing there for several seconds, she straightened her shoulders. "We should go in, dinner is ready," she murmured.

Inside, she pasted on a smile for appearances, though Jen's glow eclipsed everyone at the table. Once plates were filled, Andrew lifted his glass, inviting everyone to do the same.

"I want to propose a toast...." He reached out and took Jen's hand in his. "To Jen, for saying yes. To Noah, for coming home. And to Lily, for being her usual generous self."

Lily's smile wobbled just the tiniest bit as they touched rims and sipped. It was clear that Andrew and Jen were completely happy and it created a bittersweet ache in her chest. Andrew squeezed Jen's hand and grinned. "It's as good a time as any," he said. "We came here tonight to...well, Noah, you're my brother. I came to ask you to be my best man."

"And I want you to be my maid of honor," Jen added, beaming at Lily. They both looked at Noah and Lily expectantly.

Lily gaped; Noah looked down at his plate. After a few seconds of silence, they looked at each other. Best man. Maid of honor. Dresses and tuxes, cake and flowers.

At the thought of having to walk up an aisle in a gown...Lily felt the color drain from her cheeks. She couldn't do it. Even as a bridesmaid, she'd be a complete fraud.

At her stunned silence, Jen's face took on a stubborn expression that Lily recognized as her "I'm getting my way" look.

"I...I thought you'd want Lucy." Lily struggled to come up with something to say to cover the confusion in her heart. She hadn't been to a wedding since her own failed attempt. It had been easy to make excuses not to attend over the years. A conflicting schedule, an illness. She had never breathed a word of it to anyone.

But she couldn't make those halfhearted excuses this time. Because right now this wasn't about *Lily*. It was about the best friend she'd ever known, and she felt guilty for hesitating for even a second.

"Lucy is seven months pregnant. Besides, the one I really want is you."

Lily had no response to that. If she were getting married—which she most definitely was not, not now and not in any future she could envision—it would be Jen she'd want beside her.

"Of course I'll do it," Lily replied, reaching over and taking Jen's hand, giving her fingers a squeeze. "I'm honored. You just took me by surprise, that's all." She smiled, feeling as if she was breaking inside. "I've never been a bridesmaid before."

"And Noah," Jen went on, her voice soft. "You're Andrew's brother. His flesh and blood. It would mean so much to him. And…to your father, don't you think?"

Lily studied him, saw the battle waging within. He blinked—was that a sheen of moisture in his eyes? She knew he'd never made it back for his father's funeral. Had he even found time to grieve in the midst of all his troubles?

He gave a small cough and acquiesced. "Fine. I'll do it."

"Wonderful!" Jen bubbled over, taking a drink of wine and leaning into Andrew's shoulder. "I told you," she chided her fiancé. Then she beamed at the two of them.

"And, Noah, I'm sure Lily will help you, won't you, Lil? Noah will need a tuxedo." She winked at Noah. "Besides, women do tend to know what needs to be done for weddings."

A lump clogged Lily's throat. Of course she knew what needed to be done. She'd been through it all before. The anguish of seeing Curtis walk away from her before the vows had ever been spoken pierced her heart even now. And Noah…how was he feeling about being asked? He'd only just arrived home from the hospital.

Lily met Noah's despairing gaze, her plans of a relaxing and complication-free school break suddenly out the window. What had they both gotten themselves into?

# Chapter 2

While Jen bubbled away about the wedding plans and Andrew broke in occasionally with news of the Rescue Ranch, Lily remained very aware of Noah on her right. He said little, instead focusing on his meal and speaking to Andrew about the horses he'd be working with. Lily was wondering if she'd ever get time to catch her breath. All she'd agreed to was delivering a box of groceries, and somehow before the end of the day she was maid of honor and agreeing to guide Noah with his share of best man duties.

"We set a date," Jen announced. "The second weekend in August."

"That's only six weeks away!" Lily put down her fork with a clatter.

Jen poured more wine into Lily's glass before topping up Noah's. "We didn't want to wait. And we wanted to have it before you had to be back at school and, well, at some point Noah will be going back to work, I suppose. And that brings me to the next question. I…I have another favor to ask."

Lily's hand paused on the way to her glass. "Another favor?" She tried hard to keep the hesitation out of her voice. There was no way for Jen to know how difficult Lily would find simply being her maid of honor. The woman was planning her wedding after all. The most important day of a single girl's life. The day that was supposed to come along only once in a lifetime.

"I want you to make my dress, Lily. I don't want some off-the-rack factory dress. I want something that's just me."

Lily's lips fell open. She couldn't stop the rush of emotion at being asked. A woman's wedding dress was the most important article of clothing she would ever wear, and she would only wear it once. Lily's heart was touched by bittersweet emotion. "Oh, Jen."

"I don't know of anyone who could do this any better than you. We can take a day to go to Calgary to shop for materials. It would mean so much."

She could feel Noah's eyes on her, assessing. Lily had made only one other wedding dress before, and it hung in her closet as a white reminder of past mistakes. In one hour she had thought of her failed attempt at matrimony more than she had in the past few years. "Of course I will," she replied quietly. "I'm pleased you would even ask."

As she and Jen chatted about styles and material, Lily could see Noah out of the corner of her eye, providing a welcome distraction. The hinged salad utensils had solved any serving issue earlier, but she was suddenly aware of him struggling to slice into his chicken. He put down his fork and used his knife, but without his other hand, there was nothing to anchor the meat to the plate. Her eyes stung quite unexpectedly. Perhaps he had good reason to be cranky, certainly a better one than she could claim. Life for him was one adjustment after another as an amputee. Even something as simple as eating a meal had its challenges. It was easy to forget that when he was so full of pride and determination.

And she was sure that the last thing he would want was sympathy. What on earth could she possibly say that would help, and not cause embarrassment or humiliation?

She took a breath and turned to face him. "Would you like me to help you with that?"

The table went silent. Lily wished Andrew or Jen had said something, rather than pretend not to see him struggle. Now they were staring at her as if she'd committed a sin.

Noah picked up his fork and attempted to cut through his chicken with the blunt side of it. But even Lily could tell that the breast was just a little too thick, and that he wasn't as coordinated with his left hand as he would have been with his right. "Noah," she said quietly, all the while feeling Andrew's and Jen's shocked gazes settling on her face. But she focused on Noah.

"I can manage. I am not some two-year-old that needs help cutting his food." There was a hard edge to his voice and it was no less than she expected. And yet to avoid the obvious was wrong, and the only thing she could think of was to be forthright and honest.

"Of course not. And I would imagine you will find it

easier when you get a prosthetic. Until then…there is no shame in asking for assistance now and again."

He put down his fork and glared at her. "Again, I don't recall asking for your help."

"You need not ask for it to be offered."

The look he gave her was so complicated she found herself entangled. It was amazement at her persistence and gratitude and anger and annoyance all bound together with a tenuous thread of vulnerability.

He put his fork and knife on the plate and slid it to the side. Without any fuss, she picked up his knife and fork and cut the remainder of his chicken into bite-sized pieces. She laid the utensils back onto his plate and gave it back, picked up her own fork and took a bite of pilaf as if nothing had ever happened. It tasted dry in her mouth, but she was determined not to make a big production out of it.

"Thank you," he said quietly.

The talk around the dinner table resumed, but Lily couldn't get that haunted look in his eyes out of her head.

After dinner Noah and Andrew went into the backyard with coffee while Jen and Lily tidied the kitchen. Lily looked out the window over the sink as she dried a plate. Noah stood an inch or so taller than his brother, his wide back accentuated by the taut fabric of his shirt. A curl went through her stomach when she remembered how he'd looked at her when she had offered him her help.

"Andrew is so glad Noah came home to recuperate," Jen said, taking the dishcloth and wiping off the counter. "We weren't sure he would."

"Why not? This is his home." Lily tore her eyes away

from the view and looked at her friend. Jen's lips were unsmiling.

"He's stubborn. At least in that, he and Drew are alike. I think by Drew offering him a temporary job it helped. Noah's so independent, he would hate to be taken care of." Jen put the pilaf pot into the dishwater and turned to Lily. "Thank you for helping today. You really were a lifesaver. Juggling both businesses with wedding plans is proving a challenge."

Lily carefully dried the wineglasses and put them in the cupboard. "Summer holidays are slow. I thought about lending him a hand occasionally."

Jen smiled. "Of course you did."

Lily's nose went up at Jen's knowing tone. "What does that mean?"

"It's what you do, Lily. You make curtains and cook for potlucks and quilt crib sets." Jen smiled. "Lucy told me about the set you did for the baby. You do a wonderful job taking care of people."

Lily tried to accept the remarks as a compliment, instead of with a sting. She had always been that way. There had been times growing up that her little touches were all that made home bearable. Times when it had seemed she was the adult and her mother the child. As a result she'd seemed mature for her age.

"Maybe so," she replied, "but I doubt Noah would cotton to being 'taken care of.'" Lily rested her hip against the counter and twisted the dish towel in her hands. "The only way he would let me straighten up at all was to insist he pay me to do it."

Jen smiled then. "Like I said, stubborn."

Lily regarded her friend with suspicion. "Of course I have no intention of taking his money."

Jen stepped forward and put her hand on Lily's arm, smiling softly. "Of course not. We could have hired a maid for him, or nursing care. He could have hired them himself, if it weren't for his pride getting in the way. But that's not what he needs most, Lily."

Lily's gaze was automatically drawn to the two men again, sipping coffee and talking, though what they were saying wasn't audible in the kitchen.

"I know," she said quietly. She pictured him tugging on his cowboy boots with one hand, so determined to do things on his own. "He needs a friend."

"He couldn't ask for a better friend than you. I know I couldn't."

Lily couldn't resist her friend's heartfelt words, and pushed away the sad feelings that had been resurrected today. She loved Jen like a sister. "Friends I can do. At least you don't have to worry about us dating." She folded the dish towel and put it down on the counter. "Remember, Jen, I don't date cowboys. I should also have said, soldiers." She offered a cheeky smile. When Jen and Andrew had been working through their problems, Lily had made the comment about cowboys glibly and it had become a bit of a running joke between the two friends.

Staring at Noah now, though, she realized she had only been half kidding. There was a certain something about him that caught her attention—and held it. And that would be a mistake.

Jen laughed. "You and Noah? I can't picture it. Two more bullheaded people I've never met. It'd be like mixing oil and water. If I know Noah, this situation is only temporary. Once he gets adjusted, has time to think, he'll be making plans for his future. All I know is we're glad he's here now. Andrew needed the help with the stock and now he gets to have his brother as his best man. And this is a difficult time for Noah. It's fitting that he should be surrounded by family. Right now, we're the only family he has."

Noah said something to Andrew and Andrew laughed, and then Noah joined in. Something warm flooded through Lily at the sound of the laughter. In it was a sense of belonging, of being included.

Lily's gaze once again fixed on Noah's tall profile. Turned this way, his injury wasn't even noticeable. He looked strong, healthy, gorgeous.

She dropped her eyes quickly. No. That didn't matter. Not in the least. Jen was quite right in saying they weren't matched at all. And the last thing Lily was looking for was a boyfriend.

"Anyway," Jen went on, oblivious to the sudden turn in Lily's thoughts, "you handled him just like he needed tonight. He accepted it differently than he would have from me or from his brother. No fuss, no beating around the bush. He'll appreciate your plain speaking, even if he doesn't say it."

Lily took the clean pot and put it in a drawer. There was plain speaking…and then there were some things that just shouldn't be said at all.

It was only for a few weeks. She could be practical for that long. Absolutely.

Noah grabbed the twine in his gloved hand, heaved and lifted the bale at his side. He staggered a few steps and put it down again with a soft oath and a kick at the golden hay. Sweat trickled down his back. It wasn't so much the weight as the abrupt shift in balance he had to adjust to. He gripped the twine again, and lifted, this time planting his feet wider and distributing his weight more evenly. Once the bale was steady, he headed for the nearest fence in an awkward gait.

Working for Andrew was both a pleasure and a pain, he thought, as he cut the string and folded the knife back up using his thigh and left hand. He distributed the hay to the horses waiting most impatiently for their feed, pausing to rub the nose of a particularly old gelding. Andrew had brought this group nearer the barn for medical attention, rather than letting them graze on the sweeter, green grass of the pasture. Noah admired what his brother was doing, establishing a Rescue Ranch. If he hadn't supported the idea, he might have resisted selling his share to Andrew last year.

But he'd thought he'd be a career soldier. He'd never anticipated being back in Larch Valley again. Certainly not as ranch hand to his younger brother. *Oh, how the mighty have fallen,* he thought bitterly. Not that he held it against Andrew; his brother had been great. But it was a temporary thing, only until he adjusted and got clearance to return to duty. For now it kept him busy and in shape, two things that would speed his recovery.

He reached out and rubbed the nose of the mare, Pixie, one of the thinnest of Andrew's latest rescues. There was definitely something satisfying in having the freedom to work away all day on the ranch, with the sun and the fresh air for company. It provided as much healing as the endless rounds of therapy and doctor's appointments. He hated the poking and prodding, the endless talking about *how* he'd been injured, as if they expected him to fall apart at any moment. Treating him with kid gloves. He shoved another flake of hay into the corral. He'd made a mistake, that was all. As angry as he got sometimes, he thanked God every day that he'd been the one to suffer the consequences. It had been an error but it was his error, and his consequences.

Yet, that wasn't what people saw. Even with Andrew and Jen, everyone saw the injury first, rather than the man.

His mind thought back to Lily and how she'd offered to cut his meat that first night. She certainly hadn't given him the kid-glove treatment. He'd completely surprised himself in the backyard when he'd apologized and then explained about the moodiness. It was more than he'd revealed to anyone.

He didn't know what was in store for him, but he'd spent enough time deployed to know that he had to keep busy and that he'd die being behind a desk somewhere. And yet the army of today tried to keep its soldiers in service. So where did that leave him? He couldn't deny his abilities were compromised due to his handicap.

He shoved the last of the hay into the corral. Handicap, huh. He hated that word. Handicap, cripple, amputee. He'd heard them all and didn't accept any of them. And yet he had no alternative word to describe himself, either.

Most of all he hated needing help. As he reached the barn, he sighed, absently rubbing the ache in his right bicep, the only part of his limb that remained. Not long ago he'd been a commander of men. From there to needing his chicken cut in pieces. He lashed out and kicked a plastic tub sitting by the tack room door.

"Rough day?" Lily's sweet voice had him spinning around.

"What are you doing here?"

Lily looked pretty again, in a white sundress with some sort of stitching that made her waist look impossibly small. The slim straps on her shoulders set off her golden skin, and the wind ruffled the hem, drawing his attention to her bare legs and feet in intricate little sandals. Her toenails were painted a pastel pink.

"You really do need to work on your welcoming skills."

"You surprised me. Again. You have a habit of doing that, you know."

"No reason to shoot the messenger."

He couldn't help it; he laughed, looking her over with appraising eyes. She was a picture of femininity, and for a few seconds, he'd responded to her as a man would when faced with a beautiful woman. He'd flirted.

Until he saw her eyes shift.

"You wore a T-shirt today."

Her words were soft. Damn, she always spoke what was on her mind, didn't she! And just when he'd been thinking nice thoughts about her practical streak. He refused to look down at the empty place at his side, instead keeping his gaze on hers. She would have seen the stub sooner or later. Might as well be sooner.

"It gets too hot to wear long sleeves."

"And so that is…" She nodded slightly toward his shoulder, where a stretchy fabric covered the end of his arm.

"A stump sock." It was almost a relief to say it. "It protects the sheath, and, well, it looks nicer."

He spoke of his arm as if it were an entity separate from himself, he realized. Well, perhaps it was. It certainly was difficult to equate it with the man he'd been for years. A whole man.

"Does it hurt?"

The straightforward yet gentle question touched him, and he relaxed his shoulders. Lily didn't look away from him, or act strangely. She just said everything plainly, and yet with a compassionate concern that reached in and chased away his resentment.

"Sometimes," he admitted. "I have something that goes over top right now, getting it ready for a prosthetic. And the sock over that. Mostly it's just phantom pain."

She nodded again, her eyes liquid blue as she met his gaze. He couldn't believe he'd actually told her that much. What was it about her that put him off balance, made him tell her things? He'd have to watch that.

"Jen and I went shopping this afternoon. We got the material for her dress."

He blinked as she accepted his answer and changed the subject without offering the sympathetic platitudes he'd grown used to, or further prying. "That's good."

"Yes."

The conversation seemed to lull and Noah found himself gazing into her eyes again. He'd never met a woman as no-nonsense as Lily, and having that trait paired with such femininity was a potent combination. But that was the end of it. Even if he were interested, which he wasn't—*curious* would be a better word— what woman would want a man like him? Maybe *cripple* was a good word. He bore the scars to prove it. More than she knew. He saw the reminders every day when he looked in the mirror.

"I should get back to work."

"Oh…of course." She started to back away, then reconsidered and instead hurried forward, as if afraid she would change her mind. As she looked up at him, he saw a tiny wrinkle form in between her eyebrows and he had the sudden urge to touch it with his fingertip. Oh, Lily Germaine could be a dangerous woman if she wanted to be. It was just as well she was off-limits.

"Noah, wait." Lily stopped only a few feet away from him and looked up into his proud face. Faint freckles hid beneath his deepening tan that came from being in the sun. These past few minutes told her that things were even more awkward between them than before, and if they were going to stand up at the wedding they should at least come to an understanding. Getting through the wedding would be difficult enough without being at odds with him. A tingle went through her, thinking about how they would witness the marriage certificate together, or stand for pictures, or be seated together at the reception. Somehow she felt she needed an ally, rather than a cold stranger at her side.

"What is it?"

"I don't want things to be weird."

He laughed tightly. "Things are already weird. My whole life is different from what I'm used to."

She seized on the opening. "You see? I don't know what that means. And so I don't quite know what to say to you."

"You seem to manage quite well," Noah remarked. His cheekbones became hardened edges and his eyes darkened. "You don't miss a beat when it comes to telling me how it is."

Lily tried not to let the dark expression intimidate her. "You seemed like the kind of man that would appreciate plain speaking."

"I am." He raised an eyebrow, challenging her. "In the army I was also a stickler for insubordination."

She couldn't help it, she laughed. Oh, he could definitely be a piece of work, she thought. He was trying to provoke her. But all his stubborn ways made her far too aware of the breadth of his chest beneath the T-shirt or the way he had tiny tan lines in the wrinkles beside his eyes.

"Do you miss it?" She raised her own eyebrow. "All that bossing people around? It must be very different being here and working for Andrew."

He made an aggravated sound and turned away. She reached out and grabbed his left arm, catching him off guard and spinning him around.

"I'm sorry. That was too much."

He considered her for a moment. "Oh, I was just as used to taking orders as giving them. After all I am only a captain." She was treated to that small glimpse of a smile again. "And Andrew's all right. He made sure I had what I needed before coming back to Canada."

"From Afghanistan?"

He shook his head. "No, Germany. That's where I did most of my recuperating."

"But he didn't go see you, did he?" Lily imagined what it would be like to receive such a call about a family member. Would she run to her mother's side? She rather suspected she would, and for the first time in a long time she wondered about the life Jasmine was living.

Noah pulled away from her arm. "I'm glad he didn't."

Lily gasped. "Why? Surely having your family around you…"

And just like that, Noah's expression closed, as it had the first time they'd met.

"They only send family over if there's a good chance you won't make it back," he said stiffly. "So I'm glad Andrew never needed to come."

Lily felt very small all of a sudden. There was so much about Noah she didn't know, didn't understand. She wondered how he was making out keeping the house tidy, cooking, all the menial jobs left at the end of the day when he was done at the ranch. She had considered asking him to let her help while she and Jen were doing dishes that first night. Jen had looked exhausted during their excursion today, and Noah needed someone to help. Why not her?

"I'd like to help you, Noah. Even if it's running a vacuum over the floor and taking you to appointments. I know you have appointments, lots of them. And why bother Jen and Andrew when I clearly have the time?"

Noah spun on his heel, striding back to the barn. "I don't need a nursemaid. And my own truck will be here soon."

"Oh, for Pete's sake, I never said a word about nursing!" She scrambled after him, her sandals slapping on the concrete floor of the barn. "Why are you so determined to refuse assistance?"

"Because I need to learn to do it for myself."

"But you don't have to do it all at once, do you?"

He reached for a halter hanging on a hook and a lead, which he looped around his neck. He went back out to the small corral, whistling for Pixie, Lily's sandals sounding behind him. The small bay mare trotted over, and hooking the halter over his wrist he opened the gate and slid into the fenced area with her.

"Can't you find another pet project?"

"I hardly consider you a pet." She couldn't stop the

acidic reply and it brought a burst of laughter from his lips. She got the feeling he didn't laugh that often these days. She only wished she didn't feel as though it was at her expense.

She watched, amazed, as he lifted his upper right arm and slid the halter over the stump, and then used his left hand to rub Pixie's head, scratching beneath her forelock. Then he deftly retrieved the halter, slid it up past her nose and over her ears. Once it was secure, he took the lead from around his neck and hooked it on the ring at the bottom.

He led the horse to the gate and with his fingers and hips, maneuvered the gate open and closed again. It had taken him barely a few more seconds than it would have if he'd had two good hands for the task.

"What are teachers making these days? If you need the money…"

Lily's nostrils flared. "It's not about money. I'm fine."

He led the horse back to her, looked down his perfectly straight nose and said, "Then why me? And leave Jen out of it. Even if she is your best friend. Do you feel sorry for me?"

"Oh, please. You make it impossible for *anyone* to be sorry for you."

"Good." With a cluck, he started toward the barn and the veterinary area at the front.

She trotted after him. "Maybe it's my way of saying thank you."

He kept walking. "Thanks for what?"

Oh, he was infuriating! Why couldn't he just accept her help without needing to know the reason? A reason she didn't quite grasp herself. Was he right? Did she need a pet project? She remembered Jen's words—how she was good at looking after everyone. And for one sad moment she considered that Jen might be right.

Doing for others kept her from looking too closely at how lonely her own life was. And damn him for making her remember it. She searched her mind for a plausible reason she could give him. One that perhaps also held some truth.

"For serving your country."

He smiled that tight-lipped smile again. "Right. Well, don't bother. It happens. We were all pinned down during an insurgent attack. I was just the unlucky one that got hit."

That raised more questions than answers, but Lily knew to pry further would get her nowhere. "You don't think what you did was extraordinary?"

He halted, dust rising in puffs from the tracks of his boots. "You know what I think, Lily? I think you're so determined because you're bored. This is farming area. Summer's a crazy time. And here's poor Lily with nothing to do, so she makes wounded Noah Laramie her course for extra credit."

The way he spoke made her blood boil, partly because of the insolence behind it and partly because she already knew it was just a little bit true.

"You want to know the one thing I learned when I moved to Larch Valley? People help each other. It was an amazing concept to learn. When someone needs a hand, it's there. How on earth do you think your brother got the Rescue Ranch started? I helped Jen then, too, and with renovating the bakery. Now if it makes you feel better to pay me, by all means. I certainly wouldn't want to wound your male pride."

Noah started walking again, the horse trudging along behind, unconcerned with the arguing going on. "Ouch."

"It's more than that, Noah. Has it occurred to you that you need to get fitted for a tuxedo? Shoes? That you have duties as a best man? What about a bachelor party? Have you thought about that?"

She stood back with a satisfied smile at the blank expression on his face. "Ah, so you haven't. Tell me, do I strike you as the kind of woman who wants her escort to show up in jeans and boots?"

His nostrils started to flare. Well, good. Noah was pretty transparent, whether he thought so or not, and she seemed to get her own way best when she stood up to him. "Moreover, do you think Jen and Andrew want that, either?"

"Andrew said he's just pleased I'm home to see it."

"Yes, and Jen is planning her wedding. Her one-and-only wedding, Noah. Do you know what a wedding means to a woman?"

"Everything."

Her stomach quivered. "Yes, everything," she breathed, remembering the dress hanging in her closet. She'd never had the heart to get rid of it. "A woman wants her wedding day to be her fairy tale. All her dreams come true." She wanted to help give that to Jen. The kind of wedding that Lily had never had. One with a happy ending. Proof that it could happen.

"Is that why you didn't say more at dinner the other night?" He angled his head, looking at her curiously. "Because I saw your reaction when the wedding talk started, remember? Why is that?"

Lily squinted against the sun as she looked up at him. How did the conversation suddenly get turned around so that the spotlight was on her? "Jen is my friend. I would do anything for her. Even stand here and argue with your stubborn head. I consider it part of my maid of honor duties."

"I warn you, Lily. I'm not pleasant to be around."

"Tell me something I don't already know," she challenged.

"I mean it, Lily."

"So do I." She reached out and put her hand on his left forearm as the lead rope trailed out of his palm. "I am their friend, and you are their family. Doesn't it make sense that we should try to be friends, too?"

Once she said it she knew it made the most sense of any argument she'd put forth. "Friends" was safe, wasn't it? The skin beneath her fingers was warm and firm and she looked up. Her gaze caught on his mouth, the finely shaped lips with the perfect dip in the centre.

He said nothing, and her breaths grew faster, more shallow as the moment held in the hot summer afternoon.

Pixie got tired of standing around and nudged Noah with her nose, sending him off balance and forward. Lily's hand gripped his forearm and her other reached for his T-shirt as their bodies bumped together.

Her breasts were flattened against his rib cage and she felt the quick rise and fall of his breath. His deep-set eyes looked into hers, wide and with an awareness that hadn't been there before. For a second it almost seemed he leaned closer, but then she blinked and his jaw tightened as he stepped back, steadying her on her feet with his hand and tightening his grip on the lead.

"Friends," he stated, though she detected a sliver of skepticism in his tone. "We'll see, Lily. We'll see."

He walked away, Pixie trailing behind, leaving Lily with nothing to do but watch his retreat.

## Chapter 3

Lily picked up Noah in her compact car. When he came out of the house, he had a small bag over his shoulder and sunglasses shaded his eyes. His jeans were neat but well faded and broken in, the way a good pair of jeans was meant to be. Despite the heat, he wore a long-sleeved T-shirt in brown, the right sleeve pinned up to cover the stump sock.

Lily briefly remembered being breathless, pressed up against his chest. It was just as well they only had the wedding and summer vacation when they'd be seeing each other on a regular basis. After that, she'd be back teaching. And she'd be focused on what she needed to be focused on. Work. Routine. And who knew what was in store for him?

"Thanks for the lift this morning." He opened the

door and slid in, only to find his knees pressed against the dash.

Lily laughed at the comical sight of his legs folded up in the small space. "My lord, you're a giant for this little car. Handle's in the middle, between your legs."

He reached for the lever, heaving a sigh of relief when the seat slid back and he could extend his legs a little bit. He put his bag on the floor between his knees. "It isn't quite a Humvee, is it."

He seemed in better humor this morning, despite the day they had ahead of them. "It suits my needs," Lily replied lightly. "It's practical and economical."

He twisted, reaching across with his left arm to grab the door handle and slam it shut. It took him two tries and a low grumble to get it latched so that the little red dash light went out. His good mood seemed to dissipate as he slid his glasses onto the top of his head. "And you are a practical woman, aren't you?"

She prided herself on her practical streak, and yet the way he said it felt like a criticism, not a compliment. He reached across himself once more and grabbed his seat belt, crossing it over his middle and fastening it. She put the car in gear and started out the drive, heading toward Main Avenue and from there to the highway to take them north. She felt his eyes on her and returned the look when they stopped at a stop sign. She forced a smile. "I try to be."

"It is an unexpected trait," he mused, shifting and settling into the upholstery. "You're so..." But he broke off, turning his head to look out the window.

"I'm so what?" Her heart tripped a little bit. It shouldn't really matter what Noah thought of her, but somehow it did. Maybe because, even though she'd

known him such a short time, she already had a sense
of his strength and honor. Even his bouts of grumpiness
were understandable under the circumstances. She realized she didn't truly care if he *liked* her, but it was important that he *respect* her.

"Never mind."

"No, I want to hear it. I'm so?" She did want to know
what he thought. She'd spent a long time in her mother's shadow, and people expected her to follow in her
mother's footsteps. Jasmine Germaine always seemed
ethereal. Beautiful, wispy, moving with the breeze. She
had never seen the need for roots the way Lily had. She'd
moved them more times than Lily cared to count when
she'd been a child, all the while insisting something
bright and shiny was around the corner. All Lily had
wanted was some stability. To have the same bedroom
more than a year at a time. Time to be a kid.

It had been her mother who had been popular, and
loved, a beautiful and fragile butterfly with a handsome
man on her arm. Lily had always faded into the wood-
work when Jasmine was around.

"I was just going to say…"

She noticed a few spots of color on his neck. Was he
embarrassed, for heaven's sake?

He cleared his throat. "You're very pretty, Lily. Your
name suits you."

She stared out at the highway as heat flooded her
cheeks. Noah thought she was pretty?

But she wasn't the pretty one. That was her mother.
Lily was the practical, steady one.

"My compliment doesn't please you."

She kept her eyes on the road. "I'm just not used to
anyone calling me pretty, that's all."

She could feel his gaze on her and she was resolved not to look away from the pavement.

"What do they call you, Lily?"

She took a breath and remembered what Jen had said at dinner. That she looked after people. "They call me handy to have around."

Noah's rusty-sounding laugh filled the car. "Well, you are that."

His deep chuckle wrapped around her. Was he flirting? A lightness filled her body, something that felt an awful lot like happiness. Was Noah Laramie actually capable of flirting?

"So which do you prefer, Noah? The pretty or the practical?"

Dear Lord, she'd gone and flirted back! What was wrong with her? When he was around she seemed to forget her common sense.

The air in the car grew heavy as the question settled. The smile slid from Noah's lips. "I didn't think the two had to be mutually exclusive. And what difference does it make which I prefer?"

"It doesn't," she answered quickly, but the words came out clipped. It couldn't make a difference. They were just friends for the time being. She certainly wasn't fishing for more.

But Noah's gaze bored into her, seeing far too much. She felt him shift in his seat so he was partially facing her. "It's perfectly allowable to be both, you know. There's nothing wrong with it."

The breath she'd been holding came out in a wisp and she tried to smile. She didn't want to be judged on her looks, yet knowing he found her attractive sent an expansive warmth through her. "Thank you, then, for the compliment."

They drove on for a few minutes more before his voice broke the silence again.

"Lily?"

"Hmm?"

"What do you want me to see when I look at you?"

Her hands grew slippery on the steering wheel. What did she want from Noah? The answer came back swiftly: nothing. She did not want to get personally involved with him. Friendship was far enough. She thought he was a good person in a difficult situation. But anything more…not again. She'd keep her life ordered and complication free, thank you.

"Your future sister-in-law's best friend," she replied, reaching over and turning up the radio.

She heard him chuckle beside her, and it made her curious. "What?"

He leaned his head back against the back of the seat and closed his eyes. "If nothing else, you keep things interesting."

The weight that had seemed to hover over the conversation dissipated like a fine mist. She couldn't help the smile that curved her lips in response. "Is that a good thing?"

"Very good. I tend to live in my own head a lot. You help me stop doing that when you're around."

"What kind of things do you think about?" All the headlines lately seemed to talk about returning soldiers and post-traumatic stress. Surely losing an arm in a firefight was grounds for some serious trauma. She found herself wondering what things he suffered that she knew nothing about.

"Oh, you know. What to have for breakfast. What shirt to wear."

"In other words, none of my business." She glued her eyes to the highway, put on her blinker and passed a transport truck as they climbed a hill.

He still had his eyes closed as he answered. "Stuff that talking won't solve," he said, his voice low.

She risked a glance and saw he still had his eyes closed. "Are you tired?"

Noah nodded, just a little, opening one eye to squint at her. "A little. I didn't sleep much last night."

"How come?"

"In my own head again."

She had wondered if his arm pained him frequently, but instead now pictured him lying awake thinking. Wondering if he dreaded his doctor's appointments. Wondering if it was memories of combat that kept him up while the rest of Larch Valley slept.

Wondering if he'd been thinking about her the way he seemed to sneak into her thoughts lately.

"Are you worried about today?"

He shrugged, and she spared another glance sideways, seeing how his eyelashes lay against his tanned cheeks. "What's in the bag?"

"Mostly paperwork. The army's part of the government. There are forms about forms and so on."

"About your discharge?"

"So many questions today," he replied drily, opening his eyes.

"We're going a hundred and ten on the highway. Not like you can get away, is it."

That at last got a smile from him. "I can always refuse to answer."

"But you won't because…"

She was teasing, but when she turned her head at his prolonged silence the mood quieted to nearly somber. She could see the deep blue of his irises and the black pupils within them. Her face heated as she forced her attention back to the road where it belonged.

"I'll be damned if I know, Lily. I haven't spoken to anyone about this unless I was ordered to."

She wasn't sure how to feel about being his confidante, and yet she wanted to know the real Noah. "Maybe it's easier because you don't really know me," she suggested.

"Maybe," he agreed. He leaned his head back against the headrest again. "Anyway, I'm not discharged. I'm what they call a temporary category."

She hadn't considered he was still truly in the army. She'd never seen so much as a uniform around his house. "It sounds like they don't know what to do with you."

He chuckled. "Maybe not. The idea isn't so much to know where I'll end up, but to give me the time to get there, I suppose. Then figure out where I'll be sent to next. Right now I'm being paid to get better." He frowned. "It feels ridiculous."

"Why?" She kept her eyes on the road, but she could sense his frustration anyway. "You were hurt doing your job, and it's only right you don't suffer financially while you recover, right?"

"I guess."

"So the agenda today is…?"

"Following up with the doc, talking to a head shrinker, and physio."

Lily couldn't help it; she laughed at the matter-of-fact way he put it. "Psych follow-ups, you mean."

"Yes. In case there's mental and emotional trauma after the fact. And believe me, it's far nicer when you get debriefed when you're healthy. It's a vacation. I missed out on that part when I was in Landstuhl."

She swallowed. It was different hearing him verbalize the possibility of PTSD. He'd admitted to internalizing things too much. The Noah she'd seen so far seemed unlikely to have such problems. But maybe he was just good at hiding them. Maybe her impressions were completely off base.

It wouldn't be the first time she'd misjudged someone's character. Curtis had turned out to be a very different person than she had hoped. Not nearly as strong as she'd thought, for one.

Not nearly as committed, either.

She pushed back the painful memory and focused on the present. She was also helping Noah get fitted for his tuxedo today. "I think you're more likely to be traumatized by what comes *after* your appointments today."

"I think you might be right," he agreed, sliding down in the seat a little more so his knees were nearly against the dash, and closing his eyes once more.

A few moments later she looked over and his lips had fallen open, relaxed in sleep.

She had to be very, very careful. Because she was starting to like Noah Laramie. Too much.

Lily read a book and drank coffee while she spent the day in waiting rooms outside the physio clinic, the psychiatrist's office, at the pharmacy, and at the Area Support Unit while Noah paid a visit with paperwork in hand. It was midafternoon before they left the Currie Barracks and made their way to Macleod Trail to the formal wear boutique. Noah was already looking tired from his day of poking and prodding.

"We can do this another day."

Noah sighed and shoved his pack into the backseat. "That means another trip to town and prolonging another physio day. I'd rather just get it done. Besides if we don't, the first thing Jen will do is remind us how few days there are until the wedding."

Lily shut the car door and led the way to the store. "You're probably right. I'll try to make it painless."

Inside they were greeted by a pleasant salesman who took one look at Noah's arm and then raised his gaze politely to Noah's face.

"We're here to rent a tuxedo," Lily explained, as Noah stared around him at suits, shoes and novelties.

"Is the wedding party registered here?"

"No...the groom has his own tux. We'll only be needing the one."

"Sir?"

Noah turned from looking at the silver flasks at the counter and straightened at the word *Sir*. Lily had the sudden thought that perhaps he missed that particular word. It was as indicative of his former life as the uniform, she would imagine. She wondered why he wasn't wearing his dress uniform for the wedding. She hadn't even thought to ask. She wondered if it was his decision or Andrew's request.

"May I take your measurements, sir?"

Noah and Lily followed the salesman to a back portion of the store, where the clerk retrieved a form and a measuring tape. After filling out the information, he procured his tape. But as he began to stretch it out, Lily saw him hesitate next to Noah's arm. His cheeks suddenly colored and he stepped back.

"I'm…I'm sorry, sir." He stammered and then cleared his throat. "I don't know if you're comfortable with… I mean I…"

Noah's eyes darkened. "You mean *you're* not comfortable."

Lily sensed the impending storm. Noah had had people poking and analyzing and asking questions all day. Getting fitted for his tuxedo was definitely not a good idea. He was tired and she felt the frustration coming from him.

The clerk swallowed and bravely met Noah's gaze. "I simply don't want to presume, or inadvertently hurt you."

"Noah." She stepped in front of him and caught his gaze, hoping to send a well-meaning caution. "I think he's just unsure. It's awkward, that's all."

"Dammit, Lily," he warned in a low whisper. "I didn't want to do this in the first place."

"Then why not wear your dress uniform?"

For a moment Noah's gaze held hers. "Because for this one day I am not Captain Laramie. I am the brother of the groom."

"May I proceed, sir?"

A muscle in Noah's jaw ticked. Lily thought maybe everyone would be more comfortable if she used the tape measure. The clerk could note the measurements, and Noah might lose some of his stoic resentment.

"I'll do it," she said, loud enough that the attendant could hear. "Or we'll do it together." She lowered her voice, put her fingers over Noah's. "Is that okay? Someone needs to measure you."

She saw him swallow. Other than the afternoon when

they'd been pressed together, they had avoided touching. Suddenly her great idea seemed intensely intimate, and her tongue slipped out to wet her lips.

"Fine, you do it," he said sharply, his gaze dropping to where the tip of her tongue had disappeared back into her mouth.

Lily took the tape from the attendant and smiled. "I do a fair bit of sewing." It was an understatement, but right now she just wanted to keep everyone happy. "Just tell me if the line isn't exactly where you want it."

Her fingertips grazed the muscles of Noah's shoulders as the tape stretched across the breadth of him. She measured down his left arm, meeting his eyes only briefly when she murmured words about using the same length for the right—it would be pinned up out of the way anyway. She heard him catch his breath as she wrapped the tape around his slim waist, and she had to remind him to relax and let the breath out. The fabric of his shirt was soft and warm against her fingers, and butterflies tumbled in her stomach as her hands rested against the button of his jeans for a few breathless moments.

This wasn't what she'd had planned when she'd told herself she was going to keep Noah at arm's length. The way she was responding, and the way he was holding himself so rigidly, told her an arm's length away was still too close.

"I need to do your chest," she said quietly, and she reached around him. She guided the tape measure beneath his arms, her fingers touching his right bicep lightly as she adjusted the tape. Did it hurt? Did it feel odd to move that part of his arm without the rest of it attached? His heart pounded against her hand as she brought the ends of the tape together. Touching him this way made her too self-conscious to ask. She read out the measurement instead and the man put it on his clipboard.

"Now there's just the inseam," he chirped, oblivious to the tug-of-war going on between Lily and Noah. "You should have on proper shoes to measure that," he explained. "You're what, an eleven?"

Noah nodded. As the salesman scurried away to retrieve dress shoes, Noah's voice came from above, deep and husky. "Lily…"

"There's a chair over there. Why don't you sit to change your footwear," she blurted, more affected than she wanted to admit by the rough way he'd said her name. She did not want to be the pretty girl who'd lent a hand. Someone who had his attention now, when he needed her, but would one day be forgotten. It was better to keep it strictly platonic.

Noah hesitated the smallest instant, and for a minute she was afraid he was going to say something more. But he went and sat and pushed off one boot with his toes. The second required more pushing, and she gave in and knelt before him, gripping the heel and sliding it off his foot.

"I hate this," he admitted in a low voice. Lily's eyes stung. Grouchy Noah was a challenge, but a Noah who had started to trust her was far more difficult to handle. In only a short week he'd started accepting little bits of help, like the drive today to his appointments. She almost preferred the stubborn, irascible man to this one. It was easier to keep her distance from him. Easier to keep her thoughts in line with where they should be.

The salesman arrived with a shoe box. Lily took the shoes, unlaced them, and put them on the floor for Noah to put on his feet while she talked to the salesman about what style tuxedo they wanted to coordinate with Andrew's. She wouldn't do everything for him.

When she turned back, Noah's cheeks were red. He had the toe of his right shoe holding down the right-hand lace of the left shoe, while he tried to negotiate the other tie into a semblance of knot and bow with one hand.

"Dammit!" he finally exploded, sitting back on the bench and closing his eyes while his jaw trembled with frustration.

"Could you give us a moment?" Lily asked the salesman in a whisper. When he'd discreetly left, she went to Noah and sat on the bench beside him.

"Noah—" she began, but he cut her off.

"Don't," he commanded, and she recoiled from the venom in his voice. "Don't you dare try to placate me or say it's understandable or whatever it is you are going to say. I can't stand it."

All the platitudes she'd had on the tip of her tongue, the ones about needing time to adjust and how things would get better and it was understandable to be frustrated fled, driven away by the force of his words.

"All right."

For several minutes she waited, feeling the vibrations of resentment lengthen and weaken. He finally reached over and took her hand. "I'm sorry."

"You have nothing to be sorry for." Relieved, she turned on the bench so that her knees touched his. "You are allowed to feel the way you feel."

"Helpless? Is it okay for me to feel helpless?"

"How can I answer that without saying any of the things you've forbidden me to say?"

That drew a reluctant smile from his lips. "Touché."

"Look, we're almost done. Why don't you just let me tie them this once."

"Because I need to do it myself."

"Why?"

His eyes glittered at her, angry and resentful. "Because I do, okay?"

"Does this have to do with your wounded male pride?" She tried to lighten the mood but he didn't smile. Oh, no, a smile would have been preferable to the searing gaze he treated her to. There was an intensity to Noah she couldn't deny, and it drew her to him no matter how many times she told herself it wasn't smart.

"Yes," he said simply.

Something sizzled in the air between them. Lily looked away first. "We can argue about this later. Right now the salesman is wondering what the heck is going on. Will you let me tie them, please?"

He nodded, and she squatted down, deftly tying the laces while he clenched his jaw tightly and stared past her to the change rooms, his gaze closed off and unreceptive.

Every one of his struggles seemed to hit her square in the heart. He was so proud. She knew he hated it every time he attempted something and failed. His occupational therapy would teach him tricks to manage everyday tasks, she was sure. He just wasn't there yet.

Lily beckoned the salesman over again and took the tape measure in hand once more as Noah stood up, shaking down his pant legs. Suddenly she seemed to realize exactly where she was measuring—his inseam. Embarrassed, she couldn't find it within herself to meet his gaze. She tried a smile on the sales assistant, knowing it was futile to think he didn't sense her discomfort. "I think you can do this one?" she suggested.

The man took the tape back and deftly made the measurement. Lily couldn't help it, she finally risked a look at Noah, and her lips quivered as he waggled his eyebrows at her. He knew. He knew why she'd suggested the salesman take the measurement and he was teasing. Her heartbeat took a little lift. After his outburst, a sense of humor was like a ray of sunshine.

"Fantastic," the clerk said, beaming. "Let's try on some styles to be sure, shall we? The four-button notch is a great choice. What colors for the vest and tie?"

"Just white," Lily replied when Noah shrugged. "This is why you needed me with you," she chided, offering a small smile. "You wouldn't have had a clue on your own."

"Hey, I've had my wardrobe supplied for the last few years," he replied. They could see the clerk hovering at a rack, fiddling with hangers but obviously listening in. Noah leaned forward and said in a stage whisper, "That happens in prison."

Lily gaped and fought hard not to laugh. She turned her forehead to Noah's chest, hiding as soon as she saw the clerk's eyes widen. Inaudible giggles shook her chest as she felt his smile next to her temple. His joke took her so much by surprise she had no opportunity to guard against it.

"Oh, come on, you know now he's wondering what I was in for and how I lost my arm," he murmured, his breath warm in her ear.

"You're terrible."

The smile faded; she could feel it as the warmth at her temple disappeared. "It's been a rough day. I don't want to lose my temper again. I'm sorry, Lily, for being so short with you. For allowing myself to get frustrated. It's just safer to have fun with it. Maybe I need to start laughing more."

While they were waiting, Lily leaned back. "Does this feel like a prison now? Being ripped out of the life you knew?" She searched his eyes, marveling at how the layers of Noah seemed to be getting unwrapped today— both good and bad.

"Sometimes. When I get frustrated, like I was with the shoes. Or when I just miss the life. I thought I was a career soldier. It's tough to be a civilian after this long."

"Ah, here we go. Four-button notch with a white vest and tie." The clerk put the clothing on a hook in a dressing room.

Noah reached for the safety pin holding his sleeve, but he couldn't seem to get it to release properly. After a half-dozen tries and a healthy sigh, he turned back.

This time she didn't ask. He was tired and his patience was at the breaking point. He needed to get this over with and get out of here.

She reached for the pin, odd circles of nerves twirling around her insides as she touched his stump for the first time through the sleeve. It felt like any ordinary arm, only it was wrapped beneath the shirt and ended above the elbow. She wasn't sure what she'd expected. Something harder, less pliant perhaps. She was careful, not knowing if it was still tender to the touch.

"The wedding is in August. I think we'd better plan on pinning you twice. Once with the jacket for the ceremony, and then with the jacket off for the reception due to the heat. I can help you with that. I'm a whiz with pins and things. No one will even be able to see it."

She clipped the safety pin closed and smiled up at him, the edges of her lips trembling.

"You don't need to."

"As maid of honor, I consider it one of my duties."

"No, what I mean is that I'll be able to do it myself."

Lily frowned. Despite needing her help today, he wasn't showing any signs of letting up. In the meantime, he was frustrating himself to death.

"I'll be out in a few minutes."

He took the clothes into the change room while Lily and the clerk waited. The clerk had said very little since Noah's surprise revelation.

It took slightly longer than it would have normally, but Noah finally stepped out from behind the door and Lily caught her breath.

He was stunning. His eyes gleamed above the fine lines of his cheekbones, his dark hair mussed slightly from pulling his T-shirt over his head. His tan set off the snowy white of the shirt, which he'd buttoned to the second top button. The vest lay taut against his flat stomach, and the jacket was unbuttoned. The shirt was tucked rather unevenly into the trousers. All in all, he looked like a man at the end of the day rather than the beginning, and it was arresting.

"The tie," she said, reaching forward and buttoning the top button. "We won't get the full effect without the tie."

The skin of his neck was warm against her fingers, and she fought the feeling that this whole afternoon was something a girlfriend or wife should be doing, not a recent acquaintance or sudden bridesmaid. He swallowed and his Adam's apple bobbed against her fingertips. She slid the silk tie around his neck and fumbled her way through a Windsor knot, remembering quite painfully performing the same task for a very young, very fresh-faced groom. Lord, she'd been so young, and so naive, so sure everything was going to work out the way they'd planned. She saw the empty sleeve at Noah's side in her peripheral vision. Surely Noah had had dreams of his own. How many had been quashed by the loss of his arm?

"Andrew will help you on the day. I'm afraid I have had less experience with ties than safety pins."

He couldn't look down with her hands holding his chin up, and she noticed the smooth line of his jaw. There were no missed shaving spots today.

Lily then put her hands on his lapels and drew the jacket closed, buttoning up the four buttons. Andrew had said his tuxedo was similar, and she knew the two of them would look handsome standing at the altar together.

At the altar. Lily's hands grew cold at the thought. Everywhere she turned lately there seemed to be a re-minder, making her relive her failures over and over again. Perhaps it was good that there wasn't much time before Jen's big day. It would be over and Lily could go back to the business of forgetting.

She stood back, assessing his appearance. The sleeve would be tucked up neatly on the day. And she'd walk up the aisle in the pale pink dress she'd already started cutting and pinning.

At the front, she would move to the left, beside Jen. She'd never be caught as the one in the white dress. It wasn't that she was against marriage. Not at all. She'd just already learned it wasn't for her. Not everyone was as lucky as Andrew and Jen.

"You look very handsome," she said dutifully, as the

assistant picked and pulled at the coat a few different ways, making alteration notes.

"Even if it's not my dress uniform?"

Lily stepped back, putting distance between them. She almost wished he was wearing it, if that would make him seem more of a stranger. She had to ignore the physical attraction that had woven its spell this afternoon. That was all it was. Attraction. Perhaps a smidgen of curiosity. Nothing more.

"You can take the man out of the uniform, but not the uniform out of the man, I see."

"Being out of it was not my choice." He reached for the dressing room doorknob and then looked over his shoulder. "None of this was my choice, Lily. My mistake, maybe, but not my choice. Don't forget that."

Lily stared at the closed door for a few moments. What could he possibly mean, his mistake? And it felt very clear that he wasn't just talking about his injury but the current situation, which included her. She wanted to feel relieved at the stinging rejection. Starting something with Noah was not on her agenda.

But it stung just the same, and she retrieved her purse from the floor to hide just how much.

## Chapter 4

Noah disappeared back into the dressing room to change again. He spent a frustrating few minutes putting the pin back in his sleeve, cursing under his breath as the pin sprung open and dropped to the carpeted floor. He didn't have to do it himself. He could have asked Lily and she would have performed the task in an instant.

But she'd done enough for one day.

When he stepped out of the change room, he was completely buttoned and snapped. Lily rose from the bench and came to him, her lips curved up in a reassuring smile. He'd felt so helpless, so…impotent…when he'd needed her help with the shoes. It was demoralizing when you were trying to impress a woman. And he was trying to impress her, he realized. He wasn't sure how or why her opinion had started to matter, but it did.

"If I could just get you to sign here, sir, and pay for

the deposit," came the clerk's voice from behind them. He was still holding the clipboard.

Noah reluctantly broke eye contact with Lily and followed the clerk to the reception area where he dug out a credit card for the rental deposit. He'd probably been too harsh earlier, speaking to the salesman. But he wasn't used to the stares yet, or the way someone's eyes automatically darted to his empty sleeve first and then to his face. He wasn't used to looking completely inept in public, either, or losing his cool.

And he wasn't used to the way Lily had looked at him, and touched him. The gentleness of her fingers, the way the feel of them against him made him feel more of a man than he had in many weeks. Which was foolish. She didn't want him. They were merely thrown together. The last thing she'd want was a man with his scars. The touch on his stump today was as close as she was going to get to seeing his wounds. He didn't want the ugliness of war to touch her the way it had him.

And yet he found himself telling her things he couldn't bring himself to say to Andrew, or even to his army buddies when he one-finger typed emails to them.

He took the pen in his left hand and painstakingly signed his name to the document and credit card slip. He scowled at the uneven letters that looked the equivalent of a child's scrawl. Learning to write with his opposite hand was yet another one of his challenges.

The clerk stared at the card and then the signature and paused. Noah stiffened, but was determined to hang on to his temper. He knew the clerk was only doing his job, comparing signatures. "I used to be right-handed. I'm having to relearn to write with my opposite hand."

The clerk flushed deeply. "I'm sorry…I mean…I didn't realize. I'm required to match the signatures…."

Lily put her hand on Noah's arm. The gesture was reassuring and he exhaled. He couldn't fault the man for sticking to his orders, even if it was an inconvenience to him. "It's okay. I know you're just following procedure."

Lily spoke up, squeezing Noah's wrist. "If you like, I'll give you my credit card number."

"No, this will be fine," the clerk assured them. He lifted his chin. "There won't be a problem, sir."

Noah pocketed his wallet again and they left. Once they got into her car, he let out a gigantic sigh.

"I'm so sorry, Noah. For all of it."

"This is why I hate going out. I spent my entire day either being stared at or poked. I should be able to sign my own damn name! A five-year-old could do better."

"Give it time. I'm sure the occupational therapy will help."

Noah let out a bitter laugh. "Do I strike you as a patient man, Lily?"

"Not particularly."

He turned his head to look at her. Lily put the car in gear and headed out toward Highway 22. "Do you want to stop for dinner on the way back? We haven't really eaten all day."

"If I have to see one more person today…"

Lily spluttered out a laugh. The aggravated tone reminded her of the old *Honeymooners* reruns her Gram had watched on the television. But she understood his need for quiet. She couldn't blame him for not wanting to spend any more of his day in public. She suddenly wondered if part of his reluctance to be in the wedding had to do with feeling on display. She certainly felt that

way, and she had nothing as gossipworthy as a war injury to contend with.

"Fair enough. No restaurant then." But it was going
to be early evening before they got back. She couldn't
just drop him home. The only thing they'd had during
the day was a coffee at a drive-through.

"Why don't you let me cook you dinner?"

They were stopped at a light and she looked over. His
jaw was so firm, so defiant. He needed to relax, needed
a night away from Lazy L and doctors and reminders.

"At my house. You haven't seen my house yet. I have
lots of groceries and a bottle of wine I've been saving
for when I had company."

He raised an eyebrow and her lips twitched. "Sue me,"
she said carelessly. "I don't usually sip alone."

"That actually sounds good."

"Then it's a date."

At Noah's shocked expression she backpedaled.
"Well, obviously not a real date…"

Silence fell in the vehicle once more as the light
changed. As they accelerated down the highway, Lily
wondered how much deeper she was going to let herself
get in before she started bailing out.

Noah's first reaction to Lily's house was surprise.
She unlocked the front door to the stuccoed duplex and
they stepped inside. It smelled of vanilla and something
lightly floral. The small foyer was painted a warm, welcoming yellow. As he followed her past the stairs and
to the kitchen, he was surprised at her color choices.
The same yellow was repeated on the walls there, with
splashes of chocolate and terra-cotta lending a cozy feel.
The colors were repeated on pottery canisters, and a tall

potted orange tree sat in a corner by a south window. He smiled. If the landscape was slightly different, he'd almost feel he was in a hacienda rather than a duplex in suburbia.

"Make yourself at home," she said, putting down her purse.

To the right was a living room, and the colors there picked up the red tones. Caramel furniture and cherrywood floors mellowed the deep shade of the walls. He wandered to the doorway and stared at a painting on the wall. It was a cacophony of flowers in yellows, reds, purples, so vivid the blossoms almost seemed to jump out at him.

"Is there something wrong?"

He turned around, looking at Lily standing in jeans and a plain pale blue T-shirt, holding a bottle of wine in her hands. "It's just that this wasn't what I pictured your place to be like."

He'd come to somewhat accept her help. Dinner for two at her house wasn't really in the plans. But the thought of going out somewhere to be gawked at again had been unbearable. It had seemed like a good solution at the time.

Right up until the moment she'd made a point of insisting it wasn't a date. As if he needed a reminder. He was starting to realize she was a dynamic, competent woman. And today he'd demonstrated how he could neither tie his shoes nor write his name. Not exactly date material.

"What did you expect?" She went to work on the cork, and he saw the way her shoulders curved as she manipulated the corkscrew. Her dark hair lay over one shoulder and he had a momentary urge to go over and push it aside, so that it cascaded down her back. But after this afternoon, that was a very bad idea. He took a step backward and put his hand in his pocket.

"I expected lighter colors. Pinks and blues, maybe."

"I like earth tones," she responded, finally getting the cork out and retrieving two glasses. "They make me feel warm and comfortable and content."

"It's a very nice house."

"It's not very big, but there's just me."

And now tonight he was there. He wondered how much socializing Lily did and if she had teacher friends. If she entertained, if she dated. He accepted a glass of wine, murmuring his thanks and taking a small sip. It occurred to him that while she had been given a crash course in Noah Laramie, he knew next to nothing about her.

It also occurred to him that he wanted to know more. Maybe it was his military background, but he liked to get a complete picture about who he was dealing with. It made for a more level playing field. Lily knew far more about him than he was comfortable with, while she was surrounded by secrets. Surely he could find something to fault. It would make it easier not to like her quite so much.

He walked to the door that opened to the small back deck. "What brought you to Larch Valley in the first place?"

Lily took a bag of tomatoes out of the fridge and lined them up on a cutting board. "Work. I had my degree but no job. LVHS was looking and I applied. It's a lot easier to find a job out of province."

"But so far from home...you're from back East, right?"

Her knife paused for a moment. He wondered why the slight hesitation and watched as the blade moved again, finely chopping the red flesh of the tomato. "Yes. Ontario."

"What about your family?"

The knife rested on the cutting board then as Lily looked up. "Is this the interrogation equivalent of *get to know you better?*"

He grinned then, knowing he'd inadvertently struck a nerve. He'd gotten the impression that Lily had few faults beyond her stubborn nature. But there was something here. And it felt wonderful to turn the spotlight on someone else for a change. He got tired of being the focus of scrutiny.

"Sorry. Occupational hazard. I was feeling a little at a disadvantage. Not really fair for you to see all my dirty laundry now, is it."

A reluctant smile tugged at her lips. "I suppose not. But my life really isn't very interesting."

He left the view from the door behind and went to stand near her at the center island, watching as she heated olive oil and garlic in a pan and added the tomatoes. "No one grew up in a bubble," he said simply. "'Fess up."

She sighed, stirring the mixture with a wooden spoon. "My mom still lives in Toronto. There was only ever the two of us, at least after my Gram died when I was small."

"Does she visit here a lot?"

A dry laugh greeted his question. "No, she's never been here. We sort of keep our lives…separate."

Lily focused on the bubbling tomatoes rather than on Noah. Wasn't he just full of inquiries today. Innocent questions, too. Only they weren't that innocent at all.

The last thing she wanted to do was get into the complicated relationship she had with her mother. Or why they didn't see eye to eye on almost anything. They'd stopped talking mostly, just to avoid arguing.

Noah put his hand over hers on the spoon. "I haven't seen my mom since I was seven."

His fingers were warm and slightly rough and felt good on the smooth skin just behind her wrist. "I know." She thought of the young boy he must have been, left with his father and a baby brother. At least Lily had grown up with a mother, for all her faults.

Still, she appreciated the confidence, and the fact that he'd shared a tiny bit of information about his childhood. His hand slid off her wrist and she avoided his eyes, instead reaching for a bunch of fresh basil and chopping it for the sauce.

"I'm sorry about your dad, too." She scraped the basil into the sauce and put the cutting board down on the counter. "I know you didn't make it home for the funeral."

Noah's face twisted and she felt guilty for causing him more pain. "Oh, Noah, I'm sorry. I didn't think it would make you feel worse."

Noah shook his head. "In some ways I'm just glad he doesn't have to see me like this."

"Noah!" Dismayed, she forgot her earlier promise to keep the evening nontactile, and she reached out, gripping his forearm in her fingers. "Surely you don't think he would care about your injury. That it would make a difference."

His gaze met hers. "I don't know. He always seemed so proud that I was a soldier. Said that if I wouldn't be a rancher, this was the next best thing. Somehow I can't escape the feeling that I failed him. It made going to his grave pretty difficult."

"But you did go."

He nodded. "Andrew drove me when I first got back. It was my duty to go. Andrew's made his peace. I don't think I have yet."

"A parent loves their child, no matter what the disappointments. And I can't imagine your father was disappointed in you. He must have been very proud." She squeezed his arm and smiled.

And yet she knew there was a false note to her words. Jasmine had never accepted Lily's version of life. She'd accused her of limiting her options. While the words had never been said, Lily knew her mother was disappointed in her choices.

"That was a very nice diversion, Lily, but we were talking about you." Noah slid his arm out from beneath her touch and grabbed the wooden spoon, taking a turn at stirring the sauce. "So a job brought you to the Larch. What made you stay?"

"I've made my home here," she said finally. "I love Larch Valley, I love my job, and I've made friends. What more could I ask for?" She stopped short of saying it was the kind of home she'd always wanted. There was stability and order and a routine that was comforting. She'd never liked living life on a whim. She liked going to the grocery store and knowing the cashier by name. She enjoyed seeing the neighborhood kids grow and change. And knowing she had people like Jen and Andrew and the Hamiltons as a surrogate family was a blessing.

"It's a good place to call home," he agreed.

Lily watched him wander through her kitchen and bit down on her lip. It was silly that she should be feeling drawn to him in any way. Their lives were drastically different. But the things that made up Noah were hard to resist, and each time she saw him face a new challenge she felt connected to him a little more. He was strong and brave and a little bit angry. And his motives seemed to have very little to do with her, which was a refreshing development. It was clear he wasn't interested in her romantically. The look on his face when she'd said the word *date* had spoken volumes. She'd had to hastily backtrack before he started thinking she did have a thing for him.

Lily shook her head slightly. She should be relieved. After all, if he wasn't interested in her, then it was only herself she had to worry about.

She put water on for pasta and took a sip of her wine, wanting to change the subject. The past was where it should be—behind her. It was better to talk about the future. "What are your plans for after the wedding?"

He frowned, the scowl marring the handsome perfection she'd glimpsed when his face was relaxed and smiling.

"I don't know. I suppose I'll start talking to someone about new positions and postings. At some point I have to get back to work, and the sooner the better."

Lily let out a slow breath. Why was she worried? This was nothing more than an itty-bitty attraction. A few months and Noah would be gone again anyway. He certainly wasn't looking for a relationship. And neither was she. Knowing he would be putting his uniform back on and heading to a new base made him just a little bit safer.

"Your condition won't make a difference, then?"

"It all depends on my rehab and doctor's orders. Who knows what limitations they'll put on me. But they try to keep people who've been injured in the service these days. They'll rustle something up. I've got rank and experience going for me."

She dropped her shoulders and made her hands busy stirring the sauce. That was it then. He wouldn't be staying. Any elemental attraction of the moment on her part wouldn't be a concern. So why couldn't they make standing up for Andrew and Jen fun, instead of a chore?

Why couldn't they just clear the air and get it over with? Why not just tell him why she was dreading it so much?

But the words refused to come as she slid spaghetti into the boiling water and went to the cupboard for pasta bowls.

"Well, that's good then. At least you can reclaim something of your old life, right? A few months and you could be back in uniform and captain again. That must make you happy."

"Sure."

Yet as he said it, she saw a shadow lurking behind his eyes, and she got the feeling the sentiment came laden with conditions.

"And we might as well make the best of this wedding business, don't you think? I mean, you're only here a short time, and I'm not looking for anything romantic, so why don't we just agree to keep it light? We might as well have fun."

Yet, even as she said it, she kept feeling the way his chest had been wide and strong beneath her hands this afternoon, the way she'd had to damp her lips with her tongue as he'd come out of the dressing room with the tux on. Just who was she trying to convince here? Many more scenes like that and he *would* start thinking she had designs on him.

He stepped forward, putting his glass down on the countertop. Lily's heartbeat seemed to pause for a millisecond before starting up again slightly faster than before. He was only a breath away from her, and her hands itched to reach out and draw him closer. She didn't want entanglements. But she did want *him*. Not that she'd admit it in a million years.

"You don't strike me as a keep-it-light kind of woman," he said softly, his deep voice penetrating right to her core.

"Oh, but I am." She panicked, scuttling away as the pasta threatened to boil over, knowing it had been many years since she'd allowed herself to "keep it" anything. "I definitely choose *keep it light* over *hot and heavy.*"

She turned her back to him, attending to dinner, but the way her senses were clamoring around, she knew *hot and heavy* was exactly what had been running through her mind.

Lily carefully took the cardboard box out of the backseat of her car and shut the door with her hip. Andrew's truck was gone and so was Jen's car. She'd just leave the supplies and head back home. She could do with a day to tidy up her own place and possibly even spend an hour or two on the deck with the latest paperback she'd picked up at the drugstore.

The door to the house was open and she stepped inside, marveling at the transformation since Jen and Andrew had gotten engaged. Gone was the plainness that she'd seen during her first visit. There was fresh paint on the kitchen walls, and the yellow and white accents were brought out even more by Jen's subtle touches. Lily went through to the living room and put the box down on the sofa. Inside, Jen would find the stationery she had ordered as well as the materials to put together table centerpieces of floating candles and silk flower petals. She reached out and grazed a finger over a cool glass bowl. There'd been nothing like this at *her* wedding. It had been rushed and simple and…

Footsteps clumping up the porch steps pulled her out of her thoughts. As the front door slammed open, she pressed a hand to her chest before rushing to the kitchen to see what the commotion was about.

Noah was at the sink, water rushing into the stainless steel basin as he added soap to the water. "Dammit, dammit, dammit," she heard him mutter.

"Noah?"

He spun, water flying everywhere, his face blank with shock at having her appear before him. He turned back and shut off the water. "Give me a hand here," he commanded, and she immediately went forward.

"Did you hurt yourself?" For a moment she felt a shaft of panic that he might have done something to his one good arm.

"No. Beautiful's foaling and Andrew's in Calgary with Jen. I can do it but…" He shoved his hand in the sink and swished it around. "This is stupid. I need to scrub up and I obviously can't scrub my own arm."

Relief rushed through her as she stepped forward. "I'll do it for you." She grabbed the antiseptic soap and began working his fingers through her own. "Why didn't you use the sink in the barn?"

His voice came from above as she worked the soap with the spray from the tap. "The faucet broke yesterday and we didn't get a chance to fix it yet." He chuckled as she continued, her fingers working in a most businesslike fashion, the warm sound doing swirly things to her insides.

"Lily?"

"Hmm?"

"You need to go up past my elbow."

She blanched a little. A farm girl she was not, but she dutifully scrubbed and cleansed until she dared any germ to get in her path.

"There," she breathed once she was done. Even a job as brusque and businesslike as washing his hand seemed intimate these days. In fact, since their meal the other night, she'd barely been able to think of anything else.

"Thanks. Now I'm going to need your help."

"My…my help?" She stammered the words out, her fanciful thoughts scattering. Washing hands was one thing, but she'd never birthed anything in her entire life. Nor had she had any burning desire to. "Noah, I don't know…."

He looked down at her, so solid and confident she felt like ten times a heel.

"Beautiful will do the work herself. I'm just there for backup. But I don't even have a full set of hands, Lily. If I need something, it would be helpful for you to be there to hand it to me."

She nodded mutely, staring down at her jeans and white sneakers. What in the world was she getting herself into?

She trotted after him to the barn, his long strides eating up the ground between the two buildings. As they neared the door, he offered her an encouraging smile. "Relax, Lil. Keep your voice soothing and soft—it'll be comforting. Imagine you were having a baby and how you'd like it…no bright lights, no loud noises, just soothing and comfortable, right?"

Lily blinked back stinging tears and squared her shoulders. He couldn't know how his words hurt. Maybe it was the renewed experience of being involved with a wedding or the fact that every time she saw Lucy and Brody together she was reminded. She'd thought she'd done a good job of forgetting and moving on. But lately it seemed to hit her from every corner. Once upon a time she had wanted children for herself. She and Curtis had talked about it, agreeing to wait until after they were finished school and both working before starting a family. A girl and a boy. Lily held back a sigh. Once upon a time she'd dreamed of a happily ever after that didn't exist. A happy ending that she was no closer to now than she was before.

But if Noah was willing to do this one-handed, she could find the wherewithal to help.

They stepped inside the dark barn, quiet except for some shuffling from the stall nearest Andrew's clinic space. Noah grabbed a box and slid inside the stall, simply watching as the mare lay on the bed of soft straw.

"Shouldn't we do something?"

"Not yet. Hopefully we won't have to." He spoke in a low voice. "I can't believe Andrew's not here. We knew it would be soon, but we kind of expected a late night, not a midmorning birthing."

Lily looked around her. The mare lay on her side, breathing heavily, the whites of her eyes showing. The straw was dark beneath her and Lily got a horrible feeling.

"Noah..." She stared pointedly at the spot, but he only smiled.

"Her water broke, just like a woman's would. That's all."

"You've clearly done this before." Maybe he didn't need her help and she could escape to the house.

"I grew up here. Of course I did, many times." He smiled at her, and it seemed to light up the dim stall. "Some of my favorite memories are of the three of us down here late at night when a mare was foaling. Afterward Dad always made us hot chocolate. Sometimes, if it had been a very long night, we got to miss the morning of school."

"He indulged you."

Noah nodded. "Not often, but sometimes." He kept a close eye on the mare. "This time I thought we'd have the resident vet in attendance. We don't know much about her history, previous foals, nothing. Jen basically rescued her from the side of the road."

Lily was familiar with the story, and the fact that Noah's agitation had subsided helped to calm her, as well. Her eyes widened as one hoof emerged, then another. She held her breath as she waited.

After several minutes without progression, Lily saw Noah's brow pucker. "Hand me the towel," he said softly, and Lily bent to retrieve the soft cotton from the kit. She watched, fascinated, as Noah crooned low words to the horse, amazed as he used the stump end of his right arm to anchor the towel against the tiny hooves as he wrapped it around and then gripped the fabric in his large hand.

"What are you doing?"

"Giving her a little help."

Mesmerized, Lily watched as Noah worked on his knees, easing the hooves toward the mare's feet rather than out, inch by inch. "Good girl," he murmured, sweat beading on his forehead. Lily saw his bicep bulge as he tugged gently but firmly.

The head and shoulders appeared and Lily gaped, unable to turn away from the beautiful sight. For a few moments mother and foal rested, and then it was over. Head, shoulders and hindquarters, with only the tips of the foal's feet left to come.

"Hello, gorgeous," he murmured warmly, running his hand over the foal's head. "Look at you." He sat back on his heels. "What a girl. Barely needed a bit of help."

"Why aren't they moving?"

He smiled up at her, a big celebratory smile that took her breath from her lungs. "They're resting, see? And in a moment she'll be up and then I'll need your help for just a few moments more."

"You didn't need my help at all." She stood by the stall door, only a few feet away, but she could feel the relief and joy emanating from him.

"I might have, though. A little pull is nothing. You never know if there are going to be complications. I'm glad you were here."

Suddenly Lily was, too. She'd seen a side of Noah that was beautiful. Capable and strong, but gentle, calm and affectionate. She smiled as the mare struggled to rise and the umbilical cord broke.

"A clean break. Fantastic. Can you hand me the iodine? It's just there." He pointed.

She opened it and watched as he gently doctored the umbilical stump.

"Great…look at that. Mom and baby and all's right with the world."

The last word faded away slightly, and Lily caught a glimpse of telltale moisture in his eyes. She rushed forward, looking up at him, searching for signs of pain. What if he'd overdone it? She was pretty sure foaling wasn't on his list of physio activities. "Noah? Are you okay? Did you strain something?"

He shook his head, moving past her. He grabbed the kit in his hand and led the way out of the stall. "No. I just realized I've missed this."

She trailed after him. "The farm?"

"I'm usually in the middle of places where *nothing* is right with the world, you know? That's why I'm there. To try to fix it."

There were times she had paused to wonder about his past, about what he'd seen in his years as a soldier. If his experience had affected him in the ways she read about in the paper or saw on the news. The thought that he might have to suffer through that as well as his physical injury made the July day suddenly seem cold. "Do you have nightmares or anything?"

He shook his head. "No, nothing like that, thank God. It's just a whole other world from here, and I think I got used to it. Numb. But in some ways those are lost years. I lost touch with Andrew. And with my father. When I found out he was sick there wasn't any way I could come home. Now it's too late."

"I'm sorry about Gerald."

"Nothing we can do about it now. Sometimes all you can do is move forward." He clenched his jaw after he said the words, and she wondered what he was remembering.

He walked to the barn door and she followed, turning her head to stare at the stall again. "Should we leave them?"

"I'm just going to wash up again and come back. There will be more to do in the next few hours, but nothing I can't handle until Andrew returns."

In the kitchen once more, Lily put on a pot of coffee and made Noah a sandwich. She put it before him and stood back, letting her hand rest on his shoulder briefly.

He crossed his left hand over and covered hers, the contact searing her skin. There was something here, something begun much earlier. For a second she considered removing her hand from beneath his, but then she remembered the look of happiness on his face as the foal had been born, and she found she could not pull away.

He pushed his chair back and her heart jumped.

He stood, holding her fingers still within his as he faced her. For long, quiet seconds he gazed into her eyes, the deep-set blue pulling her in. He pressed the palm of his hand flush against hers, then twined their fingers together.

"Noah," she breathed, a warning lost in a sigh.

He took the last step forward and dipped his head, touching her lips with his own.

# Chapter 5

Noah's lips were warm and rich from the heat of his body and the taste of the coffee. With a sigh, Lily melted against him, feeling his wide chest against her breasts as she lifted her face to him, curling her hand around the nape of his neck while her other hand remained entwined with his.

He moved their joined hands so that they were pressed against the small of her back, pushing her closer into his body, and the kiss deepened. It had been a long time, too long, she realized, since she'd kissed a man. Since she'd wanted to. Her lashes fluttered as he murmured against her lips and her hand slipped down over his shoulder, avoiding his partial arm and sliding over his ribs instead.

When they broke off the kiss, Lily stepped back, even though what she really wanted was to curl up inside his embrace and feel cherished there.

That in itself was reason enough to back away.

"We shouldn't have done that," Lily blurted out as Noah's keen eyes pinned her to the spot. With a breath of panic, she realized that with a slight movement he could have her close again.

"That bad, huh."

Bad? She studied his face but he didn't look as though he was joking. It hadn't been bad in any way, shape or form. It had been fantastic. That was why it was a mistake. But she knew admitting it would be an even bigger error in judgment, so she stayed silent.

"I beg your pardon." The air between them seemed to turn quite chilly now. His lips became a thin, inaccessible line. "I overstepped. It was an interesting morning."

Damn, now she'd gone and offended him. That hadn't been her intention. "There is no need to beg my pardon." She tried to smooth it over by offering a conciliatory smile. "We both know there can be nothing between us, right? It just happened. That's all. As you said—it's been an interesting morning."

Interesting wasn't the half of it. She'd seen a side of him that was unexpected; gentle, quiet, tender even, as he helped bring the foal into the world. She was usually immune to that kind of sentimentality, instead choosing to see the big picture. And the big picture here was that Noah was at an in-between place in his life and would be leaving as soon as he was able. If she kept on, she would be a casualty. She must be losing her edge.

Noah sighed, turning away and going to the sink for a glass of water. "Seeing the mare and foal…it reminded me of what it was like to be home before. When times were simpler. Sometimes it feels so strange, being here, being in this kitchen." He drank deeply of the water and put the glass on the counter.

"You've been gone a long time. Maybe too long."

He nodded. "Yes, in some ways, the army became my home."

A home away from here, Lily reminded herself. A home he wanted to return to. She was realizing it more every day. It had been foolish to give in to the kiss. Keeping it light was how it had to be. *This time* she had her eyes wide-open, and he would be leaving. She had to keep herself from caring. And sneaking kisses didn't help with that objective at all! She needed to find a way to put some distance between them.

Noah rested his hips against the counter and stared toward the hallway that led to the stairs. "I haven't even been through my things, do you know that? I've stayed in the rented house, been here for a few meals at Jen's nagging."

Her insides seized as he talked about being home; he couldn't know how the truth of his words resonated within her. Home was something she hadn't had, not really. Not with a deep history like Noah's. For a moment she forgot about the kiss and the upcoming wedding and how she needed to keep her distance while at the same time keeping things amicable. No, he'd touched a nerve. Here he had a perfectly fine home—where he was wanted and welcomed and he seemed to be turning his back on it when he should need it the most.

"Perhaps you should go up. This is your home. I don't know why you'd feel odd coming back to it. I'll bet there are all kinds of things left up there."

Lily went to the far counter, tidying up the sandwich fixings while Noah studied her with sharp eyes. She couldn't meet his gaze. Did he realize how much he was taking for granted?

"I'm not the same boy who left."

"So what? It doesn't change who you were, or the fact that that boy was the reason you became the man you are now. It doesn't change that Andrew is your brother. Or that he worked very hard to make sure you came home to get well. It means a lot to him that you're here. Maybe more than you realize."

"So you think I'm ungrateful?" He pushed away from the counter.

Did she? Lily pondered that for a moment. "Not ungrateful, exactly," she amended. "I think you have tunnel vision right now. It's understandable. A lot has happened to you."

He looked down at his arm. "You think?"

Lily knew that whatever she'd gone through was nothing compared to Noah, and it had left invisible scars as well as the obvious. He had a lot to work through. But it bothered her that he suddenly seemed to be taking Andrew and Lazy L for granted. He had sold out his share. Andrew had brought Noah home because that was what real families did.

"What I think is I need to get going and you need to check on Beautiful and her baby. And then I think you need to spend some time reacquainting yourself with Noah Laramie. Your room would be a good start."

"And I suppose you want to help me with this, too."

Lily grabbed the cold cuts and put them back in the fridge, keeping her hot cheeks away from Noah's astute eyes. She was already in too deep simply by caring. By going now, she would be away from the temptation of kissing him again. "You've fought my help since the beginning," she pointed out, turning from the fridge and leveling him with a stern look. "This time I agree with you—I think this is something you need to do on your own."

"Right."

He went to the door and out onto the veranda. "Where are you going?" she called after him.

"To check on the mare, like you said."

Lily picked up her purse and stared after his retreating figure. He was angry, and a part of her felt badly for being blunt. But another part of her wondered if any of what she'd said had penetrated his thick skull…and if it might make a difference.

Andrew had taken over with Beautiful and the new filly the moment he'd arrived back at Lazy L. When Jen had asked about naming her, Andrew had given her an indulgent smile and a knowing look at Noah. "Women, they have to name everything like it's a pet."

But Noah had interrupted, remembering the look of awe on Lily's face as the foal had been born and his first words to the latest addition to the Lazy L herd.

"Gorgeous," he said. "Her name is Gorgeous."

Andrew had laughed and Jen had been delighted.

But now they'd gone out to the barn together and Noah was left in the farmhouse all alone.

Maybe Lily was right after all. Maybe he did need to remember the boy he'd been. It was as if there was a distinct line in his life. One side said *before the army* and the other said *in the army*. But where was he now? Certainly not out, but not in, either. And there had been some good times here. Good times like the ones he'd remembered today.

He took the stairs slowly, wandering up to his old room. The door was ajar, and he pushed it the rest of the way open, flicking on the light switch. The window blind was down, and he crossed the room to open the slats, letting in summer evening light. He turned the light back off and stared around him. Nothing had changed. Nothing. It remained exactly as it had been when he was nineteen and heading to boot camp. For a few years he'd returned during his leaves, but Andrew and his father always seemed to be at odds and it hadn't been enjoyable. And since then, he'd barely been home for visits, and then only short ones. He hadn't been home in five years. And now he regretted it.

The navy comforter was unmussed on the bed, the shelf on the wall still contained his softball and hockey trophies. On the scarred pine dresser was the framed photo of his graduation from boot camp. Another of the day he'd become an officer. It was clear Andrew hadn't touched a solitary thing in here. Nor had Gerald. What had they been waiting for? The boy he'd been wasn't the man who had returned. Seeing his things waiting for him should have been comforting, but instead it made Noah feel even more like a stranger. What had happened to that young, idealistic boy? Where had he finally left him behind? Afghanistan? Bosnia?

The truth was that the house at Lazy L didn't actually feel like home anymore. He felt more relaxed, more contented, in the little rented house closer to town. Today as they had watched Beautiful's foal being born…that had been the first time that he'd really felt things click into place. He'd missed things about being on the farm. He'd remembered some happy moments when it had been the three of them all together.

Lily had been with him. And he'd been a fool and kissed her.

Noah sat heavily on the bed, hearing the box spring creak under his weight. He had let her simple touch carry him away, and then he'd slipped completely under her spell the moment her lips touched his. He'd been wanting to do it ever since the day he'd tried on the tux and her arms had come around his chest.

And practical, pretty Lily had been darkly sweet. He hadn't anticipated the punch to the gut response. Noah ran his hand through his hair, frowning. And then what? Even if he wanted to take it further—which he had, at least at the moment—he couldn't. He couldn't let her see him the way he was now. He couldn't bear to see her soft smile turn to horror, and that's what would happen if she saw what war had done to him. An army life was no life for her, but it wouldn't matter because as soon as she saw the marks it would be over. He could learn to rewrite his name, he could learn to tie his shoes and drive a car again. But he couldn't take the scars away. He couldn't change a single, damn thing.

His jaw hardened and he got up from the bed. One kiss and here he was, thinking about her and reminiscing in his old bedroom. What good would it do to remember? Not a bit that he could see. When he'd said that the boy he'd been was gone, he'd meant it.

He shut the door behind him with a firm click. When he'd said kissing her was a mistake, he'd meant that, too.

But then he leaned against the door frame, closing his eyes. Somehow he had to find a way to keep his attraction to her at bay. No more moments of weakness. The wedding was coming up, and for the sake of peace he would somehow manage to keep things amiable between them. He enjoyed her company. There was no reason to make the wedding a tense affair. He'd lock up whatever feelings he seemed to be developing, because no good could come of it. And when the wedding was over, he'd see about his options for the future.

Back in the part of his life that made sense.

"Noah."

He opened his eyes, startled by the sound of his brother's voice saying his name. He turned his head, saw Andrew at the bottom of the stairs. "Hey."

"What are you doing up there?"

Noah schooled his features. He didn't want Andrew to know how he was feeling about the house or about Lily. Lily was their friend. And Lazy L... It was clear to Noah that Andrew was really proud of what he was doing. Lily's words still rang in his ears. Andrew had wanted Noah to come home. If Andrew was trying to make up for lost time, he was too late. Their father was gone. The years were gone. What they had to work with was *right now.* And as much as he had no desire to hurt his brother, he couldn't look too far into the future yet. It was simply too big, too daunting.

"Just checking out my old room."

Andrew nodded. "You got a minute for a walk? I want to talk to you about something."

"Sure."

Noah looked at his bedroom door once more before going down the stairs. He pulled on his boots while Andrew waited on the porch, and then went outside. Wordlessly they started walking, heading toward the west hay field.

The sun was still in the sky but its light had mellowed as summer suns do. The blades of grass held a rosy hue, and the scattering of clouds across the sky had pink and lavender underbellies. It was Noah's favorite time, when there was slow warmth and the day was gently sighing that the work was done. At this time of day sometimes it was hard to believe he'd ever left.

"I'm glad you were here today," Andrew began. They slowed their steps, stopping before the boundary of the field, watching the grasses wave in the wind. "I didn't expect the mare to deliver."

Noah thought back to how relieved he'd been to see Lily in the house. It had been a long time since he'd helped a mare foal and he'd been afraid. Doubted that he could have handled any complications with one arm. But Lily had been there, backing him up, and he'd felt strong and capable when she'd beamed as the foal stood for the first time on wobbly legs. He swallowed hard. "I was glad to do it."

"You've been more help than you know, Noah. This summer would have been impossible without you being here."

"You would have hired someone."

"It's not the same as family."

Noah got an uncomfortable feeling in the center of his chest. Andrew hadn't looked at him while he was speaking, instead staring off into the distance. He didn't want to disappoint Andrew. It had been good, connecting with him again. But if Andrew was hoping for more…

The uneasiness grew as neither said anything for a few minutes. Finally Noah broke the silence, nodding at the hay field. "Just about time for the second cutting, don't you think?"

Andrew nodded. "Dawson said he'd do it. Look, I asked you out here because I have something to tell you."

And he didn't sound the least bit happy about it, Noah realized. Was it Jen? The ranch? Noah? "Just come out with it then." He hooked his thumb in his front pocket and faced his brother square on. A clean cut healed best.

Andrew met Noah's gaze and admitted, "I invited our mother to the wedding."

Noah's breath came out with a whoosh. "What? Our mother? Do you even know where she is?" He hadn't seen his mother since he was seven years old. He'd seen his father's heartbreak after she'd abandoned them, had seen how Andrew had been so confused and had kept waiting for her to come home. At seven, he had understood certain things slightly better than his little brother. But she hadn't ever come back and he'd never gone looking.

"She's been in Grande Prairie all along. I've seen her. Twice."

"But for the wedding…" Noah understood this was a big deal for Andrew. He even understood that Andrew wanted their mother there. Jen's parents would be there. It was a natural time to want family to be together. But they weren't a real family. It had all the potential of a big disaster. Maybe he wasn't well versed on other best-man duties, but this was one time he felt up to the job. And right now that was delivering a heavy dose of realism.

"Are you sure that's a good idea? I know you want her there, but think about it, Andrew. She hasn't been back in Larch Valley since she walked away from it. Memories are long here. You know that."

"Of course I do. Believe me. It wasn't exactly a picnic when I came back, you know. And there's always the chance she won't come. But she's the only family we've got, Noah. How can I not ask?"

"It's your wedding, and your decision," Noah replied.

"What about you, though? Noah, you've just come home. I don't want to upset you."

"And you haven't. Surprised, yes. But to me, she is a stranger. I accepted it a long time ago. She didn't seem to care about family all the years she was gone. I don't expect any of that has changed. It's one day. If it's what you want, I'll manage."

Andrew sighed. "There's more, something I should have told you long ago but didn't know how."

"More?" He let out a harsh laugh. He thought of standing up with Lily at the wedding, knowing how beautiful she was going to look and how he kept trying to hide his scars from her. Now there appeared to be family drama added to the mix.

"Gerald was not my biological father."

Nothing Andrew could have said would have surprised Noah more. Gerald had raised them both. "What are you talking about? Of course he was."

But Andrew shook his head. "No, he wasn't. And he was the one that made Mom leave. She was having an affair when I was conceived. But when she did it again, it meant the end of the marriage. And he refused to let her split us up. She left rather than face a big custody battle."

"And this is supposed to make me feel better?" Anger rushed through his veins, revitalizing him after the initial shock. "The fact that we're now half brothers?"

"Is that what bothers you? Not the affairs?" Andrew's words were laced with incredulity.

"I knew about the affairs. For the most part anyway. I heard more of the arguments than you did." Noah's anger had flashed and was now fading away. "And you're my brother, no matter what. What makes me mad is that you kept it from me."

He took several steps away, needing to walk, to expend some of the emotion bundling up inside him. Was *nothing* in his world staying the same? Through it all, he'd held on to Lazy L and the presence of his brother for stability while the rest of his world changed. Now that seemed to be slipping through his fingers, too.

And when Andrew had come asking to buy him out, he'd said nothing.

For the first time in days he almost felt the presence of his right arm even though it no longer existed. He could feel his hand balling into a fist, the cording of muscle as he longed to punch something in anger. But the bone and muscle and flesh were gone. Never in his whole life had he felt so impotent.

He stopped, hung his head and fought to calm his breaths, trying to make the sensation go away. "You should have told me."

"I don't expect you to understand it all in an evening. God knows I didn't," Andrew said quietly, coming to his brother's side. "And I knew about the parentage thing since before I left for university."

"That long." He couldn't keep the bitterness from his voice.

"It was what caused the rift between Dad and me. I wish I'd had the chance to make peace with him when he was alive. He was a good father."

Noah swore softly. "I had no idea. I really didn't."

Andrew put his hand on Noah's shoulder. "Our mother loved Dad in her way. She knew we'd have a better life with him than we would with her."

"You've had more time to think about it than I have."

"I know. I didn't tell you before because I was still trying to make sense of it myself."

The firm hand slid off Noah's shoulder and Andrew took a step back.

"Noah?"

"Yuh."

"This doesn't change that you are my brother. In every way. Remember that."

Noah heard Andrew's boots scuff away in the grass, but he stood a long while, looking out over the waving hay field. He'd only just started feeling that he was getting his life back. And now he felt more alone than ever.

# Chapter 6

The punch bowl held the remnants of a pink punch, the soda pop in it now flat and tasteless. Pink, lavender and white bows topped a paper plate hat trimmed with ribbons, and plates and pastry crumbs were scattered over the pink tablecloth. It was the remnants of a frilly, girlie bridal shower. As maid of honor, it had been Lily's duty to host. And it had been fun.

Hostess duties had kept her occupied over the afternoon, but now, looking at the mess left behind, Lily couldn't stop the sadness that crept into her heart. She had never had a shower. Planning to run away had meant that no one was supposed to know. There had been no silly games, no punch, no bows and cards and presents to unwrap. There'd been no bachelor party for Curtis, either. This afternoon Noah had taken Andrew, Dawson and Clay golfing in lieu of a stag party. It was all so very traditional. Predictable.

Thinking about it wore her out, and Lily simply didn't have the heart or ambition to clean everything up now. She turned her back on the messy kitchen and headed for the stairs. She had to keep her hands busy with something else. The wedding was only days away and she still couldn't seem to get the waist right on Jen's dress. She could work on that instead, and later, when the echoes of laughter and well-wishing had faded, she'd put her house to rights.

Upstairs, Lily slipped the dress over her hips and reached behind her, pulling up the zipper. She studied the mirror, tugging gently at the strapless bodice. Her figure wasn't a match to Jen's, so the fit wasn't quite right, but she could tell if there were puckers or pulls where there shouldn't be. The organza overskirt was being particularly fussy to work with and she was struggling with the waistline. She smoothed and tucked with her fingers, frowning in the mirror. It should have been Jen trying it on now, but she and her mother had taken her shower gifts back to her house. Lily frowned, working with the fabric, trying to see where the adjustment should be made. She wanted it perfect for tomorrow when Jen came to do the final fitting.

She sighed, knowing that this wasn't quite breaking her promise to herself. After all, if she'd had a dressmaker's dummy, the dress would be on it now instead of her. When she'd vowed she'd never put on a wedding dress again, this wasn't exactly what she'd had in mind. And she supposed it had been a rash pronouncement, one made in anger and mostly out of hurt and disillusionment.

If she'd really meant it, she would have thrown away the dress. The one that still hung in her closet. The one with the chiffon overskirt that had taken days to get just right...

She stared at the closed closet door for a long moment, then unzipped the zipper of Jen's gown and hung it on its special hanger. She put it in the closet and her hand rested on a white opaque bag. She'd managed to keep the overskirt flat and flowing just right in the end. If she could only see it on... Once again she wished for the dummy to help solve her problems. Her brow puckered. Did she dare? Even thinking about putting it on felt like tempting fate.

She remembered that day so clearly. The rush for the flight, the excitement of checking into the hotel room and the surreal moment of putting on her wedding gown. The moment of sadness as she missed having someone to help her with her hair, her crystal necklace that she'd made herself. Then the sadness giving way to excitement when Curtis had knocked on the door.

She took the bag out of the closet and laid it gently on the bed, unzipping the zip as if it was Pandora's box. But nothing emerged from the plastic beyond a wistful sense of nostalgia.

She'd designed the dress herself, going through pages of scrapbook paper until she got it just right, and she'd saved up the money she'd made working weekends for her mom to buy the material. She ran a finger over the fine chiffon, smiling at the memory of paying full price for the fabric so her mom wouldn't know what she was up to. Stolen moments she'd worked at it, measuring, cutting, stitching, while she and Curtis had been making plans. He'd been stashing away enough money to pay for their trip, ready to go the moment she'd had her birthday and was legal.

Lily bit down on her lip as she took the gown out of the bag. In those days she'd designed and sewed many of her own clothes, thinking of opening her own boutique while Curtis worked alongside his father. She'd dreamed of teaching her own daughter to cut and stitch. She unzipped the hidden zipper and stepped into the pristine white creation. She moved the hasp of the zipper upward, sucking in a bit to get it to the top. It fit. It was a little snug in the chest, but her figure was much the same as it had been when she was eighteen and full of dreams.

She went to the mirror and stood, staring at the fine stitch work. Spaghetti straps held the simple bodice, which draped and gathered at the side. The satin underskirt felt luxurious against her bare legs, while the chiffon fell with a long, soft ruffle down to the hem. Not a pucker or misplaced fold in sight.

Lily raised her arms, gathering the cloud of her hair into a twist, holding it with one hand while her eyes searched the reflection in the mirror.

"Is that Jen's dress?"

Lily jumped at the sound of a deep voice, releasing her hair in a tumble about her shoulders and catching her toe in the folds of the skirt.

"Noah!"

"You must not have heard me knock."

She pressed a hand to her heart, supremely embarrassed that he had found her in such a state. "So you just came in?"

"The door was unlocked. I saw your car and figured you were home. I take it your guests are gone?" He took a hesitant step inside her room, not waiting for her answer. "That's beautiful."

The compliment both touched her and cut like a knife. "You could have knocked harder," she snapped. The last thing she needed was Noah prying. If she'd heard the knock, she could have at least scrambled out of the gown and into her jeans again. She'd never meant for anyone to actually *see* her in the dress. Let alone the man she hadn't been able to erase from her thoughts. The memory of their kiss was stuck in her brain with disturbing clarity.

"I'm sorry. I wanted to show you something." His eyes looked sincere enough. Lily let out a breath and told herself to relax.

"Show me something?"

He nodded, a slow smile lighting his face making him look years younger. "I came to take you for a ride."

Lily understood immediately where the little boy smile had come from. "You finally got your truck."

"Yup."

"And you came to show it off."

"Yup."

"And I suppose taking Andrew or Jen for a drive wouldn't have sufficed." She grabbed at the opportunity for distraction, taking the focus off her appearance. He looked so hopeful she couldn't resist teasing him just a bit.

"I got it yesterday and drove the boys to the golf course today. I'm just on my way home and thought I'd stop."

She had to turn away from the pride in his voice. She was happy for him. Not being able to get around on his own had limited his freedom, and she understood how difficult it must have been for a man like him, who was used to being self-reliant. And yet she was reminded that every step of his recovery was one step further to his getting on with his life, and here she was, pathetically dressed up in a wedding dress that should never have seen the light of day again. She wished she'd never taken the garment bag out of the closet.

"Come for a drive with me, Lily."

There was something in his voice that called to her even though she couldn't say exactly what it was. But it almost sounded like need, a little thread of tension through the celebratory facade. And as much as she'd never admit it out loud, she liked being needed. Even if this development put him one step closer to being out of her life.

She twisted her fingers together, hating the mix of feelings that seemed to keep cropping up with planning Jen and Andrew's big day. She'd been contented here, buying her house, settling into her job, making friends. She'd even managed to avoid talk of babies and marriage and dating. Now Lucy was nearly due and Jen was alight with nuptial plans and she couldn't escape Noah even when she tried. Not that she'd tried very hard.

A few hours driving in a truck with Noah, away from white dresses and shower leftovers sounded very nearly like a perfect way to spend an afternoon.

"Just let me change," she replied softly. The sooner this gown was off and put away, the better. It had been a stupid thing to do, to take it out and try it on in the first place. Even if she did now remember how to fix the skirt.

"I'll wait, then," he answered.

Lily inhaled and exhaled twice, trying to calm her nerves as Noah's steps sounded on the stairs. He'd sought her out, as a friend. As someone to spend some time with. That was all.

She had to remember that he had apologized for making the mistake of kissing her. *She* was the one making a lot of something out of nothing, only because she was attracted to him. She stared at her reflection one last time.

Maybe she should simply relax. What was the harm in spending time, enjoying his company? She didn't have to worry about him falling in love or wanting anything more permanent that she wasn't capable of. It seemed pretty clear that he didn't think of her in *that way*.

And maybe she should just stop thinking, full stop. She pulled at the zipper and it slid down a few inches before getting jammed. Lily closed her eyes, told herself to relax and tried jiggling it up and down. How could it be stuck? It might have something to do with the fact that it was slightly too tight, she grimaced. She sucked everything in as best she could, but nothing. It was well and truly caught.

She went to the door and called downstairs. "Noah? You still there?"

"Yeah." She heard his voice come from the kitchen and she sighed.

"I seem to have run into a snag."

He came to the bottom of the stairs and looked up. He wore a plain T-shirt today in black, a pair of faded jeans hugging his lower body. Her eyes fell on his stump sock and she realized that working a zipper wasn't going to be easy for him, either.

"I've caught the zip."

He grinned. "Oh, dear."

Now he was teasing! Infernal man. And when had he developed dimples? She didn't seem to remember that detail before, but as he grinned up at her she saw two subtle indentations mocking her.

"Could you help? Please?"

"Since you asked so nicely…"

He came up the stairs toward her and she got a warm curl right in the center of her belly. He was coming to help with the dress, nothing more, but seeing him take the stairs one at a time, coming to her bedroom, seemed very intimate indeed. Her tongue darted out and wet her lips.

Noah reached the top step, stopping directly in front of her. She tilted her chin up to see his face. There was something in his eyes she hadn't seen before. The blue was deeper, the pupils larger, drawing her into the dark shadows, making her wonder what was behind them. Desire pulsed through her, shocking her with its potency as her well-intentioned self-talk went flying off on the summer breeze.

"Turn around," he commanded, the words soft but an order just the same, and she obeyed, giving her back to him, reaching behind and pulling her hair over her shoulder. His fingers toyed with the clasp and she realized that she was very happy for the fact that this dress, unlike Jen's, wasn't strapless. She wasn't wearing a bra underneath. All she was wearing was a pair of plain white bikini panties.

Each breath going into her lungs was torture as his warm fingertips played with the mechanism.

"It's stuck in the lining." Frustration rippled in his voice. "I can't get a good enough hold on it with one hand, and I don't want it to tear."

She nearly told him it didn't matter, but then she would have to explain it was not Jen's dress and she didn't want to open that particular can of worms. "What if you held the lining back and I tried to move the zipper up or down? You can be my eyes, tell me which way to go."

He pinched the fabric and she extended her right arm behind to grip the zipper. "Move it up," he said, and all the while she could feel the heat of his body oh-so-close to hers. Trying to suck things in was even harder when it felt as though every cell in her body was expanding.

She pulled up, felt it give a little.

"Down, just a bit, then up again."

She obeyed, following his directions, until his fingers closed over hers and pulled the zipper down. All the way down, to where it ended at the hollow of her spine.

Noah focused on the fabric caught in the mechanism rather than on the delicious curve of her neck. He wanted to kiss it something awful, but she was already wound up tight and tense all over. Knowing it set his body on fire, and he forced himself to concentrate on the zipper and not the pale skin revealed by the cut of the dress. Even pinching the fabric was proving difficult, and required all his attention.

But seeing her in a wedding gown had damn near gutted him, even if it wasn't her own. He'd never seen anything so beautiful, and knowing Lily had made it with her own hands had only added to its charm. Marriage had never even been on his radar, but Lily made him start to understand the attraction. He didn't know why she had Jen's dress on, but Andrew's eyeballs were going to be knocked out at the wedding.

The way his were right now as together they pulled the zipper to the bottom and a wedge of creamy white back was revealed to his gaze. The fact that she wasn't wearing a bra only fueled the flames.

The dress gaped at the waist and he caught a tempting glimpse of skimpy white underwear. She had two tiny dimples at the top of her tailbone. He wanted to touch them with a finger. Wanted to touch the skin that was scented with vanilla and almond.

But undressing a woman in a wedding gown was something he never intended to do. And now, with his body scarred and disfigured, he knew he had to step away. She'd made it clear each time she backed off that she wasn't interested in him in *that* way. And could he blame her? He had a difficult enough time dealing with his injuries. It was different for a lover. There were some things you could never expect a woman to overcome.

He stepped back, swallowing hard, exerting restraint and keeping his fingers to himself. "There you go. Good as new. I'll wait for you downstairs."

Lily heard his footsteps muffled on the carpet of the stairs. She gathered the sagging skirt up in her hands and rushed back into the bedroom. She let the gown drop to the floor and hurriedly shoved on her jeans and put on a bra and light sweater. Good as new indeed. If he only knew.

She'd wanted him to touch her, so badly she had ached. She'd wanted to feel his fingers on her skin, wanted him to slide the straps off her shoulders and she'd wanted to turn into his embrace, feeling his warm body against hers.

But he'd turned away, and she just thanked God she hadn't been brazen enough to do it and make a fool of herself. Clearly he was not feeling the same incendiary attraction that she was.

She had to stop thinking of him this way. He'd made it clear that Lazy L was just a pit stop on the road to his recovery, and that was just fine with her. But she couldn't get him out of her mind. And she wasn't thinking about him in a best man kind of way....

Now he was waiting for her to go for a drive, and her body was still humming from the simple contact of his fingers on her skin. How could she possibly go with him? But if she backed out now he'd know how desperately he'd affected her. No, she had to go downstairs and act as if nothing had happened. She grabbed a hair elastic and wound her hair into a ponytail. She would go for a drive with him. They would have *fun* and forget all about this one-sided sexual attraction business. And she would not allow herself to feel let down that instead of kissing her again as she wanted, he had walked away.

It was for the best. Kissing Noah wouldn't lead anywhere.

When she went downstairs she found him outside on the deck, looking at the long range of mountains to the west. "Sorry about the mess," she said, going out to meet him. "That's all right. I was just admiring the view." He didn't look at her, just rested his elbow on the wood railing while the sun glinted off his hair. "How'd the shower go?"

"Oh, as you'd expect. Lots of women talking about girlie things and a predominance of the color pink." She smiled softly. "You wouldn't have enjoyed it at all."

"You might be surprised. Women and food in one location. It's hard to find a downside."

Lily smiled shyly, remembering once again how his

fingers had felt on her skin. "Noah Laramie, are you flirting with the maid of honor?"

He paused for a minute, as if deliberating an answer. What he said wasn't at all what she expected.

"It's been a long day. I felt the need to get away."

Somehow Lily found the courage to ask what she was dying to know. "So you came to me?"

"Yeah." He smiled at her, just the hint of his dimple taunting. "Yeah, Lily. I came to you."

Lily struggled to keep everything normal. "You must be relieved to have some measure of freedom these days," she remarked, leaning her elbows on the deck railing, trying to shift the subject. His admission had made her heart beat way too fast. "No more putting up with my driving."

"Your driving wasn't so bad." He smiled, treating her to a sidelong glance before gazing back out over the trees and fields. "But I'm glad I don't have to inconvenience you and Andrew anymore."

"I don't think either of us minded."

He paused for a few moments, as though he was on the verge of saying something but changed his mind. He rolled his thumb in a circle. "Even so. I don't like to be beholden to people."

She wasn't offended by his independent streak any-more; she admired it. Even if it did make him stubborn to deal with at times. At least he knew what he wanted and didn't back away from it.

"So, where are we going?"

He turned away from the view at last. "The mountains. I've been staring at them for nearly a month. With working and appointments and wedding plans, there hasn't been an opportunity to go."

Lily nearly mentioned that if he'd said something she would have taken him, but she didn't want to spoil the moment for him. "Then let's go."

Lily locked the deck door behind them and followed him out the front door, grabbing her purse from a hook and locking that door, as well. It didn't matter how long she was in Larch Valley or how safe she felt…locking her door was a matter of habit. A remnant of the city living she'd experienced all her life.

Noah went to the passenger side of the truck and opened her door. It wasn't fancy, not like Andrew's huge diesel with all the bells and whistles, and it wasn't even brand-new; it was a few years old with some miles on the odometer. It didn't matter to Lily; she knew it represented freedom for Noah. It still had that new car smell from detailing and it suited Noah's needs just fine.

He hopped up into the driver's seat and started the engine. Lily stared at the console as he put the truck into gear. Everything normally on the right-hand side of the steering column was now on the left, within reach of his good arm. A round knob was installed on the wheel for ease of steering. Before hitting the gas, Noah turned his head and looked at her, his expression so full of boyish happiness that she laughed. He seemed almost like a teenager getting a driver's license for the first time.

"This," she said, buckling her seat belt and nodding at the driver's controls, "is pretty cool."

"Isn't it?" He let off the brake and pulled out into the street. "A few mods and I'm ready to go." He turned a corner, heading for the dusty side roads. "You don't mind the scenic route, do you?"

"Not at all."

The roads were paved but without lines or shoulders,

and constructed like a grid, so each one either went north and south or east and west. As they passed through rolling ranchland dotted with spruce trees and grassy fields of beef herds, Noah tilted his head toward the stereo. "You want some music?"

There was a CD in the deck and Lily hit the play button. They enjoyed the day and the music without words for several minutes as they came out at the highway, heading north to Longview. It was nice not to feel the need to make conversation to fill uncomfortable gaps. Noah seemed to enjoy driving so much that she slid down in the seat a bit and crossed her left ankle over her right knee, getting comfortable.

At Longview they turned onto the road leading to Kananaskis and the Peter Lougheed Park. Here the dwellings were even more scattered; at times they drove for miles without seeing a soul. They climbed as the road moved northwest, up through the mountains, sharp faces and peaks and cattle ranging freely. Once they slowed down to watch a gathering of bighorn sheep on the jagged rocks, with ragged coats and little ones with nubbins for horns at their sides. Lily thought of the foal and finally broke the silence.

"How's the baby doing?"

Noah looked over briefly, a smile lighting his face that seemed to heat the cab of the truck. "She's fine. Her mama, too."

"Did Andrew name her?" She knew Jen had christened the mare, and she hoped the baby wasn't called "the foal" all the time. She deserved a proper name.

"I did."

He didn't look away from the road this time, and Lily

thought she saw a slight blush infuse his cheeks. "You did? You named an itty-bitty baby horse?"

"You're teasing me."

"I am, yes." She rested her head back on the seat with a smug smile. "So, what did you name her?"

"Gorgeous."

Lily laughed. "Beautiful... Gorgeous...it fits. Bit sentimental for a tough old soldier like you, though, don't you think?"

He pulled into a lay-by spot at the crest of Highwood Pass and put the truck into Park. He half turned on his seat to face her. "Is that how you see me? A tough old soldier?"

He wasn't smiling anymore. She wondered if she'd hit a nerve or if there was something bothering him, as she'd suspected earlier. "I don't know. Sometimes."

He turned off the ignition and opened the door to the truck, sliding out and shutting it, leaving her sitting alone.

There was something bothering him. Something beyond dealing with his injury. Lily got out of the truck, too, and followed him to the edge of the paved parking space. She hesitated. The earlier lightheartedness of going for a drive was gone, and instead he was very nearly unapproachable. She was getting used to his mood swings by now. If he had sought her out rather than his brother or even Jen, then there had to be a reason.

She went to him and laid a hand in the space between his shoulder blades. "What's wrong?"

The muscles were so tense beneath her fingers. Had he had bad news? Was it to do with his latest physio appointment? The change had occurred when she'd called him a tough old soldier. She rubbed gently. "Noah, what's happened? Is there something wrong with your recovery?"

He shook his head. "No, nothing like that. Physio is going well."

"Then what?"

He turned to face her. "How much do you know about Andrew? About our parents?"

"I know that your mother left when you were very young and your father raised you."

He nodded, but his lips formed such a thin, forbidding line Lily knew there was more to the story. "Is this to do with your parents?"

"I'm not sure it's for me to tell."

She reached out and grabbed his wrist. "If you didn't want to tell me, you wouldn't have brought me here. You might as well come out with it."

The tense lines of his face eased a little. "There's that practical streak again."

"You can thank me for it later." She softened as his eyes seemed to ask her to understand even though he hadn't yet said the words. "Let me help you, Noah."

"Andrew dropped a couple of bombshells the night Gorgeous was born. One is that Gerald was not his father. We're only half brothers."

Lily tried to hide her shock. Jen hadn't breathed a word, and she knew from talk around town that Andrew had always been considered Gerald Laramie's upstart boy. But for Noah not to have known…and especially now, when family was so important.

"And does that change anything for you?"

"Of course!" He pulled his arm away from her hand. "No, not really. I don't know."

"What does it change?"

"Everything I thought I knew. Andrew's known since high school, and yet no one bothered to say a thing to me. If I'd known..."

"Ah yes." Lily had played this game often enough and could guess what was going through his mind. "If I'd only, right? Only there is no point because the past cannot be changed." She knew that well enough, too. Just as much as she knew letting go was easier said than done. "Does it change how you feel about Andrew?"

"Of course not!" He took a step backward. "He's my brother."

"If that's the case, then you will come to terms with the rest. Just give it time."

Noah walked away, kicking at some random stones that were on the asphalt. "Andrew and Jen have invited our mother to the wedding."

Lily's lips dropped open. "The mother who left you when you were children."

"Yes."

"When did you see her last?"

Silence, with the only sound the odd vehicle passing by and the breeze through the grass and fireweed.

"When I was seven."

"Oh, Noah." He didn't have to say any more. This wedding was going to be difficult enough for him. She'd understood that from the start. She knew he didn't much enjoy being out in public, being stared at and whispered about behind hands. In a city of strangers it was bad enough. But in Larch Valley, where everyone seemed to know everything, it was worse. To ask him to stand up at the wedding, knowing the truth, and to face his mother after all these years...

"Are you scared?"

"Scared?" He wrinkled his brow as he stared at her. "Why would I be scared?"

"Of seeing her? It would be understandable." She went to him and laid her hand on his arm.

"She's little more than a stranger to me, Lily. I know why she left. I stopped hating her for it long ago. It was why I joined the army. For a new start."

He stared out over the mountain range, and Lily felt the wall go up again, the transparent yet tangible barrier of self-protection.

"I didn't come here to talk about my mother."

"Then why did you?"

His gaze plumbed hers for long seconds. "Because today was the hardest day I've had to face yet, and at the end of it…"

He broke off and looked away.

"At the end of it?" She prodded gently, holding her breath, feeling the connection zip between them again, drawing them together.

"At the end of it, the one person that seemed to make sense was you."

## Chapter 7

Lily tore her eyes from the green curves of the valley below. Perhaps they weren't so different after all. They'd both made choices based on what they *didn't* want out of life and along the way found a measure of peace in belonging—him within the army and her in Larch Valley. Now all of that was being ripped away bit by bit for Noah. The life he'd made for himself wouldn't ever be quite the same again. Andrew was the only family he had left now that Gerald was gone, and the two of them had held on to this family secret, keeping Noah in the dark. Either way, she didn't know whether to be thrilled or afraid that he had sought her out after a difficult day.

"The afternoon with the guys didn't go well?"

"It went as well as I should have expected." There was a harshness underlying the words.

"What went wrong?

"Andrew loves to golf. I thought it would be a fun afternoon. The two of us, Clay, Dawson. I would play chauffeur. Some laughs, a few beers and a steak sandwich at the clubhouse, you know?"

"But?" She prompted him to continue. His eyes had turned a steely dark blue that she recognized as his stubborn, frustrated look.

"But I felt like an idiot. I drove the cart and played caddy and laughed along, but the whole time I was thinking about how Andrew had known about this for years and no one had bothered to let me in on the secret. And then I was sitting waiting as everyone else was playing. And I couldn't, because I can't golf with one arm."

"And so you felt useless."

"Yes."

Lily's heart ached for him. Noah was not useless. He had so much to give. So many talents, so much insight and intelligence. She hated that he'd been made to feel less just because he wasn't physically capable of hitting a ball with a silly club.

"Andrew should have seen how hard it would be for you and suggested something else," she replied sharply. "I know, I know," she continued as Noah started to open his mouth. "It's his wedding. But still, Noah. A little consideration. After all, he's the one that dropped the bombshell, too." She put a hand on her hip.

Noah's jaw softened with surprise. "Are you defending me?"

"Someone has to, don't they?"

Without warning, he reached out and pulled her close, against his chest where his heart beat strong and true. A few stones rolled beneath her sneakers as her weight shifted. "Thank you," he whispered into her hair. "I was feeling pretty selfish."

She inhaled deeply, absorbing the scent and warmth of him before standing back from his embrace and looking up. "You? Selfish? There isn't a selfish bone in your body."

He shook his head slightly, while his hand still rested at the base of her spine. "Oh, yes, I am. I've done nothing but think of myself lately."

"You earned that right."

"It struck me today that I've avoided town, avoided people, because I'm different now. People look at me differently, talk to me differently. It's why I hesitated when Andrew asked me to be his best man. Today I got a taste of how it will feel to be up at the front of that church. Like I'm on display."

Noah always seemed so take charge; hearing him voice his insecurities surprised and touched her.

"You never felt like that in the army?"

"In the army you're all in there together. Take a look at my company picture sometime. We all look…"

"Alike," she finished. "Did you tell Andrew how you felt about it at all?"

He shook his head again. "Not really. I just let it ride."

A van pulled into the parking lot and Noah removed his hand from her back, their cocoon of privacy broken. They walked back to the truck, pausing and leaning up against the hood as the summer breeze ruffled her hair, sending little pieces scattering out of her ponytail.

"So you asked me to come with you…"

"I needed to talk."

A small smile crept up Lily's cheek. Beyond any of the times she'd nearly died from wanting his touch, at this moment right now she felt closer to Noah than she had since they'd met. Closer than today when he'd seen her in the dress, or in the barn or at his house or measuring tuxedos. Did he realize how silly it sounded? He was a champion at keeping his feelings to himself. She supposed it had to do with the macho idea that men didn't discuss their feelings. And yet he'd wanted to talk. To her. For some reason it meant a lot for him to tell her why.

"Why me, Noah? Why not Andrew, or Jen?" She asked it quietly, then held her breath.

The answer didn't come right away. The van unloaded a group of tourists who were not concerned with Noah and Lily but more about taking a picture by the sign that marked Highwood Pass's claim to fame—the highest paved point in Canada. Noah ignored them, instead murmuring softly, "Come here."

Lily obeyed, taking his hand, and he moved her to a spot in front of him. His arm came around her, pulling her back against his body that still leaned against the truck, tucking her head beneath his chin. It felt good to be held. Safe and secure and wanted.

"I told you because I trust you, Lily. Not sure why. I'm not even sure how. Maybe because you didn't grow up here and it's easier. Maybe because you always tell me the truth. But I trust you."

Lily closed her eyes. It was true that when they spoke she was very plain. But there were so many things she hadn't told him. Things she didn't want him to know. Things she hadn't wanted anyone to know. Even Jen knew nothing about Curtis, or why she and her mother had become estranged. And Jen was the closest thing she had to family.

And yet, she trusted him, too. Noah would never judge her. She knew it as surely as she knew this wedding was going to be difficult for both of them.

"I don't like weddings, either." She admitted it and instantly felt better. Somehow with Noah she could stop pretending.

"You don't?" His head moved against hers as if he were trying to peer around to see her expression.

She let out a light laugh. "No, I don't."

"But you are always helping Jen and making the dress and seemed, I don't know, excited."

How could she explain that while she loved her life here, sometimes she still felt the need to put a happy face on for the world? That the woman people saw wasn't the true Lily? She kept that part of her locked up safe and sound.

"Jen is my best friend and it's my problem, not hers. I wouldn't upset her for the world. Just like you didn't want to lay it on Andrew. You grin and fake it. Today's shower was one of the hardest things I've ever had to do."

"Fine pair we make."

"Do you suppose they knew how much trouble we'd be when they asked us?"

Noah laughed, the motion bumping against her back and she leaned more into his shoulder. He gasped slightly at the contact, and Lily felt a quick panic, wondering if she'd hurt him accidentally.

But if she had, he didn't let on. "I thought all women dreamed of weddings."

Ah, there it was. Lily blinked, the words sitting on her tongue. She could explain about the dress today, about the hurt that had never quite gone away. But in the end she couldn't do it. Not all of it.

"My mom never got married. In fact…I never even met my father. She was always, oh, I don't know, open to opportunities. More of a free spirit. Still is. But I think that's when I started hating weddings. At first it was my friends being flower girls. And then just…resenting her, I suppose. She was a seamstress, you know. She'd make these gorgeous dresses, but they were never for her. They would hang on the rack, all white and lacy and shining and all I wanted was for her to put one on and get married and settle us down, instead of moving from place to place all the time. I used to wonder why she spent hours on something she believed so little in. But her motto has always been to love deep and love often. And I suppose she did it because they were beautiful and because it paid the bills."

Noah squeezed her close. "I didn't know. You sound like you were a very lonely girl."

Lily clung to the words and to the feel of his strength surrounding her. "I suppose I was. It was always a different apartment, a different school, new kids. It was why I fell in love with Larch Valley. For the first time in my life I felt like I belonged somewhere. And I'll do this for Jen—dress up in a pink dress and carry flowers and craft centerpieces—because she's the family I found here."

"And I am…?"

The words hung in the air as the tourists piled back in their van and pulled out of the lot.

"You are someone who needed a friend. And you are Andrew's brother, so that makes you family, too."

"I don't want to be an obligation to you."

"You've never been an obligation." Her heart stuttered as she blurted it out, a fearful beat that suggested maybe she'd admitted a little too much. "Do you know what I see when I look at you, Noah? I don't see your limitations. I see a strong, determined man, and before you know it you will be going back to the life you love, too."

A lump formed in her throat at the last words. It was the danger of getting to know someone. Of caring. They always had another life waiting somewhere, didn't they. She'd known from the start he was merely recuperating. That he had every intention of going back to his life in the army. And why shouldn't he reclaim his life?

But she'd let herself get close anyway. It didn't matter how many times she'd told herself it was for the best. Heck, she'd even convinced herself that knowing he would be going back to active duty made him safe. He would not ask for more than she could give.

She turned within his embrace, so she was facing him. For a few moments their gazes caught and held, and they both knew there was more than friendship— obligatory or not—at work. And then a recognition that the inevitable must happen in the end. He was a soldier. It wasn't something he could just quit. It was as much *who* he was as *what* he was.

"So," she said quietly, "we'll get each other through it. You'll grin and bear it. And you can look at me and remember I really dislike the color 'petal pink' and the smell of lilies."

"It's a deal."

She stepped out of his embrace, knowing she must and yet wanting so much more. Perhaps it was enough that they'd silently seemed to acknowledge the attraction. Now it was dealt with and maybe even put aside for the greater good.

But as they got back in the truck and headed home,

Lily could only remember how good she'd felt being held by him and how close she'd come to telling him the real reason she dreaded weddings so much.

The platter of grilled steaks was down to juices on the plate and the tray of brownies mere crumbs when Noah approached her. The rehearsal party was winding down, now reduced to wandering with cups of coffee or tea. Lily had helped Jen set it up right here at Lazy L—two of the new tables Jen had bought for the balcony seating at Snickerdoodles, white linens and fresh-cut flowers that Lily had snipped from Agnes Dodds's considerable garden. She'd visited with Mr. and Mrs. O'Keefe, chatted to the minister and his wife, made plans for the following day with Jen.

And the whole time, all she could think about was Noah, and how he'd confided in her, and how much she wanted to feel his arm around her again.

"Do you want to get out of here?" Noah's rough voice tickled her ear.

The low invitation sent her pulse fluttering. "I can't yet. I promised Jen I'd help clear up."

"I need your help with something. I can wait for you."

She smiled then, letting the end-of-the-day warmth and the relaxed atmosphere woo her. "Oooh, mysterious."

He chuckled, the sound low and sexy. Lily looked at him, liking dressed-up Noah. Not the jeans and T-shirts of his everyday life, nor the formality of the tux tomorrow, but a pair of chocolate-brown cotton pants and a lightweight tan shirt. The cuff was rolled up on his left arm, the other side pinned to hide the end of his stump. She stacked a few more plates and angled him a questioning look. "Dare I ask how you rolled up your sleeve, Mr. Laramie?"

"I don't suppose you'd believe me if I said my teeth."

She snorted and then bit down on her lip. "Funny. But no." She turned, holding the plates before her and smiling up into his face. "You are much easier to be around when you are not so grumpy."

"I must be losing my touch."

Hardly, Lily thought as she forced herself to slide away, taking the dishes to the kitchen. Since they'd gone for that drive, he seemed to be more in his stride than ever. Maybe talking had helped restore some of his confidence. He certainly had a way of keeping her attention.

Mrs. O'Keefe was drying the last of the glasses when Lily poured herself a cup of tea. The brew was hot and soothing and she took a moment, listening to the mother-daughter chatter about plans and big days, and for the first time in years she missed her own mother. She missed the Saturday afternoons when Jasmine had made tea and they'd baked butter cookies. Or when she was older, sitting with sketch pads together, designing clothes, stealing ideas from each other's drawings. Her mother had always encouraged Lily's sense of daring and adventure. But the moment Lily had dared to actually use it, the result had been disastrous. Jasmine had been the first one to point out what a horrible mistake she'd made. And Lily had never picked up a sketch pad again.

"Lily?"

Jen's voice pulled her out of her woolgathering and she forced a smile. "Sorry?"

Jen came over and took Lily's empty cup. "You need to go home. We can't have a tired maid of honor tomorrow."

"But I am supposed to help you." She shook off the memories and smoothed her hands down her skirt. "Not the other way around."

"It's nearly done now anyway. And Mom's here. And I'm running on adrenaline anyway." Jen's face was lit up like a candle, glowing with happiness. "You've done so much. The dress…" For a second Lily was afraid Jen was going to cry. But the wobbly smile straightened. "The gown is perfect. Just be at my house at two, ready to get dressed, okay?"

"Okay." Lily was helpless in the face of so much happiness. She didn't begrudge her friend one iota of it. She gave Jen a quick hug. "I'll be there."

She looked out the kitchen window. Noah was climbing into his truck, but he paused and gazed back at the house, as though he was looking for her, asking her to follow him. She took her purse from a hook behind the door and wished everyone a good-night. Went to her car and got in behind the wheel. Drove into town and down the main drag toward her subdivision at the far west end.

But partway there she turned south, headed toward the little gray house where she knew he was waiting. He had asked for her help. And as much as it frightened her, she knew that whenever Noah asked for her, she'd be there.

Noah's truck was parked in the driveway and Lily pulled in behind it. He'd said he needed help with something. Considering the wedding was tomorrow, she hoped it had nothing to do with his tuxedo. His continuing therapy meant he was getting stronger, and the work on the ranch had kept him in shape. But surely everything still fit. The measurements had only been taken a little over a month ago.

The door was unlocked, and Lily walked through the quiet house to the back door. She found him sitting on the step, his arm folded over his knee as he stared past the back fence to the line of shrubs marking the back alley.

"Nice night," she commented softly.

"We survived."

"It helped having a partner in crime."

Lily smiled, sitting down beside him, the hem of her skirt tickling the back of her ankles. Noah had stood beside Andrew at the front of the church as the pianist played a Rachmaninov rhapsody and the minister issued directions as she was walking. It had all felt scripted and silly and with his back to the minister, Noah had rolled his eyes at her, making her smile bloom. They'd walked through the order of service and then it had been over. Jen's mom had placed the simple pew markers on the ends of the benches during the rehearsal, and in the morning, Kristin, the local florist, would deliver the floral arrangements. It had been particularly well-organized in true Jen fashion.

As she sat next to Noah, saying nothing in the twilight, she felt an emptiness open inside her. These moments happened more and more often as Jen's big day approached. Lily had never had a wedding rehearsal. Never had pew markers or special cloths for tables or a maid of honor. And she'd been okay with it, because she and Curtis had made their own plans.

She sighed. She would get through tomorrow.

At her sigh, Noah shifted over a few inches closer

and put his arm around her, pulling her close so that her head fit into the curve of his shoulder.

She wasn't the only one dreading the formalities. Somehow they'd both get through it. She'd make sure of it.

"Busy day today." He spoke quietly; it fit the softness of the evening.

"Busier one tomorrow. First the ceremony and then the reception and dance."

"Yeah."

"So what's the emergency?" She stayed where she was, wanting just a few minutes more of the accord she seemed to find when she was in his embrace. "You said you needed help with something. Is it the tux?"

"No, the suit's great. They even pinned the sleeves in place during the final fitting. All I need to do is put it on. It's…" He hesitated. "It's the dance."

Her mouth formed a round O. "I see."

His breath fanned warmly on her hair as he turned his head the slightest bit. "I never thought of it until today when Jen was talking about Andrew dancing with her mother and she with her father tomorrow night…and I realized that I'll probably have obligations, as well."

"Not if you don't want to. I'm sure if you explain… Jen won't hold you to those traditions."

"I still have two legs, Lily. And I work really hard to avoid anyone making allowances for me. Or excuses."

"Don't I know it." It was one of the things that drove her crazy—his stubbornness—but also something she admired so much. He worked so hard at being self-reliant.

"We're going to dance together, Lil."

He shortened her name and it sent curls of intimacy

spiraling through her. Dancing with him tomorrow would be easy. There would be people there, friends and guests and it was expected. But here, tonight, she was afraid.

"It'll be fine, don't worry," she reassured him lightly.

But at her flippant tone he removed his arm from around her shoulders and got up from the step, moving inside, leaving her sitting in the cold that settled over the open prairie on a clear night.

She shivered, felt guilty. He had honestly asked for her help and she had brushed him off, simply because she cared about him too much. Because she wanted him at least as much as she *didn't* want him—perhaps more. Because she was *afraid*. Even to her, that reasoning was flawed.

She got up and followed him inside. He was standing in the middle of the living room, the protective wall he tended to build around himself back in place again. What was it that made him so easy for her to read? Why did she want to?

"I'm sorry, Noah. I didn't mean to make light of it. Of course you're self-conscious."

Noah turned, seeing Lily silhouetted by the pale light coming through the back door. Did she really think this was about him being embarrassed about his arm? He couldn't care less. But perhaps it was better this way. Maybe it was better than her knowing that what he really feared was disappointing her tomorrow. She had been there for him for weeks, and he knew she was dreading the wedding as much as he was.... He wanted to leave her with a good memory of the day. She deserved it. Suddenly he stopped caring about what he looked like, or what people said; he just wanted to be able to dance with her and not have it be a disaster. He wasn't even sure if he could hold her properly.

"I can't hold you the traditional way," he admitted. "And I don't want us to try to figure this out in front of a hundred people tomorrow."

"What do you want to do?"

"I want to dance with you."

"Now?" Her lips parted as she took two steps forward. His memory was assaulted by the soft smell of her perfume, a little bit floral, a little bit citrusy as she'd leaned against him outside. He wanted to be that strong man for her, just this once.

"Now," he murmured, closing the distance between them. "Away from everyone. Just you and me." He swallowed, wondering how it was he wanted to confide in her the very reason he was afraid. Wanted to tell her about all the doubts he was having about what he'd done, where his life was going, the upcoming decisions he knew he had to make. It was more than a physical demanding, though there was definitely that aspect. His body's reaction to her was loud and clear.

The trouble was, he wanted to share everything with her, and he was afraid she'd hand it right back to him with a no-thank-you. How could he expect her to overcome his disfigurement when he could hardly stand to look at himself in the mirror? He couldn't hide the missing arm. But he had successfully hidden the other angry effects of that morning in the desert.

"My right arm is less than half and I…I don't want you to be turned off tomorrow. Hell," he breathed, unable to look into her eyes any longer, turning away from the pity he saw there. "I'd give anything to have two good arms to hold you with right now."

The silence bore down on him until he heard the sound of her steps behind him. There was the click of the stereo and the sound of her putting the remote control down on the shelf. Soft music played quietly behind him and every muscle in his body tensed. He could imagine holding her close, moving their feet together. Why was it that at these moments, he would swear he could still feel his hand, longing to reach out and touch her? To feel her hair between his fingers? He closed his eyes, unable to fight the tingling sensation as his brain's memory warred with reality. Hating it and yet trying to imprint it on his memory anyway.

And then her hand was there, warm against the flat of his back. "Then dance with me, Noah."

Slowly he turned, saw her looking up at him with caring and acceptance. He'd hidden things from her for so long—bouts of phantom pain and discomfort and the annoyances of having to deal with mundane tasks. He'd gotten quite good at it. But now, she held up her right palm and he placed his left one against it as her body came closer to his; only a whisper apart. He could not pull her close as he wanted, and held himself stiffly, hating his injury more now than he had in any moment since he'd awoken in Kandahar after the firefight.

And then Lily reached out with her left hand, slid her arm around his back and pressed her body lightly against his.

He swallowed, wishing for the first time for a prosthetic so he could at least pretend to hold her as a man should.

He cupped her hand in his and shuffled his feet along

to the music, feeling her sway with him as they took small steps in the dark living room. In years past, he would have used his right hand to stroke her back, or toy with the hair at the back of her neck. Tonight he could do none of those things. Tonight he was more attracted to her than he'd ever been to any woman, and he was helpless to do anything about it, even as they quietly moved in a slow circle. Tonight he wanted to explain to her about all his injuries, to show his scars. But to do that would be sending her away, and he couldn't do it. Not yet. So he prayed that she held on and that the song wouldn't end too soon.

Lily bit down on her lip, the feelings pulsing through her raw and real. She'd realized right away that by holding her right hand traditionally, he would not have a hand to put at her waist. Instead, she'd put hers around him, moving carefully so she wouldn't bump his arm. As a solo voice and guitar wooed the air around them, their feet had started moving, and his fingers had tightened over hers almost painfully.

He could have simply gone against tradition and not danced tomorrow. But instead he was allowing himself to be vulnerable, to do something despite his disability, despite how it would look. She was glad…so glad. Being held against him, swaying with him in the dark was the sweetest thing she'd ever known.

Her hand slid up his right shoulder blade, stroking against the cotton, every fibre in her body vibrating with life, like smooth ripples on a pond. With a mixture of wonderment and fear, she let her fingers glide over the crest of his shoulder and slowly, testing, over the tricep of his arm, to where she felt the silicone cap beneath his shirt.

His muscles tightened beneath her touch, his whole body alert, and she held her breath, moving her finger-tips back to the line of his shoulder, up to his neck, across the line where his hair met his collar. And back down again, wanting, needing to know all of him.

"Lily," he whispered, but she cut off any refusal he could utter.

"I don't want to pretend it doesn't exist," she whispered, letting her hand rest where his collarbone met his shoulder. "It's part of who you are."

"Only a part," he whispered bitterly, his feet halting.

But she looked up at him, his dark eyes mere shadows shining down at her. "Yes, Noah. Only one part. Why won't you share it with me?"

He seemed to struggle for a few moments for an answer. When it came, his voice was rough and raw, as if it physically hurt to speak.

"Because I want to be perfect for you."

At that moment, Lily felt herself going. Sliding out of the life she'd built for herself into a place so painfully sweet it stole her breath. There was nothing she could do to stop the rush of feeling.

"You are," she whispered. She took her hand from his and framed his face with her fingers. "Oh, Noah, you are."

His eyes glittered at her as the music stopped. With his left arm free, he looped it around her waist and pulled her against his chest. Then he lowered his head and kissed her until all the reasons against them scattered like the stars.

## Chapter 8

"You look beautiful, Jen."

Lily stood back, staring at her best friend, who simply beamed as she stood in the middle of the bedroom. Lily blinked back a small tear as the photographer snapped a candid photo of the two of them together. The intrusion was a welcome one for Lily. The last thing she wanted to do was get overly emotional today. Knowing there was always the chance of being snapped, she kept her features well schooled.

Jen reached out and took her hand. "And so do you. The dresses are so lovely, Lily. I can't thank you enough."

Lily felt the sting again and covered it by giving Jen a quick hug. "You are a gorgeous and happy bride," she whispered. "That's all the thanks I need."

She turned away and retrieved the bouquets still sitting in their tissue and boxes on the bed. "Now you are ready. I have the ring and you have your flowers and there is a surprise for you outside."

"A surprise?" Jen rushed to the window. "Oh, Lily!"

Lily smiled. "We can't have you going to the wedding in my old car, can we? We're going to ride in style. But she's not much for speed. We should get going."

With a delighted giggle, Jen rushed to the door and outside, holding up her tiny train as she tripped down the walk. Lily sighed and followed, carrying a small bag with makeup fixes and the ring. Outside she met Jen by the side of a horse-drawn black buggy.

"Wherever did it come from?"

Lily laughed, she couldn't help it. Jen had planned the day meticulously, but she hadn't suspected a thing. "Mrs. Dodds knows a lot of people. It's from Noah and me."

"You two…" Jen paused, her hand in the driver's and her toes on the foot plate. "You really are a pair, aren't you."

Lily shook her head, denying the flash of elation she felt at being paired up with Noah for real. She motioned for the driver to help Jen up to the seat. "No, we're not," she replied, following suit and settling on the cushioned seat. She refused to let Jen see how complicated it all was. Especially after last night. The memory of those few stolen minutes still made her dizzy. Remembering his mouth on hers, or the way his arm had pulled her tight against his muscled body. "We're friends, that's all. That's what you said you wanted," she reminded Jen. The last thing she wanted was for Jen to know she and Noah had kissed. More than once. It was fragile enough without outside interference.

With a flick of the reins by the driver, the buggy jolted and they were on their way.

"Besides," Lily continued before Jen could reply, "today is your day. Your wedding. Noah and I should be way down on your list of discussable topics."

"I can't believe it's happening." Jen's hands fidgeted in her lap. "For so many years, I thought we'd lost our chance, you know?" Jen's eyes lit with anticipation.

Lily smiled, pushing back the bittersweet memory of her own wedding excitement only moments before it had gone so desperately wrong. Jen would have a perfect day. Lily would make sure of it.

"Are you nervous?"

"A little." Jen pressed her hand to her belly. "I don't know why. I've wanted this since forever."

"Just remember who is waiting for you at the end of the aisle," Lily advised, running a hand over the skirt of her pink dress. Noah would be standing at the front with Andrew. Noah would be in his tuxedo. The same Noah who had held her and danced with her and kissed her last night until she was sure her heart would break with love. The strong, irascible man had shown her his vulnerable side. And it had turned everything she thought she knew on its head.

*Noah.*

"Oh, Lily, listen!"

The church bells were clanging in the summer breeze and Lily's smile wobbled. It wasn't fair to make comparisons. But when had life truly been fair? She wouldn't begrudge her friend this moment for all the world. But it wasn't fair that Lily had been cheated out of one wedding, and it wasn't fair that now, when she finally fell in love again, it was with the wrong man.

They pulled up to the church as the bells ceased pealing, the photographer pulling up behind in his car and getting out. "Give me a few minutes to get into position," he instructed, while Jen's mom and dad waited on the church steps.

Lily got out of the carriage and took Jen's flowers while she got down, holding the skirt gingerly and revealing white satin pumps. Lily straightened the gown, then brushed her hand down her own, smoothing out any wrinkles. It had been Jen's wish that they both wear strapless gowns, but Lily suddenly felt self-conscious in the obvious concession to femininity. What would Noah think, seeing the floor-length pink confection? How would he look at her as she stepped onto the navy carpet runner? Things between them hadn't ended well last night. She had apologized, of all things, stammering and babbling while he stood motionless in the center of the room. She'd had her hand on the doorknob when he'd finally spoken, saying her name and how he would see her at the wedding.

He'd been in control, and she'd felt all at sea and needing to run. Or at least she thought he'd been in control.

She arranged her hair over her shoulders, making sure the pearl-headed pins holding back several curls were secure. What would he say the moment he took her arm to leave the church? And then there were pictures, and being seated together, and...

Her breaths shallowed and she felt slightly lightheaded. Oh, this would never do. She couldn't truly be in love with him, she decided. It was the wedding spinning a spell, weaving fanciful magic. It was all the time they'd spent together, that was all. She'd been careful not to go out on more than a few dates with any one man for years, avoiding entanglement.

But that had all changed when her best friend had

asked for a favor. And perhaps that long drought had made her thirsty. And Noah was too tempting to resist.

The fact remained that he would be returning to his army life. It had just been last night, and the wedding preparations, and the music in the dark. It would have enchanted anyone. He had kissed her, that was all.

She squared her shoulders, inhaling deeply, the scent of flowers and fresh-cut hay and sunshine filling her nostrils as she climbed the church steps ahead of Lily and her parents. She hid the bag of makeup beneath the guest book table, removing the large gold wedding band and slipping it over her thumb for safekeeping. She smiled at Andrew's friends, Clay and Dawson, who were in suits rather than jeans and boots, and acting as ushers today. Clay threw her a wink as he stepped inside the sanctuary door, escorting Mrs. O'Keefe to her seat while the pianist played something soft and pretty.

And then the music stopped and Clay and Dawson took their own seats.

Lily turned to Jen, who was already holding her father's arm, and adjusted the simple veil over Jen's shoulders. "See you at the front," she whispered, smiling.

She turned and took the first step onto the carpet, clutching her bouquet until her knuckles turned white.

Andrew was there, standing at the bottom of the steps, but it wasn't his face that held her attention. It was Noah's, beside him, his deep blue gaze warm with something so intimate she felt herself flush all over. The makings of a smile flirted with the corners of his mouth as his eyes telegraphed his approval. *You look beautiful,* they seemed to say. She blinked, wondering why on earth she should feel the need to cry walking up the aisle as a bridesmaid.

And oh, he looked so handsome, so straight and tall, his broad chest highlighted by the cut of the jacket and the white tie bobbing at his throat as he swallowed.

Then she was at the front, on the other side of the altar from him, and with a shaky breath, she turned her attention to the woman at the door of the church.

The music swelled and the congregation rose as Jen entered, the town sweetheart, the woman who had somehow wound herself into the hearts of everyone present. Lily couldn't help the smile that lit her face when Jen's and Andrew's gazes met, so filled with love and hope.

Something made her glance over at Noah and she saw a tiny wrinkle in his brow. He stared at Jen and then looked over at Lily, a question in his eyes. She had hoped he wouldn't remember. Wouldn't recall that the dress she'd worn that day had been different. But he hadn't just seen it, he'd touched it, the tiny straps and the zipper along her back. She shivered as she remembered his fingers on her skin.

The minister opened with a prayer and the giving away of the bride. He asked the question—if anyone opposed the marriage they should speak now—and Lily froze, her heartbeat stuttering as her fingers clenched the roses and sweet peas painfully. This was where her own fairy tale had ended. She bit her lip and tried to focus on the minister's words instead of her memories, but it didn't work. The flurry of excitement, the angry words, the tears. She had never spoken the vows, or put on the plain gold ring, or tasted the first kiss of marriage. It had all ended with a single word. *If anyone has reason why these two should not be joined... Yes.*

But the minister moved on and the rest of the ceremony happened in a daze. Lily held Jen's bouquet during the vows, and while she and Andrew sealed their marriage with a first kiss. She saw Andrew's lashes fall as he leaned in, and an image of Noah in the dark flashed through her mind like heat lightning. Her lips tingled, remembering how she'd melted against him, let him into all the dark corners of her heart, how little fingers of need had clung to him even as the kiss had softly ended. Their eyes met while Jen and Andrew kissed, and Lily knew he hadn't forgotten, either. His hooded gaze dropped to her lips and back up, leaving her as breathless as if he'd kissed her.

A soloist from the church sang as Jen and Andrew signed the wedding register. Then it was Lily's turn, and Noah's. He held her flowers as she sat at the small table, signing her name on the witness lines. She tried not to think of how sexy he looked, all done up in his tux, holding a posy of white peony roses and pale pink sweet peas. When she finished, she met his eyes briefly as she took back the flowers, their fingers grazing. The slight contact played havoc with her senses, a jolt from her fingertips to her core. She watched, fascinated, as his tongue came out to wet his lips.

She wondered how on earth it could feel as if they'd held a conversation over the past half hour when the ceremony had prevented either of them from uttering a word.

Then he moved away, taking his place at the table and with concentrated effort, signed his name where designated. Lily noticed the letters were much neater than before. Day by day he was improving. Day by day he was one step closer to rejoining his life.

And then the ceremony was over, and her fingers gripped her bouquet tightly as her right hand rested on

Noah's arm. Amidst the recessional and the clapping, they made their way down the aisle and into the bright sunshine.

There were a blessed few moments where confusion reigned as the church emptied. Noah shifted his arm, catching Lily's fingers within his own instead. "You look amazing," he murmured, leaning close to her ear as guests spilled out into the parking lot and green grass surrounding the church.

Lily smiled up at him, determined to put things back on an even footing. "Thank you. And you look very dashing."

He smiled back briefly, but then it faded. "Lily, about last night…"

She felt that familiar turning in her tummy that happened every time he spoke to her with that soft, but gruff voice. And yet the day was difficult enough without adding their troubles to it. "Let's just forget it," she suggested. "Why don't we try to enjoy the day? We're partners in crime, remember?" She let her eyes twinkle up at him. "It isn't right to admit to hating weddings while you're attending one, I suppose."

"So you're just using me to survive the festivities?"

If he only knew. But the truth was, even if she did feel something for him she had never expected to feel again, nothing had changed. What did she want from him? Certainly not marriage. The very idea sent an ache pulsing through her, and a panicky need to keep things as uncomplicated as possible.

"Why don't we just enjoy each other?" Lily saw the photographer bearing down on them and squeezed his hand. "We're friends, and I like you. A lot, in case you didn't notice." She attempted a saucy smile. "Let's just

leave it at that. Can't we have fun in the time we have?"
If he caught the note of desperation in her voice, he ignored it.

Noah paused, and their gazes tangled for a few moments before his eyes lightened. "Sure we can. Although
fun is something that hasn't been on my radar for a
while."

"Then maybe it's time."

"Miss Germaine? Mr. Laramie? I need you for wedding party pictures."

Lily gathered her skirt in her fingers. "Come on then.
Let's get this over with. I can bear it if you can."

The photographer gave orders, arranging the two
couples on the church's stone steps with the large double doors behind them. There were pictures with Lily
and Jen together, their skirts and flowers artistically arranged, and shots of the two brothers. There were many
photographs with Jen and Andrew while Lily and Noah
and the guests that hadn't gone to the community hall for
the reception watched. One woman stood apart from the
others, slim and almost drawn within herself, as though
she was trying to be inconspicuous. But Lily twigged
to something about the fine cheekbones, and the deep-
set eyes. The resemblance wasn't immediately apparent, but it was there.

"Is that her, Noah?" Lily whispered. "Standing over
by the shrubs?"

"Yes, that's her." There was an underlying note of
steel in his voice.

"Did you speak to her?"

"And say what? Hello is not enough. And anything
more is unthinkable."

Still, he refused to look over at the woman and Lily squeezed his fingers. "You're right."

Andrew called their names again and Noah sighed with irritation. "What happened to fun? I am duty bound to remind you of the color of your dress. Pink, Lily. Very, very pink."

He winked at her, tugging her hand again and leading her to where the bride and groom waited. "Fun. It's what you said you wanted. So come on."

The photographer wanted pictures of only the maid of honor and best man, and he had chosen the shade of a poplar tree for the shot. Noah leaned lightly against the trunk while Lily rested against his right shoulder, disguising his pinned-up sleeve. She hesitated as his mouth twisted in a grimace, but he quickly gave her an encouraging smile. "It's fine," he murmured, settling her back against the hard length of his body. Noah's left arm looped around her, and in a stroke of ingenuity the photographer had him hold Lily's flowers loosely while she crossed her right hand to rest on his wrist.

"You smell good," he whispered, making her smile.

"It's the sweet peas," she replied, holding the pose for the shot.

"No lilies, Lily?"

"No, thank God. I can't imagine what my mother was thinking when she named me."

"Beautiful, exotic, sweet."

Lily's pulse leaped at the softly whispered words. She couldn't see his face as they held their positions. "Mr. Laramie, I do believe you're flirting."

"You might be right, Miss Germaine."

This was better, Lily thought. Even if her feelings for him were the real deal, what was important was that she didn't act on them. No grand declarations of love or expectations of commitment. A firm belief that this was only temporary. Yes, that was the ticket. The more she thought about it the more sure she was. She could give herself permission to feel. It was human after all, and she wasn't callous or bitter. She simply had made decisions about what she wanted from life. And she had to remember that Noah hadn't said a word about loving *her*. The worries were for nothing.

"Lily? He's asked us to move."

"Oh, right, sorry." She took the bouquet from his hands and smiled brightly. "Are we done here yet? I could use something to drink."

"I'll find out. Two seconds."

He strode back across the lawn toward her. He'd removed his tuxedo jacket and had hooked the collar by a finger, holding it over his shoulder. Lily wet her lips. "Well?"

"We're free to go. Andrew and Jen will be taking the carriage over to the reception. We can take my truck."

"Sounds good to me."

She followed him to the parking lot and gathered her skirt around her as she got up into the cab. Just before he shut the door, he chuckled. "Nice shoes. They're not actually glass slippers, are they?"

Lily flushed. She might not like pink, but she'd been unable to resist the shoes. They were slides, with a transparent band across the top of her foot adorned with a satin ribbon, and a transparent two-inch heel. She knew they were ultrafeminine and fanciful. But she'd adored them the moment she'd slipped them on. "Of course not."

Noah went around to the driver's side door and hopped in. "Okay, Cinderella, let's get you to the ball," he remarked drily, starting the truck and putting it in Reverse.

Lily stared out the window to hide her flaming cheeks, somehow feeling she was riding in a pumpkin after all.

The toasts had been made, the cake cut, and the dee-jay was playing music quietly until it was time for the first dance to be announced. Lily freshened her makeup and came out of the bathroom to find Noah and his mother, Julie Reid, in a corner, speaking quietly. Lily paused, retreated to where she wouldn't intrude. And yet she wanted to be close by. She recognized the tight set of his jaw and the way his skin seemed taut across his cheekbones as he kept his countenance polite. The words they said were too low to be heard, and she didn't want to eavesdrop. She just wanted to be there.

Julie put her hand on Noah's sleeve but he didn't move to take it. Nor did he pull away. Sympathy flooded through her. Imagine meeting a parent for the first time in over twenty years, and doing it publicly. How would she have reacted if Jasmine had shown up tonight?

But then her lips fell open as Noah smiled at his mother. Not a big smile, but a definite pleasant curving of his lips. She put back her shoulders, pasted on a smile of her own and stepped forward.

"There you are!" She went up to his side and took his hand, giving his fingers a reassuring squeeze. "The dancing is about to start."

"Lily." His smile got bigger as he said her name. "Lily, this is my mother, Julie Reid." He paused, seemed to struggle for a moment and then simply said, "This is Lily, Jen's maid of honor."

"Hello," the woman said, her smile faltering as she looked a long way up at her son.

"Please excuse us," Noah said politely, nodding at Julie before taking Lily's hand and going back to the reception room.

"How did it go?"

Noah surveyed the room blandly. "Fine, I guess. We're strangers, Lily. We both know it. It wasn't as difficult as you might think. I'm glad she came, to be honest. It's been good for Andrew. Maybe good for me, too."

The deejay announced the first dance and Lily and Noah halted by the cake table, watching Jen and Andrew take the floor, their permanent smiles still bright on their faces, eyes only for each other.

The bridal couple had chosen to forgo a traditional parent dance for the second song, instead making it a blend of couples: Andrew with Mrs. O'Keefe, Jen with her father, and Noah and Lily.

"This is it," Noah said, but Lily heard the tension in his voice. The memory of last night came to her, fresh and beautiful as they walked to the dance floor together. Noah took her hand in his but his body remained stiff. Lily swallowed and stepped a breath closer. "Noah," she whispered.

"What?" He looked down at her, a spare, cold glance that told her how difficult this was for him despite their practice run. Or maybe because of it.

"Dance with me, Noah." She slipped her hand onto his waist and held his gaze. She could feel the warmth of his skin through his crisp shirt and white vest.

His feet began to move and hers followed, her eyes never leaving his. She could tell the moment he started to relax, the moment his hand softened in hers and his rigid posture settled beneath her fingers.

"Thank you for all you've done, Lily."

"I promised, didn't I?"

He smiled a tiny smile. "Yes, you did."

"And I never go back on a promise, remember?"

He moved their joined hands and touched her cheek with a fingertip. "I remember. Even when I tried to force you to."

"Yes well, you should be glad you didn't succeed. I mean, you'd be left without a dancing partner tonight."

"I'd be left without a friend, as well. Even if she is wearing pink."

"How very cruel of you to bring that up, Mr. Laramie," she coquetted.

"I don't know what your issue is with pink, after all. It suits you."

"It goes back to something my mother said once."

Several beats of music passed. "Are you going to enlighten me?" He angled his head, regarding her curiously. "Surely you're not going to leave it at that."

Lily remembered the moment quite clearly. When she'd been crying in the hotel room and Jasmine had been helping her out of the gown. *"Really Lily,"* her mother had said disparagingly. *"White? You had to go for white? Pink suits you so much better. White is so predictable."*

It had hurt her terribly at the time, as if she cared about a dress when all her plans were being washed away like a dirty secret.

"Lil?" His voice was soft now, and she realized there were two tears on her cheeks. Mortified, she sniffed, taking her hand from his back for a moment to hurriedly wipe them away.

"Don't say anything, please," she begged quietly. "Smile and dance. That's all I want from you."

When the song was over, Lily took her hand from his and walked away.

## Chapter 9

Lily took several deep breaths to regain her composure. She'd fought hard against the memories today, but there were times that they sneaked around her defenses so easily. The smell of the flowers, or the step onto the carpet runner. As much as she had told herself she was over it and it didn't matter, she still bore the scars of that awful day.

But she couldn't leave yet, not when there were still traditions to be upheld. The bouquet had yet to be thrown and several more minutes of dancing before the bride and groom would sneak off for a very brief honeymoon. It would be bad form for the maid of honor to leave before the bride and groom. Besides, what explanation could she give? Certainly not that the whole day was a reminder of broken dreams and crushed hopes. And definitely not that her feelings for the best man were getting in the way. The last thing she wanted was for Jen or Andrew to put their hopes in that direction.

Guests now took the floor as the music changed to something with a solid dance beat, and Lily went to the punch bowl, pouring herself a plastic cup of the sweet pink drink to keep her hands occupied. It only took seconds for Noah to be at her side again.

"What just happened?"

She took a sip and focused on the line of dancers on the floor. If she looked at him now he'd know that it was him affecting her. She hadn't quite spoken the truth when she said a dance was all she wanted from him. And yet she was sure she didn't want more than that, either.

The plain truth was that when she was with Noah she didn't know *what* she wanted.

"Nothing."

"Lily."

His hand stopped the progress of her cup and she looked up at him in annoyance as the punch sloshed close to the rim. Sometimes she liked him a whole lot better when he wasn't so clued in. She sighed. "Just let it go, Noah. It doesn't matter."

Noah released her wrist, but didn't move away from her. He'd promised to stick by her side during the wedding, knowing she wasn't looking forward to it any more than he was. But this went beyond a simple promise.

He swallowed, looked down at her profile. She was so beautiful. She'd done something curly and wispy to her hair, tiny pearls shimmering from within the dark strands. Her skin glowed next to the pale pink of the gown, begging to be touched. He reached out and touched her bare shoulder, craving the sight of her eyes locked on his. He wasn't disappointed. At the moment his fingertips grazed her soft skin, her head turned and her gaze clashed with his.

He let his finger trail over her shoulder and down her arm, the touch so light it skimmed over her skin like a soft breath. "What are you doing?" She whispered it and he barely caught the words, but he saw them form on her lips and he smiled.

*Seducing you,* he thought suddenly, smiling. It sounded ridiculous. They had kissed last night, and today he'd touched her as it had been required. But seduction was something different. Seduction demanded a conclusion. And he knew that was out of the question. No, he wouldn't seduce her, wouldn't let it go too far. There was too much undecided in his life to complicate things further. Too many decisions he was putting off making, weighing him down. But he couldn't seem to stop the simple caress, either.

"I'm touching you. Do you want me to stop?"

"I…"

Her hesitation did wonders for his confidence. He didn't want her to see what was beneath the surface, but knowing that he had the power to make her lose her words, the power to make her sigh into his mouth as they'd kissed… She had run out of his house last night and he'd thought it was because he had gone too far. That he had repulsed her as she'd touched his arm. But now, he saw the top of the strapless bodice of her dress rise and fall with the force of her breath and he knew she was feeling it as strongly as he was.

But they were here, in the Larch Valley Community Center with his brother and new sister-in-law and old friends and his mother in attendance. He scanned the crowd. He saw old schoolmates and local business owners, like Jim Barnes, who still owned Papa's Pizza, and Agnes Dodds, who'd rapped his fingers with a ruler in elementary school and now ran the local antique store. This was no place to broadcast that he lusted after the maid of honor. No, not lusted. Lusted was too superficial, and there was more to Lily than that.

She moved one single finger against his as his hand trailed past her wrist. A brushing of contact that somehow said *no, don't stop*. That said she was feeling it, too.

And for once Noah didn't want to think about the mistakes he'd made, or if his recovery was on schedule, or what choices he'd have to make about how to serve his country. For once he wanted to live in the moment. To think only about the gorgeous woman whose hand was twined with his and whose eyelashes now lay demurely against her cheeks as she avoided looking at him.

"Can I take you home?"

His question was rewarded by her lifting her head, giving him a glimpse of the piercing blue of her irises. "We can't leave yet."

He took a step backward. Perhaps he'd misread.

"But I'd like that. Later."

She smiled up at him, sweetly, and without the edge he was used to seeing. It hit him in the gut with the force of a punch. Noah nodded. "Let me know when you're ready."

To be in each other's pockets now would be too obvious. For one, he was already having a difficult time not touching her. They had to mingle, speak to others rather than gazing into each other's eyes the entire time. He checked his watch. "I'm going to go talk to Clay for a bit," he said to her, finally letting her fingers go. "Enjoy yourself."

He forced himself to leave her there, walking over to where Clay stood at the side of the floor. Talking to him about looking after Lazy L in Andrew's absence wasn't nearly as interesting as spending time with Lily.

But it was the right thing to do.

Once Jen and Andrew had thrown the bouquet and garter and escaped under a shower of rice, Lily made herself busy at the head table, packing wineglasses into a padded box.

"What are you doing?"

She jumped at the sound of his voice, especially when she'd just been thinking of him again. The way he'd touched her earlier had nearly sent her up in flames. Now he was right behind her, so close she could feel the warmth of his body, and her fingers shook as she placed the last of the special wedding glasses in the tissue.

She took a breath and closed the box. "The bride and groom glasses. Jen asked if I'd pick them up."

"Then are you ready to go?"

She bit down on her lip. She shouldn't accept the drive home. Anyone here would give her a lift. She was getting far too involved with Noah.

But as she looked up into his strong, handsome face, she knew it didn't matter. It was Noah that she wanted to be with. It was Noah's humor and understanding that had made today bearable.

And it was Noah she trusted.

"Yes, I'm ready."

There were no more options, no more diversions or prevarications. Lily was going with him. And she was still unsure of what she wanted the night to bring.

They resumed walking, out the double doors to the

parking lot. The sound of the dance beat a steady rhythm behind them, a muted thump that seemed incongruous in the otherwise quiet night. It was the time of day Lily loved best, when the light hadn't quite faded from the sky, leaving it a swirl of indigo and lavender and peach, and the first stars poked through the curtain of falling darkness. Their steps slowed as they walked to Noah's truck, making crunching sounds on the gravel.

Conversation would have felt out of place. Noah opened her door and held the box of crystal while she got in. What was between them now was too fragile, too tenuous to spoil with conversation. She had needed him today. She'd needed his steady presence; she'd needed the distraction he provided.

She still needed it.

Noah got in, started the engine and made the short drive to her town house.

As he idled the truck on the street, she knew she didn't want to go in alone. She didn't want to go upstairs and remove her bridesmaid gown with an empty house and a head full of memories for company. She didn't want to face the postwedding letdown that already felt hollow in her heart. Somewhere along the way she'd started needing him. She'd started trusting him. And the simple truth was that there was no one else she wanted to spend time with tonight. She wanted to be with him, not because he kept her mind off other things, but because the air felt a little bit colder when he wasn't around to warm it. Because he'd touched her in ways she hadn't been touched in a very long time and she wasn't ready for it to end yet.

"Do you want to come in? I can put on some coffee."

She looked over at him, his features highlighted by

the colored lights of the dashboard. The tie that had been so precisely knotted earlier was loosened and at a crooked angle against the crisp collar of his shirt. The tuxedo jacket buttons were undone, the inky-black material flowing away from his body as he put the truck in Park. A memory flashed through her mind, of Noah coming out of the change room, looking slightly rumpled. But that image had nothing on the deliciousness of the real thing before her now.

She wasn't prepared to want him this much.

The moment held, tethering them together by some invisible force, until his eyes warmed and he replied, "I'd like that."

The house was dark as Lily fumbled with the keys, unlocking the front door. Once inside, she went to the kitchen, turning on the under-the-counter lighting. Noah followed behind, looking tall and elegantly gorgeous in his tuxedo. Lily's hands shook as she prepared the coffeemaker and flipped the switch. Nerves fluttered through her stomach, over her skin, making her doubt the wisdom of inviting him in. She didn't want to be alone, but being alone with Noah was dangerous, too. This was going further than the physical attraction that kept demanding to be acknowledged. She wanted more. But how much more? Everything? The very thought made her drop the spoon from her hand. In all these years, she'd never been faced with this choice.

She picked up the spoon again and got out the sugar bowl. Maybe it was just the wedding. If she could only convince herself of that! Weddings made people crazy, isn't that what everyone said? She had to break the wedding day spell. The first step would be getting out of the pale pink gown.

"If you don't mind, I'd like to change."

Noah took a step forward, his body blocking her passage. "What if I do mind?"

She swallowed. Tried to be annoyed that he'd stopped her, but a delicious shiver feathered over her, simply in an elemental response to his nearness.

Another step, and he reached out his hand, placing it over the smooth fabric covering her ribs, down over her waist. "You look beautiful."

"Noah…"

But he wasn't deterred, not by the gurgle of the coffee brewing or by her weak protest. His right foot joined his left, leaving only a breath between them. "Beautiful. Like strawberry ice cream." His hand moved up, his finger tracing along the fine stitching and pink crystals at the top of the bodice.

She couldn't breathe, couldn't think.

His mouth descended, toying with hers. "Soft." His kiss was barely a glance on her lips. "And sweet." And his tongue touched her bottom lip, tasting.

She had no defense against his gentle persuasion. Her hand twined with his hair as she drew his head down, kissing him fully, tasting the sweetness of champagne and cake, the tartness of punch and the seductive flavor that was simply Noah.

The passion rose so quickly between them it pulled her breath out of her lungs. His body pressed her backward so that she was bolstered by the kitchen counter, and his hand braced on the granite edge. And still the kiss went on, Lily's head tilted back so that the tips of her hair touched the satin back of her dress. Noah's lips slid from hers and down the column of her neck, gentling as he tasted the skin there before moving back up and pulling her earlobe into his mouth.

It drew a quiet moan from her, and they paused as the sound echoed through the kitchen. And in that soft, prolonged moment, everything caught up with her. This was too much, too fast, too everything. They had to stop. It would only end in heartache, and the ache would be hers.

She let go of the resolve that had held her together throughout the day and everything came flooding back. The chapel in Las Vegas, Curtis, their parents, the hope crushed. And in that moment, she started to cry. Quiet, heartbreaking tears. All she'd ever wanted was a place to belong. A home. And she'd thought she'd found it in Larch Valley.

But Noah had changed that. He'd changed *everything*. The satisfaction she'd built into her life here was no longer enough. And he was offering her no more than a few kisses. It was all he *had* to offer.

"Lily…" His voice was tortured, pulling her close to him. "Lily, don't cry. You *never* cry."

His hand was on the back of her head, tucking her against his shirt that smelled of starch and cologne. No, she never cried. She was always upbeat Lily, who hid those hurts inside. She was tired of being that person. When had she last been able to truly be herself? When was the last time she'd let someone see who she really was?

"What is it?" He whispered the question in her ear, sending shivers down her spine as his breath warmed her hair. "Tell me."

Lily sighed against his shirtfront. How could she possibly explain to him how she had come to care so deeply, in such a short time? That being with him had thrown the rest of her world into flux. "I don't know if I can."

"Does it have something to do with the dress you had on that day?"

"I should have known you'd remember," she whispered, blinking against a new onslaught of tears. She hadn't wanted to tell him about Curtis, but it was far better to do that than probe her feelings for him out loud. "When you saw it and thought it was Jen's…"

"But it wasn't." He rested his chin on the top of her head, the pressure comforting. "I knew when I saw Jen step onto that runner today. Was it yours?"

She nodded, sniffling. "Yes."

He said nothing more, just held her close for several minutes.

Finally Lily pulled away and looked up into his face. That steady, strong face that had seen so many things during the years. After wars and battles, she knew her past would seem trivial to him. "It seems silly," she whispered, putting a hand against his chest, a flimsy barrier between them. "Look at you, and what you've been through. This is nothing compared to that."

"Everyone has their own crosses to bear. Just because yours is different than mine doesn't make it any less important. Or any less difficult. So are you going to tell me what happened? Was it divorce?"

It was a logical conclusion for him to make. "Oh, Noah, it was such a long time ago."

He smiled then, a soft, indulgent curving of his lips. "And you call me stubborn." He reached down and took her hand, tugging it until she followed him to a chair in the living room. And then he sat, pulling her down with him so she was on his lap, her skirts billowing out around them. Gingerly he settled his right shoulder against the plush upholstery and she wondered if his arm was paining him after the long day. Carefully she leaned toward his left side, her hand circled his neck, and she looked down at him, memorizing each angle and tiny wrinkle. He was beautiful, she realized. Not just on the outside. Inside, too. Obstinate, and sometimes prickly, but that was just a cover.

It would be so easy to fall completely over the edge into love. But perhaps telling him the truth would be enough to put some space between them.

"When I was eighteen, I ran away to be married. His name was Curtis and we had been planning it for months. Just waiting for my birthday so I would be legal. He was in first year university and I was nearly finished high school."

Noah didn't ask questions, just kept his arm solidly around her, stroking her bare arm with his fingers. Sitting there, snuggled up in a chair, Lily felt secure and comforted. Noah wasn't just a good-looking guy she was attracted to. Somehow they'd become friends over the past weeks. Somehow she'd found herself telling him things she hadn't revealed to another living soul. And it felt good to finally tell *someone* about it. She looked into his eyes, the inky color of deep twilight, marveling at the change in her heart. She had never wanted anyone in Larch Valley to find out about her previous mistakes. But it was easier to reach into the past for explanations than to confess her present feelings.

"Curtis saved up his money. His family was a lot better off than we were and so he squirreled away funds to pay for the hotel and the plane tickets. My mom was a dressmaker. I already knew I could sew my own dress, so I bought the material on the sly and designed it."

The hand on her arm stopped moving. "You designed it? The dress you had on? That's amazing."

"I was always drawing new ideas. I made most of my own clothes back then." She realized she hadn't designed anything new in years, and missed the feeling of the pencil in her hand, the way the lines felt as images translated from her head to paper. She sighed. "I lost a lot of my dreams that day, Noah."

She slid farther down on his lap. "We made it to Vegas. We even made it to the chapel. But when we got to the part about objections, the door opened. And there were Curtis's parents, and my mom."

"Oh, Lily." Noah's voice was soft in the darkness. "They stopped the wedding."

"Legally we could have continued. I was eighteen, an adult. But Curtis's parents, who'd always been good to me…" She swallowed, remembering how she'd felt small and ugly and worthless. "They made it very clear that I wasn't the kind of girl that he should marry. Dating was one thing. I guess they'd never realized how serious we were. I was a nobody. And he was destined for bigger and better things than an unfortunate marriage."

"And what did Curtis say?"

She laughed then, a bitter sound in the dark. "Our plan had been for him to finish school, go into business with his father as agreed. I was going to design, and open a little boutique. Funny how that plan evaporated once his father said if we went through with it he'd be cut off."

"He walked away from you?"

"Without a second's hesitation. Left with his parents and me standing at the altar, so to speak."

"Then he didn't love you."

Lily's heart seemed to sink to her feet. It hurt to hear him state the truth. What did she expect from Noah? Not love, certainly. He would leave, as Curtis had. He would do his duty. And she would be left behind again. No one had ever cared enough to stay. "Oh, I know. Believe me."

"No man who ever loved you could ever walk away."

And just like that her heart soared up, back into her chest again. What was it about Noah that made her feel special? Worth it? She'd never been worth the trouble before.

"What about your mother?"

His question drew her out of the sweetness of the moment. Lily's answering laugh was bitter with cynicism. Her mother had been a real piece of work, too. For a woman so concerned with *feelings*, she had been astonishingly immune to Lily's pain, even as Lily had left the chapel in tears. "Oh, my mom called them a bunch of snobs and then proceeded to tell me it was for the best. I had to endure hours of her saying how I'd been foolish and too young to put my life into one person when I had my whole life ahead of me, full of adventure. I didn't want adventure."

"And so your heart was broken and nobody cared."

"Yes." She whispered it.

"Now I know why you don't like weddings."

"I would never have said anything to Jen. I know it doesn't make sense. They love each other and I'm happy for them. At the same time...Curtis said he loved me, too. And yet it was so easy for him to leave. I'm not sure I believe in love that lasts forever. At least not for me."

She sat up slightly, looking down into his eyes. Now she wondered if Jasmine had somehow been right after all. How much time had she wasted, lamenting old dreams instead of finding new ones? When was the last time she'd let herself have an adventure? Instead she had settled for something else, an imitation of the dream she'd wanted. She had the home she'd always craved, but it felt empty. Look what happened when she finally let go of the rigid control she usually exerted over her life. She was on the brink of being hurt just as much this time as last, and it wasn't worth it.

"My mom always said life was too short to fall in love only once. She called me predictable and small-minded when I said I wanted something other than the life she had."

"Is she happy?"

The question surprised her. Was Jasmine happy? She'd always insisted she was. She'd always seemed like this free spirit that lived in the moment, beautiful. Lovers had come and gone. Some of them had been good to Lily and she'd secretly hoped for a father, but that had never happened. But what about now? Lily didn't know. Other than dutiful cards on birthdays and Christmas, she hadn't spoken to her mother in many years.

And she felt ashamed that she had to answer, "I don't know."

Noah sighed, and Lily asked, "What about your mom? Did she seem happy to you?"

"No. She's spent her whole life looking for happiness and never finding it. Not with my father and certainly not with her second husband. I'm not angry at her anymore. And yet, it's hard to let go when people hurt us. When people we are supposed to be able to count on let us down. Even," he added quietly, "when that person is yourself."

He understood.

"She's not a particularly strong woman, Lily." His eyes were nearly black in the darkness of the room. "Not like you."

No one had ever called her strong before. Reliable, sure. Ready to do a favor, yes. But no one had ever seen to the core of her the way Noah could. She'd tried to use her past as a barrier to their relationship, expecting him to back away. But instead he'd broken straight through it.

And while it was a relief to finally let down that guard, it was scary. Because Noah, like everyone else she'd cared about, would be leaving, too. What was the alternative? Marriage? She'd be a disaster as an army wife, left home alone while he was deployed. And what about children? How could she subject children to life as army brats, moving from base to base, school to school, knowing how difficult it could be?

She pushed herself off his lap, wiping her fingers beneath her eyes. "I must look awful. I'm going to change. But help yourself to coffee."

Before he could reply, she rushed to the stairs and up to her room.

Noah was not permanent. No more than Jasmine had been or Curtis had been. She had to remember that.

It was just as well that his recovery was well in hand and that there were only a few weeks left until she would be back to work.

Because wishes were pointless, and now that the wedding was over, it was time she started making a break. It would be best for everyone.

# Chapter 10

It had been a long day.

Noah had done the bulk of the chores himself, and it had taken him longer than he liked. Pixie had bumped his right side hard when he'd gone into her stall, and he still felt the ache in his shoulder. And on top of it all, it had been the middle of the night before he'd gotten to sleep. He simply hadn't been firing on all cylinders today.

He'd lain there thinking of Lily, turning what she'd told him over and over in his head, thinking about her and the wedding, and about the army and Lazy L until it all blended together in his head. The result was he'd awakened even more confused.

What did Lily want from him? A friend? More than that? She had confided in him, and he'd encouraged it. He'd never done such a thing in his life. Dating had been a superficial way to put in time, to appease some of the loneliness and longing, but he'd never been in love. There hadn't been time. He'd always kept things light. He'd been careful to keep it casual on both sides, not to create expectations he couldn't fulfill.

But Lily was different.

Now, as he struggled to open a box of pasta, he scowled. She had managed to get past the usual barriers. And last night…last night he'd come very close to forgetting about everything *but* her and how much he'd wanted her.

He ripped at the cardboard, resulting in a nasty paper cut. "Dammit!" He let go of the box, sticking his finger in his mouth, and the package dropped to the floor, scattering bits of rotini all over the kitchen.

He was in a mess, tired, angry, and unable to even put on a Band-Aid. Sometimes it truly felt like two steps forward and then one step back, never advancing as quickly as he wanted. Why did the simplest things have to be so difficult?

"Noah?"

Lily's voice had him swinging toward the door. She stood on the other side of the screen, peering in. He took his finger out of his mouth and watery blood formed around the cut. He grabbed the tea towel from the counter to cover the finger.

"Hang on." There was no time to clean up the mess. He shut off the burner and went to the door.

She wore jeans today, and a copper-colored T-shirt that clung to her curves. Beaded sandals were on her feet. She looked just as attractive this way as she had yesterday in her gown and pearls.

"Lily." He pushed the door open, inviting her in. She stepped inside and reached into her purse.

"You forgot this last night," she said quietly, holding out his tie. He stared at it, remembering how he'd slid it from around his neck as he'd pressed his body against hers.

"The formal wear shop will want it back with the tux." Lily gave the tie a slight shake, drawing him out of the memory.

He reached out to take it, then realized he couldn't. The last thing he should do was get blood on a white tie.

"What have you done?" Lily put the tie on a bookcase and grabbed his hand. She pulled off the tea towel, looking at his finger. "You cut yourself."

"It's just a paper cut. That happens to be bleeding a lot."

She bit down on her lip as she gripped his finger. "Where are your Band-Aids? I'll put one on for you."

"I'll do it myself." He pulled his hand away, feeling like a child. "The stuff I take to keep the swelling down makes my blood a little thinner, that's all."

He spun away, heading for the bathroom. He didn't need her to do every little thing for him. Good Lord, he could care for himself! He found the kit beneath the sink and flipped it open, using his teeth to tear a bandage from a perforated strip. He ripped it open—again using his teeth—and tried to wrap it around the finger.

The plastic wrinkled and stuck to itself. He reached for a replacement, ripping too hard and destroying another Band-Aid.

He swore, then leaned against the sink, breathing heavily.

Last night he'd felt like a normal man. Last night his

decision had made sense, and he'd felt as if he could handle anything. And he'd known that a life behind a desk, stuck within four walls was not the kind of life for him. But today he couldn't even put on a Band-Aid. Now Lily was here, looking as pretty as ever, and the last thing he wanted to do was disappoint her. She'd had too many disappointments.

What a mess. If he backed away now he knew how it would look to her. As though what she'd told him about her past made a difference. And to let things go forward would be a mistake. Where could they possibly go? He certainly couldn't love her the way she wanted. The way she deserved.

"Noah?"

He spun around as her voice startled him, and smacked his injured arm spectacularly on the door frame.

White-hot pain radiated through his stump, nearly bringing him to his knees as he caught his breath. Lily, the feminine, beautiful Lily, cursed in alarm as he started to slip, then slid beneath his left arm, bolstering his weight.

"Come sit down," she said, urging him toward the dining area and pulling out a chair. He sank into it, closing his eyes and baring his teeth to keep from crying out. It wasn't just the stub. It was his entire arm, right down to the fingertips that were no longer there.

Phantom pain. Now and again it struck, sometimes after a bump or for no particular reason at all. Today, when he was especially tired, it had been worse than usual, flashing off and on, tingling. But now it was a searing line that took his breath away.

"Oh, Noah. What can I do?" Lily's panicked voice

came from his right and he forced his eyes open. Her bright blue gaze was focused on his face, guilt on each delicate feature.

"It's not your fault. It's been a long day. And I wasn't watching where I was going."

Cold sweat beaded on his forehead. This was not how he wanted it. He wanted to keep this part of it hidden from her. The part of his injury that reduced him to a quivering mess. Most of the time he coped. But there were times it took him unawares, and all he could do was wait it out. Times when he was tired, or stressed, or if he simply overexerted himself. A frustration and a symptom to be expected, the doctors said. Listen to your body, they said.

If only it were that easy. Right now his body was screaming at him.

"Is there medication I can get you?"

He shook his head. The over-the-counter stuff was useless.

He looked up at her, recognizing the expression of helplessness on her face. Lord knew, he'd felt that way often enough when he'd seen his soldiers get wounded and had been unable to make it right. Speaking to them at the airfield as they were being patched up. Or as they were being prepped for transport to Germany. He hated that the boot was on the other foot now.

Icy-hot daggers shot down his arm and he gritted his teeth. She had trusted him with the story of Curtis. Could he trust her, as well, to see the scar he bore?

"Can we ice it or something? There must be some way to help," she insisted.

He caught his breath as the muscles spasmed in protest. At some point, someone was going to see his stump without its protective covering. As the muscles seized, he knew he needed to do something to help the pain, and that of anyone, Lily would be the most practical nurse.

"Heat relaxes the muscles. There's a pack in the medicine cupboard."

As she left to retrieve it, he tried to roll up his sleeve. But it had rained this morning and he'd put on a long-sleeved cotton shirt, making the chore even more challenging. When Lily came back, she put the pack on the floor and unpinned his cuff.

"Roll it up," he said.

She tried, but there was too much fabric and the roll was too tight over the muscles that corded just below his shoulder.

"You've got to take it off," she said.

The stabbing pain continued and he breathed through gritted teeth. "No."

"Yes." She went in front of him and began working the buttons.

"Lily, no," he said weakly, as she slipped each button from its hole, unable to fight her beyond putting his left hand over her wrist, stopping her movements. He didn't want her to see him this way. It was too ugly.... It would be a sight she would remember each time she looked at him. A man covered in ugly scars. Not the Noah who had danced with her in the dark.

But she pushed his hand away and kept on until the last button was undone and she spread the sides wide to ease it off his shoulders.

Then she saw.

And she cried out, the sound filled with the shock of the sight before her.

He knew what she was seeing right now. The angry

red marks, the puckered scars of the cuts caused by the shrapnel. A beast.

"Oh, Noah…I didn't know." Her breath hitched with emotion. "Why didn't you tell me?"

"I didn't want you to see," he whispered, turning his head away.

Noah wasn't a man who wept. He hadn't cried in the hospital, or when he'd gone to his father's grave site, or when he'd seen his mother for the first time in over two decades. But at this moment, he was unable to stop the tears from coming as Lily stood back, covering her mouth and staring at the vision before her. The tears formed, hot and bitter, sliding over his lower lashes when he blinked.

Lily gaped at the sight of his battered skin. My God, the pain he must have gone through. Not just the arm, but several red scars from his chest to his abdomen. She looked into his face. Noah was crying. *Crying.* The sight nearly undid her, seeing the pain and shame on his face. But he shouldn't be ashamed. He had done nothing wrong, nothing to deserve the cuts that marred his body.

They did not define him. Not to her. To her they were medals, badges of his strength, his dedication, his sacrifice.

Lily sniffed, wiped at the tears on her cheeks, and saying nothing, stepped forward, easing him out of the shirt, taking it and laying it gently over another chair. Questions flooded her mind about what had really happened to him, questions she was afraid to ask amid the profound sympathy she felt, not only for his injuries but because it was clear to her that the marks they left behind caused him a deeper pain that hadn't yet begun to heal. Not all of his scars were on the outside, she realized. They had left their mark on his soul, as well. And that was something she could understand very well.

"What can I do to help you?"

He swallowed. Reached over and removed the shrinker covering the stump, revealing the entire wound to her eyes for the first time. She bit down on her lip at the sight, at the supreme trust that the gesture meant. She remembered dancing with him and his whispered words of wanting to be perfect for her. And he was, in many ways, naked before her now. His trust in her was the most humbling experience of her life.

"Just give me the pack," he said, taking it from her hands. He anchored one side in his armpit, then wrapped it around, feeling the warmth seep into the muscles, relaxing them and easing the spasms.

She moved a chair closer to him, sitting on it. And then she covered his fingers with her own, holding the pack in place.

"I had no idea, Noah." She said the words gently, needing to acknowledge what she'd seen and show him it didn't matter.

"You weren't supposed to," he replied, his chin jutting out defiantly. "No one was."

"Why?"

He turned his head and stared into her eyes, a mixture of pain and defiance in his gaze.

"Why do you think? It's ugly. I'm a mess of scars and incisions. No one should have to look at me this way," he said, turning his head away. "What woman would want a man like this?"

In that moment, Lily bled for him. He had always seemed so sure of himself. Yes, he'd had challenges, but he'd always been so determined to move forward.

How could she have missed it? Of course his self-image would have suffered. He'd done a good job of hiding it, but not tonight. Tonight she was seeing it all. And what she saw was a man not defined by his scars but by the strength of his heart.

"Did you think I would be repulsed?"

"Aren't you?"

"Absolutely not."

The words settled around them. Had she been shocked, seeing the extent of his wounds? Yes. It had been unexpected. But repulsed? Not in the least. Her only thought had been of the pain he must have endured.

Lily eased the pack off his stump. "What else can I do?"

Noah didn't reply, so Lily stood, cupped his chin in her fingers and lifted it so he was looking into her face. Then she touched her forehead to his, closing her eyes. His body stiffened; she knew he was fighting her but she was determined to wait.

"What can I do, Noah?" Her voice was barely a whisper, but she heard him swallow. She framed his face with her hands, touching her lips to his, carefully, lightly. Trying not to cry. The time would come to cry later. Right now he was in pain. How long had he been toughing this out alone?

"Massage helps."

Without a moment's hesitation, Lily went to his side and began kneading the muscles. The flesh was strong and firm beneath her fingers, and she marveled at the sight of the scar tissue and shape of the tip as she worked from his shoulder down his bicep. Noah closed his eyes and she felt the tension seep out of him as she pressed and kneaded gently.

Shadows fell in the room as the sun moved around toward the west side of the house. Lily's hands slowed, moved beyond his right arm to the back of his neck, working the warm, smooth skin beneath her fingers. Touching him the way she'd wanted to for weeks now. Learning the shape of him, the hardness of his body from the life he'd led. Flawed, but beautiful. She massaged his other shoulder, the one that now bore the brunt of all his daily tasks, and down his left arm until she was in front of him again. He stood up from his chair and reached for his shirt, holding it loosely in his fingers.

He would have put it on but Lily stayed his arm with her hand.

"Don't. Not yet."

She reached out a fingertip and touched each scar, each angry red ridge of tissue. She bit down on her lip as she explored, feeling a reverence she hadn't expected. What sort of man suffered such an injury and returned so strong, so determined? Each scar made him more of a man in her eyes, not less. The love she'd felt before was nothing compared to the feeling swelling her heart right now.

"How did you get these?" she asked finally, looking up.

"The explosion that took off my arm also sent little pieces of shrapnel everywhere. I got peppered."

What atrocities had he seen? She could only imagine what it had been like in the theater of battle. "You've never said much about that day."

"What was the point?" His voice was quiet, husky. "It was early in the morning, before dawn. Things had been quiet for days. It happened so fast, and I was asleep. I pulled on my combats and grabbed my rifle. Three of my men were pinned down. I went in to help. Then the grenade went off. I hadn't put on my vest."

A muscle pulsed in his jaw. "It was a stupid mistake, careless. I knew better. I was an officer, for God's sake. Not some green kid on their first deployment."

Lily could see it playing out in her head and suddenly things became clearer. Did Noah blame himself for making a mistake? She hated that he doubted himself for even a second. He was only human. "And the men?"

"Finished their deployment safe and sound. I think they made it home ahead of me, actually."

"So you saved them."

Her hands rested on his chest, feeling the rise and fall of his breathing, the beating of his heart that accelerated beneath her touch. He'd sacrificed himself. And the fact that her hands on his skin seemed to cause his body to respond sent a thrill through her.

"No. I screwed up and got lucky," he murmured.

"Would it have changed anything? If you'd had it on?"

He was silent for a long moment. "I suppose not. It wouldn't have saved my arm. But I still have to live with the marks, always reminding me, you know?"

She leaned forward the slightest bit and pressed her lips to one of the scars, closing her eyes and wishing she could make it go away.

"You don't have to pretend, Lily." He quivered beneath her lips and hands. "I saw your face."

"I am not pretending anything." She lifted her face to him, determined he know the truth. Knowing he *deserved* the truth. "Whatever you think you saw, you're wrong. I am not disgusted, Noah Laramie." She swallowed thickly, overwhelmed by her emotions. "I am in awe."

"In awe?" He cleared his throat, stepping away from her a little, his lips dropping open in surprise. "Don't be ridiculous."

But she nodded, surprised at the soft sound of her voice as she spoke the absolute truth—in a way she had never spoken to another man before. "I *am* in awe of you. Of your strength, and your courage, and your compassion. It hurts me to know you think so little of yourself that you hid from me. You never have to hide from me, Noah. Don't you know that now?"

She reached out and ran her fingers over the rough skin, heard his sharp intake of breath and smiled softly. "You're beautiful, Noah."

"Lily…"

The lump in her throat grew until she could hardly speak. "You're beautiful to me," she whispered. And held her breath, knowing that he was everything she hadn't wanted. And that despite it she wanted him more than she wanted breath. More than she'd wanted anything in her entire life.

Noah wrapped his arm around her, tucking her head against his shoulder. How had this happened? He was in love with her. He'd never been in love with anyone in his life. He'd never wanted to be. And she'd blustered her way in with her pragmatic ways. Lily had never said a single word she hadn't meant. So he knew she meant what she said now.

And it was just his luck that when he finally fell into something so impractical, he had no idea where his life was going. The well-ordered path he'd set for himself was gone, obliterated in the dust of his injury.

"I love you, Lily."

Where the words came from, he had no idea. But they fell off his lips like a blessing.

Lily stepped out of his embrace and stared at him, her eyes wide. But not with pleasure, he noted bitterly, absorbing the unexpected hit. Her eyes were wide with dismay and denial, and he wondered if he'd been wrong about her always telling the truth. Had she only said what she had to make him feel better?

Was she capable of that? He couldn't, wouldn't believe that of her.

"You can't love me." Her voice was a harsh rasp in the quiet room as she shook her head.

He clenched his teeth together, disappointed that the one time in his life he'd said those three words to any woman they were not reflected back. "I can love you. And I do. But whether or not you accept it is up to you." The words came out cold, flat, as she stepped away from him.

This was why he'd never gone in for the whole relationship and feelings thing. In the army, he knew what was expected of him, and what he'd get in return. Love was another matter. It was fickle and unpredictable. Like right now.

"If you're better, I should go." Lily's face was pale now, as she skirted around him to retrieve her purse. He marveled at how something so intense could change a hundred and eighty degrees in the blink of an eye. Moments later she went out the door.

He let her go.

He had let himself get caught up in the moment, and he'd shown his hand. You couldn't force someone to love you. And you couldn't force someone to stay. Gerald's and Julie's failures had taught him that.

He'd been a fool to think, even for a moment, that this would be any different.

## Chapter 11

Lily stared at the rain dripping down the kitchen window. She stirred the hot chocolate in her mug, sipping the rich drink occasionally when the thought occurred. The remnants of a batch of chocolate chip cookies sat in a tin. She felt slightly ill and pushed the container away.

Noah had said he loved her.

She braced her forehead on the back of her hand. What a horrible mess. He wasn't supposed to have feelings. She was supposed to be the one with feelings, and they were supposed to be curable. She had been so certain it had only been a few kisses and friendship on his part. But not love. What kind of future could they have?

Noah was already married. To the army. She'd known it from the beginning. Each day she realized it more. When she saw him recovering. Heard him talking. As her own feelings had deepened, it had been her comfort, her protection. He couldn't have two loves, and she knew his first love was always the service.

Until two days ago. When she saw his scars and realized how truly and deeply she'd fallen.

When the doorbell rang she jumped, sloshing chocolate over the side of the mug and onto the tablecloth. Perhaps it was Jen. She and Andrew had only gone to Montana for a few days of privacy as a honeymoon. The bell sounded again and Lily got up, hoping Jen didn't ask any questions about why she was in flannel pyjama pants and a T-shirt on a rainy afternoon. She didn't want anyone to know that she was in a funk over a man.

Not just any man. Her best friend's new brother-in-law. A man who was only in their lives during a pit stop in his career.

But it was Noah on her step when she opened the door, standing under the eaves in full dress uniform. The rain dripped in a steady beat behind him, and Lily paused, momentarily stunned by the sight of him. The soldier, with the proud and tall bearing, his beret creased precisely over his short, dark hair. And there were medals over his heart.

A whole new Noah she hadn't imagined.

"Can I come in?"

Dumbly she stood aside, opening the door so he could enter. What was he doing here? In a second of brief panic, she thought he was going to announce he was leaving. But it wasn't time yet, was it? Could it be?

Had he come to say goodbye? She certainly hadn't given him any reason to stay....

As Lily shut the door, Noah held out his hand. In it was a bouquet of sweet peas, deep pink and purple. "No lilies," he said quietly. "And no light pink."

Lily stared at the blossoms as she took them from his hands. How had he remembered what she'd carried in her bridesmaid bouquet? She was touched by the sentiment despite herself. "I'll put these in water," she replied, trying a tentative smile.

Noah reached up and removed his beret, holding it in his hand. His gaze fell on Lily, soft with concern. "Are you feeling okay?"

Lily felt her cheeks bloom. She was in flannel sleep pants and a blue T-shirt, and her hair was in a messy ponytail with bits coming out of it. She looked a fright. Not a bit of makeup graced her face. And she was sure her eyes had dark circles beneath them as she hadn't been sleeping well, either. The last thing she wanted was for him to guess the truth—that she was moping over him. "I'm fine. Just lazy on a rainy day, that's all."

"You're sure?"

"I'm sure."

She went down the hall to the kitchen in search of a vase while Noah took off his boots. She took advantage of the few extra moments to put away the tin of cookies and roll the chocolate-soiled tablecloth into a ball, tossing it into the laundry room. As his footsteps came closer to the kitchen, she hurriedly pulled out her scrunchie and twisted her hair around, forming a coil and anchoring it with the elastic.

He stood at the entrance to the room, and she wished, if he were going to say goodbye, he would just do it and get it over with.

"You're in your uniform." Immediately she felt foolish for stating the obvious, but a small smile curved his lips slightly.

"And you're in your pyjamas."

He stepped forward, moving to stand before her so that she had to tilt her head back to see his face. She had promised herself that she would keep her distance. But now, looking up into his face, it almost felt as though she was begging for his kiss. Which wasn't too far from the truth.

His thumb touched the corner of her mouth. "And you've got a bit of chocolate right here."

The spot burned where he touched, and her lips fell open as her chest cramped. Desire began its insistent throb, and she grabbed onto the word *chocolate* to try to distract herself from the way his hand felt against her skin. "I made cookies," she breathed. "Would you like one?"

"No, thank you."

The pause filled out, growing with unsaid words until Lily could stand no more. What was he doing here? Why was he in his uniform? Was this the end? If so, why wasn't she feeling relief? Why did the thought of him going back to his life leave her with an empty hole of dread in the pit of her stomach?

"Where have you been, all dressed up?"

"A funeral in Drumheller."

The lightbulb flashed on in Lily's mind. "The soldier from the news the other day."

He nodded.

It had been in the papers and on the television the day of the rehearsal, she remembered. But he had said nothing to her about it, and she had assumed he did not know the young corporal who had been killed. But that wasn't the case at all. She realized he'd kept her out of that side of his life completely. The same way he'd hidden his scars from her.

"But you didn't say anything at the wedding."

"What would have been the point?"

"But you knew him?"

"He was in second battalion. I'm a captain in the regiment. It was my duty to go since I was able."

A captain in the regiment. Clearly, he had been motivated by duty—the same duty that would take him back to the forces. Lily was suddenly grateful she hadn't echoed Noah's sentiments back at him the other night. She'd been so tempted. The words had been there, right on the tip of her tongue, scaring her to death. It would only have made everything more difficult, though, in the end. And watching him go away was going to be hard enough.

And yet she couldn't find it within herself to be bitter about it. Noah was different from Curtis, or the father she'd never known. If he left, it was for the right reasons, not because he was weak. No, it was just the opposite. It was his strength, his convictions that would take him away. He'd never once pretended otherwise.

"I'm sorry," she murmured, turning away and picking up her mug of now-cold chocolate. She dumped it down the sink and ran water to rinse out the mug. "It must have been difficult for you."

"It's always difficult. Worse for the families, though."

And that, Lily reasoned, was exactly why she had to let him go. Easier to lose him now, after a few weeks. Because she knew Noah would never be happy unless he was in the thick of things. The army was his Big Adventure. And she couldn't bear being the one left behind. It was a world he chose not to share with her. In all the weeks they'd known each other, she'd never even seen his uniform until today. He'd shut her out of that part of his life. Maybe he had said he loved her, maybe he'd even thought he meant it.

But loving someone meant sharing. And he had never asked her to share in his world.

Nor had he asked for Lily to share hers.

"Why don't you come in and sit down?" She led the way to the living room and sat in a single chair, leaving the sofa for him. Sitting beside him would be too tempting. She would want to touch him. To sit close by him. She would lose her resolve, her perspective, if she let him too close. At least in the single armchair she had some level of protection from his touch, had a hope of remaining logical.

He perched on the edge of the sofa, placing his beret on his knee and toying with the edge. In the silence, she realized he looked exactly as she pictured officers would look when they were about to deliver bad news. Irritation flared. She wished he would just get on with it. But despite her sloppy appearance, she wanted him to see her composed, so she locked the annoyance away and prayed for calm.

"I haven't seen you in uniform before." She folded her hands atop her knee. "Does it feel good to be back in it again?"

Noah wrinkled his eyebrows, as if she was a puzzle he was trying to solve. "A little. Lily I came here to—"

"You've made such great improvement." She cut him off, forcing a smile. She didn't want to hear the words yet. "I bet you can't wait to get back to the service now that the wedding is over and you're healing so well."

Noah's chin flattened and he straightened his back. Whatever he'd started to say was gone, she realized.

"Yes, the doctor said I'll be getting my prosthetic soon."

"That's wonderful." She tried to picture him with an artificial limb, but it wouldn't gel. No, to her he'd always be Noah in faded jeans and a pair of dusty cowboy boots with his shirtsleeve pinned up. That was her Noah. Not this stranger in a pressed and precise uniform. She didn't know how to speak to this man, so official and somber. "Have you found out when you go back to work?"

Again his expression was impossible to read. It amazed her how he could do that. There had been so many times she'd seen his feelings and thoughts so clearly, and yet other times when he was able to close himself off. She held her breath waiting for the answer, hating how awkward and heavy the air felt in the room.

"Anxious to get rid of me?" He raised one eyebrow coolly.

If only it were that simple. She laughed lightly, without her heart being in it. Anxious for him to leave? Never. But needing for it to happen so she could move on? Absolutely. "You've made a point of letting everyone know these few months were just a stop in the road. The army is your life."

"It has been, yes."

"So what now? You said before you'd have to talk to someone about what role your service would take, right?"

Noah got up off the sofa abruptly and went to the fireplace, his back to her. Lily's heart stuttered, struck by the clean, starched lines of his uniform, the gold stripes on his sleeve standing out in bright relief from the dark green. She needed him to just make the break, to walk away as she knew he would. He seemed a stranger to her now, and she missed his grumpiness almost as much as she missed how easily he'd smiled the past few weeks. That man was gone. Perhaps the one before her now was the man he'd been all along. Maybe this was the real Noah and she'd fallen for a fantasy.

"I have some options," he replied. Then he turned, tucking his beret beneath his right arm, close to his body. "Lily, about what I said the other night…"

"You don't have to explain." She tried to make the smile sincere, but couldn't, not when it hurt just to see him again. "It was a rough night. I understand."

His lips thinned. "You think I didn't mean it?"

The last thing she wanted was for him to take back the words. The only thing that would be worse would be hearing him pretend to mean them. He couldn't, not really. It occurred to her that she didn't know him nearly as well as she thought she did.

"You were hurting. And it was very emotional, Noah. For both of us. This whole time has been, don't you think?" It certainly had been for her. She hadn't planned on falling in love with him, either. But looking at him only reinforced her decision. She could not be an army wife. She wasn't the kind of woman who could keep the home fires burning and be happy. She wasn't the kind of woman who could handle a husband keeping a major part of his life separate from hers. She needed total commitment. She needed to feel like a part of his world, not an appendage to it. She had spent too many years tagging along at the mercy of her mother's life to do it again.

And he needed someone who could stand behind him. She wasn't sure she could be that strong. Not and still be happy. She would hate being the one left behind, wondering where he was, feeling alone. She knew it as surely as she was breathing. And whatever feelings they had, even if it was love—would be poisoned by it.

"I've done nothing but think since you left. About you, about the army, about life…"

"Noah…" She stood, unsure of where he was going, but getting a bad feeling that she wasn't going to like what was coming next.

He stepped forward and grabbed her hand, squeezing her fingers. "I meant what I said, Lily. I love you. I certainly didn't expect it or want it, but I won't pretend otherwise, either." He lifted her fingers and pressed them to his cheek. She fought against wanting to believe him and needing to remain objective. He loved her despite himself. She needed more. She needed everything. Even when she doubted everything even existed.

"You have always been honest with me, from the first day when you told me to stop being a baby and accept some help. I can never repay you for all you've done. Never."

She slipped her hand off his cheek, touched beyond words but with a frisson of fear at hearing him declare his love again. A love out of gratitude? It felt hollow, false. "I don't want you to feel obligated."

"It has nothing to do with obligation, Lily, don't you see?" He refused to give up. "I know it's sudden, but you…the things you said, the way you touched me when you saw my scars…Lily, that was extraordinary. You are extraordinary. I understand that you are afraid. But I don't want to let you go."

She blinked, feeling as if held hostage by her own love, responsible for his feelings and terrified of meeting him halfway. He had been through so much, and she had been there for him. She'd wanted to be. But was it enough to base a life together on? She already knew the answer.

He took her hand again. "Will you marry me, Lily?"

Lily felt none of the excitement that should accompany such a proposal. All she felt was dread and disappointment and a very real fear of what her answer must be. The deep blue of his eyes was bright with hope, the touch of his hand on hers earnest and true. But what would her life become? She'd made her home here. She was happy, wasn't she? And with Noah, she would have to move. Give up her job, a job she loved. And even if he didn't travel for work or go overseas, there would be changes in posting and having to start all over again. A new job, new people, each time withdrawing further into herself. He would have his life in the army. And she would be invisible.

"I can't." And she pulled her fingers out of his and walked away to the kitchen, trying to put some space between herself and his imploring eyes. For a beautiful, flashing moment she had a vision of what it would be like to be his wife. Wasn't being the wife of a soldier better than being without Noah? But that moment was fantasy, not reality. She had made herself a family here. The only family she'd ever known. And a soldier's life held no guarantees. His scars bore the proof of that.

She paused by the kitchen table and put her hands over her face for a few moments, trying to compose herself. Noah still stood in the middle of her living room, and when she turned back to face him he looked as if he'd been struck. Why couldn't they have just kept it light, and been friends as they'd said all along? Why did love have to get involved and ruin everything? She closed her eyes, remembering the look of anguish on his face as his scars had been bared to her. She had wanted him to realize that those scars didn't matter, that they didn't make him less of a man. She had wanted to help, give him strength. But love meant more than that. Love meant thinking of the other person first.

She swallowed, the sight of him looking so strong and tall in his uniform branded on her mind. It had been easy to forget when he'd been working at the ranch. But she knew in her heart the army would always come first for Noah. How could she ask him to stay? He would resent her for making that demand, the same as she knew she would come to resent him if he asked her to leave behind the life she'd built.

She opened her eyes, and said the words she knew she must, even though it was tearing her apart.

"Noah, I'm sorry. But this is for the best. I would not make you happy. I'm sure of it."

His eyes iced over and his jaw tightened, covering the hurt she'd glimpsed. He stared at her a long time, until she looked down at her feet, feeling his censure.

"You are not the woman I thought," he replied, his deep voice rife with disappointment, the words cutting through her like a blade. He put the beret back on his head, using his hand to angle it precisely. As he went to the door, Lily started to follow, but his harsh words stopped her.

"Don't worry. I'll show myself out."

When he'd arrived, she'd expected him to announce his leaving, and he was. But she hadn't thought it would be this way, with anger and hostility. A few minutes later the front door shut quietly, a click rather than a bang. But that click held as much condemnation as any words might have.

* * *

Noah's decision had been made, and Lily's response did nothing to change it.

He leaned on the fence, watching the mare Beautiful and the filly, Gorgeous. Silly, feminine names, both of them, and yet they suited. He reached up, tilting the brim of his hat down against the noonday sun. This was home now. These fields where he'd grown up, this stable filled with horses once more. The wide-open space and sunshine and peace and quiet.

Andrew sauntered up, giving Noah a clap on the back and then joining him at the fence.

Married life clearly suited his brother, Noah realized. There was an air of contentment surrounding him that Noah had never seen before. It was as if he was exactly where he belonged and satisfied with it.

The only time Noah had felt more out of place was when he'd stepped off the plane, seeing his brother for the first time in several years.

He'd handled things all wrong with Lily. He should have told her the truth. Made her understand. That had been his plan but it had gone all wrong. He knew the battles she'd fought. She needed a home, a place to belong. Her mother had hauled her from pillar to post during her childhood. He knew how she felt about Larch Valley. But dammit, he had enough pride that he'd wanted her to choose him *for him*. Not because of a decision he'd made. So he'd kept quiet and watched the relationship crumble around them. Maybe she did love him. Just not enough.

The filly cavorted through the paddock, making him smile and drawing him out of his dark thoughts. He gave a nod in her direction. "She looks good, doesn't she?"

"Sure does."

Andrew reached down and plucked a strand of timothy that grew next to the fence post, began chewing on the end. "You're sure this is what you want?"

Noah nodded. He'd thought long and hard lately. He couldn't go back to the life he'd had. It was physically impossible. And he'd discovered the alternative wasn't what he wanted, either. It was time he came home, and stopped avoiding all the things that had kept him away. He just hadn't planned on doing it alone.

"I'm sure."

Andrew's wide grin split his face. "Good. That's real good, bro."

Noah laughed. "You say that now, but I'm used to being the one giving the orders, little brother."

"There's no one I'd rather be partners with. Let's go tell Jen. She's got some lunch ready, too."

As they walked to the house, Noah wondered what Lily was doing on a Sunday afternoon. He'd had plenty of hours to mull things over since leaving her town house, to think about what had happened. The sunshine and fresh air and physical labor had helped clear his mind. And the one thing he had figured out was that he hadn't imagined her feelings. Lily was easy to read. She wasn't capable of being false or manipulative.

And the way she'd responded to his kiss had been genuine. The trembling touch on each of his scars, the waver in her voice when she'd said he was beautiful... that wasn't for show.

The only conclusion he could reasonably come to was that she was scared to death.

Either way, he'd decided to leave the army before he'd ever proposed, and come what may, he was happy with that decision. He'd been as guilty as Andrew of running away from home. The army had filled the gap for years. Now it was time to let go of old resentments and be back where he belonged. With his family. He and Andrew were partners in Lazy L now, and it was a decision that simply felt *good*.

And now, being in Larch Valley on a permanent basis meant he could put his energies into fighting for Lily. Because she expected him to give up. She expected him to walk away just as Curtis had.

And that was the last thing he intended to do.

## Chapter 12

Jen was elated at the news and gave Noah a gigantic hug, and then proceeded to lay out a lunch of soup and sandwiches. The three of them were just sitting down, talking about plans for the ranch, when the sound of an engine broke through the chatter. Jen stood up and went to the window, looked at Noah, and back to the door. "It's Lily."

Noah's insides twisted and the bite of sandwich in his mouth turned dry. He hadn't seen Lily since the day she'd turned down his proposal. He'd planned on seeing her again when they could be alone. Talk. Not with an audience who knew nothing of what had truly transpired between them.

"Lily, come on in. We were just having lunch. Do you want some? There's plenty."

Lily stepped over the threshold and froze as she saw

him, her expression a blend of surprise and awkwardness. He looked down, missing how she used to look at him with welcome in her eyes. Noah forced himself to swallow the bread and sliced turkey before lifting his head to acknowledge her. "Lily," he said quietly.

Lily jerked her head away and smiled at Jen. "I can't stay. I just wanted to drop off the stuff from the reception." She handed over a box. Noah noticed her hand was shaking the tiniest bit. Had she been anxious to get rid of Jen's things? Were they a reminder of how things had gone so wrong between them?

"Thanks, Lil. I appreciate you bringing them over."

A moment of silence fell, filled with awkwardness. Noah watched as Lily pasted on a smile. He knew it was forced, and that it was made worse by his being there.

"It's okay. It's just your flutes and the centerpiece from our table. A few other things I thought you might like to have as keepsakes."

Andrew hopped up from the table to take the box. "I'll put it upstairs," he volunteered.

"I thought you'd both like to know that Lucy had her baby this morning," she added.

Noah watched Lily's face carefully. Color swept into her cheeks as she avoided his gaze. He remembered her saying once that marriage and children weren't in the cards for her. For a moment he imagined how beautiful she'd be carrying a child. His child. The image was stunning.

"Oh! Boy or girl?"

"A little boy, Alexander. I ran into Brody at the café this morning. He's one proud papa."

"A boy." Jen beamed at Andrew. "There'll be no living with him now, will there. And named after Lucy's father."

"As the first Navarro grandchild should be." Andrew laughed.

Noah pushed back his chair and gathered up his plate and bowl, taking them to the sink. Andrew and Jen, Brody and Lucy...everything was fitting into place in their worlds. But not in his. He was satisfied he'd made the right decision, leaving the army, but it didn't quite work without Lily.

"I'll let you ladies catch up," he said, his voice low. Without saying another word to Lily, he slid past her and out the door. He wouldn't torture her further by being in the way here. But it wasn't over. He'd find a way to fight for her.

Lily watched him go with sadness in her heart. The little looks they used to exchange, the warm smile he often greeted her with was gone. She hadn't expected to see him here, not on a Sunday. It had been difficult staying away, though she knew it was for the best.

But his reaction to seeing her today left her feeling even more down, if that were possible. She knew it was too much to expect he would be the same smiling Noah after what had happened between them. Feeling awkward was understandable. As Jen and Andrew talked about baby Alexander and made plans to visit Lucy, Lily slipped out the door. Somehow they had to make things right. She would feel awful if the last words they had were angry ones. It wasn't what she wanted him to take back with him, wherever that was going to be.

She found him in the barn, in the tack room tidying

the already neat shelves. She stood quietly in the doorway, watching his movements. "Noah?"

He sighed, put down the bridle in his hand and turned. No smile, no welcoming warmth in his eyes. "What can I do for you, Lily?"

His brusqueness made words catch in her throat before she could set them free. "You could stop hating me, for starters."

She saw his throat bob as he swallowed. The tension in his eyes softened the slightest bit. "I don't hate you."

"I'm glad. Because I don't like how we left things. We were friends, first. I want to be that again." She didn't want this to be the pattern in her life. She and Curtis had never seen each other again after it had gone wrong. Noah was too important to lose altogether. Somehow they had to make things right, not marked by bitterness and regret.

"I don't know." He picked up the bridle again and went to hang it on its proper hook.

"Noah, when you go back to the service, I don't want it to be with anger at me. Maybe that's selfish. But we shared a lot more than just those last few days. That's what I'd like you to remember. Not how it ended."

He gave up any pretense of working and sat on a sawhorse, his long legs stretched out in front of him.

"I'm not going back."

"Not going back… What do you mean?" Lily felt the color leach from her face. But his uniform the other day…and the way he'd spoken… Her knees wobbled as her emotions reeled. Did this mean he wasn't leaving? That he would be here in Larch Valley? For a brief moment she rejoiced. Then she remembered she had turned him away. She had been the one to refuse.

Had he actually said the words at her house? Or had she simply assumed by his appearance that he was being taken off his temporary status? Had he been let go because of his disability?

Once again, she didn't know the answers. He hadn't let her in. Once again, he hadn't trusted her. She tasted the bitterness of futility in her mouth.

"I applied for a voluntary discharge. I'm not going back into the army. I'm going into partnership with Andrew instead. Trading in my stripes for cowboy boots."

The light was dim in the tack room, but Lily could see enough to know he was completely serious. "But… but…" she stammered. The army was everything to him. He'd said so. There had never been any doubt. "When you came to the house the other day…"

"You made it very clear my proposal was unwelcome."

His steady regard sent her nerve endings skittering. "You had on your uniform," she insisted.

"I had been to a funeral."

"And you never said…you never mentioned you were even considering this!" She backed up slightly, leaning against the doorjamb, letting it support her. That was the trouble, wasn't it. He *never* said. He kept her in the dark.

His smile was small, cold. "Why does it matter? I'd made my decision before then anyway."

Leaving the army, putting his life as a soldier behind him for good? It didn't make sense. His whole identity was wrapped up in being a soldier.

"Why? The army is everything to you. You told me it was your *home*." She took a step inside the room, putting her hands in her jeans pockets. She was so tempted to go to him, and knew she must not.

"The army made up for a lot of things that were missing in my life. For a lot of years, it was my family. But in the end, I knew I'd only be going back in an administrative role." He waved his hand, encompassing the tack room. "I can't be shut up in an office, Lily. I would be grossly unhappy. I need to be outdoors. Where there is room to breathe. I wouldn't be able to go back and be with my men again. And Andrew's here, and Jen. I love this place, always have, even when I had to get away from it. I think I started to remember when we delivered Gorgeous."

They were good reasons, but Lily's heart sank, knowing that she wasn't included in any of them. Emptiness opened up inside her. Never in her life had she felt so utterly left out.

"You're not going, then."

"No."

"You might have told me that the other day." She lifted her chin, torn between wanting to cry with relief that he wasn't going and fear that he would want more from her than she could give. She knew it was unreasonable and unfair. She knew it made no sense to want him to stay when her heart still quaked when she thought of marriage.

"And would it have made any difference?"

The quiet question struck her with the precision of an arrow. Would it? If he had come right out and said he was planning on staying in Larch Valley indefinitely, would her answer have been different? She would have her life, her job, her friends. No moving around, none of the weeks alone while he was away. And then she pictured herself standing at the front of the church, as

Jen had with Andrew, and her chest contracted as panic threaded through her.

Noah boosted himself away from the sawhorse and came to stand in front of her. Her breaths shallowed at the mere nearness of him. Her fingers itched to reach out and touch him, to gather the light cotton of his T-shirt in her hands. "I tried to tell you what I'd decided, but you didn't want to listen. You were so afraid, so bent on pushing me away that I knew."

"Knew what?" She dared a glance upward, into his eyes. Saw his jaw tighten as he clenched his teeth. Her gaze dropped to his lips and for a moment he seemed to lean closer. Then his expression changed, just a hint of sympathy entering his eyes as he withdrew the slightest little bit.

"Knew that you were too afraid to say yes."

Her eyebrows shot toward her hairline as the spell surrounding them broke. "How could I know you were staying here? Yes, I was afraid! You were asking me to leave my home behind, my job! My life that I've built here!"

"I was asking you to share your life with me, Lily."

She turned away from the earnestness in his eyes. Took several deep breaths, trying to calm the frantic beating of her heart. She had desperately wanted to share herself with a man before, and it had gone so very wrong. Love was one thing. And she did love him. How could she not? But marriage, that was quite another. The act of giving your life to one person for safekeeping forever. Or until they decided to hand it back to you.

"You're scared." Noah came forward and spun her around with his hand. "The idea of marriage scares you to death, I know that. I knew that when I asked you!

Don't you think I'm scared? Do you know how hard it was to tell you I loved you?"

"I'm sorry it was such a burden!" Her eyes flashed up at him. Why did she continually feel as though she was an obligation? She needed him to share his life with her, as well. If only he could see that!

"Don't do that!" he yelled, exasperated. "That's not it at all, and you know it!"

"I can't let myself love you, don't you see that?"

He gave her arm a little shake. "Look at me, Lily. I've done nothing but think about how I would support you. Worry about how my physical challenges might affect a relationship." He let go of her arm and ran his fingers through his hair. "Dammit, woman," he muttered, quieter now. "I wasn't even sure how to hold you on the dance floor. How would I manage making love?"

The backs of her eyes stung at his honest admission. She'd known all along about his insecurities. "Do you really think I care about any of that?" Her voice was raspy, raw with all the emotions she was trying to hold back.

"I worried about it and I asked you anyway. Because I thought you trusted me. But I realized something even more important. I realized that this had nothing to do with me being in the forces or working Lazy L. This has to do with you and what you're really afraid of."

A knot tightened, grew in Lily's core. Afraid? Hell yes, she was afraid. She'd never wanted this. Never wanted to feel so strongly again. Never wanted to be tempted to throw it all away for the love of one person. She'd sworn she'd never do it again. She'd had to keep reminding herself that he was temporary. She'd felt safe in knowing it. But now he wasn't temporary, and somehow the fear remained.

"You want love with boundaries, Lil. It was okay when you knew I'd be leaving again. I thought so, too. When I first got here, all I wanted was to get better and get back to the regiment."

"What changed?" Lily chanced a look up, feeling moisture on her cheeks but ignoring it.

"You changed me. You made me look at things differently. I told you things I hadn't talked about with anyone ever. You helped me when I needed it but let me stand on my own two feet, too, like the day we delivered the foal." He lifted his hand and grazed her cheek with a finger. "You made me feel like a man again."

"Noah, don't…" Her voice broke on the last word, but he persisted, his soft voice relentless. He cupped her cheek.

"I was safe when I was going away. It's not marriage that you doubt, Lily. Your problem is that you don't believe in love. Not the forever kind."

He leaned forward and kissed her forehead gently. "The kind I want to give to you."

Lily savored the touch of his lips on her forehead before forcing herself to back away. Was he right? Was that the nagging feeling that she couldn't escape?

"Maybe I don't," she confessed. She pressed her hands to her hot cheeks for a moment, trying to find the words to explain all that she needed, wanted. "Maybe I don't believe in it because I've never seen it."

And then it was like beams of light into her mind and heart. That was it, wasn't it. The reason why Jasmine had never settled on one man. The reason why she'd moved from relationship to relationship, taking Lily with her. She'd simply been searching and coming up empty. Looking for the mate to complete the other half of her soul and never finding him. The reason why she'd been so flippant about Lily's relationship with Curtis, insisting it wasn't real.

And she'd been right. She'd been right because the real thing was standing before her right now and she knew what he was offering wasn't enough. That was what she was afraid of. Not of loving him. She couldn't help but love him. But that one day he'd realize he'd made a mistake and it would be over. That *his* love wouldn't be forever.

She fled the tack room, needing to get out of the dark corners and into the sunshine where she could breathe. She had to find the words to tell him what she wanted. If she could even consider jumping into love—into marriage—it needed to be on her terms.

She just had to be strong enough to ask for it.

His boots sounded on the concrete and she wiped her eyes, trying desperately to ignore the uncertainty rolling around in her stomach. She could do this. She sniffled, straightening her shoulders. For the first time, something mattered more than protecting herself. She could say the words. She could ask for what she deserved. The way she'd never been able to face up to anyone she'd loved ever before.

He stopped at the edge of the barn, in the breach of the door just behind her.

And when she turned to face him, it was with eyes that saw the man she loved, the man she would always love.

"Noah, I love you."

In a split second he had her pulled tight against his chest. He kissed the top of her head, bathed in the warmth of the sun. She returned his embrace, knowing they needed this as a starting point. Needed to let their love be the foundation for everything else, if they had any hope of making it work.

"But you have to listen to me." She pushed back, putting her hands on his upper arms in a way she wouldn't have dared only a few short weeks ago. "Because we can't go on this way. You're right about one thing, I am scared. I'm terrified. I'm scared because I can't go through life being invisible."

"I see you," he replied, bending his knees slightly so that their eyes were level. "I see a woman who is caring, and compassionate, and funny, and selfless…."

"That is just the outside! That is what I want people to see. Noah, I'm a woman who spent her life trying to please other people. The one time I tried to do something for myself was when I ran away with Curtis. And it went spectacularly wrong. And so the time has come for me to be selfish."

She looked into his eyes, praying for courage to say what she had to say. "I know the reason my mother kept us moving from place to place. She was searching for, and never finding the person she wanted to spend her life with. Oh, Noah, I would share all my life with you. But you have not shared with me. There are times I have felt so left out, so in the dark and feeling like I didn't know you at all."

"You know me better than anyone," he protested, and she felt her pulse give a little kick. But she had to stay on course.

"I knew the Noah that came home, the Noah that was wounded and the Noah who was working his way through healing. I shared things with you about myself because I felt I could trust you…and that did not come easy to me. I fought my feelings for you so much. I didn't want to love you, but I always knew you would be going away and I thought my heart was safe."

How wrong she'd been. The night she'd seen his body laid bare to her, she'd felt a love so big, so pure, it had changed everything. And she'd started to realize how little she truly knew about him. About his hopes and dreams, because he had kept so much hidden from her.

She reached out and took his hand, needing the connection as she gathered the strength to continue.

"When you showed up in your uniform, I thought you had come to say goodbye. Instead you proposed, and all I could see was a question mark. When would you be going back to duty? Where would we live? What would you be doing? How could I find a life again? I realized I had not once seen your uniform, although you had claimed that the army was the most important thing to you. I didn't know you were going to the funeral even though it could have easily come up in conversation. The most important thing in your life was the one thing you didn't share. Even the details of your injury...those are sketchy at best. The bits you allowed me to see." Emotion tore at her throat. "I can't live that way, Noah. I can't. I'm not strong enough. Or confident enough. I would always be wondering, waiting for the dream of being with you to end."

Noah took a step back, staggered by what Lily had said. Had he done that? Had he really shut her out? He thought back to their conversations, their moments together. Had he truly discussed his plans with her? His doubts about going back into an army where he didn't fit anymore? His longing to be with family? How he'd felt contented back at Lazy L in a way he hadn't expected?

He hadn't. And as they stood there in the summer sunshine, he realized that when he'd proposed, he'd asked her to take a leap with him when he'd barely made a single step himself.

He met her gaze and saw her eyes, wide and sorrowful, shining back at him. "You're right. I asked you to share my life without sharing mine with you."

She nodded.

He swallowed, wanting to explain how he'd felt, not sure if he could. Never in his whole life had he discussed his feelings this deeply. But he loved her. And he would do anything to put the smile back on her face. To feel her hand in his. That was more important than being afraid.

"I didn't think you loved me, you see," he began. "I kept telling myself you couldn't, not in my condition. I didn't know what the future would bring. All I knew was that I felt better—happier—when I was with you. But when the time came to decide what I wanted to do, I was selfish, Lily, and I was wrong. I tested you, and that wasn't fair. I had to know you loved me for me, not because I was staying in Larch Valley or because I was moving away to be a part of the service again. I've been married to the army my whole adult life. And suddenly it wasn't enough. I wanted *you*. I needed you to want me that much, too. I didn't want the rest to matter, and because of that I didn't see I was shutting you out. I'm sorry, Lily, so sorry. I never meant to exclude you."

"You left the army because of me?" Her voice was a tiny whisper.

"You see?" He ran his hand through his hair, leaving the dark spikes standing on end. "I didn't want you to bear the responsibility of my choices. I never wanted you to feel I expected something of you. I didn't leave

*for* you—I left *because* of you. Because you showed me
there was more in my life than I imagined. You showed
me the possibility of a new start. And one I prayed to
God you might someday want to share."

He reached out, running his thumb over her cheek,
touching her lips before letting his hand fit the curve of
her neck. "I have never been in love before. After my
parents, I was sure that it wasn't something I wanted.
Even now, I see how lonely my mom is. I watched Dad's
pain after she'd gone. Oh, Lily, you never trusted in a forever kind of love before. I'm here to say you don't have
to. Just trust in me. I won't betray your faith. I promise."

The sob came out before she could stop it, a small
hiccup of emotion as she wound her arms around him,
holding him close. "I knew the night that we danced and
you said you wanted to be perfect that I'd fallen for you."

"Before the wedding?"

"Oh, yes." She smiled against the fabric of his shirt,
absorbing the feel of his unique shape against hers, the
scent of him that was just Noah. "Saying no to you was
the most difficult thing I've ever done."

"Harder than being left at the altar?" There was a
note of incredulity in his voice. She nodded and peered
up into his face.

"Absolutely. I never loved him the way I love you,
Noah. If I didn't love you so much, I wouldn't have had
the courage to say what I did today."

She knew as a concept that didn't make much sense,
but it was true. Her love for him made her stronger. Gave
her the desire to fight for the life she wanted.

Her heart clubbed at her ribs. His deep eyes were
questioning, with just a hint of challenge that she adored.

It wasn't what she'd planned, wasn't what she'd envisioned, but something greater than logic propelled her to kneel before him, holding his left hand in hers, pressing a kiss to the work-roughened skin. "Noah," she said clearly, her voice ringing out into the summer air. "Will you marry me, Noah? Will you take me, with all of my faults, all of my weaknesses, all of my scars? Because I love you, Noah. More than I ever thought possible. It doesn't matter where we live. As long as we're together."

He tugged on her hand, lifting her to her feet. "Lily," he said gently, "do you know how many times you have humbled me? With your caring and compassion and strength. It would have been impossible for me not to have fallen in love with you."

Lily's eyes misted with tears. "Is that a yes?"

He laughed, a sound filled with happiness and emotion. "Yes, of course it is. I'll marry you. The sooner the better. I'll be damned if I'm letting you get away again."

He pulled her into his embrace, sealing the engagement with a kiss. "Definitely not letting you get away," he murmured against her mouth.

The clatter of footsteps interrupted the moment before an exclamation cut through the air. Lily's and Noah's heads turned together to see Jen and Andrew coming through the barn. Jen stopped abruptly, put a hand to her mouth.

"Drew! They're not…are they?"

Lily felt a giggle, a warm, expansive bubble of happiness rise within her. Noah's arm held firm around her waist as they faced Andrew and Jen together.

Jen rushed forward, her jaw slack with surprise, but elation beaming from her eyes. "When did this happen?"

Lily laughed, enjoying her friend's surprise. "Pretty

much the morning you asked me to deliver those groceries," she admitted with a laugh.

"Lily's in the market for a matron of honor," Noah added, the smile Lily adored curling its way up his cheek.

"You're getting married? Oh, my word. And to think we were inside being worried…" She hugged Noah for the second time that day, before standing back and shaking her head, as if she still didn't quite believe it. "I hate the word *matron*, but this is one time I'll wear it. Gladly."

Andrew caught up with Jen and placed his hands on her shoulders. Happiness glowed from his face. "It's true? The two of you?"

Lily nodded, while Noah answered, "It took some work."

Andrew barked out a laugh while Jen rushed forward, claiming Lily in a hug this time. "Oh, you guys!" she wailed, stepping back and dabbing at her eyes. "And oh, Lily, just think, this time you'll be making your own wedding dress! It's so perfect."

Lily looked up at Noah, knowing Jen knew nothing about the dress still hanging in her closet. It was time to let it go. It was time to put the past behind her and look forward to a kind of future she'd only dreamed of. Noah's eyes glowed at her, strong and true, and she smiled.

"I've made the last wedding dress I'm ever going to," she announced, squeezing Noah's hand. "I think a shopping trip for something shiny and new is in order."

The two couples chatted happily about future plans until Jen stopped up short. "Wait a minute," she said, turning to Lily, her expression flat with mock seriousness. "I seem to recall it wasn't that long ago that you said you didn't date cowboys."

Lily grabbed Noah's hand and stepped on tiptoe to kiss his cheek, but he turned at the last second and caught her lips in a sweet, brief kiss.

She turned to Jen, now understanding why it was her friend seemed to glow from within all the time. She smiled, and curled into Noah's side.

"You know how it is," she remarked to Jen, while her gaze remained locked with Noah's. "I guess I'd just never met the right one."

\* \* \* \* \*

We hope you enjoyed reading

# THE LAST MERCENARY

by *New York Times* bestselling author

## DIANA PALMER and

# HER LONE COWBOY

by reader-favorite author

## DONNA ALWARD

Both were originally Harlequin series stories!

Escape with romances featuring real, relatable women and strong, deeply desirable men. Experience the intensity, anticipation and sheer rush of falling in love with **Harlequin Romance!**

Look for four *new* romances every month from **Harlequin Romance!**

Available wherever books are sold.

SPECIAL EXCERPT FROM

**H** HARLEQUIN®

*Romance*

*Read on for an extract from Michelle Douglas's
first book in the **WILD ONES** duet,
HER IRRESISTIBLE PROTECTOR.*

"I'VE NEVER SEEN anything like this in my life," she whispered. On impulse she turned to him. He did something with his paddle so the kayak barely moved in response to her movement.

The half-light softened his face, turning him into a sort of soft-focus angel. The longer she stared at him the more he came into focus. And then he smiled. She blinked and forced her eyes back to the front.

She clenched her eyes shut.

Her breathing grew more erratic rather than less. She tried telling herself it was the exertion of paddling, but it wasn't. Mitch had a smile that could make a woman forget which way was up. A flicker of heat licked low in her belly. Mitch had a kind of face that could make a woman forget vows she'd made to herself—vows to never fall for him again, to not expose herself to his treachery.

They landed against the beach with a tiny bump and scrape. Mitch vaulted lightly out and she barely noticed the gentle rock from side to side because he steadied it again so quickly. He reached out to take her hand. "Keep your shoes on. The shells are sharp."

She put her hand in his, all of his latent power pressed against her palm, and curled around her fingers in undiscovered promise as he pulled her upright and helped her step out of the kayak. Her heart fluttered up into her throat, nearly smothering her. "Thank you." Her voice came out breathy, thready.

He let go of her and she had to lock her knees to stay upright. She glanced around, forced herself to feign interest in her surroundings rather than the man beside her. At the very back of the cave, where it was darkest, a couple of straggly plants clung to the rock—obviously a place where the tide rarely reached. "It'd be possible to hide away from the world in here."

She had a sudden vision of a thick blanket spread on the smoother ground beyond the shells, a bottle of champagne, strawberries…

She shot a look at him from beneath heavy eyelids—took in his wide shoulders, the depth of his chest and those rippling biceps.

He'd be sheer heaven to touch.

She lifted her gaze to find him staring down at her.

He backed up, his face suddenly tight. "Pick your shell, Tash."

The warning in his voice slapped her like a dash of icy water. She snapped away and crouched down, scrabbling wildly. This… this desire was just a carryover from eight years ago when she'd been a crazy stupid teenager.

Except…

Her hand closed around a shell—a fan, grey on the outside and pink on the inside. She rose to her feet. "Thank you."

*Thank you for the adventure.*

*Thank you for the reminder.*

Without another word they climbed back into the kayak and paddled away.

*Don't miss HER IRRESISTIBLE PROTECTOR*
*by Michelle Douglas, available July 2014.*
*And look out for the second book in Michelle Douglas's*
**WILD ONES** *duet, THE REBEL AND THE HEIRESS,*
*available August 2014.*

# HARLEQUIN®
# Romance

Save $1.00 on the purchase of

# HER IRRESISTIBLE
# PROTECTOR

by Michelle Douglas,

available July 1, 2014,
or on any other Harlequin® Romance® book.

Available wherever books are sold, including most bookstores,
supermarkets, drugstores and discount stores.

---

**Save $1.00**

on the purchase of
**HER IRRESISTIBLE PROTECTOR**
by **Michelle Douglas**
available July 1, 2014, or
on any other Harlequin® Romance® book.

Coupon valid until September 3, 2014. Redeemable at participating retail outlets
in the U.S. and Canada only. Limit one coupon per customer.

**52611533**

**Canadian Retailers:** Harlequin Enterprises Limited will pay the face value of this coupon plus 10.25¢ if submitted by customer for this product only. Any other use constitutes fraud. Coupon is nonassignable. Void if taxed, prohibited or restricted by law. Consumer must pay any government taxes. Void if copied. Millennium1 Promotional Services ("M1P") customers submit coupons and proof of sales to Harlequin Enterprises Limited, P.O. Box 3000, Saint John, NB E2L 4L3, Canada. Non-M1P retailer—for reimbursement submit coupons and proof of sales directly to Harlequin Enterprises Limited, Retail Marketing Department, 225 Duncan Mill Rd., Don Mills, ON M3B 3K9, Canada.

**U.S. Retailers:** Harlequin Enterprises Limited will pay the face value of this coupon plus 8¢ if submitted by customer for this product only. Any other use constitutes fraud. Coupon is nonassignable. Void if taxed, prohibited or restricted by law. Consumer must pay any government taxes. Void if copied. For reimbursement submit coupons and proof of sales directly to Harlequin Enterprises Limited, P.O. Box 880478, El Paso, TX 88588-0478, U.S.A. Cash value 1/100 cents.

5 65373 00076 2   (8100)0 11929

NYTCOUP0614